Single
Bald
Female

Single Bald Female

Laura Price

MACMILLAN

First published 2022 by Macmillan
an imprint of Pan Macmillan
The Smithson, 6 Briset Street, London EC1M 5NR
EU representative: Macmillan Publishers Ireland Ltd, 1st Floor,
The Liffey Trust Centre, 117–126 Sheriff Street Upper,
Dublin 1, D01 YC43
Associated companies throughout the world
www.panmacmillan.com

ISBN 978-1-5290-7424-6

1 3 5 7 9 8 6 4 2

A CIP catalogue record for this book is available from the British Library.

Typeset in Sabon by Jouve (UK), Milton Keynes
Printed and bound by CPI Group (UK) Ltd, Croydon, CR0 4YY

Visit **www.panmacmillan.com** to read more about all our books
and to buy them. You will also find features, author interviews and
news of any author events, and you can sign up for e-newsletters
so that you're always first to hear about our new releases.

*For anyone touched by breast cancer,
infertility or simply bad luck in love*

Imposter syndrome

I haven't thought this through.

As the taxi pulls up outside the poshest hotel on Park Lane, I spot the red carpet with a gaggle of paparazzi on either side. I had planned, naively, to change into my shoes in the loo, minimizing the amount of time I have to spend in these ridiculously high heels before I go in. Now I realize the entrance is *outside* the hotel, so I'll have to traipse down the red carpet in my trainers and probably end up on some sort of sidebar of shame before the evening is out.

'Hold on,' I say to the cab driver, who is tutting impatiently as he eyes the cars queued up behind us in his rear-view mirror.

I rummage through my backpack to find the heels that Aisha lent me from the fashion cupboard just a few hours ago. I could barely walk five steps in them in the office, so knowing my luck I'll probably fall slap on my face in front of the paps. I strap them up, instantly wishing I'd bothered to fix the chipped paint on my toenails.

A minute later, I push open the heavy black door and step down onto the tarmac, thankful for the hotel porter who lends me his arm for support. I shove the tatty rucksack under my armpit. Perhaps I'll start a new trend, the backpack clutch.

I'm starstruck for a second as a well-known breakfast newsreader makes her way inside to the flashes and clicks of the cameras. When the coast is clear, I totter behind, keeping my head down. But it seems the paps got the memo, their cameras immediately falling silent in recognition of my status as mere magazine new girl. They could at least have *tried* to feign interest.

Inside, I head straight to the cloakroom to dump my bag, then take a deep breath before walking into the main room. I look around for Aisha, Leah or Tabitha, longing for a familiar face. They went ahead at lunchtime to set up while I stayed behind to hold the fort, but now I'm regretting having to walk in to the most glamorous event of the glossy magazine calendar on my own.

Just inside the entrance, women in sparkling gowns parade down another red carpet, stopping to perform immaculate hand-on-hip poses before a huddle of photographers. When they reach the end of the velvet carpet, they pick up champagne flutes from precariously balanced trays and head towards the sign that reads 'Luxxe Women Awards'. I may only have moved up a few floors at the same publishing house, but it's a different world.

'Jess, you made it!'

I turn to see Tabitha Richardson, ever the fashion editor, towering above me in heels even higher than the ones she wears around the office. Draped in a stunning, floor-length ivory gown with her glossy blonde bob shaped at a sharp angle, she is every inch as A-list as the guests.

'You look incredible,' I say, admiring the way the silky material glides over her hips and suddenly feeling wildly underdressed.

'Aw, thanks hun. Your jumpsuit is very . . .' She looks me up and down. '. . . quirky.'

I suck in my ribcage and glance down at the tight black top and adjoining trousers, which are already giving me camel toe. It was a last-minute change directed by Aisha to rectify my

2

earlier wardrobe malfunction and I'm assured it's on trend, but I'm longing for the comfort of my own clothes. I had set aside my favourite LBD, the one with the plunging neckline that always gets Johnny's approval, but as soon as we realized you could see the huge plaster on my chest, Aisha ordered me to change.

'Ready for your first Luxxe Women Awards?'

'Terrified,' I say, glancing around at the gaggles of well-known faces hugging and greeting each other as if they've been friends for decades. At my old magazine, I was used to doing live interviews and occasional presenting, but the Cake and Bake Show wasn't exactly a red-carpet affair. This is another league, and I've been out of the women's-magazine game too long for any of these people to know who I am.

'You'll enjoy it,' Tabitha says, looking over my shoulder. 'It's my first one back after mat leave so I better go work the room.'

She marches off, slotting into a circle of people and greeting them with hugs and kisses. I stand outside the group but she fails to notice my presence. When they've disbanded, I try to keep up with Tabitha as she paces across the floor.

'Would you mind introducing me to a few people?' I say.

She stops marching and turns to face me. 'Oh my gosh, of *course*. I thought you knew everyone.'

Hardly. The whole idea of me coming along to the awards tonight was to shadow Leah before she goes on maternity leave and I take over as acting editor for real. Since Tabitha has been at *Luxxe* for three years, I figured she'd show me the ropes.

I spot someone I recognize. 'Isn't that . . .?'

'Yep,' Tabitha says, grabbing my wrist and pulling me towards the woman so that I almost stumble on a bunched-up bit of carpet. 'Come on.'

'*Darrr-ling*,' Tabitha says, leaning in for a hug and elongating the word as if they're childhood friends. 'How *are* you?'

There's an awkward moment as the woman fails to recognize Tabitha and she has to introduce herself again. Then Tabitha puts a hand on the small of my back, as if encouraging a shy toddler. 'This is Jess, our new starter.'

'Actually, I'm joining as acting editor,' I say, shaking the woman's hand and wondering if Tabitha has acknowledged that I'm technically now her boss.

The woman looks from Tabitha to me, then over both of our shoulders. 'There's someone I should go speak to. Nice to meet you both.'

Tabitha calls after her. 'Wait, I wanted to ask you . . .'

She chases after her, and I'm on my own again.

I spend much of the reception behind the comfort of a high table, clinging to my phone in one hand and champagne flute in the other while I pluck up the courage to introduce myself to at least one of the women I've admired over years of reading *Luxxe*. Having spent my entire career at Harcourt House Publishing, I'm familiar enough with my new colleagues, but it's been years since I've written for women's magazines, years since I've encountered the mega-stars you meet at these events. I could walk up to Paul Hollywood and he'd hug me like a long-lost friend, but in the world of female celebrity, I'm a nobody.

'Found you!'

Relief floods through me as Aisha appears, looking flustered as she juggles a smartphone, portable flash and a terrifying robot-arm contraption with a video camera balanced on the end of it. 'Sorry, it's always a nightmare running around doing the socials. I'm going back to the red carpet – have you done your picture yet?'

I shake my head. I'd never dare hog the limelight with all those actual celebrities getting their photos taken, but I wouldn't mind a glamorous pic for my new Insta.

'Come on,' she says, grabbing my hand and dragging me back towards the entrance. I'm grateful to have known Aisha since we were interns. The fact that I already had a friend at *Luxxe* was one of the things that persuaded me to apply for Leah's maternity cover in the first place. It's weird that I'm now going to be Aisha's boss, but at least with her handling all things digital, we have boundaries. Plus, we've made a pact to keep it professional at work.

'Are you sure you can't see it?' I say, gesturing towards my jumpsuit, aware of the giant plaster beneath it.

Aisha takes a step back and examines the top half of my outfit. 'Jess, you look smoking. Now come on, let's see your best pose.'

I stand up straight against the backdrop of sponsor logos, still adjusting to the borrowed heels. I force a smile in the hopes of disguising how utterly out of place I feel.

Aisha reappears from behind the lens and shakes her head. She steps over the velvet rope and bends me into position like I'm Stretch Armstrong. 'Don't move.'

She clambers back over and takes a series of photos, then nods her head, satisfied. 'I've got to help the social team get ready for the ceremony. I'll send you the pic as soon as we get the cards uploaded.'

I nod in thanks, eager to get off the red carpet and out of the spotlight.

As she walks away, Aisha stops and turns to me again. 'I almost forgot. Break a leg! You'll absolutely smash it.'

I make a face. Being here in my new role is nerve-wracking, but it's not like I'm going up on stage or anything. I do a double-take. 'Wait, what?'

Aisha gives me an encouraging smile. 'Your presenting debut!'

I freeze on the spot. 'Sorry?'

Her face drops as it dawns on her that I really don't know what's going on. 'Wait, Tabitha didn't tell you?'

Suddenly everything is moving in slow motion. I'm pretty sure I'm about to be told I have to go on stage in front of a room full of game-changing film directors, podcast hosts and entrepreneurs. 'Tabitha didn't tell me what?'

'Leah went into labour,' Aisha says, softening her voice. 'Shit, Tabitha said she'd tell you. Leah was going to call you as well.'

I think back to my brief exchange with Tabitha when I arrived. She had plenty of opportunity to tell me that our boss had gone into labour, though she did seem a bit flustered. And now it makes sense why Leah didn't answer when I returned her missed call in the cab.

'Hang on,' I say, reaching out for Aisha's hand to steady myself. 'Is Leah OK? It's too early for her to have the baby, isn't it?'

Aisha shakes her head. 'She's fine. It's only a few weeks early. I'm so sorry, I thought you knew.'

'Right. OK. Shit.' I run through the implications in my head. If Leah has gone into labour early, that means she'll be starting her maternity leave with immediate effect. Which means, as of tomorrow, I am officially acting editor of *Luxxe* magazine. Which means . . .

'Do you think you'll be OK to present the big award?'

Shit. The last time I went up on stage was to discuss the pitfalls of soggy bottoms with Mary Berry in front of an audience of cake enthusiasts as editor of *Perfect Bake*. But this is different. I'm so new to *Luxxe* that nobody knows who I am, nobody knows I'm taking over from Leah, and I've never edited a women's lifestyle magazine before. Why would anyone take me seriously?

'It's literally two sentences, saying the name of the winner, handing over the award and then you walk off,' Aisha says, glancing down at her phone. 'I'd offer to do it, but I'm stuck on the front row doing the socials. Just head backstage five minutes before you go on and they'll get you miked up and give you your lines. You'll be fine.'

'OK,' I say, nodding my head in an attempt to convince myself I can do this. I've done it before, just for a different style of magazine, to a different audience. If I want to be offered a permanent role when Leah comes back from mat leave then I need to smash it from day one. Just rip the plaster off, as my dad would say.

Half an hour before the ceremony begins, I hobble outside to call Johnny, my ankles already blistered from the heels. November air shocks my cheeks as I nudge past the smokers to find a spot on the kerb.

Within seconds of dialling, his smiling face and chocolate-coloured hair fill the screen and I feel the tightness in my chest melt away. If anyone can calm me down, it's Johnny.

'Hey, Ginge. Look at you, all glammed up,' he says, his almond-shaped eyes not quite lining up with mine. 'How's it going in there?'

It all pours out like verbal diarrhoea. 'The editor has gone into labour and I have to go on stage in, like, an hour. Shit, shit, shit, I think I'm having a stroke.'

'Deep breaths,' he says, miming inhalation and gesturing for me to copy him over the phone. As I try to inhale, he speaks again. 'Jessica Dawn Jackson. Do I have to remind you that you were named New Editor of the Year last year? That you made editor of a magazine before you even turned thirty? You are more than capable of doing this job. It's just women instead of cakes. OK?'

'You're right,' I say, taking a long breath out. Women instead of cakes.

'Whatever you do, don't look at the crowd,' he says, accustomed to speaking in front of clients and big boardroom meetings. 'And remember you're the smartest, most beautiful woman in the room.'

I smile. Johnny has been so supportive while I've worked myself into a tizzy over the last few months trying to jump from the world of baked goods to a women's lifestyle glossy.

I blow a kiss at the phone screen, instantly calmer. 'Thank you.'

He pretends to catch it, then smushes it against his face.

'Loser,' I say, rolling my eyes.

'Love you too,' he says with a wink.

On my way back to the function room, I pick up a glass of champagne from the human tunnel of drinks trays and take a few sips. Then I walk into the hall with my head held high, channelling Johnny and his Big Lawyer Energy. I find my seat on the front row, next to a familiar face, Stephanie Asante. She is hovering on her own, so I introduce myself before the nerves can set in.

'I'm Jess,' I say, making for a left-sided air kiss. She goes to the right, holding out her arm for a hug so that we end up almost kissing on the lips.

'You'd think I'd be used to this sort of thing by now,' she says, holding up both hands in apology.

My guard drops as she smiles back at me and we take our seats. Up close, she is even more flawless than she looks online, her skin glowing under just a lick of blusher. Women like her are the reason I wanted to work at *Luxxe* – not to write the usual features about how effortlessly beautiful she is, but the whole inspiring story of how she made it from a Hackney council estate to leading her own women's empowerment network. Of course, *Luxxe* is giving the big award to someone who landed her own fashion empire via the Bank of Mum and Dad, but I'd love to see it go to someone like Stephanie next year.

'Are you shortlisted too?' she says.

'Me? God no,' I say, as flattered as I am flustered. 'I'm actually taking over when the editor goes on maternity leave. Only she literally just went into labour and now I have to present one of the awards.'

'Oh wow. Are you bricking it?' she says, drawing back her lips. 'I shouldn't admit this, but I still shit myself every time I do one of these things.'

I laugh, relieved that even the leader of a women's empowerment network gets nervous about public speaking. 'I am very much bricking it.'

'You'll be amazing,' she says. 'What were you doing before?'

As the seats fill up around us, Stephanie and I chatter away. She seems genuinely interested in why I'd leave a job where I got to test cake every day for one where I have to go up on stage and speak, semi-sober, in front of two hundred people. After five minutes banging on about how I spent my childhood sticking pictures of women into my own homemade magazines, I think she gets it. There's no need to tell her the real reason why I left.

As the lights go down, I feel a buzz in my stomach. A series of presenters dole out awards including Influencer, Icon and Entrepreneur of the Year, while the winners parade on stage to heart-rate-raising tunes like 'Firework' and 'Girl on Fire'.

When it's almost time for Tabitha to present the Fashionista award, I head backstage, my stomach fluttering as if I'm teetering on the cusp of the Big Dipper at Blackpool Pleasure Beach. I find her pacing nervously in the wings.

'Would you mind if I run through my lines?' I say, clutching the card that has just been thrust into my hands as a technical assistant attaches a mic to my jumpsuit.

'Sure,' she says, her own face pale with nerves. 'But quickly. I'm on in a sec.'

I look down at the card and reel off the lines. '. . . and the winner is . . . Sophia Henley-Jones!'

'Perfect,' Tabitha says, but I can tell she's barely listening as she flaps her own card. I don't blame her. I can't concentrate on a thing right now either.

'Good luck,' I say, as she hears her cue and heads out onto the stage.

And then it's me.

You can do this, Jess.

I totter onto the stage, summoning the image of an audience of baking enthusiasts, which is somehow nowhere near as scary. But as I reach the top step, I stumble slightly, my left heel catching on something as my right struggles to join it. I style it out, making a mental note not to attend any more events in heels I haven't worn in.

I continue towards the podium, reaching the lectern and clutching it like a life raft. I unfold my notes, my fingers shaking so badly that the pages flutter about.

'G-good evening,' I say, leaning forward and repeating myself until the mic picks up my voice. 'I'm J-Jessica Jackson.'

Whatever you do, don't look at the crowd.

As soon as Johnny's voice comes into my head, I'm OK. I can do this.

'I'm Jessica Jackson and I'm acting editor of *Luxxe*,' I say, finding my bearings. *Focus on the script.* 'And, er, judging by that entrance, you can probably tell why I'll never win Woman of the Year.'

A loud cackle comes from the audience and a ripple of

laughter follows it through the room. I glance down to see Aisha, who smiles at me from the front row.

Just a few sentences, that's all you have to say, then you're done. I shield myself behind the lectern and try to relax my legs. Deep breath.

'It's an honour to be here tonight,' I say, my muscles beginning to soften. 'Not only to celebrate the ninth annual edition of the Luxxe Women Awards, but also to present the most prestigious accolade of all, the Woman of the Year Award.'

There's a whoop from the audience. Aisha again, buoying me on. I'm getting into my groove now.

'At just twenty-eight years old, this woman has achieved more than most of us will in a lifetime. Not content with her award-winning fashion and beauty lines, TV show and a whopping half a million Instagram followers, she is now the proud author of the new *Sunday Times* bestseller, *How I Wear It*. Ladies and gentlemen . . . SOPHIA HENLEY-JONES!'

There's a split second of silence and a cough from the audience. Then the whoops and cheers begin as Sophia makes her way across the stage, her long black ballgown trailing behind her as she swoops towards me with a beaming smile. A dangling earring clinks against my Britney mic as she hugs me so tight I feel the air squeezed out of my lungs.

'It's So-FY-ah,' she hisses into my ear, her voice acidic. As soon as she pronounces it to rhyme with Mariah instead of my erroneous So-FEE-ah to rhyme with Maria, I realize my faux pas. Why didn't Tabitha tell me?

'I'm so sorry,' I mouth, mortified. 'So sorry.'

I step backwards so I'm out of shot, trying to remember which way I'm supposed to exit the stage. Then I'm running down the steps as fast as possible, making my way towards the bar, where I intend to find Aisha and get very, very drunk.

Felt cute, might delete later

'Everyone knows it's So-FY-ah, you numpty,' Lauren says into my ear as I step outside the hotel, phone balanced on my shoulder as I juggle the leftover goodie bags from the event.

It's hard to tell if the half a magnum's worth of champagne has helped or hindered me as I stumble down the front steps. Pros: I was loose enough to hold my own in a four-way conversation with Britain's top podcast host, a transgender activist and an Olympic gold medallist. Cons: I'm going to have a raging hangover on my first day as acting editor tomorrow.

'How was *I* supposed to know?' I clamber onto the back seat of the taxi.

'Don't you remember when she did that reality TV show about her super posh Chelsea life with her ultra-rich crisp-heir hubby?'

I laugh. When we lived together, Lauren and I would spend every waking hour watching 'structured reality' shows, to the point where we knew the exact inheritance of every mining, jewellery and confectionery heir on television.

'Well I've just made a right tit of myself in front of some of Britain's hottest celebrities then,' I say.

'I'm sure you didn't,' Lauren says. 'These people are too busy caring how they look on Instagram to worry about you butchering someone's name.'

'Yeah, you're right,' I say.

'Do you think she sabotaged you on purpose, this Tabitha?' Lauren says.

'Nah,' I say. 'She just wasn't paying attention. She's just come back from maternity leave, so she was probably as nervous as I was.' Although I must admit, there's a part of me that's not so sure.

'Well, good luck with everything tomorrow,' Lauren says, yawning. 'We need to talk about the wedding when you get the chance.'

'Yes, we do,' I say. Lauren's wedding is another thing on my endless to-do list, but I've struggled to find time for it lately with the whole new job thing. 'Tomorrow, I promise. I'll let you get off to bed,' I say, before hanging up.

In the back of the cab, I open my camera reel and flick through the photos Aisha sent. In the majority, my eyes are half-closed or I'm holding my arm at a weird angle. But there's one of me on the red carpet where I look vaguely passable.

I open Instagram and flick through the celebrity red carpet pictures on *Luxxe*'s account before I navigate to my profile. At *Perfect Bake*, I left the social media to the experts. Until recently, my last post was one of me and Johnny that I'd taken in the early days of Instagram, when everyone still used the X-Pro II filter and that chunky black frame that made everything look vintage. I started using it again when I decided to apply for the acting editor job and Aisha told me I needed to 'build a brand'. Since then, I've been trying to post regular pictures in an attempt to look like an achingly cool magazine editor, despite the fact that my camera roll is ninety-two per cent cat pictures.

I select the red carpet shot where I don't look entirely hideous and post it with the caption: *Heading into my first #LuxxeWomenAwards*. Then I refresh the page and wait for likes.

13

Three minutes later, there are no likes, and I wonder if I should delete it. Until two weeks ago, I was the editor of a baking magazine. No one is going to give a shit about me standing on a red carpet pretending to be someone I'm not. They're probably slagging off my outfit and rolling their eyes as they scroll.

I stare out of the window at Trafalgar Square, empty but for a few clusters of pigeons, some homeless people and the odd drunk stumbling home. A couple walk arm in arm, gnawing on fried chicken drumsticks with their free hands.

I open Instagram again. One like. Aisha Parker.

A second later, a little heart flashes onto the screen. A comment.

@Aisha_Parker_ You look smoking, Jess! Welcome to the Luxxe fam! xx

Several refreshes later, there's another like and a second comment.

@JohnnyWest That's my girl, working it! So proud of you x

I'm greeted at the door by a sleepy Oreo, who rubs himself against me, performing a figure of eight around my legs. I reach down to stroke his little head and he gives me an appreciative purr.

There's a light on in the kitchen, so I make my way through. The table is laid out with cling-filmed bowls of sticky rice and Johnny's signature Thai green curry, which he must have made from scratch because the pestle and mortar are out and there's a scent of lemongrass in the air. I reach into the open bag of prawn crackers and shove a handful into my mouth.

I slip off my heels, wincing at the blisters on both ankles. Desperate to rip off the jumpsuit, I reach an arm behind my back to undo the zip with my prawny fingers, but it gets stuck halfway down.

'Here, let me help you.'

I turn to see Johnny in the doorway, tumbler of whisky in hand and pyjama bottoms slung low.

I face away from him as he eases the zip down to the base of my spine, letting the top half of the jumpsuit fall around my waist. He plants delicate kisses on my neck as he slips a hand around my waist and pulls me into him.

'I could get used to this sexy new look,' he says, cupping one hand under my chin as he gently pulls my neck towards him.

As I turn to kiss him, I realize I still have the huge plaster across my chest from the hospital tests last week – the reason I had to wear this stupid high-necked jumpsuit in the first place.

Johnny sees it at the same moment and stops kissing me.

'How did it go? Shall I warm this up for you?'

'Look at you, cooking up a storm on a school night,' I say, quickly pulling the jumpsuit back up as he ladles rice and curry onto a plate and takes it to the microwave.

'Well, it's not every night my girlfriend does her first Luxxe Women Awards, is it?'

He puts the kettle on as I talk him through the events of the evening, including how I mispronounced the name of one of the UK's most well-known fashion influencers.

'How did you say it?' he says, looking bemused.

'I said So-FEE-ah and apparently it's So-FY-ah.' I smack myself on the forehead like an idiot.

Johnny laughs, putting one hand out to the side in a camp expression and saying 'Oh, So-FY-ah, darling!' with the poshest accent he can muster. Then he returns to his lovely, mild Mancunian twang. 'As if anyone would have known that.'

Hearing him take the piss, it hits home just how trivial my predicament is, and I snort with laughter. When Johnny and I first met, we bonded over our shared northernness, the way we both said 'grass' instead of 'grarse' and 'bath' instead of 'barth'. We would stand on the left side of the escalator to piss off the rest of London's mardy commuters. Whenever I've felt out of place as a state-school-educated northerner in the South, he's always had a knack of making me feel like I belong.

'I'm sure you were brilliant,' he says, passing me a cup of tea and returning to take my plate out of the microwave.

'Thanks for waiting up.' I watch him squeeze fresh lime on top of the plate of rice and creamy Thai green curry. He scrapes the sauce off a couple of prawns and puts them on the floor in front of Oreo, who gobbles them up in seconds.

As he puts the plate down in front of me, I realize I'm ravenous. I hoover up the curry like a gannet while Johnny takes my phone and plugs it in to charge for me.

'I'm proud of you, Ginge,' he says, massaging a knot in my shoulder.

I can't help but smile. This is high praise from Johnny. In my early twenties, I'd meet guys in bars who were gushy from the off, calling me 'beautiful' to try and get my knickers off, but they'd run a mile once they got what they wanted. Johnny took a year to tell me he loved me, and a month before he even paid me his first compliment. 'You're quite fit, you are.' Coming from him, it meant the world.

As I eat, I relax into his touch, relieved at how much better things are between us. When I first heard about the acting editor position, I knew it was my chance to leave *Perfect Bake*, even though it would mean spending all my evenings and weekends preparing for the interviews. It made things tough between us, not only because he wanted me to spend that time with him but also because he didn't understand why I wanted to leave the baking mag in the first place – I'd only been editor for a year. He went on about how 'obsessed' I was with Instagram and how I never had time for him any more, yet it was perfectly fine for him to spend a weekend working on a case, as if his career was more important than mine.

Then one day I came home to find he'd put up the pictures I'd been nagging him about since the day we moved into the flat, including the special print he'd made of my very first *Perfect Bake* cover. Ever since then, he's been Mr Supportive.

'Mm,' I say, moaning at the massage, feeling a combination of sleepy and sexy all at once. I push away my plate and turn to kiss him, then slowly stand up, pulling him towards me in a way that says yes, tonight you are getting it. 'Let's go to bed.'

Instagram vs reality

'Did you see we were trending on Twitter?' Aisha says, as I walk into the office on Tuesday morning.

I make my way over to my desk, peeling off the long, tailored red coat that I gave myself as a gift when I got the job at *Luxxe*. I'm a little groggy from the booze and the short night's sleep but, back in my own trusty heeled boots and skinny jeans, I feel confident in my skin again. Then there's the ever-so-slightly glowy feeling from last night's spontaneous sex . . .

'Let's have a look,' I say, excited for my first proper day in charge. Even though I no longer have Leah as my support blanket, I'm feeling psyched, if a little terrified.

I check out the buzz around #LuxxeWomenAwards on Twitter, then I switch to Instagram to see how my own post is doing. The love-heart icon shows I have hundreds of likes and seventy-three new followers, including Stephanie Asante and the editor of our biggest competitor. I refresh my feed and click on the photo I posted last night.

Two hundred and fifty-four likes. That has to be my best-ever performance, even better than the one where I announced my new role the other week. I study the photo again, thankful Aisha was there to style me into the perfect red-carpet position, my left leg in front of my right and my face turning slightly off to the side.

Beneath the picture, there are now dozens of comments from friends, PR contacts and magazine readers. They range from the fire emoji from Lauren to *So lovely to meet you! xx* from Stephanie Asante. *The* Stephanie Asante, commenting on *my* pictures. I feel like Beyoncé.

I scroll through the list of new followers, scanning for anyone I should follow back and clicking into a couple of profiles that sound familiar. Then I notice a new notification. *Johnny West has tagged you.*

I click through to the picture, which he must have posted on his way into work. It's the same red carpet shot, with the caption, *So proud of my magazine extraordinaire girlfriend @Jess_Jackson_Luxxe! Good luck on your first day!* He's added the flexed bicep emoji and two kisses at the end. *Aw.* Johnny *never* posts on Instagram – he's one of those silent observers who just browses and occasionally likes things, but he's only ever posted two pictures, both of which were of his bike. That makes it doubly cute that he's being so supportive of my career move. I make a mental note to return the gesture somehow. I know Johnny has been going through a hard time at work too, but I haven't been able to pay him much attention these last few months.

I'm about to shut the app when the heart symbol flashes up again, that little chemical hit that keeps me hooked to the 'gram for hours on end. I have one new follower, @LittleMissAvo, who seems to have had a liking spree of my last few posts. The tiny avatar shows a scantily clad brunette with abs to rival Jessica Ennis-Hill's, and I can't help but click on her profile for a look. She has twenty-two thousand followers to my meagre eight hundred and sixty-two (no thousands). The line at the top says, *Followed by Tabitha_Richardson__, Aisha_Parker_, PerfectBakeUK + 14 more.*

I cast my eye over her grid, which alternates between food

and profile shots. As I take a closer look, I realize they are body-positivity posts – each split-screen image has her in hot pants and sports bra, showing off her washboard abs and perky breasts, then a comparison shot from a different angle revealing just the tiniest patch of cellulite. There are a series of no-bullshit hashtags, from #InstagramVsReality to her own bespoke tag #LittleMissAvo, and for every body-positivity post, there's a food collage calling out taste-free 'diet' alternatives in favour of full-fat cakes and traditional puds. Now this is a girl after my own heart.

Another split-screen post catches my attention a little further down her grid. There she is, in a tailored suit and six-inch heels, posing in front of an indoor water feature, coffee cup in hand, looking the consummate professional. Next to it is a make-up-free selfie, greasy hair pinned back but still looking gorgeous with a pile of papers on top of what looks to be a desk in her bedroom. The caption reads:

Pic 1: When you're all spruced up to hit the head office at your fancy new firm. #RunningInHeels. Pic 2: When you're pulling your fifth all-nighter to prep for the *most terrifying meeting* at said fancy new firm. #ImposterSyndrome, much?

I immediately click 'Follow Back'. This is exactly the sort of woman I want to feature in *Luxxe* – someone who cuts through the bullshit and tells it like it is, not competing against other women but empowering them, showing them that success doesn't come without hard work.

'I *love* her!' Tabitha says, appearing from nowhere behind my desk. 'She's so refreshing, isn't she? And I *wish* I had those abs but fat chance of that after having a kid.'

I close the app, keen to remain professional. Even though I'm looking out for new people to feature in the mag, I don't want Tabitha to think I'm messing around on social media. I'm not about to squander the job I've been working up to for almost twenty years.

It was in my early teens, mesmerized by *Sugar*, *Bliss* and *J-17*, that I proudly proclaimed I was going to grow up to be a magazine editor. While my friends coveted clothes from Miss Selfridge or the latest make-up from The Body Shop, all I wanted was A4 paper, printer ink and Pritt Stick so I could put together my own problem pages and invent real-life stories.

It helped that I had Mum's buy-in. She and I would pore over the pages of glossy magazines while she described the glamour of Covent Garden, where she'd worked as a waitress at Simpson's in the Strand before she moved up north to be with Dad. She indulged my dreams of editorship, telling me that when I was rich and famous, she would be my plus one at lavish launch parties, hoping one day to meet Cliff Richard, her free pass. Dad would shake his head in mock disgust, but I could tell it delighted him to see Mum and I so close.

My parents were only just breaking even from running the tea rooms they'd bought in our little Yorkshire village when I was ten, so money was always tight. But Mum having a sister in London meant they could just about afford to send me down south for two weeks of work experience when I was fifteen. I still remember the day Mum waved me off, packing me up with sandwiches and a suitcase as if I was leaving for a year. Looking back at the house as Dad's car turned out of the end of our road, I could still see her there, waving on the driveway in her slippers and pinny over her favourite frock. When I unpacked that evening at Aunty Cath and Uncle Paul's, I discovered she'd hidden a tin-foiled batch of lemon drizzle in my suitcase with a note that read: *Knock 'em dead, Jessie. We are so proud of you. Love Mum and Dad x*

Those two weeks were everything I imagined they would be. Taking the train and the Tube from Peckham to Soho each day felt impossibly grown-up. Even though I didn't get a single word in the magazine and my days were spent fetching sandwiches and cans of Diet Coke for the editor, it was a thrill to see the articles before they went to press, to transcribe pages and pages of important interviews and to watch the editor in her corner office, sipping on coffee from a tall cardboard cup while typing away on her gigantic Macintosh computer. This, I was certain, was my world.

Once the IT guy has given me access, I work my way through Leah's emails, catching up on commercial partnerships, budgets and the flat plan for next month's pages. The timing would have been perfect if I'd actually got the whole three weeks in the job before she went on maternity, but I ended up with just a week and now I have a gazillion questions to ask her.

At ten a.m., I catch up with Miles, the publishing director. It helps that I already reported to him as editor of *Perfect Bake*, so I know what he likes and doesn't like. Miles isn't interested in the nitty gritty of the monthly pages – as long as the cover looks good and we've hit revenue targets, he's happy. It's a relief not to have someone micro-managing me, but on the other hand it means asking Tabitha when I have questions about the day-to-day running of the mag, and I don't want to come across like I don't know what I'm doing.

I blag my way through an impromptu stand-up meeting, re-assuring the team I have everything in hand – which, of course, I will have, just as soon as I catch up on all the loose ends left from Leah's early departure. Even though it's only mid-November, we're well into next year's issues, so it's all about fresh starts and how to achieve your dream career, both of which are topics I'm au fait with. When it comes to the fashion and beauty pages, I'm less comfortable – that's Tabitha's domain. I could reel off a thousand words on the ins and outs of Cronuts, duffins and other bakery hybrids in my sleep, but I'm not quite up to speed on paper-bag waists, or whatever's in fashion these days. Thankfully, *Luxxe* is less fashion, more lifestyle – think features on feminism, relationships and careers.

Mid-morning, I make my first slip-up, emailing the wrong freelancer about a vegan weddings article she pitched but which Leah ended up commissioning from a different writer. For a moment, I wish I could take the lift back down to my old floor, where I felt so at home I kept half my wardrobe under my desk. Then I remind myself why I left – you know you've fallen out of love with baking when even a triple-layered Biscoff cake doesn't get you excited.

I remember how enthusiastic I was when I started at *Perfect Bake*. I'd been working for Leah on a teen glossy when the publisher announced plans to launch a baking title with a tiny budget and an even tinier team. With my experience baking with Mum in the family tea rooms over the school holidays, I was the natural choice for features writer. *The Great British Bake Off* was taking off and the magazine grew just as fast, with me being promoted to features editor within a couple of years, and then editor a couple of years later. Mum would strategically place copies around the tea rooms, proudly telling every customer that her daughter wrote for the magazine.

Our biggest win was creating a title that appealed as much to teenage baking enthusiasts as it did to older dab hands, and I remind myself I want to do something similar with *Luxxe*. Although I can't make significant changes as acting editor, I can focus on making every bit of content as inclusive as possible, so an article about how to dress like a fashion editor is as relevant to a size eighteen cisgender Liverpudlian as it is to a size six trans woman from Brighton. Growing up in

Yorkshire, I never felt seen by these magazines – everything was so London-centric. I vowed that if I was ever in charge, I would make sure my magazine applied to every woman.

By lunch time, I'm hitting my stride. I check in individually with each member of the team, letting them know that I'm open to new ideas and I want to learn as much from them as they might from me. We've been friends for years and I thought she might feel weird about me becoming her boss, but Aisha is excited about me joining the team and has tons of ideas for how to transform our print content for the digital realm. The rest of the staff are enthusiastic and pumped to have their pitches heard.

But when it comes to Tabitha's turn, she reels off what seems to be every single nugget of knowledge she has acquired in her three years at *Luxxe*, as if she's determined to show me how capable she is. '*Miles doesn't like too many pieces on menstruation.*' '*Hygge is so 2016.*' '*Oh, we'd never put a reality-TV star on the cover.*' I know what she really means is they'd never put a *working-class* reality-TV star on the cover, but I'm not about to challenge her just yet. I do my best to make it clear that I'm not out to test or threaten her in any way, but when I start talking, she's barely listening, distracted by something on her phone. She's going to take a while to crack.

Leah's news makes its way to us around four o'clock, when Tabitha squeals from behind her desk. 'It's a boy!'

We crowd around her screen, taking turns to peer at the picture that Leah has sent to the team WhatsApp. In the shot, a bare-faced Leah snuggles a tiny, pale-looking creature with a full head of hair against her chest, her wife's head smushed up beside her. She looks exhausted but glowing.

Our beautiful little miracle was born Tuesday 14th November at 12:20 p.m., weighing 8lbs 2oz. Mummy, Mama and baby are doing just fine but mummy needs a strong Scotch after a gruelling 20-hour delivery. We are so, so in love xx

Leah's message ends with a little blue love heart. Below it, Tabitha has replied:

Oh my goodness, congratulations! There is nothing quite like those first few days with your precious little one. Enjoy every moment! Xx

We're all distracted for at least half an hour, cooing and awing over the baby and speculating about what she might call him. Leah and I kept in touch after I went to *Perfect Bake*, and I know how desperately she wanted to become a mother. She and her wife jumped through years' worth of hoops trying to make it happen before eventually getting pregnant with donor sperm. It's especially poignant that they've finally had a healthy baby.

I remember how she joked when I went for the *Luxxe* job that I'd probably be knocked up myself by the time she came back from maternity leave, but I've always hoped Johnny and I would get married first – if he ever asks. At the moment, babies and nappies couldn't be further from my to-do list – I've just got my dream opportunity in editing a magazine I've loved for years. I'm not about to throw it away.

Keen to establish a routine as the first in and last out of the office, I stay at my desk until seven, looking at the layout of the upcoming issue on the flat plan while sifting through mounds of emails from PR girls with names like Sapphire and Arabella offering to send me to the Seychelles in exchange for a feature. It's a step up from the free cakes I was sent every day at *Perfect Bake* in the hopes that they'd make it onto our socials, but I'm desperate to establish myself as a serious editor instead of taking advantage of freebies.

Despite hoping the Tube would be less busy by this hour,

I'm standing with my neck bent against the doorway and my other shoulder squashed into the armpit of a businessman who smells of stale beer. I stare into the carriage of lemmings, every single one of them engrossed in their smartphones. It's not exactly what I pictured when I fantasized about this lifestyle with Mum, but then none of it is quite the same now that magazines are folding left, right and centre. I'm grateful to have a job at all in this climate, let alone to be working at one of the few magazines that is actually thriving.

'The next. Station. Is. London. Bridge.'

I clutch my backpack to my chest as the commuters barge past me, elbowing their way out of the carriage like bath water flowing through an open plug hole. Then the tub is filling again, people pushing, handbags everywhere, outspread *Evening Standard*s filling all available space.

The flat in Clapham was supposed to make our lives easier. A straight Tube line south from the City for Johnny and a single change from Soho for me – if it wasn't for the hell that is the Northern line. Still, for the first few years that Johnny and I were together, I was living with Lauren down in Crystal Palace while he was all the way north in Stoke Newington. Whenever I made the trek to his, he would tell me to bring spare clothes and stay as long as I could, because he didn't want us to travel in the opposite direction unless strictly necessary. When Mum was really sick, he finally said the words I'd been waiting for: 'I never want us to travel in opposite directions, Jess. Move in with me.'

'Move down please!' someone shouts. But I can't. I'm stuck in the space between the seats and the end of the carriage, about to be wedged in by bodies.

'Fuck's sake,' someone says.

I look up to realize it's aimed at me, because I'm blocking a tiny space that I know if I move into, I won't have anything to hold onto. Then a brief case whacks me in the shin, sending a sharp pain down my leg.

A couple of weeks ago, I would have burst into tears. I would have questioned why I bother working all the hours, only to be abused on the Tube by middle-aged men who wouldn't give a shit if I keeled over and died, while other people make their money from sunbathing in the Maldives in #gifted swimsuits.

But today I shrug it off. Sure, it's been crazy busy lately and Johnny and I have had a bit of a rough patch, but things are actually pretty great. I have everything I want in life – the dream job, the doting boyfriend, the bright future.

Little Miss Avo

'I read your first article!' Johnny says, waving his phone at me with the profile of Stephanie Asante on the screen, my first article for *Luxxe*. I drafted it a couple of weeks ago and added a few quotes from a quick interview at the awards ceremony before Aisha published it this afternoon. 'I loved all that stuff about how under-represented the working class is in the media. She's cool, isn't she?'

My heart swells. I don't think I'll ever get over the feeling of gratitude for the fact that Johnny reads every single article I write. He even read half of my back catalogue when we met, just so he could bring things up on our early dates. Five years on, he remains as interested as ever.

While Johnny plates up our dinner, I go to compose a post on Instagram about my first *Luxxe* online piece. But as soon as I open the app, I'm distracted by a video.

Little Miss Avo appears in a white bikini performing handstand push-ups against a wooden pole on the veranda of what looks to be an exotic holiday resort. When she pops down from the handstand, I can actually see the flex of her tanned, toned thigh muscles and I'm mesmerized by how her breasts defy gravity even when she's upside down. Then, in the second video in the carousel, I discover her blooper reel of failed attempts. Here she is falling on her face, there she is tucking in a nipple that threatened to escape. I laugh out loud – I love this girl.

'What's funny?' Johnny says, plonking down a bowl of his weeknight pasta, which consists mostly of frozen peas and shop-bought pesto. Clearly last night's homemade curry was a one-off.

'This new influencer I've found,' I say, flashing my phone at him. 'I'm thinking of interviewing her for a piece.'

Johnny squints at the screen, briefly frowns and then shakes his head. 'You and your bloody Instagram. Put it away for once.'

Suitably reprimanded, I lock the phone screen and put it down on the bench beside me. There are only so many times I can tell Johnny I'm on it for work, and I haven't exactly convinced myself either.

Before he sits down, Johnny picks up his phone, types something, then clicks it shut, signalling he's ready to obey the phones-off-at-dinner rule that we've both been pretty lax about lately. 'So how was the vibe with Tabitha today?'

'Hmm . . .' I search for a word to describe her general attitude towards me. 'Hostile?'

'She's jealous,' Johnny says, grinding pepper onto his pasta. 'Someone with your stratospheric career waltzing in as her new boss? Anyone would be threatened by that.'

Perhaps he's right – I wouldn't want to step on anyone's toes. But I can't help thinking it's the other way round. Tabitha is so experienced, so knowledgeable about fashion, that I feel pretty inadequate next to her. Until recently, I thought Sandro was a pizza chain, not a fashion brand.

'Could you take her out for lunch, get her on your side?' he suggests. 'Keep your enemies closer and all that.'

'Good shout,' I say, wondering what Tabitha would make of the way I'm funnelling pasta into my gob like I haven't seen a meal for a month. I've rarely seen her eat anything that isn't quinoa.

Johnny takes a sip of his wine. The buttons of his shirt are pulled slightly taut around his middle and there's a single strand of chest hair poking out. I've been trying to get him to do some sort of exercise, but last time I broached the idea of him cycling to work again, he muttered something about the high incidence of cycle-related deaths in London.

'How's work, anyway?' I say, keen to figure out how to get him motivated.

Johnny shrugs. 'Ah, you know, the usual. Did I mention your dad called me again?' He stabs his fork into multiple bits of penne. 'He's worried about you, you know.'

Shit. I need to return one of Dad's missed calls, just like I need to call Lauren about the wedding, but I've got enough on my mind. I'll call him on the weekend.

While Johnny clears the plates, I pick up my phone to post my article, but I find myself gravitating to Little Miss Avo's profile again. She's exactly the sort of person I want to interview – strong, smart and funny, yet apparently petrified about a job that I'm sure she's probably more than qualified for.

I click on the link in her bio and navigate straight to the 'About Me' page of her blog, where I'm met with a full-screen image of her, sprawled across a swanky hotel bed, one tanned shoulder exposed and her Kate Middleton-esque hair covering her breasts. The bio reads: *Mia King, 23. Full-time solicitor, part-time bullshit detector. Trainee at Mackenzie Paige in Manchester.*

'Oh my God, she works at your firm!' I say, remembering the #ImposterSyndrome post. I *thought* that water feature looked familiar.

'Who?' Johnny twists around from the sink to glance at me.

'This new influencer I've found. Mia King?'

He gives me a blank look, then shakes his head. 'Never heard of her.'

'Could she be one of your new trainees? Maybe you could introduce me.'

He turns his head back to the sink. 'I've only met the ones in the London office.'

'OK,' I say, starting to type out a message. 'In that case, I'm sliding into her DMs.'

'Wait!' Johnny turns off the tap and wipes his soapy hands on his trousers. 'Put your phone away a sec.'

'What's up?' I abandon the message and push my phone to the side.

Johnny comes back over to the kitchen bench and sits down opposite me. He lets out a sigh as if he's been holding it in for a month, then he gulps. 'I wasn't going to tell you this yet but . . .'

'J, what is it?' I see the dejected look on his face.

'I didn't make partner.'

'What?' Making partner at his law firm is like a life-or-death scenario for Johnny. He's been working towards this forever. 'But I thought the decision wasn't for another few weeks?'

He sighs. 'Erica told me I wasn't going to get it.'

'When?'

'A couple of weeks ago.'

'What? Why didn't you tell me?'

He picks at his fingernails. 'You were starting your new job. You had enough to worry about.'

I *knew* there was something he wasn't telling me. He may have been supportive, but he's been so moody lately, one minute miles away staring out the window and the next making plans for our summer holidays.

I take his hand. 'I'm so sorry. You'll get there, though. I know how much Erica rates you.'

Erica Paige is your typical alpha female, surviving on four hours' sleep and waltzing around the office in her power suits without ever looking the remotest bit tired. She made partner at thirty-four with three children under the age of six and somehow still found time to set up a women-in-law symposium. But despite her intimidating demeanour, she's a nurturer, taking Johnny under her wing when he is struggling, championing diversity and welcoming all the trainees as if they were her own children.

'Wait, how did you know she wasn't in the London office?'

'What?' Johnny is distracted by something on his phone.

'Mia King,' I say.

'What do you mean?'

'Well, you said you'd never heard of her, but you knew she wasn't in London. So you must have known she was in the Manchester office.'

He makes a face. 'I just assumed because I hadn't met her, she must be in Manchester,' he pauses, then adds, as an afterthought, 'because I've met all the London trainees.'

'But you're up in Manchester every month and the office is tiny.' I pull up her Instagram and scroll to find the image to show him, but a selfie with a pastel pink background catches my eye. I recognise the iconic dining room at Sketch because we profiled it in an afternoon tea feature for *Perfect Bake* – and because Johnny went there for a dinner that Erica put on to help integrate the trainees with some of the senior associates.

I look up at him. 'Didn't you go to that dinner at Sketch in September?'

Johnny looks off to the side, scratching his nose. 'Oh yeah,' he says, his voice going up an octave. 'Let's see what she looks like again.'

32

But before I have the chance to show him my phone, I'm distracted by the hand that appears, resting on the table, just in shot, beside Mia. I pinch my fingers to zoom in on the unmistakable dark hair that expands from the wrist, then the silver cufflinks – the ones I had engraved for his birthday. I'd recognise that hand anywhere.

'J, you were sitting *next* to her.' I thrust the phone in his face. 'Why would you—'

My stomach drops.

This isn't a coincidence, is it? She *wanted* me to find her on Instagram. She followed me right after Johnny posted my picture.

The words take a while to form. 'Is there . . . is there something going on with this Mia?'

Johnny jolts his head back into his neck and for a moment I doubt myself. 'What? Of course not! I just forgot I'd—'

'You forgot you'd met someone who you sat next to at an intimate dinner and who you presumably see once a month in an office of, what, ten people?'

Something flashes up on his phone. We both glance at it at the same time, but before I have chance to read the message banner, he's turned it face down on the table.

'Who is that?' My heart rate is rising, the sudden feeling of dread taking over my bowels.

'No one,' he says, turning it towards him then putting it face down again. 'Just work.'

I put my hand on my chest to steady myself and I speak in the calmest voice I can manage. 'Why do I get the feeling you're lying?'

Johnny makes a sort of pyramid with his hands around his nose, inhaling deeply with his eyes closed. When he removes his hands, I see he's shaking.

'Johnny, what is it?'

The words come out quiet, like a child 'fessing up to getting crayon all over the wallpaper. 'I'm an idiot, Jess. I've fucked up.'

He gulps, then raises his head to look at the ceiling. I follow his gaze and notice he's put the wok back on the wrong hook again.

'What have you done?' I say, my heart thumping in my chest now.

'Mia and I . . .'

He looks at me, like I'm supposed to finish the sentence, but all I can think of are her perfect, perky breasts, bouncing up and down in her white bikini.

'Mia and you *what*, Johnny?' I can barely breathe. A punch to the gut, swift and sharp.

He shakes his head again, like it won't be real if he doesn't voice it out loud.

'It was just one time, I swear. I was wasted . . .'

Just one drink

'You need to eat something,' Aisha says, pushing the bowl of sweet potato fries towards me and waving one in front of my face. 'Come on, just a few, or I'll have to pull out the big aeroplane moves.'

I barely slept last night. I was a zombie all day around the office, my eyelids swollen like watermelons from so much crying. I'd get distracted by an email or a meeting for around five seconds before it hit me afresh, a swift kick in the stomach every time I remembered that the person I love the most has committed the cruellest betrayal.

I push a chip into my mouth and try to chew it; it tastes like cardboard. I'm running on empty but I can't eat. I can't stop crying. As I relay it all to Aisha for the third time today, I feel hollow.

He tried to wriggle out of it at first, telling me they'd just had a drunken kiss on a work night out last month in Manchester. But I knew he was lying. It all makes sense now, the way he'd been off with me about spending so much time engrossed in my work, and then suddenly one day he comes home all jolly and handy around the house, trying to seduce me with home-cooked meals and DIY. *Guilt.*

I can't even say her name without venom rising up my throat. I pushed him and pushed him until he told me the truth, or his version of it, the gradual drip-feed of information hitting me blow by blow as I discovered the extent of his betrayal. Mia, it turns out, is the Rising-Star Trainee Who Can Do No Wrong who started at Johnny's firm after the summer. They had sex – just once, he swears – and when he told her he had a girlfriend, she threatened to find me and tell me everything.

'And the worst part of it is he left for Manchester this morning,' I say, puffing air out of my nose as I realize how much of a mug I must look. 'He could have called in sick, told them he couldn't make it this month, *anything*. But no, he's literally gone back to the scene of the crime to spend the next two days with *her*.'

'So how did you leave it?' Aisha says, passing me a napkin to stem my tears.

I huff as I recall the hideous screaming, crying fight that followed us from the kitchen to the living room and eventually to the bathroom until I finally collapsed into bed at four in the morning while Johnny slept on the sofa. He suggested I could sleep with someone else if I wanted, to 'make things even', as if that could somehow magically fix what he'd done. I told him it was over; there was no way on earth I would stay with a cheat.

'And then he had the cheek to say he wants to marry me some day,' I say, laughing at how ridiculous it sounds.

Aisha screws up her face. 'Bit late for that, isn't it?'

I nod. When Johnny and I first met, I was sure it would just be a fling. We were both on the singles table at a wedding and I instantly gravitated towards his northern accent, which felt like home. He was too young, too good looking, too successful to be anything other than a player, and I knew he wouldn't be up for anything serious. It was only after we'd been dating for a month that I found out Johnny had shuffled the table plan so he could sit next to me. He'd seen me in the church, asked the groom who I was and then rearranged the little teacups that denoted our names on the table. It always tickled us that I'd never find out if I'd have hit it off with Uncle Nigel. Now that little private joke feels pathetic.

'Hey,' Aisha says, squeezing my hand. 'I hate that he's done this to you. He's a prick.'

But he's not a prick. As much as I hate him for betraying me, the Johnny I saw last night doesn't compute with the guy who plugs my phone in to charge because he knows I panic when it goes below twenty per cent. It doesn't compute with the man who always lets me go first in the bath or shower, who rolls up slices of ham and serves them to the cat as a gourmet meal when he thinks I'm not looking, and who will always forgo the last Rolo, the last crunchy corner of lasagne, the last *anything*, for me.

I thought we'd get married someday. It's not like I wanted the big white wedding. I'd always pictured us in a registry office with a few close friends, like Mum and Dad did. The sort of love that lasts forever, or at least until death do us part.

'He actually said she "listened" to him,' I say, making air quotes with my fingers and immediately hating myself for it.

Aisha rolls her eyes. 'For fuck's sake, is he after the cliché of the year award or what?'

'But what if he's right?' I say, fingering the stem of my margarita glass. 'I *have* been absorbed in my job. I *have* neglected him, I suppose. I didn't even know he'd failed to make partner.'

Aisha waggles a finger at me. 'Don't you *dare* blame yourself for this. The whole "she listens to me" thing is the oldest trick in the book.'

She's right, of course, but there's a part of me that thinks Johnny isn't like that, that he really did feel like I wasn't listening to him. He's been through a lot, what with Mum, and everything with his dad, and now failing to make partner.

'I don't know if I could forgive him,' I say, swirling the dregs of my cocktail.

'I know you love him, but he's a dick for doing this to you.'

I want her to tell me I'm crazy not to forgive him, that he regrets it as much as he says he does. I've been ignoring his calls all day and going over and over the conversations in my head, but I can't see how we could ever go back to normal. I'm exhausted from thinking about it.

'I still can't believe it was Little Miss Avo,' Aisha says, shaking her head. When I told her everything in the office at lunchtime, she instigated a bitchy scroll through Mia's grid before we both ceremoniously unfollowed and blocked her. Aisha tried to console me by saying things like 'you're way smarter than her' and 'guys prefer something to grab onto,' but the fact is he slept with her, and now every time the image comes into my head I feel it in my bowels, a full bodily reaction to what he's done. I know it wasn't her fault if she didn't know he had a girlfriend, but she wanted me to find out, didn't she? She wanted to hurt me.

I need to stop going over and over this in my head.

'Enough about me,' I say, trying to brush away the thoughts of Miss Perky Avocados that are threatening to take over again. 'I want to hear all about your date with the painter.'

'If I'm going to tell you about my love life, we're going to need another drink,' she says, gesturing for the bartender's attention.

'Bottle?' I say, pointing to the prosecco at the top of the list.

'This is why you're my kind of wing woman, Jessie J.'

Half an hour and a glass of prosecco each in, Aisha has talked me through her latest string of disastrous matches. From the teacher who sent her voice notes every day for six weeks only to ghost her as soon as she suggested meeting up, to the banker who flew her to New York for a date, only for her to find out via a deep Facebook stalk in the airport that he was engaged to be married, she makes a convincing case for me to stick with the cheating boyfriend rather than hit the dating scene.

'And then he had the audacity to ask me to repay the air fare,' she says, swigging another gulp of prosecco. 'Like, I'm sorry, but if you're going to fly your date halfway across the world without bothering to tell them you've got a fiancée back at home, you can bloody well stump up the air fare.'

I shudder at the thought of Johnny doing something so deliberately deceiving. But what he did wasn't exactly much better.

'So the painter?'

She huffs. 'He was alright, but he bored on about himself for two hours. I sent him a text afterwards, like "nice meeting you but I didn't feel a spark", and he sends me this whole tirade of abuse.'

'What did he say?'

She picks up her phone and scrolls to find the message, shaking her head as she reads it back:

'It's fine, I could tell you would be high maintenance and frankly you are not my physical type either. I hope you find what your looking for. "You're" spelled y-o-u-r, naturally.'

I laugh properly for the first time this evening.

'High fucking maintenance?' she says, her mouth agog. 'I mean, who does he think he is? He met me for two hours!'

'Wow,' I say, genuinely shocked by some of the stuff she tells me about her dates. 'What did you say?'

She looks down at her phone again.

'Dear Patrick, I was actually trying to be kind by telling you I didn't feel a spark. In truth, I thought you seemed like a

LAURA PRICE

self-absorbed prick. Oh, and you might want to learn the difference between "your" and "you're". Love, High Maintenance x'

I almost choke on my prosecco. I wish I had Aisha's balls.
'Did he reply?'

'Oh yeah,' she says, tapping her finger again and reading
out the message:

'Just remember this is what your missing out on.'

She turns the phone to face me, showing me a full-frontal
image of a stocky, hairy-chested man, standing in front of a
mirror, his head cut out of the shot and his erect penis peeking
out over the top of the bath.

'Jesus Christ,' I say, batting the phone away and checking
behind me to make sure no one else has seen it. 'Why would
anyone think you wanted that?'

'Vile, isn't it?' she says, finishing her prosecco and topping
us both up. 'Anyway, we move on. I've got a date this Friday
with an Aussie surfer.'

She swipes through her phone and shows me a picture.

'I approve,' I say, picking up my glass and cheersing her.

For all of five minutes, I almost forgot about Johnny and Mia.

'I need you to teach me the dating apps,' I say, returning
from the loo half an hour later, buoyed by several rounds of
drinks.

Aisha spits out a mouthful of prosecco, sending droplets
of liquid onto my hand. She stares at me, laughing for a
moment, then her face goes serious. 'You're not joking, are
you?'

I shake my head. 'I'm going to sign up for online dating.'

Aisha stares at me like I'm batshit crazy. 'You don't think
you're slightly rushing into things?'

I shrug. 'Johnny's in Manchester with some twenty-fucking-
three-year-old he clearly fancies the arse off. If I'm going to be

40

single, I need to get straight back on the horse. I'm not exactly getting any younger.'

'But you literally broke up with him last night,' Aisha says, looking uneasy. 'You don't even know if it's definitely for good.'

'I'm not saying I'm going to go on Tinder and find my future husband tonight,' I say, reaching for the bottle and pouring us each another glass. 'It's just a dabble, you know, see what's out there?'

'I can tell you exactly what's out there,' Aisha says, glancing at her phone as if it's to blame for every single date that didn't work out. 'Did you listen to anything I just said? Online dating is chucking yourself to the lions. They'll rip you to shreds.'

I know she is jaded from years of relentless swiping and disappointment, but still I want to give it a try, if only to take my mind off Johnny and Mia. I know Johnny wants to speak to me; I know he's trying to make amends. But the more I think of him in Manchester with her, the more I need to protect myself.

I shrug. 'I want to do something reckless for once, you know? I'm not going to shag anyone. It's just a distraction.'

'So you won't go on any dates?'

'No way. Not yet anyway.'

Aisha perks up. 'Well, to be honest it takes about three weeks to set up a date on the apps these days. You're WhatsApping for about a week and then you're either pen pals for life or they ghost you.'

'There you are,' I say, already feeling better that there's no immediate threat from signing up. It'll just be nice to have a swipe and see what's out there. Dip my feet into the waters of single life, as it were.

'Alright, fine,' Aisha concedes. 'I'll show you the craic, but only if you promise not to do anything stupid. I wouldn't be a very good friend if I sent you off for some kind of rebound shag.'

The thought of dating fills me with dread. I know Johnny and I aren't perfect, but when I hear about other people's relationships, I'm always glad to be with him. We're forever taking the piss out of other couples, sniggering at the way a lawyer friend of his puts his hand over his wife's wine glass when he thinks she's had enough, and rolling our eyes at those couples who put each other down in front of their friends.

'Sure you're ready for this?' Aisha says, taking my phone and searching for a dating app to download.

I nod my head, increasingly determined to get back at Johnny. I'm conscious I have to lead the editorial meeting first thing tomorrow morning and I need to leave early for my hospital appointment. Then again, Aisha's hangovers are so extreme that I'll look positively sober next to her anyway. I down my drink and ask the bartender for a couple more glasses.

'Right then,' she says, downing the dregs of her prosecco and slamming the glass on the edge of the bar with a flourish.

While Aisha scrolls through my photos to find a suitable profile shot, she gives me her dating 101, talking through the different apps and why online dating is 'a numbers game'. She explains that Tinder will give me exposure to a critical mass of available men but half of them will ghost me; Happn will ensure if I pass a single guy in the street, I'll be able to contact him; and Bumble will give me the apparently feminist opportunity to message the guy first. I don't see the advantage of being able to message first – surely I can do that with the other apps anyway – but I nod along with my teacher.

Aisha starts typing. 'What do you want to say about yourself?'

I stare at her. 'I don't know . . . I'm thirty-one, ginger, um, sort of single?' Saying the words out loud makes me reluctant to do this at all, but I force myself to picture Johnny with Mia.

'He knows that from your picture, dipshit. I'm going to have to take matters into my own hands.'

She writes: *Recently back on the market. Looking for a reason to delete this app.* Then she taps in a string of emojis: a dancing girl, a cat, a cocktail glass and a pink ring doughnut.

'What's that supposed to mean?'

'That's your profile,' she says. 'Emojis are the modern-day language of love. Anyway, no one reads this shit.'

'Right,' I say. 'Is there a "heartbreak on board" badge?'

Aisha raises an eyebrow. 'Jess. The first thing you need to know about dating apps is that you are not, under any circumstances, to tell the truth. It's like a CV. Write the good shit, leave out the bad.'

'So don't mention the five-year relationship that I may or may not still be in?'

She rolls her eyes. The further we go with this, the more nervous I feel about putting myself out there. But it's only a distraction.

The bartender approaches just as Aisha is explaining the concept of benching, which she says is when a date doesn't want to meet in person, but still continues to send messages. He opens his mouth as if he's about to say something, then shakes his head, picks up the empty prosecco bottle and replaces it with two fresh glasses, then slinks away again.

'So he's putting you on the subs bench, if you see what I mean?'

'OK . . .'

'Most guys put their height in their profile,' she says. 'If there's no height, that means he's short. If the guy has a photo with a kid, he'll usually put "child not my own" or similar. If he doesn't put that, he has a kid. Probably a wife. Oh, and if there's no photo of a kid at all, it's even more likely he has one.'

'Right. So to be clear, I'm looking for guys *with* kids in their profiles?'

'Exactly,' Aisha nods.

This is all very confusing, but I'm happy to humour her. 'OK. What next?'

'We start swiping,' she says.

I take a swig of my drink.

We work our way through pilots, musicians and traders, dismissing lawyers and fellow journalists in case we come across any of Johnny's or my past and present colleagues. I swipe left and right, watching as the different men disappear like discarded jacks in a pack of cards.

'Wait a second, isn't that . . .?' I pause with my finger over a familiar freckled face with vibrant red hair and beard, clad in sunglasses and apparently piloting a yacht. *Marcus, twenty-eight, designer.*

'Well, if it isn't Hot Coffee Guy,' Aisha says, grabbing my phone to take a closer look at his profile.

When I was at *Perfect Bake* and Aisha was already at *Luxxe*, we would watch this guy performing his elaborate coffee routine in the office canteen. We would speculate over whether he'd been a model in a previous life.

'Surely he isn't single?' I say. He's so unbelievably hipster, I always figured there'd be some achingly stylish musician girlfriend waiting in the wings.

'It says you've just crossed paths with him.' Aisha waves the phone at me.

It makes sense – we're right outside the office, so either he's still up there or he's somewhere in this bar.

'Do I swipe right?' I suddenly feel nervous about the idea

of snogging – or worse, being rejected by – someone I see in the office on a daily basis.

Aisha screws her face up. 'I'm not sure. I . . .'

But I've already done it, my thumb clicking on the little heart to the right of the screen.

Immediately, my phone vibrates and a notification pops up on the screen. *It's a crush!*

'He likes you,' Aisha says, rubbing her palms together while looking around the bar to see if she can locate him.

'Should I message him?'

'I dunno, Jess.' She looks down at her phone. 'It's getting late. I need to get off soon.'

I should really leave too. Tabitha has a whole host of ideas she wants to pitch and I want to make sure I put my own stamp on the magazine before anything is set in stone. I was meant to do it before Leah left, but now I have about a week to put together a killer presentation for Miles for our tenth anniversary issue. I really should go home and get a good night's sleep so I can focus. But the more I think about Johnny and Mia in a hotel in Manchester, the more I'm dreading going home to an empty flat.

'You do it,' I say, handing her my phone before I change my mind.

'Are you sure?' She looks uneasy.

'I just want a little flirt,' I say. 'Maybe a drink with him?'

So apparently you're 100m away from me. Office or bar? she writes.

I peer over Aisha's shoulder as we stare at the screen. *Marcus is typing.* The typing stops. Then Marcus is typing again.

I look up from the screen and see him – directly parallel, on the other side of the bar. He locks eyes with me and gives me a flirty smile.

I do my best ventriloquist impression as I try to communicate to Aisha that he is literally four metres away. She clocks him and gives him a little wave.

Drink? he writes.

Aisha looks at me, cautiously holding out the phone for me to take it.

I take a deep breath and type into the chat box.

Meet you outside in five.

'Jess!' she says, gently thumping me under the bar so he can't see my reaction.

'What?' I say. 'It's just a drink. I'm not going to do anything with him, I promise.'

She sighs. 'I don't want you to get hurt.'

'I'm already hurt,' I say, feeling a twinge in my chest as the heartbreak hits me again. I can't believe Johnny had the gall to suggest that we could "get even" if I slept with someone else. Nothing I do could ever match up to what he's done, how much he's hurt me.

'OK, but just . . . be careful, yeah? Message me in an hour, let me know how it goes. Don't do anything I wouldn't do . . .'

'As if,' I say, getting up from my stool, hugging her goodbye and promising to message her a full progress report within the hour.

But when I stand up to go to the loo, I almost fall into the door frame. It's not like me to be wasted two nights in the same week, but then it hasn't been a normal week. I steady myself on the toilet, glancing at my phone with its fifteen missed calls from Johnny, but my eyes are glazing over. I vow to get a pint of water before I leave the bar, then I truss up my hair with my hands and sweep it over my forehead.

I know I shouldn't do this, that I should go home and sleep

off the alcohol so I can go in to work early. But I can't stop thinking about Johnny with Mia.

I'll just go for one drink. That way, I've done nothing wrong, just a harmless flirt. Yes, that's what I'll do.

Just one drink.

It's complicated

I'm pinned up against the exposed brick wall of a Soho speak-easy, Marcus's arm propped up beside me, hemming me in. He's standing so close I can smell the tequila on his breath.

So much for drinking a pint of water. The moment he saw how tipsy I was, Marcus declared he needed to play catch-up and took me for tequila shots at a bar around the corner. He had me licking salt and lemon from his hand within minutes. The next thing I knew, we were descending the steps to a base-ment speakeasy, declaring the secret password and ordering overpriced gin and tonics before settling into a quiet corner at the back.

'I always thought you looked too serious to be out drink-ing on a school night,' he says, flirting with his ridiculously beautiful lips.

I don't know whether to be offended or flattered – the fact is, I would never normally be out drinking in the second week of a brand-new job. But alcohol and thoughts of Johnny are making me behave out of character.

'It's been a rough week,' I say, looking down at the floor.

'Want to talk about it?'

I wouldn't know where to start. I'm fairly sure Johnny and I broke up, though I'm aware there are many logistics to sort out, like the fact that we live together and share a cat, for starters. Maybe once we've put a proper full stop on it, I can begin the whole twelve steps of grief thing, but right now I'm in limbo. Then there's Tabitha, who's shot down every idea I've had so far this week. And I don't even want to think about my looming hospital trip.

I turn my face towards Marcus, my nose just inches from his. His eyes really are extraordinarily blue.

'Nope,' I say, taking a swig of my gin and tonic.

'Me neither,' he says, cheersing me.

I smile and take another swig of the bitter liquid. The more intoxicated I am, the more it numbs the pain, though I keep remembering I have work in less than ten hours.

We move on to the topic of *Luxxe* versus *Perfect Bake* and how I'm liking it 'on the other side'. I don't want to bitch, but as soon as he asks me about 'the girl who wears all those crazy outfits', I know he's talking about Tabitha. I didn't realize how much pent-up frustration I had, but she's done everything she can to make me feel maximum unwelcome since the Sophia debacle. Casually 'forgetting' to include me on email invitations, giving me the minimum information about whatever we're supposed to be working on, then making comments in front of everyone, like, 'Sorry, Jess, I thought you knew.' She's supposed to report to me, but she seems to think *she's* the boss.

It turns out Marcus does a cracking impression of Miles. He has me in fits of laughter over his assessment of editorial from the perspective of the mystical land of design. We bond over our shared gingerness and how we are the only genuine redheads in the publishing house. Within an hour of his company, laughing over our observations of everyone else in our office, I feel like a weight has lifted. I hadn't realized quite how inferior I've been feeling at *Luxxe*. Marcus feels like an ally.

'Enough taking the piss out of me and my team,' I say. 'Can we discuss your absurd coffee routine?'

I might have run a food magazine, but I've never seen anything like the fuss Marcus makes over his coffee. I tell him about the observations Aisha and I have of him operating his wanky drip coffee contraption while the rest of us brew our Nescafé in two seconds flat.

'You'll have to try it someday,' he says.

'I'll stick with my mug of instant, thank you very much.'

He takes the piss out of my rapid style transformation. It turns out he loved seeing me coming into the office all red-faced and sweaty from a morning gym sesh, before I showered and changed into my *Perfect Bake* uniform of skinny jeans and one of the countless pairs of boots I kept under my desk. I've only made minor changes, upgrading to the occasional pair of heels, my tailored coat and a bit more daytime lipstick.

'You've really been analyzing me,' I say, lifting an eyebrow.

'Well, when there's a woman as gorgeous as you sauntering around the office every day, it's kind of hard to concentrate . . .'

My mouth opens just a touch, my head dropping back against the wall behind me, exposing my neck to Marcus. My eyes find his for just a second too long, and then he is taking a step towards me, his whole body pressing me up against the wall.

Warm lips on mine. The taste of tequila, gin and prosecco combining in my mouth as his tongue attacks mine, hot and wet.

It is completely different from kissing Johnny. Marcus's lips are much thicker, plump like lilos, grazing mine.

I kiss him back, faintly aroused by the firm torso against my waist and the hand on the back of my neck, fingers touching the small baby hairs, making them stand on end.

And then he is pushing closer into me, grinding his crotch into mine as he performs a sort of vertical version of the worm against my body.

He nibbles my neck, leaving a trail of kisses down to my collarbone, making me shudder with pleasure. Then there's the thrill of kissing him in a public space, where anyone could walk in on us. He slips a finger into my blouse, tracing it slowly down to my breast.

'What's this?' he says, his finger having located the huge plaster that still sits on my chest.

'Nothing,' I say, snapping his hand away and doing up the top button of my blouse. I found the lump more than two months ago and I've been told several times it's probably hormonal.

Marcus mutters something under his breath and returns to kissing me on the lips, but I'm suddenly sentient, aware of the empty bar around us and the realization that I'm betraying Johnny.

'Stop,' I say, pushing him away. I look down at my phone to see a stream of messages from Aisha. The clock reads ten past midnight. *Shit.*

'What's up?' He steps back.

'I'm sorry,' I say, suddenly desperate to get out of here, desperate to get home. 'I shouldn't be doing this, I'm still . . . I'm not . . . I have to go.'

Marcus looks put out, but produces his own phone and concludes we should both go home. We retrieve our coats, sheepishly walking out into the cold Soho air together.

'Maybe we could get a drink another time?' he says, trying to keep up as I march towards the Tube station, desperate to shrug him off.

I stop suddenly, braking in the middle of Oxford Street. 'Marcus, look, I'm really sorry, I'm sort of in the middle of things with my boyfriend. I can't . . .'

'Umm . . .' he says. 'But I found you on Happn?'

'I know.'

51

'So I thought you were single.'

'Yeah, I know,' I say, feeling like I might be sick the minute I board the train. 'I'm sorry.'

'So you're not . . .?'

'It's complicated,' I say, pushing past him and stumbling off towards the Tube.

The morning after the night before

I roll over onto my right side, peeling open one eye. My mouth tastes like I've swallowed the rotting carcass of a skunk with a side order of durian fruit. My head is throbbing. The fuzzy red lights on the alarm clock show 08:15. *Shit.*

I sit up straight in bed, reaching for the glass of water but finding it empty. I don't remember getting home. Oh God, oh fuck, oh shit, I kissed Marcus.

I throw back the cover and find myself still dressed in yesterday's clothes, my blouse still intact. I must have stumbled home from the Tube gone midnight. Anything could have happened to me.

I search around for my phone and find it on the floor beside my bed, stacked up with messages from Aisha. I'm going to be late for work and it's only my third day in charge.

Holding my hand against my forehead as I pad to the kitchen, I fumble in the medicine drawer and pop out two Nurofen from their foil strip. I chug down a pint of water and put the kettle on while I get dressed. I'll throw some coffee in a travel cup and drink it on my way in, then I'll shower at work so I'm swiped into the office not long after nine. I'll just have to ply myself with toast and try to act sober so I can get through the day.

*

I'm still wasted as I board the Northern line at Clapham Common, jamming myself into a tiny slot in the rammed carriage. I button my coat right up to my neck, even though I'm sweating. I'm desperate not to see anyone I know among the morning commuters.

I open my phone to read the messages from Aisha, then I see the text from Johnny.

Hey Ginge, hope you're OK. Just wanted to wish you luck for your appointment today. Will you call me as soon as you come out? Xx

I lurch forward as the Tube pulls out of Clapham North. *Shit.* I'd almost forgotten I get my hospital results today. The last week has been such a whirlwind, it's hardly been at the top of my mind.

I check my calendar. I have a few hours to go to work, make like a brilliant acting editor while doing my best impression of a sober person, then get the Tube to the hospital after lunch. I can do this.

I open WhatsApp to read the messages from Aisha that I was obviously too drunk to reply to last night.

21:43 How's it going?

22:03 Did you snog him?

22:45 Going to bed. Hope you're behaving yourself! Let me know you get home safe please Xxx

07:01 Did you get home safe? x

07:14 Let me know you're OK, starting to get worried xx

07:35 Jess? You alive? xx

I message her back when the Wi-Fi signal returns at Elephant and Castle.

08:45 Feel like death. Still drunk. Send help. Please could you tell Tabitha and team I'm running late? Home emergency . . . Xx

The beauty of Miles being on a different floor is that he

won't notice I'm late – not that he would care, as long as I get the job done.

Aisha texts back immediately, saying she'll invent something about a plumber.

08:46 But only if you fill me in on EVERYTHING! Did you snog him?

08:47 Um, yeah. Please don't tell anyone. I feel rotten . . .

Aisha texts back with the crying face emoji. Don't feel bad! Johnny cheated on you, remember? Did it feel good to get it out of your system?

I spot an empty seat and slump into it, pretending not to see the other woman who was making her way over. You snooze, you lose.

I've lost Wi-Fi again and I don't even know what to reply. I don't feel good *at all*. In fact, I feel horrendous for stooping to Johnny's level, going straight onto a dating site before we've even had a chance to talk it over. What was I thinking?

08:51 Shall I tell them the meeting's rescheduled?

Shit, I'd completely forgotten I'm supposed to be leading the nine a.m. catch-up meeting. I reply to Aisha, asking her to reschedule it for ten a.m. to give me a bit of time to resuscitate myself.

I make it into the building just after nine fifteen, keeping my head down as I walk through reception and straight to the communal shower rooms.

As I strip off, I feel soiled. My head is pounding so hard I have to try and rein back the thoughts that are charging through my brain at a hundred miles per hour. What kind of person goes on a dating site and chews the face off a colleague the literal day after she breaks up with her boyfriend? I'm as bad as Johnny. At least he cared enough to remember my hospital appointment.

It is then that I feel the sour taste of bile rising at the back of my throat and the sweat spreading up my neck, making my head feel as if it's on fire. I'm going to puke . . .

I make it to the loo right before I vomit clear liquid everywhere. I empty my guts then collapse in a heap next to the toilet bowl. I've barely been able to eat anything over the last thirty-six hours. Lauren may call it the heartbreak diet but it's alien to me. I can't remember the last time I couldn't stomach a bowl of pasta.

I glimpse down at my naked body slumped on the floor. I disgust myself. Who in their right mind would hire me as the editor of a magazine? They'll never offer me a permanent job after this.

I allow myself five minutes of wallowing before I find the strength to crawl under the shower and turn the heat to as steaming hot as I can manage. I'll get cleaned up and force a few slices of toast down. Then I can focus on the mountains of paperwork and meetings I have lined up either side of my hospital appointment this afternoon.

It's going to be a long day.

Call me Rose

'Jessica Jackson?'

I look up to see a lady in her sixties or so, with the same smiling eyes as Mum. For a second I want to wrap my arms around her and breathe in the smell of flour and icing sugar that always clung to her hair from whatever cakes she'd been baking that day. I snap myself out of it. She is not my mum.

'Come with me,' the nurse says, a warm smile spreading across her face as she cradles her clipboard in her arms.

I scramble to put my laptop away, conscious of not wasting valuable hospital time. As I get to my feet, I still feel unsteady, the hangover headache escalating despite the painkillers. I clutch my fourth cup of coffee.

'Did you bring anyone with you today?' she asks. I shake my head, feeling instantly guilty about Johnny.

I follow the nurse down the corridor, around a corner and through a set of doors. I'm expecting her to lead me to another waiting room where I'll sit for the usual half hour, plenty of time to get through a few emails. But instead she turns left and walks us straight into a tiny, windowless consulting room, where I find the doctor already seated at the table.

'Hello Jessica. I'm Mr Patel. Please, take a seat.'

The doctor's face is wrinkled and cracked, but his eyes offer a glimmer of a younger man.

57

'Sorry, got coffee,' I say, putting the cardboard cup down on the table and dumping my bag as I sink into a wipe-clean chair, grateful for the seat. I want this day to be over so I can flop on my bed and sleep for nine hours.

'Don't worry,' the nurse mouths, sandwiching me in between her and the doctor.

'Jessica, we've received your test results,' says Mr Patel. 'I'm afraid it's bad news.'

His eyes are fixed on mine as if he wants me to speak next. I feel the blood start to drain from my face.

'The results show a malignant tumour in the left breast,' he says.

In *the* left breast. Not in *your* left breast.

I stare at him, unable to speak, willing him to continue.

'We'll need to put you through a course of treatment.' He pauses for effect, then continues. 'We won't know for sure until we've done further tests, but it's most likely we'll need to give you chemotherapy to shrink the tumour, then surgery, then probably radiotherapy. It could take around eight months.'

'Malignant?' I turn to the nurse for confirmation. 'Does that mean it's cancer?'

Of course it's cancer.

'Yes,' the doctor says. 'It can be hard to take in, initially, but Nurse Raymond here and the entire team will provide you with all the support you need.'

'Call me Rose,' she says, as if that's the most important thing to consider right now.

'But they said it was a hormonal cyst.' That's what my GP told me, then the consultant confirmed it with an ultrasound. They were both so sure it was normal for a woman of my age, even though I'd told them my gran died young from breast cancer. I only went back for another check-up because it hadn't gone away after almost two months and I couldn't be sure it wasn't getting bigger. That's when I had the biopsy with the giant needle, but by that point I'd had several doctors tell me it was nothing.

They must have made a mistake, mixed up the scans. It can't suddenly be cancer.

'We understand you'll be anxious it wasn't found sooner, Jessica,' says Mr Patel. 'But the good news is we found it and we're going to make sure we get you the best possible treatment.'

'Will I lose my hair?'

Nurse Rose crinkles her nose as she nods at me. I can't help picturing Little Miss Avo's beautiful glossy hair, then poor Britney when she had her breakdown, all chipmunk-faced and bald.

'Try not to worry about that for now, lovely. The team here are fantastic. We have everything you need to help you through it.'

Rose unfolds her age-blotted hands to reveal a wad of pink leaflets, which she slides towards me. I glance at the middle-aged woman in a fuchsia head scarf on the front of one pamphlet. My thoughts turn to Mum. 'What type of cancer?'

'Invasive ductal carcinoma. It's also what we call oestrogen-receptor positive, which means it responds to oestrogen. We'll have to put you on a course of hormone-suppressing drugs, and if you're on the pill, you'll have to stop taking it. But we'll need to do some more tests first.'

'I've got to call my work.' I don't have time for this. I have to put my absolute all into this job.

'I think, given the circumstances, your work will understand if you're a little late,' she says, touching me on top of my hand.

Mr Patel looks down at his notes and then back at me.

'Nurse Raymond and our brilliant team will go through every-thing with you in the coming days, Jessica.'

I open my mouth to tell him it's Jess, but I stop myself.

'Now, there's one thing. In pre-menopausal women such as yourself, chemotherapy can lead to a loss in fertility levels. You are . . .' He scans his notes, checking for my date of birth with that magical doctorly ability to calculate an age within three seconds. 'Thirty-one. Yes, it's likely you'll be on tamoxifen, that's the hormone suppressant, for ten years. At forty-one, you may find it very difficult to conceive, but there are options . . .'

This isn't happening. Practically everyone I know is settled down and getting married. Johnny said he wanted to marry me some day, and I know he wants kids. I've read enough women's magazines to know that fertility falls off a cliff at thirty-five and now I have the added curse of cancer. Maybe I'll *never* be a mum.

'There's all sorts in here,' Rose says, patting the pile of leaflets in front of me as if they hold the cure for cancer. 'Hair loss, egg preservation . . .'

'Egg preservation?' I remember a feature on egg freezing for single women in their twenties and thirties. The expert in the piece had called it 'Russian roulette' because the chance of a successful pregnancy from frozen eggs was so low.

'There are various options for preserving your fertility,' Mr Patel says. 'We can make you an urgent referral to a special-ist as you'll need to get this all done before you start chemo.'

Chemo. A montage of images flashes through my mind. Mum hooked up to the cannula, the drip feeding her chemicals that would knock her out for days. The first time I saw her bald, her pale scalp plucked like a chicken. Holding her hair back, trying to keep Dad from seeing her bent over the toilet bowl, crippled in pain. It would have broken Mum's heart if she'd ever imagined me going through what she went through. She'd be distraught to think I might never have kids, might not give Dad a grandchild someday.

Oh my God, I'm going to have to tell Dad.

My gaze shifts to a patch of peeling paint on the wall behind Mr Patel. A crisp curl of cream, like white chocolate shavings on a wedding cake. I want to reach past him to peel it off, like a scab.

'OK,' I say. 'I'd like to make an appointment for egg preservation please.'

Women are like tea bags

The key won't work. Why won't it work? I twist it left, twist it right, but it's stuck, the handle won't budge. I thump my fist on the hard wood.

'Jess? You alright?'

I turn and look down from the top step. Our neighbour, Clara, stands at the gate, immaculately dressed in Breton-striped jumper, jeans and suede boots. Baby Alfie is wrapped up in those stripy blankets from JoJo Maman Bébé that every yummy mummy in Clapham seems to own these days.

'I'm fine,' I say, turning my back to her. 'Wrong key.'

'You sure, hun? I've got time to pop in for a cuppa.'

Bingo. The key turns, the door opens.

'Really sorry, Clara. I'm fine. Talk another time.'

I open the door just wide enough to slip through the gap and slam it shut behind me. Then I run straight down the hallway and into the loo, missing the toilet bowl and vomiting into the sink. Memories of last night's tequila slammers flash through my head, but it's as if I'm imagining a different version of me. One who doesn't have cancer.

I lower myself onto the cold tile floor. From this angle, I can see all the spots I've missed – the stains on the bottom of the toilet bowl, the dirt beneath the sink. Must clean more thoroughly next time.

'*Tumour.*' I say it out loud, spitting the 't' as if to expel it from my body. I hate that word. It's growing and mutating inside me, trying to take over my body. I feel the panic rising in my chest, threatening to suffocate me. I'm struggling to breathe as I lie down and rest my head on the cold floor.

My phone vibrates against the tiles, jolting me upright.

Johnny.

I tap the green button, the first time I've answered his call in two days. I leave the phone on the floor, my head lying next to it as his voice emerges from the speaker. Oreo appears then, swiping his tail against my face as he rubs his scent all over me.

'Jess? Thank God you picked up. How was it? I thought you'd call me straight after your appointment.'

I manage a vague mumble from the floor, my head feeling drained and shaky.

'I've been calling you for ages. Are you OK?'

It takes every bit of energy to roll onto my front and push myself up from the tiles, easing myself into an upright position against the bathtub.

'I have cancer.'

'What?'

I sit in silence, letting the word sink in on both ends of the line.

'I knew I should have gone with you.'

'You weren't to know.' We'd broken up. *He cheated on me.*

'I'm coming home. Stay on the phone, OK?'

'OK,' I say, summoning every bit of strength just to hold my head straight, like a newborn whose neck muscles can't yet function.

A line of hair products stares at me from the shelf, taunting me with pictures of sleek, full-bodied redheads. Colour Goddess. Radiant Red. *Because you're worth it.*

'I'll be on my way back from Manchester soon. I'll be a few hours, OK?'

I nod. *Manchester. Mia. Marcus. Cancer.*

'Keep talking to me, Jess.'

I nod again.

'Jess?'

'What if I die?'

'You're not going to die,' he says. His legal voice, the one he uses with clients. 'We're going to take this one step at a time.'

I nod again, my gasps and sobs drowning out my own breathing.

He keeps me on the phone, talking constantly like someone from emergency services.

'Where are you?'

'At home.'

'What room are you in?'

'The bathroom.'

'OK. Go into the kitchen, OK? Put the kettle on. Make yourself a cup of tea, OK? Will you talk me through it?'

A cup of tea, the solution to everything. He's right, of course. I haul myself up from the bathroom floor, taking a moment to steady myself on the sink before I walk the few steps towards the kitchen. Oreo follows me, butting his head at my leg.

The phone is buzzing against my ear. 'Hang on, someone's calling me. It's Lauren. I need to go.'

I press the button to accept the call from Lauren.

'Jess, omigod, it's the fucking florist.'

'Hm?'

'They've messed up the flowers again. And now Lola's have said it's going to take an extra two months to make the brides-maid dresses in marshmallow.'

'Lauren, I . . .'

I open the cupboard and take down my favourite mug, the one so big Dad joked I could have a bath in it.

'Look, I know it's not necessarily what you'd pick for yourself,' I can hear her voice trembling, on the verge of tears. 'It's just really important to me that we go with the marshmallow.'

'Lauren . . .'

I fill the kettle and drop a teabag into the mug, remembering the way Mum would always put the milk in first.

'Jess, I didn't understand how stressful organizing a wedding was going to be. It's just so—' She is crying now, sniffling into the phone.

'Lauren, I need to tell you something . . .'

The comforting crackle and hiss of the kettle.

'Please don't argue with me, Jess, it's my wedding. You only get married once. At least, I hope . . .'

'Lauren!'

'Jess, let me speak.'

'No, let *me* speak. Fuck's sake, Lauren. I've got cancer.'

Silence, for once. In fact, it's quite possibly the first time Lauren has been speechless since the day that 'Hashtag-She-Said-Yes'.

A split second later, there is wailing, sobbing, almost cartoonish. I feel like I'm outside my body, unable to react to her crying. I wait for her to finish, to calm herself down.

'Are you sure?' she says, finally, composing herself. 'Could there have been a mistake? With the results?'

'I don't think so. I—'

'Could you get a second opinion?'

'It's not a mix-up.'

I hear a snotty sniffle, followed by the uncontrollable sob of a distraught child.

'But you're so young. You can't have cancer.'

65

'I know.'

'So soon after your mum.'

'I know.'

'It's just . . . it's not . . . it's not . . . fair.' There are sharp intakes of breath between each part of the sentence as she begins to hyperventilate.

'I know.' I need her to see that it's going to be fine, I'm going to be fine, but I don't know how to console her.

'Please don't cry. I'm not going to die.'

And then there is a wail, a painful, wolf-like cry that goes right through me. Maybe 'die' wasn't the right choice of word.

'Hey, hey, hey,' I say, every 'hey' an effort to stop her tears. 'They said they've caught it, it's possible to treat it. It's going to be fine.'

'Yes,' Lauren says, audibly forcing herself to snap out of it, stop crying. I hear a clunk as she puts her mobile down and then the deafening sound of her blowing her nose way too close to my ear. There's something about her distress that is giving me strength. As long as *I* can comfort *her*, I might not fall to pieces.

'You OK?' I say.

She takes a deep breath and sounds vaguely put together. 'I'll be fine,' she says. 'Do you have anyone there with you? Can I come round?'

I pour out the steaming water and add a splash of milk, then root around my baking stuff for a bag of sugar. Two spoonfuls, just like the tea Mum used to make when my periods were so bad I'd almost faint.

'Johnny will be home tonight,' I say.

'You're letting that cheating bastard back in?'

Shit. Mia. Marcus. Shit. I can't think about this right now.

'Don't,' I say, shaking my head. 'I can't deal with that too.'

'I'll cancel my last meeting and come straight over,' she says. 'Not that I'll be much use as a weeping mess.'

I laugh. 'That would be nice.'

'It's going to be OK,' she says. 'I'll be here for you every step of the way, I promise. Just like with your m—'

As soon as she starts to say 'mum', she is in tears again. All the years she was by my side when Mum was wasting away, and now she has to watch me go through it too.

'Did they . . .' She fights back the sobs. 'Did they say you're going to lose your hair?'

'I think so.'

'You're going to be . . . bald?' Britney again, that heart-breaking front-page image of her looking doe-eyed with her hair half-on, half-off, like a crazed clown.

'I guess.'

'For my . . . for my . . . wedding?'

I'm about to have chemo to save my life right after the guy I love cheated on me, and she's worried about her wedding?

'Jess?'

'I'm sure we can find a wig in marshmallow, if that's what you're worried about.'

And then we are both laughing, Lauren making hysterical hiccupping belly laughs mixed with sniffles of snot. Even though she sometimes says the most ridiculous things, I can feel how much she loves me through the phone, my stupid, blubbering emotional wreck of a best mate.

'Get your arse over here,' I say, when I can just about speak again.

'I'll bring gin,' she says.

I sit with my knees up to my chest at the kitchen table, sipping the sweet tea that I've stirred to within an inch of its life. There are several WhatsApp notifications from Aisha.

15:05 Hey Jess, you OK? Tabitha is losing her shit x

15:25 Forget about her, did your hospital appointment go OK? Xx

15:55 Haven't heard from you, you alright? Call me when you can Xx

I start to reply to Aisha when the phone starts buzzing again. Kate.

'Jess. Lauren just told me.'

Already? Bad news really does spread like wildfire. And I still need to make the call I'm dreading the most – Dad.

'I can't believe it,' she says. 'I never thought . . .'

'I know,' I say. I don't know how I'll have the energy to deliver this news to every single one of my friends and family.

'You're so young.'

'Yeah.'

I can still remember a real-life piece I read about a girl who had three different cancers by the time she was twenty-five.

'Lauren said she was going over?'

'Yeah.'

'Well, I could come over too when Colm gets home, if I can get Ella down. Or I could bring her with me now, although she's super cranky so you probably don't—'

'Thanks Kate, but don't worry.' The last thing I want is a screaming baby when I'm cancerous, shellshocked and hungover.

'You know, my aunty Pam had breast cancer and she made a full recovery. She even did a charity abseil. It's totally treatable these days, isn't it?'

'I guess.'

There are two missed calls from Tabitha and one from Aisha. I need to speak to Dad first and get it over with, but I can't help feeling an overwhelming sense of guilt. Johnny was right.

68

I'm selfish, I can see it now. I've only been thinking of myself and how I could further my own career, while my boyfriend was suffering and my Dad needed me. It's no wonder Johnny cheated.

It's no wonder I have cancer.

My mind is racing to figure out everything I did wrong. A decade on the pill, sunbeds in my teens and all those years of binge drinking with Lauren and Kate, knocking back Smirnoff Ice in skirts so short they could be belts while we waved around Lauren's brother's car keys to try and pass as old enough to get into the club. Did I bring this cancer on myself? It's not like I ever smoked or took drugs. The closest I've been to a line of coke is inhaling fumes from the vat of icing sugar we'd use to 'bathe' our freshly baked doughnuts.

Don't they say sugar feeds cancer? I can't help picturing the hundreds of cakes I baked and ate with Mum over the years – one for the customers, one for us. It had been our little ritual since I was small, but I never imagined I could end up with breast cancer. I don't want Dad to have to go through this again.

No, no, it's not my fault. Mr Patel said it's hormonal, caused by oestrogen or something. *Just bad luck*, I think he said.

I take a deep breath. Just rip the plaster off, that's what Dad always says. I turn the dial to crank up the heating. It's freezing.

'Jessie!' He sounds surprised to hear from me. My heart sinks with guilt when I acknowledge how long I've been neglecting him. He doesn't even know about me and Johnny.

'Dad,' I say, my voice already breaking.

'Love, are you OK?' He should shout at me for ignoring his calls for weeks and weeks, but he knows within an instant that I'm Not OK.

'You might need to sit down.'

'You're not pregnant, are you pet? You know what your mother always said about doing things in the right—'

'Dad, I'm not pregnant. Please sit down, you're stressing me out.' I wrap my hands around my empty mug, even though it's gone cold.

'Right, I'm sat down now. On that lovely bench your mother chose. I'm so glad we let her choose it, aren't you? It looks cracking in the springtime. Bloody freezing out here now, mind . . .'

'Dad, I've got cancer.'

No response.

'Dad?'

'Oh Jessie.'

'I'm sure they've caught it early though. It won't be like with Mum . . .' But I'm already sobbing.

'Are you sure?'

'Sure as the doctor telling me it's cancer.' My voice always goes more northern when I speak to Dad.

'I'm coming to get you. I'll set off tonight.'

'Dad, honestly, it's fine. Johnny will come to my appointments.' Will he? I don't even know if we're still together . . .

'But I'm your Dad, love.'

'I know, but I need normality. I don't want loads of people in the house.' I so badly want him to come, I so badly want him to insist.

'I'm not loads of people.'

'I know. Just let me wait and hear what the next steps are.'

'You've your mother's stubbornness, Jessie. What type of . . . cancer . . . is it?'

'Invasive ductal carcinoma, they said.' That word, 'invasive', so sinister. I picture the cancer invading my breast. 'I don't know if it's the same as Gran's.'

'So it's in your br—'

'Breast, yeah.'

I'm going to have to learn not to cringe at my father saying the word 'breast'.

'Will they have to operate?'

'They said I'll have chemo and then surgery, but there's a load more tests first.'

'You'll let me come down for the chemo, won't you? And the surgery, too.'

'Of course, Dad.'

'You never know, love, you might find it's an improvement.'

I laugh. The boiler is whirring and clicking, the room beginning to warm up.

'"Women are like tea bags",' Dad says, putting on Mum's high-pitched London accent. '"You don't know how strong you are until you're in hot water." Remember that one?'

I smile. As if I could ever forget my darling mum and all her wonderful words of wisdom. If only she were here right now.

Lauren leaves at nine thirty, the two of us hugging on the doorstep for so long I feel like she'll never let me go. I'm shattered, my eyes are sore and puffy and I'm parched from so much crying.

I strip off my clothes, put on my pyjamas and climb under the duvet, relishing the cold of the sheets against my skin. Within five minutes, Orco comes trundling in with a squeak and curls up in a tight ball on my legs. Johnny will be home any minute and if I can just go to sleep, tomorrow will be another day. I want so much for the last four days not to have happened.

I sit, stroking Oreo, his purr soothing my tense muscles. In the days after Mum died, I would sit in the same way with my parents' cat, Frostie, for hours on end. She would curl up in my lap, resigned, as if she knew Mum was gone for good and was claiming me as her replacement. It broke my heart when I had to leave her with Dad and go back to London. I wished I could explain to her that Mum hadn't left us on purpose.

As my head hits the pillow, I am overwhelmed with grief. Oreo looks up at me with his big green eyes as if to ask what's wrong. A puddle of tears forms under my face as I sob and sob, unable to control my shaking. It's the thought of Dad that sets me off. The thought of him being at home all alone, no Mum to comfort him, and the fear of his only child being sick. If Mum were there, she'd rub his back and make him cups of tea, but without her he must be lost.

I nudge Oreo off and move away from the wet patch, turning to lie on my back and cup my hand over my left breast. I used to do this as a teenager, checking how much my boobs had grown and wondering if they'd ever be too big to fill my own hand. They never were.

I've felt this lump so many times over the last few months, prodding and poking to check if it's still there. The first doctor said hormonal cysts usually go away on their own, but it didn't. It was always there, though it was hard to tell whether it had grown or changed, the signs of something sinister.

But today the lump is different, suddenly bigger and more prominent. For the first time, I can feel it not just with my fingers but also from the inside, a dull pain, like a headache inside my breast. A headache the size of a ping pong ball, glowing like an orb inside me.

I want to inflict pain on myself. I have to get rid of this parasite.

Johnny arrives home at 22:58. I know this because the glow of the digital alarm clock has been staring at me for hours.

I'm wide awake but too tired to speak to him, too exhausted to confront him about his cheating or tell him about mine, so

I pretend to be asleep. He climbs in beside me and arranges himself around me. His hairy legs feel cold against the backs of mine, but I don't flinch. He reeks of whisky. He's been drinking on the train. He rests an arm over me so that it just grazes the breast that contains the lump.

Neither of us speak. If we just lie here in silence, we can pretend it isn't happening.

Sunny D

Five other women sit around the waiting room, clad in one-size-fits-all dressing gowns. Each sits as far away from the next as possible, leaving empty chairs between them. In front of each lady is a shopping basket, just like the ones in Sainsbury's, only this time to look after their belongings while they strip down in preparation for their scans.

I pick up the bumper-sized bottle of yellow liquid and pour out a measure into the plastic cup. Keep drinking, they said, a glass every fifteen minutes. I'm pleasantly surprised by the first sip. It tastes like diluted Sunny D or a weaker version of the orange drinks that Mum would give me as a child. I gulp it down.

When they asked for a urine sample to check I'm not pregnant, I was certain I knew the result already. I could count on one hand the amount of times Johnny and I have had sex in the last month, and now I know why he was avoiding it. Since last night, we've both been making out like Mia never happened, but I insisted he go to work instead of joining me for my scans. We agreed to talk about it properly at the weekend. I don't think I could go through this whole ordeal without him, and yet I'm not ready to forgive him. Or myself.

Still, when the nurse said those words, 'not pregnant,' I

couldn't help but feel a twinge of disappointment – even though it would be impossibly ill-timed.

I reach for an old copy of *Cosmo* and flick through to the relationship pages, but soon find myself looking around at the other women, some with short pixie crops, others with shoulder-length hair. I wonder how many of them know they have cancer; how many will walk away relieved that their routine scan is clear for another year.

I'm the youngest here by far. Stripped of their own clothes and in their regulation gowns, it's hard to know how old they are, but I'd put the youngest at fifty, maybe forty-five at a push. Most of them look at least sixty.

Are you over fifty? Have you had your mammogram? reads a poster on the wall, white writing on a pink background. Pink, the colour of breast cancer.

A nurse appears in the doorway, clipboard in hand. 'Eileen?' she says. Eileen rises from her seat, dropping her copy of *Woman's Weekly* and bending to pick up her basket. She's bending all wrong, she'll do her back in.

Eileen looks about seventy, her hair cut into a short grey bob, thinning at the back. She disappears down the corridor. I wonder what stage she's at in the process.

I pick up my phone and scroll through Instagram. I double tap a picture of an exhausted-looking Kate standing next to the Serpentine lake with little Ella in a yellow woolly hat and gloves. I add a face with love hearts for eyes to a stack of blueberry pancakes on the *Perfect Bake* account. Then I land on a picture of Tabitha, posted earlier in the week, one high-heeled foot rested on her desk as she sits back in a striking Shrimps faux-fur coat. She's styled it so that it looks like she has her own private office, and the caption simply reads: *Bossing it*. It feels like a subtle way of telling me I can't expect to step into

LAURA PRICE

her territory and lead the magazine, even though that's exactly what I was hired to do.

I broke the news to Miles via an email yesterday afternoon, copying in HR. I told Aisha by WhatsApp, which felt harsh, but I really couldn't face another phone call. Both of them agreed to keep schtum until I've had the chance to figure out exactly what I've got ahead of me, and Miles said he'd ask Tabitha to hold the fort today.

I emailed the team this morning, letting them know I was taking the day off to deal with a 'home emergency' and telling them to report to Tabitha in my absence. I sent a separate message just to Tabitha to keep her in the loop, but for some reason she's decided not to respond to me privately, but to Reply All.

Hi Jess, bit last-minute as I'm sure you know the beauty pages go to press today, but thankfully I'm on top of it. Hope it's nothing too serious. Kind regards, Tabitha x

I'm irked by the kisses she puts on her emails, as if we're friends. But I can't deal with it today.

I'll have to tell the rest of them on Monday, but I'd rather do so on my own terms. And even though this is not how I pictured my first weeks at *Luxxe*, I'm determined not to let it get in the way of my career.

Fifteen minutes have passed since my last cup of Sunny D. I reach for the flimsy plastic cup, squeezing it so hard it cracks in my hands. I walk to the water cooler, sliding a new one from the tower on top of the silver machine.

'First time here?' says a voice opposite.

I look up. It's the next-youngest lady in the room. She's had her lips done, probably Botox too. Some high-flyer. I spot the fancy handbag poking out of her shopping basket and feel self-conscious about my battered old backpack.

I raise my cup of anaemic cat piss. 'How can you tell?'

'CAT scan?' she says.

I nod. The other four women have also looked up, intrigued by the sudden burst of conversation, as if someone has spoken on the Tube.

'You're very young,' she says.

I give her a polite nod.

'You'll be fine,' she says. 'It doesn't hurt.'

I want to ask if she has cancer, if she's had it, but the question feels as invasive as cancer itself.

Just as I'm thinking of a more appropriate conversation topic, the expensive woman is called in for her appointment. Her name is Fiona.

'Good luck,' Fiona says as she picks up her basket, leaving the room.

'We're going to give you a low dose of radioactive fluid, which will make any cancer cells show up on the bone scan,' says a nurse, not long after the CT scan is done. 'Don't worry, it isn't dangerous to you, but you need to steer clear of pregnant women for twenty-four hours.'

I wonder about the pregnant women in the hospital. There must be lots of them. What if I were pregnant, would I have to have an abortion? I clutch my belly. I've always assumed I'd have a baby someday.

I nod.

'Sharp scratch,' says the nurse, stabbing me with a needle way bigger than any I've seen at the GP's surgery.

It hurts more than expected, but I can't help enjoying the tangible feeling of physical pain.

'Pop your things in a locker and then we'll bob you through to the scanner,' says a different member of staff, three hours later. 'It'll take about twenty-five minutes.'

I try to unbend my arm, but I hate the feeling of being attached to a tube. I've always hated plasters, needles and anything to do with blood or hospitals. I'll never forget the tubes sticking out of Mum's nose in those final months in the hospital, her face swollen and puffed up from the steroids.

'Come through,' she says, opening a door and leading me into another room. It feels about ten degrees colder than the rest of the hospital and reminds me of a morgue.

'Take off your dressing gown and hop onto the machine on your back. I'll come back in a moment and get you set up.'

I climb onto a stretcher-like panel leading into a giant Polo mint and lower myself onto the cold, hard surface. Then I nod along as a series of different faces – radiologists, nurses, who knows what they're called – talk me through different steps of the 'pain-free process' and the importance of staying still.

'Just squeeze on this if you need to tell us anything during the scan,' one of them says, placing a sort of stress ball in my hand that's so soft it's more likely I'll squeeze on it by accident.

Once they've left the room, I stare up at the ceiling, arms limp by my sides, conscious of the tube attached to my inner elbow. Every sound is heightened, the bleeps and buzzes from the machine, the whirr of the air conditioning. As I slide into the Polo mint, I close my eyes, picturing my insides under the scanner, imagining the tumour as a glowing green mass above my rib cage.

It seems to go on forever. I'm trying my best to stay deadly still but I really need to take a deep breath and I'm afraid the movement will throw off the scans. It reminds me of clarinet lessons in year nine, when Miss Berry would make us lie on the freezing cold floor and practise breathing with our hands on our bellies. Always the class clown, Lauren would fart or burp whenever the teacher turned her back. She was so good at acting she'd manage to keep a straight face, but I would have to picture burglars and murderers to keep from corpsing. I'd inevitably get caught out.

Today I have the opposite problem, trying to think positive thoughts to keep myself from crying. I've just conjured up an image of me in a bridesmaid dress and marshmallow-coloured wig when I feel the machine start to move again.

'All done,' says the nurse. 'Go get yourself dressed and enjoy your weekend.'

I give her a smile, not exactly picturing the most relaxed of weekends ahead.

'Did you see anything?' I say, aware that the two scans will reveal whether the cancer has spread to my bones or organs. It's terrifying to think of the cells multiplying, then seeping into my liver, my lungs or even my brain.

'We're not allowed to answer that question, I'm afraid, but we'll be in touch as soon as we can.'

'Did it look normal though?' All I want is an indication, but she remains poker-faced.

'I'm sorry Jessica, we're really not allowed to comment until a doctor has analyzed your scans.'

I shut my mouth and nod because I know I'm going to cry.

I run my fingers along the buttons on the coffee machine outside the waiting room. Fair trade hot chocolate, tea, coffee, cappuccino. I pick tea, put a coin into the slot and press the start button. The machine whirrs loudly, hot water shooting out of the metal rod.

'Might want to put a cup under that,' comes a voice from behind me.

I reach for a cup and thrust it under the fountain of hot

water to catch the last drops of tea, but it's too late. The drink is already dripping over the edge and onto the floor.

'Shit,' I say, looking around the empty corridor for something to mop up the mess.

She appears beside me. A black-haired pixie, her Uma-Thurman-in-*Pulp-Fiction* bob framing her bloated pink cheeks and big, shiny blue eyes. How on earth did she end up on a cancer ward?

The girl reaches into her bag and pulls out a wad of tissues, handing a couple to me and wiping the spilt tea from around my feet.

'Rule number one in cancer world,' she says. 'Always carry tissues.'

'Thanks,' I say. 'I'm such a dizzy cow sometimes.'

'Schoolgirl error,' she says, shaking her head. 'Happened on my first day too.'

So she's a patient, not someone's kid. She's an actual cancer patient.

'You look too young—' I stop myself. *Too young for cancer.* She must have heard it a thousand times.

'It's fine,' she says. 'People say it all the time. Yes, I'm too young for cancer. Aren't we all?'

Pixie girl puts another coin into the machine, placing a new cup underneath. 'Milk? Sugar?' She seems like she already knows her way around the hospital.

'Both please,' I say. 'It's been a bit of a day.' It's been a bit of a week.

She hands me a cup and we stand awkwardly beside the machine.

'Tell me about it,' she says. 'You're the youngest person I've seen here since . . . well, me. I'm Annabel.'

Annabel holds out her tiny hand over the top of the cup. I

shake it. Her skin is dry and cracked and her face is swollen and puffy. I can't help noticing her jet-black fingernails.

'Chemo,' she says, giving me a little wink. 'Fucks with your fingernails, fucks with pretty much everything. I'm guessing you've got all that to come?'

I nod. She smiles.

'Lucky you met me then.'

Shit people say when you have cancer

What's on your mind, Jess? reads the empty white box beside the little round image of mine and Johnny's smiling faces, pressed up together with Clapham Common in the background.

I have cancer, I type, then immediately erase it. Facebook is a place for good news, like baby scans and engagement announcements. Nobody writes *I have cancer*. And yet the thought of breaking this news individually to anyone beyond Dad, Aunty Cath and my closest friends fills me with dread. This is the only way to do it. Just rip the plaster off.

Hi guys, I write. God, that's lame, but I'm not sure how else you're supposed to address your entire mass of Facebook friends. I check the number. Four hundred and eighty-three friends. I don't even know who half of them are, not least the ones who've got married and changed their names since they last contacted me, circa fifteen years ago. Maybe it's time for a cull.

I drum my nails on the silver surface before I begin to type. Hi all, I write, then delete it. Enough with the niceties. I'll go straight in and say it.

On Thursday 16th November, I was diagnosed with breast cancer. Apologies for breaking the news via the modern-day equivalent of the Christmas round-robin, but I couldn't quite face the thought of telling you one by one.

Those of you who know me well will remember that I lost my amazing mum to bowel cancer two years ago, and my gran to breast cancer before I was born. I've seen first-hand the horrific effect this disease has on people, and I'd be lying if I said I wasn't scared shitless. In fact, I've snotted and sniffled through so many tissues it's only a matter of time before I get the call to do #SponCon for Kleenex.

But Mama Jackson didn't raise me to sit back and take it, so I'm going to kick the shit out of this cancer and leave it cowering in the corner, even if it's the last thing I do – preferably while channelling GI Jane.

I'll be crossing all social appointments out of my calendar while I make way for a shit ton of chemo and my subsequent ~~amputation~~ surgery. I will try my hardest to keep you posted throughout this epic adventure, but I have no idea how it's going to play out, so please be patient. Now excuse me while I say a tearful farewell to my lovely lady lumps . . .

Jess x

My fingers are trembling as I post the status. I hate to make light of something so serious, but sharing how I *actually* feel with everyone I know feels even scarier, and I'd rather keep my most intimate fears between me and my closest friends.

I put my phone down to make a cup of tea, but the moment I start to drink it, my phone starts pinging with comments.

Aisha Parker: We're all rooting for you, Jess. You're going to kick this cancer where it hurts. Can't wait to meet your bald badass alter ego xxx

Bryony Lucas: So sorry to hear your news. Have you tried mindfulness? I've heard that a positive attitude kills cancer. Stay strong big hugs

Cath Elderfield: You are going to rock the bald head Jess don't worry take everything in your stride. Mum would be proud looking down on you. Love Aunty Cath xx

Ophelia Cossack-Daly: Jessica you are SO BRAVE. My mother fought breast cancer and won. #YouveGotThis

Eric McGinn: So sorry to hear your awful news, Jess. But look on the bright side – at least you get a free boob job! ;)

Within minutes, my inbox is full of private messages from people wishing me well and telling me survivor stories about their husband's sister's best friend's uncle's dog who had cancer. By the end of the evening, my Facebook post has seventy-three comments, one hundred and fifty-three likes, thirteen love hearts and eighteen crying faces. My phone buzzes constantly with heartfelt and well-meaning text messages and at least seven different Ryan Gosling memes with words like 'Hey girl, you've got this'.

I'm more popular than ever, and yet I've never felt so alone.

Always the bridesmaid

Lauren and Kate stare at me, heads tilted, as I recount the events of the last week. I can't quite get my head around the fact that it's only been five days since the awards – it feels like a year ago, what with finding out Johnny cheated, then snogging Marcus and being diagnosed with cancer, all in the space of thirty-six hours.

Since Johnny got back on Thursday night, I've oscillated between two states. One minute I'm angry, defiant and capable of a level of rage I didn't know I had in me. I've tortured myself by fishing for every detail – the date, the hotel, what they were drinking, what sex they had and how many times they did it. I've asked him over and over, determined to catch him out at some point, but the details are always the same – they did it once; he asked her to leave. That last part is a comfort, knowing how much worse I'd feel if she'd curled up in his arms to sleep.

We've exhausted the same arguments over and over. I've cried and screamed over the parts that hurt the most – how he disrespected me by letting her follow me on social media, as if the two of them were conspiring behind my back; how, instead of coming clean, he lied through his teeth until he couldn't deny it any more; how he must still fancy her when he sees her at work – you don't just stop thinking someone is hot because you've slept with them, especially when they look like *that*. I've made him sleep on the sofa, block Mia on social media and explain to her in no uncertain terms that they are absolutely, undeniably over, and I've pummelled my fists on his chest as I've cursed and shouted at him for ruining everything we've built.

Then I'm back in cancer shock mode. My mood plummets and the Jess who is head-strong and furious disappears. I cry for comfort and beg him to come back to the bed just to hold me and tell me it's not going to end how it ended for Mum. Then Johnny the Lawyer steps up, practical and supportive while I play the patient. He fusses around me with cups of tea and talk of practicalities like getting the right food in and making sure there's always someone to come with me to the hospital.

I remember all the good things, the reasons to stay – the history we've built over the last five years; our shared background and the way he gets me because he comes from a similar place; the way he cared for me when Mum died. But it's not just that – it's the fact that he *knew* Mum, that she loved him. If I say goodbye to him, I say goodbye to someone who got to know my mother, who'll nod knowingly and share stories about how sassy she was. No future boyfriend will ever have that.

Then I'm docile, compliant, almost numb as I allow him to organize everything around me, shutting out all the anger over Little Miss Avo. It's either the cancer or the cheating – I'm not strong enough to handle both.

'You know you don't have to stay with him just because you've got cancer?' Kate says, putting her hand over mine while struggling with Ella as the baby girl jigs up and down on her knee, pushing her tubby legs against Kate's thighs. 'I'll happily come to your appointments with you, especially while I'm on maternity.'

'Same,' says Lauren, looking radiant in a high-necked, floaty green dress that contrasts with her long blonde curls. 'You shouldn't forgive him just because of that.'

'It's not just that,' I say, though I admit I'm petrified of dealing with cancer alone and ending up single, bald and boobless.

'What is it then?' Kate says. She winces as the baby yanks at her hair. 'Last week, you were resolute that you wouldn't forgive him for cheating, and now you seem happy to forgive and forget.'

Happy isn't the word. It's more that there's only so much I can take without having a total breakdown.

I reach for Ella and move her onto my lap, holding her underneath her chubby armpits. 'You're such a cutie, aren't you? Yes, you are!' I look at Kate. 'She's so gorgeous.'

Kate gives me a toothless smile that I can tell is forced. As if she doesn't quite believe Ella is as precious as the rest of us do.

'I just . . .' I hesitate, trying to articulate the thought. 'I wonder if he's right. I *had* been neglecting him. I haven't been myself lately. I grafted so hard to get that job; I wanted so badly to leave *Perfect Bake*. I think I stopped being fun.'

Mum brought me up with this 'live for the moment' attitude where she encouraged me to never stop enjoying life, even when it gets tough. If I fancied that second piece of cake, I should have it. If I wanted to pursue a dream as a writer, I should go for it. If I lusted after the dress, I should buy it. She didn't believe in denying ourselves anything, and I grew up with a healthy appreciation for life.

That was the Jess that Johnny fell in love with. The one who danced like no one was watching and was always the last one remaining on the dance floor. The one who dragged him by the hand out to the gardens and took him skinny dipping in the pond at that first wedding together. The one who booked a spontaneous last-minute flight to Agadir without even knowing what country it was in, just because it cost £19.99. What happened to that girl?

'You *cannot* blame yourself for this,' Kate says, as Lauren nods along emphatically. 'If being busy entitled men to cheat then every guy in the world would be at it.'

I sigh. She has a point, but I still can't help feeling a sense of guilt. And then there's the other thing . . .

I didn't want to tell them about Marcus. Lauren is preoccupied with her wedding to Charlie, and Kate has enough on her plate, what with a six-month-old baby, chronic sleep deprivation, a struggling events business and what I'm beginning to think might be post-natal depression. She wouldn't cheat in a million years.

'What is it?' Lauren says, putting down her tea and reaching for my hand as I pass Ella back to Kate. 'You know you can tell us anything.'

'I cheated,' I say, looking down at the cafe table, feeling as guilty as Johnny looked that day. 'The night before I found out about the cancer, I snogged this guy from work.'

I let go of Lauren's hand as I slowly look across the table, anticipating their reactions. Since Lauren and I met Kate at sixth-form college, the two of them have been my good cop and bad cop – Lauren, the party girl, most likely to skive off school to snog someone outside the chippy, while Kate is the family gal who plays by the rules and wouldn't harm a fly. Now that Lauren is engaged, I'm expecting full disapproval from both sides.

But Lauren simply cocks her head and lets out a sigh. 'Oh, Jess.'

It's becoming familiar already, that subtle head tilt that says 'Sorry you have cancer'.

'Oh hun, you haven't been thinking straight,' Kate says. 'You were in shock.'

'Is that all you've got to say?' When Kate found out a friend of hers was cheating on her boyfriend, she staged an intervention, regaling the woman with horror stories of her own childhood and the effect of her father's cheating on her mother's life. She has a wonderfully strong moral compass. And yet, it seems cancer has given me a get-out-of-jail-free card.

'Who was it?' Lauren says.

'Some guy called Marcus.'

'Did you shag him?'

I shake my head, shuddering at the thought. If this is how guilty I am after one kiss, I can't imagine how bad I'd feel if we'd gone further.

'Well, you didn't exactly do much wrong. Nothing compared with Johnny,' Kate says, shushing Ella as she threatens to cry.

I want them to punish me, to tell me I'm a horrible person for what I've done. I don't want to get away scot-free just because there's a tumour in my breast.

'Are you going to tell Johnny?'

'I don't know.'

'That would be the end of it if I cheated on Charlie,' Lauren says, looking down at her phone. She rolls her eyes. 'Fuck's sake.'

'What is it?' I say, following Lauren's gaze to her phone screen.

'Nothing,' she says, turning it face down on the table. 'Charlie being ridiculous again.'

'What now?'

She rolls her eyes and explains how he kicked off when he found out one of their wedding guests was someone Lauren slept with in her twenties. 'And now he's trawling through my Instagram, having a go at me because I've liked Ziad's posts. What am I supposed to do, tell him he can't come to the wedding?'

Charlie's jealousy has been an issue since the day he and Lauren first got together. He scours her social media, looking for any kind of male-related activity, then berates himself for not being as buff as her exes. I thought his insecurities might have gone away once she agreed to marry him, but they only seem to have worsened.

'But Ziad was a fling; you didn't even like him,' I say, unable to fathom the root of Charlie's possessiveness sometimes. Johnny has always been the opposite, happy for me to go to the pub with a guy mate without even questioning whether I might have feelings for him. Perhaps that's a sign in itself.

'I know,' Lauren says. 'And he's a *friend*. What am I going to say, "Sorry, you can't come to my wedding because my fiancé hates the fact that we shagged six years ago"?'

Kate hmms. 'I don't know; I can see his point. If Colm had invited his ex to our wedding, I wouldn't have liked it. Maybe he just needs a bit of reassurance?'

Lauren rolls her eyes again. 'Yep, yep, I'll tell him for the millionth time that I *do* like posh boys and I *don't* mind the fact that he plays polo instead of footie. You'd think commit-ting the rest of my life to him would be enough . . .'

A waitress arrives with our food. Poached eggs on sour-dough for me, yoghurt and granola for Kate and mushroom soup with no bread for Lauren. My stomach rumbles, but I still feel sick at the thought of food.

'I just feel like if Johnny and I get married some day, we shouldn't have secrets.'

Lauren picks her phone up and shakes her head at it.

Kate glances at Lauren, then back at me. 'You're right. It'll eat you up if you don't tell him. Maybe now's a good time to bring it up? It's not like he can hold it against you.'

'I don't want anyone to treat me like a charity case,' I say. I can imagine it being like this when I walk into the office on Monday, people tilting their heads and taking on extra work because they think I can't handle it. Well, I *can* handle it. I'm not going to let cancer hold me back.

'So how's your dad?' Kate says, taking a spoonful of her yoghurt once Ella is settled in her high chair.

'He's fine,' I say, making a mental note to call him one of these days.

'You said he was thinking of selling the tea rooms?' Lauren says, putting her phone to one side again.

I feel myself seize up. I don't want to talk about this. I'd happily change the subject back to cancer or Johnny. Anything but this.

'I don't think he will,' I say. Those tea rooms were Mum's pride and joy. He'd be crazy to sell them now that she's gone.

'I could understand him wanting to move on,' Kate says. I notice she has set her spoon down and barely touched her yoghurt.

'Can we just . . .' I try not to sound too frustrated. 'Can we change the subject? We're not exactly the cheeriest brides-maids, are we?'

Lauren laughs. 'Alright. Let's forget cancer, cheating arse-holes and jealous fiancés for an hour or two. Come on, let's eat so we can go try some dresses . . .'

Four bridal shops, two bottles of prosecco and several hid-eous, baby-pink dresses later, I'm finally heading home. Kate dropped Ella off with Colm and it was nice to be just the three of us again. I got away with orange juice while Kate and Lauren were on the bubbles, but I'm exhausted from traipsing around. Still, I'm glad of a day trying on bridesmaid dresses with my two best friends instead of treading on eggshells at home.

I take a deep breath as I put my key into the door.

'How was your day?' Johnny says, standing in the doorway as I shake off my boots. 'Did Lauren find the perfect dress?'

'More or less,' I say, swerving his attempt at a kiss and walking straight towards the kitchen. Between Lauren fretting about reaching her ideal wedding weight, me worrying about how I'm going to look in a wig, and Kate agonizing over how she can no longer dress for her post-baby figure, even though she's alarmingly thin, we weren't exactly a shining example of body confidence today. Not like Little Miss Avo . . .

'I'm gasping for a brew,' I say.

Johnny ushers me into the living room and tells me to put my feet up while he makes the tea. I pat my lap for Oreo to join me and he climbs into it, curling up and purring immediately. Johnny returns two minutes later with a tray of tea and a box of Tunnock's Tea Cakes. 'Thought you might need a pick-me-up.'

'Old school,' I say, peeling the red foil off one of the chocolate domes and biting into the fluffy marshmallow middle. 'So did you get much done?'

Over breakfast before I left this morning, I gave Johnny a pep talk on his action plan to make partner at his firm. His boss, Erica, has told him he can apply again in a year, and I'm certain if he gets his head down, there's no way he won't get the promotion. Back in full organizational mode, I set him up with a notepad and encouraged him to start by making a list.

Johnny grunts like a pubescent boy.

I notice the Xbox controller and the empty whisky tumbler beside him on the sofa. 'Did you even make the list?'

He shrugs. 'There's no point.'

92

'Come on,' I say, trying to sound encouraging when actually all I feel is frustrated. He's had a whole day to get his life into gear after everything we've been through this week and, by the looks of things, he's spent it playing video games.

Johnny gets up and walks over to the drinks trolley, pouring himself a whisky. 'Rupert Smith made partner last year and he's younger than me.'

'Screw Rupert Smith,' I say, wanting to shake some sense into him. 'Focus on you. Come on, go get some paper and we'll work it out together.'

'You don't get it, Jess,' he says, back turned to me, staring out the window with his whisky in hand. 'You get everything you want in life; you've got the perfect career and you're everyone's wonder girl. I'm just Mr Average.'

I screw my face up. Usually, when he gets into his periodic slumps, I do everything I can to console him. I mean it when I tell him he's the smartest, funniest, least average person I know. But this time it's different. He *cannot* feel sorry for himself when I'm the one still reeling from the double bombshell of cheating and cancer.

'Are you seriously going to start sulking on me?' I say, increasingly angry as the thoughts of Little Miss Avo start to flicker through my brain.

'It's not just you, you know,' he says, back still turned. 'This affects me too.'

'What?'

'Cancer. You're not the only one this affects, Jess.'

I gently push Oreo off and stand up, walking over to the window to confront him. 'Are you kidding me? Are you the one who has to lose your hair? Are you the one who's going to be puking their guts up for the next six months? Are you the one putting your life on hold while you worry about whether you're going to get cheated on again?'

He turns to face me and I see that his eyes are red and full of tears. 'I'm scared,' he says, his bottom lip puffing out as he looks down at the carpet and starts to cry. 'I don't want to lose you. I can't lose you, Jess.'

My anger melts away as I look at him, completely hopeless and vulnerable. I put my arms out and pull him towards me as his shoulders shake with sobs.

To freeze or not to freeze

'Oh,' Tabitha says, looking surprised as she bounds into the office at eight on Monday morning to find me already at my desk. 'I wasn't expecting to see you.'

'Good morning,' I say, determined to be cheerful and productive. 'Why is that?'

Having seen countless people cock their heads at me with pity over the weekend, I've decided not to tell Tabitha and the team about my cancer diagnosis. Aisha, Miles and HR are all aware, but I don't see a reason for anyone else to pity me. I've switched my Facebook settings to 'friends only' so that just a handful of people can read the post I wrote on Friday.

'It's just you sent me that list of times you were going to be off for your . . . what was it, family emergency? So I wasn't sure you were coming in. I hope everything's OK?'

'Everything's fine,' I say, wondering when she'll stop being so nosy. I sent the team an email on Friday after I found out about several follow-up appointments I'll be having this week, but I didn't go into any details. 'I'm out this afternoon but I'll be coming in early and leaving late from now on. I've just got a bit of health stuff to sort out.'

It's not that I need to prove myself to Tabitha Richardson. I just want to show her why I got the job, how just because I'm not a fashion person, doesn't mean I don't have the skills

LAURA PRICE

to manage a team and edit a lifestyle magazine. Both Leah
and Miles believe in me, they've seen what I'm capable of, but
Tabitha makes me feel like she's constantly waiting for me to
slip up.

She gasps, her eyes lighting up. 'You're not . . .?'

I raise my eyebrows, willing her to finish the question.

She lowers her voice, even though the office is a ghost town
at this hour. 'Pregnant?'

I half laugh, tempted to let her believe I am. It would be a
convenient way to cover for the increasingly regular hospital
visits I'm going to be having over the coming weeks. Not that
I should have to explain myself.

'I'm sorry,' she says, shaking her head as she sets up her
laptop. 'That was really insensitive of me. I hated it when I was
pregnant with Matilda and people were always prodding and
poking me, like my belly was public property. Your secret's
safe with me, if you are.'

'I'm not pregnant,' I say, bursting her bubble.

In fact, I'm quite the opposite.

'Hello Jessica, Johnny. I'm Dr Emily Finnegan,' says the very
polished, fifty-something doctor, shaking our hands in turn. She
sits down behind her desk. 'You can call me Emily, if you like.'

'Jess,' I say.

'I understand you're here to discuss fertility options before
you start a course of chemotherapy.'

Johnny squeezes my hand. 'That's right.'

'You're very young for breast cancer.'

I give her the politest smile I can muster. Haven't heard *that*
one before.

She asks me about my family history. I tell her about my
gran, but when she asks for the details – when she was diagnosed, the specifics of her cancer, at what point it progressed – I

barely know the answers. I remember talking to Mum about it when she was diagnosed, because we wondered whether the two cancers were connected. But Mum said it was all hush-hush back then and she was just a teenager when Gran got sick. She didn't even know she was properly poorly until it was far too late. Gran was forty-five when she died.

'And what about your mother?'

I take a deep breath as I prepare to recount the details of Mum's illness. For a long time, I couldn't talk about it, and the most I tell people is that she had bowel cancer. But Dr Finnegan wants the who, the when, the how.

Conscious of Johnny's presence, I tell her about the surgery and the chemo that made Mum so sick she had multiple infections and had to quit working at the tea rooms. The day she got the all-clear was one of the happiest days of our lives, but we couldn't have known how short-lived that happiness would be.

She was never the same after the first diagnosis. She regained some of her physical strength and went back to work but her hair came back in patches and she lost all her confidence. She'd been a pillar of the village community with her Zumba classes, the book club she ran and the free baking classes she would put on for kids in the school holidays. Now she was withdrawn, taking everything much more slowly. Some days she even lacked the energy to put the cakes on their stands.

She was just getting back to her old self when we found out it had spread. By the time she got tested, it was in her lungs and liver, and it wasn't long before she had to quit work for good. Dad tried to juggle the tea rooms with looking after Mum, but he couldn't do either justice so he ended up hiring two new people. Mum declined so quickly that none of us saw it coming. She was so busy trying to protect us, putting on a brave face, that we didn't realize how bad she'd got.

I couldn't bear the thought of not being able to call her for cooking advice or put my arms around her when I was upset, all those things I'd taken for granted. Selfish or not, I wanted to keep her for as long as I could, to try and extract every story, every recipe, everything she might have told me over the next forty years. But by then it was too late, she was fading away. The day she finally started telling me her trade secrets – a pinch of chilli in her favourite chocolate cake; a dash of miso and a splash of fish sauce in her special Christmas sprouts – was the day I knew we were losing her.

'It's most likely there's no relation between your cancer and your mother's,' Dr Finnegan says, snapping me out of my thoughts. 'Breast and bowel cancer are not linked. However, there may be links between your cancer and your grandmother's, and that's something you can talk to your team about.'

I nod as if I've understood, but it's all so confusing. She moves on to Johnny, asking him about his own family history. He knows barely anything about his dad's side of the family and he clams up when she asks.

'Do you have any children, currently?'

We shake our heads.

'Have you ever been pregnant?'

'No.'

'Have you ever tried to get pregnant?'

I shake my head again, glancing at Johnny. I know he wants kids. An only child whose dad left when he was six, he always longed for siblings and swore he'd have a big brood. But we had both imagined being further on in our careers before having children, and of course there was always Mum's voice at the back of my head, reminding me I'd have to get married first. Even though she was liberal in so many ways, she felt strongly about the traditional approach to parenthood.

'I see,' Dr Finnegan says.

'Is that a problem?' Her face tells me I've done something wrong by not having kids.

'Not at all,' she says, looking up from her notepad, shaking her head. Then she blurts out what she was thinking anyway. 'There is some evidence that having children in your twenties can help *protect* against breast cancer because of the hormones released during pregnancy.'

It feels like a punch in the chest. If I'd spent the last decade having kids instead of working my way up the career ladder, I might not be in this situation now.

I look down at the floor.

'Would you like to have children in the future?'

'That's why we're here,' I say. 'Mr Patel mentioned egg preservation?'

She looks at Johnny, then back down to her desk, writing something in her notepad.

'That's one of the options we can discuss.'

'We'll still be able to have kids, won't we?' Johnny says.

Dr Finnegan looks at Johnny, then back at me. 'Well, as you may know, it's very rare for women under forty to have breast cancer. Chemotherapy targets fast-growing cancer cells but unfortunately it can't distinguish between bad and good, so it also damages living cells. That's why your hair will fall out and your fertility levels may drop.'

'So what's the solution?' I say. There has to be a solution.

'After chemotherapy, most women reach menopause around a decade earlier than average,' she says.

Menopause. That's something I've only ever associated with women in their fifties and above.

'So what are the options?' *Get to the point.*

'Some women in your position choose to freeze their eggs,' she says. 'But the chance of a successful pregnancy is extremely low.'

'How low?'

'It depends, but it could be as low as ten per cent. The eggs can become damaged in the process of extraction and defrosting. There is no guarantee of a successful pregnancy.'

I glance at Johnny, who has gone quiet. I can sense him feeling his future fatherhood slipping through his fingers. A few days ago, he was fighting for me when I wanted to end it. Now he's probably wishing he'd run off into the arms of the young, fertile Little Miss Avo.

I snap myself out of the negative thoughts. 'What's the alternative?'

'You could freeze a fertilized embryo, using your partner's sperm.' She looks at Johnny. 'Freezing an embryo would give you a much higher chance of a successful pregnancy later down the line. More like fifty per cent.'

Johnny turns to face me, nodding.

I turn from him back to Dr Finnegan. Freezing an embryo with Johnny would mean that we are tied together for life, that I can only have a baby with him. This is a decision we'll have to make in the next few days because it has to be done before I start chemo, but I don't even know if we'll still be together in a few weeks, let alone survive a course of chemotherapy together. I haven't even told him about Marcus. Our relationship is dangling by a thread as it is.

'I, er . . .' This is not what I expected, not at all. I figured I could freeze my eggs, but the embryo seems like a no-brainer if it gives me a higher chance of success.

'It's a lot to think about,' she says, giving me a sympathetic look.

'We don't have long before she starts chemo,' Johnny says, urging the consultant to give us more information on the next steps. It's all too much to think about.

She talks through the process of stimulating my period,

then injecting myself with hormones to fast-track my egg production, followed by extracting my eggs under sedation and fertilizing them with Johnny's sperm.

'Bear in mind it can be an unpleasant experience,' she says. 'It's similar to having IVF.'

Johnny looks pale. When Leah was going through IVF with her wife, I had told him about all the horrors she had described – the needles, the sore belly, the mood swings. He is probably expecting the worst.

'Given the urgency before your chemotherapy, if you're keen to go ahead, I can get you an urgent appointment at the assisted conception unit,' she says. 'Hopefully they can get you started straight away.'

Assisted conception. It sounds like the sort of place where robot arms insert frozen capsules into women's vaginas, and that's probably not even far from the truth. Now that really would be one to tell the grandkids, if we ever have any.

'OK,' I say. I can't imagine any child-free woman saying no.

'There's just one thing,' she says. 'You must be aware that the process involves stimulating the hormone oestrogen, which is what caused your particular cancer.'

'Is it dangerous?'

'We don't believe so, but there aren't enough women your age with breast cancer to give sufficient evidence. However, there is certainly no cause for concern.'

She would warn us against it if she thought it was a bad idea, surely. It's not like we're having a baby *now*. It's insurance for our future, to make sure we have the option. And after watching Mum go through chemo, I'm pretty sure I can handle a couple of weeks of bloating.

'OK,' I say. 'Sign me up.'

Extraordinary women

'So the idea is to shine a spotlight on the extraordinary women we rarely see in the pages of *Luxxe*,' I say, gesturing up at the screen. I've had the art team mock up a black-and-white magazine cover with the words 'Tenth anniversary issue – celebrating extraordinary women' in swirly font overlaying a grid of different portraits.

'Who are they, and how many covers are they going to sell?' Miles says, pausing from tapping away on his laptop.

'Top left is Ngozi Okeye, a body-positivity influencer with almost a hundred thousand followers,' I say, shuddering at the thought that I could have picked Little Miss Avo. 'Next to her is Sara González Gómez, she's basically the next Greta Thunberg, then we have trans activist Michaela May . . .'

'Her Instagram Stories are so inspiring,' Aisha says, giving me the thumbs up.

I reel off my well-rehearsed pitch. After the Luxxe Women Awards I got to thinking about how we could be more inclusive and showcase the next Stephanie Asante, who would never have got a look-in at this magazine a few years ago. It's a risk to put lesser-known women on the cover, but I've interspersed them with more famous women who've been showcased on *Luxxe*'s covers over the last decade, taking care to select the ones who still reflect the magazine's values.

If we only champion the rich, privileged and famous, we'll never be the forward-looking, zeitgeisty magazine I want us to become.

'I'm not sure,' Tabitha says, her frown so severe it's as if I've suggested putting Harvey Weinstein on the cover. 'You weren't here then, Jess, but the Lexy Banks cover we did last year didn't do so well.'

I'm prepared for this. I knew Tabitha would bring up something that happened before I started at the magazine, and I'm ready to fight for my idea.

'I understand the risk we're taking,' I say, smiling at Tabitha. 'Thing is, we've moved on such a lot in the last twelve months. Our audience is ready for this. The idea of having twenty different women on the cover is that there's someone for everyone to identify with. I want every woman to feel seen.'

'Alright, then where are the fashion designers, the models? Why isn't Sophia Henley-Jones in there?' Tabitha continues.

'I was hoping you'd help me with that – this isn't the final line-up. But I feel like we've given enough exposure to Sophia already,' I say, making a point of pronouncing it So-FY-ah. 'It's time to allow the up-and-comers to shine. Why don't you propose a few names and we'll go from there?'

I absolutely want Tabitha to be included in this process, in fact there's no way I could do it without her. But she's always so defensive, shooting me down before I've even had a chance to explain my full idea. I flick forward to my next slide. Leah has done a great job making *Luxxe* relevant to the LGBTQ+ community, but I'm determined to make my case for including even more under-represented women. I hand over to Aisha to talk through the digital side of the content plan, which includes a full social media campaign, and Instagram take-overs on *Luxxe*'s account to raise the profile of both ordinary and extraordinary women – or what we are calling 'the extra-ordinary ordinary'.

When we come to the end, everyone claps. It feels like a done deal – I don't see how anyone can argue with this idea.

But then the questions start coming, and Tabitha is grilling me on the names of fashion people I've never heard of. This sets Miles off, questioning me on budgets and the potential drop in revenue if we don't put a big name on the cover. I do my best to answer their concerns, but at the end of the interrogation, I feel deflated. This was all supposed to have happened before Leah went on maternity leave, and I can't help thinking it would have gone by without a hitch if she'd been here.

Tabitha's own pitch is killer. She wants us to produce a series of alternative covers for the tenth anniversary issue, each celebrating a different cover star from the last decade. She has proposed a digital content series that looks back on the big-gest moments in fashion, with big-name models and fashion designers already guaranteed through her connections. Miles is sold on the commercial pull of the famous faces and I feel like all my hard work persuading him towards my idea has been undone.

I slump back in my chair, defeated. Two weeks ago, every-thing was going right. I'd started the acting editor job and I thought I was with the love of my life. Now I have cancer, a failing relationship and a job that I'm starting to feel I'm not worthy of having.

'I have another meeting,' Miles says, snapping his laptop shut. 'We've got some great ideas here. Jess, love the extraor-dinary women, but as Tabitha says, we do need to keep the commercial partners happy. I'll leave you ladies to battle it out.'

Aisha looks at me, then at Tabitha, then at the door. 'Shall I make us some tea?'

*

As I walk out of the office an hour later, I spot Marcus across the courtyard. He is on his phone, smoking, with his back against the wall. He catches my eye for a second and I start to give him a little wave, but he looks away, pretending he hasn't seen me.

On my way to the Tube, I rifle through my phone, looking for the dating app. I totally forgot to delete it with everything that's happened over the last week or so, but if Johnny sees it, he'll go crazy. I locate the app and go into my profile, taking a quick look at my matches before I delete it. I click into the messages, looking for Marcus, but he's gone.

Marcus has deleted me, like it never happened.

Egg preservation

'Sorry I'm late,' Johnny says, bursting into the clinic waiting room, fifteen minutes after our appointment was due. I had to tell the receptionist to let the next patient go ahead of us and she eye-rolled me like she might strike me off the list altogether.

'Absolute shitter of a day,' Johnny says, peeling off his coat and taking his phone out of one of the pockets. 'Client meeting ran over by half an hour, then the traffic was a nightmare. And it doesn't help when Rupert Smith is swanning about like he owns the place.'

'You're here now,' I say, patting his knee and deciding against mentioning my equally challenging morning.

'I've just got to reply to this email, then I'm all yours,' Johnny says, brushing my hand away as he frantically types on his phone.

Around us, celebrity gossip magazines sit on the table, pamphlets about IVF and adoption fill metal racks on the wall and there's a fancy new coffee machine with capsules for herbal tea and coffee. A number of couples sit on the seats around the edges of the room; a few women are on their own. I imagine that most of them are desperate for children they're unable to have, while we're trying to give ourselves the best chance of having them one day too.

It's only mid-week and we've already sandwiched endless appointments between our hectic work schedules. Two days ago, we met Dr Malik, the straight-talking oncologist who's responsible for my chemo and radiotherapy regime, while Mr Patel handles the surgery. I hadn't been expecting my results, so I almost fell off my chair when he told us the CT and bone scans both came back clear.

'This is amazing,' I said, in floods of tears in Johnny's arms outside the waiting room. We still have to chemo the hell out of my breast to make sure the cancer doesn't spread, but it's such a relief to know there's nothing in my bones or organs.

Dr Malik explained that they'll have to inject a small metal marker into my tumour to track whether it shrinks during chemo, and from there he'll determine whether to give me a full mastectomy or a much simpler lumpectomy. I wonder whether I'm playing with fire by delaying my chemo to put my eggs on ice, but it's only a few weeks.

'Jessica?' A well-preened clinic assistant distracts me from my thoughts. 'Come through.'

Johnny looks up from his phone and nods at me. 'Good luck.'

There are two of them in the examination room. An older lady with a warm smile and another who looks young enough to be her daughter.

'I'm Sinéad, and this is Rita,' says the older one. 'Are you OK with Rita sitting in today?'

'The more, the merrier.' It's not like I really have a choice.

'This might be uncomfortable, so just let us know if you'd like us to stop,' says Rita. She gestures towards a raised bed with a paper sheet and a set of stirrups to hold my legs in the most mortifying position I can fathom.

'We're going to use a probe with some lube to take a look

107

inside you,' Sinéad says. 'It sounds uncomfortable but it's fine, a bit like a smear test? If you could just take off your bottom half and pop your legs in these, then pop this paper over you, we'll be back in a sec.'

Rita hands me a rectangular sheet of baking paper for my modesty and follows Sinéad out of the room. After all the ultrasounds, mammograms and core biopsies I had before the diagnosis, I thought I was pretty accustomed to the old 'we're about to look at your breasts but God forbid we actually watch you get undressed' routine, but the full vaginal inspection is a new one on me.

I wriggle out of my jeans and fold my knickers on top of the pile of clothing on the floor, then I attempt to get comfy on the bed, resting my feet in the stirrups to separate my legs out to the side. I place the baking paper on top and check my phone as I prepare for the usual five-minute wait before they return to the room.

'Fab,' says Sinéad when she comes back in and finds me undressed from the waist down with the paper in place, like a baking tray prepped and waiting for the oven.

Rita, the accomplice to the crime, hands her what can only be described as a giant white dildo attached to a machine by an old-fashioned telephone wire. If this weren't the decider on whether or not I ever become a mother, it would almost be funny.

'It's not as bad as it looks,' Sinéad says, squirting clear liquid onto the device.

'It's more action than I've had recently,' I say.

Sinéad half smiles like she's heard it a thousand times, then looks me in the eye as she holds the dildo with an 'I'm going in' look.

'This might feel a little cold,' she says.

I feel my muscles tense as she slips it inside me and slides it as far up as it will go. Then she points to the computer screens either side of the chair, moving the wand inside me while focusing intently on the monitors.

'Here you can see your ovaries,' Sinéad explains. 'The ultrasound allows us to see how many follicles are in each side, which gives us an idea of how many eggs you might produce.'

'How many do I have?' All I can see is a blur.

'There's a good amount. This doesn't necessarily mean the eggs are good, but it's a sign you have a decent supply in each basket.'

She slides out the device and hands it to Rita. Sinéad takes off her gloves with a snap and starts writing things down on a form.

'That's the hard bit over with,' she says. 'If you'd like to get yourself dressed and go back out to the waiting room, we'll meet you again in a minute with your partner.'

I can still feel the cold liquid inside me as I put my knickers and jeans back on and return to the waiting room, feeling weirdly awkward in front of the other patients. I've had the most intimate examination and yet here they all are, just next door, sipping tea.

Johnny is still engrossed in his phone when I rejoin him. 'How was it?'

'Interesting,' I say, wondering how many more transvaginal examinations I'll have to endure before this is all over.

Rita calls for us again within minutes and takes us to a different room, where Sinéad is waiting. She introduces herself to Johnny, shaking his hand.

'If you're keen to go ahead with the fertilization, we'll need to discuss dates,' Sinéad says, tapping away at her computer.

She talks us through the procedure of taking tablets to bring on my period, then the daily hormone injections I'll have to give myself, and the blood tests we'll both have to check our fertility levels and screen for diseases. Then there'll be one last 'trigger' injection that Johnny will have to administer in my bum, and finally sedation for egg extraction. It's fair to assume any romance we might have hoped for won't be coming any time soon.

'There are a few side effects, such as bloating and discomfort. Your hormones will be out of whack and you'll probably feel more emotional than usual,' she says.

I know this is a euphemism for 'you'll feel practically suicidal on a daily basis', but what's one more bombshell after cheating and cancer?

Sinéad pulls out a calendar and looks at some dates. Johnny and I find the calendars on our phones, and I can see him in my peripheral vision, shaking his head.

'I know you need to begin as soon as possible so you can start your chemotherapy,' Sinéad says, smiling. 'If we calculate the time to bring on your period then we have the final injection on . . . December eighteenth,' she says.

I picture the run-up to the festive season. The usual string of parties, the drunken nights out with Aisha. This year is going to be very, very different.

Johnny lets out a puff of air.

Sinéad and I turn to look at him.

'Sorry, it's just that we've got the Carter Moran case coming up,' he says. 'The next month is going to be tricky.'

I grit my teeth and smile at Sinéad. 'At least we'll be done for Christmas,' I say.

'There's never a good time,' Sinéad says. 'Are you OK?'

'It's just . . .' I can barely say the words before my voice cracks and I'm crying again, a solitary tear dribbling down my cheek and meeting my mouth, salty and warm. This is the time I could really do with Mum. She'd know what to say, whether

I'm doing the right thing, whether it's all worth it. It's such a huge decision.

Sinéad reaches for the box of tissues on her desk and hands it to me. I dab at my eyes, smiling, laughing, trying to be brave.

'I'm sorry,' I say, sniffling.

'Hey,' Sinéad says, patting me on the shoulder. 'This is one of the most difficult things you can go through.'

I sniffle again and nod and thank her, but the more I think about it, the more I miss Mum. She'd know what to do, she'd help me just by being here. But even if I do have a child some-day, she'll never be there to meet them.

'I'm sorry,' I say, getting up from the chair.

'That's OK, take a break,' Sinéad says, opening the door for me.

I run from the room and close myself inside the loo, sitting on the toilet and locking my head between my knees, feeling the blood rush to my head.

I let myself sob over the whirr of the extractor fan, star-ing at the spotless white floor. I just have to be strong and get through this. Johnny is offering me love, stability, and a future that includes motherhood. There's no other option.

Mannequin

I step aside to make space in the corridor for two hospital porters pushing a patient who is tangled beneath the sheets of her narrow bed. The woman's skin is the same colour as the bed sheets. Her bloodshot eyes catch mine for a second and I see a flash of something, a glimpse of a vibrant young person now trapped in an old person's body, all withered and wrinkled. I smile at her, but she looks away, reminding me of how Mum used to try and spare us from seeing her at her worst. She always wanted to keep her dignity.

I reach the purple section of the hospital, the mental health and counselling wing. Purple to cheer people up? I've made an appointment after much badgering from Nurse Rose. *We have a dedicated team of qualified counsellors who can talk to you about any of your concerns.* This will make a change from all the tests and tablets to prepare me for egg stimulation.

I reach the glass-panelled doors and stare into the corridor ahead. I'm tempted to turn back. How can a stranger possibly understand that in the space of two years I've lost my mum, been cheated on by my boyfriend, been diagnosed with cancer and finally told that I might not be able to have kids? I'm worried once I start crying, I won't be able to stop.

I push open the heavy doors and register with reception,

then keep my head down, finding a seat in the farthest alcove, praying there's no one I know here. I pick up a year-old copy of *Grazia* and thumb through the pages.

The Converse pumps appear on the ground in front of me before I see her face. 'Mind if I sit?'

She doesn't wait for me to answer. She just parks her tiny bird frame on the ripped cushion beside me.

'Those magazines are dirtier than your toilet seat,' she says.

'Gross,' I say, dropping the mag on the table and reaching into my backpack for a tube of hand gel, which I pump into my open palm, then offer to my companion.

'Annabel, right?'

'Bel to some. And hey, Jess.' She nods. I feel honoured that she's remembered my name. 'You here for your shrink session too?'

I laugh. 'Yeah, I mean, just to shut my nurse up really. I don't actually need therapy.'

'Oh I bloody do,' says Annabel. 'Actually, who am I kidding? I come here for the hot therapist. He's the highlight of my week.'

'You have a hot therapist? What time is your appointment?'

'Ten past ten . . . like, half an hour ago. But it's not like we have anything else to do with our time, is it?'

I laugh again. Little does she know I'm juggling my appointments with a full-time job at a glossy magazine, although it feels increasingly futile as I realize the extent of the treatment I'm about to endure.

'He's called Deepak, anyway, the hottie. I call him Dr Deep. I'm like, his star pupil. Or at least I'm the only one under fifty, so I think he appreciates the break from all the old biddies.'

'I think mine's a woman,' I say, checking the appointment slip. 'Guess I drew the short straw?'

Annabel opens her mouth to speak just as a door opens in front of us. Out comes a tall man with a sharp suit and thick-rimmed glasses. 'Morning, Annabel,' he says, with a wink.

'Told you,' she mutters to me not so subtly, as she places both hands on her chair for support and pushes herself to her feet.

'Have fun,' I say, and she follows him into the room, shutting the door behind her.

I emerge from therapy an hour later, my cheeks flushed and my eyes bloodshot and blotchy, much like the old lady I saw in the corridor. I know the appointment was to discuss my concerns around cancer, but I spent the majority of the time talking about Johnny. I'm still clutching a fist full of tissues.

'Trauma level on a scale of one to ten?'

I look across the waiting room to see Annabel stretched out across three chairs with her back against the concrete wall. She waited for me.

'Eight point five,' I say.

'Uff, heavy,' she says, thrusting a giant packet of Haribo sweets into my hand.

'Bought you these. Thought you might need cheering up.'

'Thank you so much,' I say, chuffed by the gesture. 'How was your date with the hot therapist?'

Annabel rolls her eyes in faux ecstasy. 'Smoking hot,' she says. 'Can't believe I have to wait a whole 'nother week till our next sesh.'

'Well, after the one I've just had with Dr Dreary, I think I need to hear all about your hour of passion.' I glance at Annabel's bob and remember Nurse Rose's advice that I find a suitable wig *before* my hair falls out. 'Fancy coming shopping with me?'

'Mate, I've got all the time in the world. Let's get out of here.'

It's the best thing I've heard in ages.

'This way,' Annabel says, leading me back towards the main entrance and in through a set of double doors. 'Prepare yourself, you're about to enter the old biddy zone.'

As we burst through the doors, a grey-haired woman in her sixties or seventies stirs behind the counter, as if we're the first customers she's seen in a year.

'Hello dears,' she says, looking us up and down. 'Are you after anything in particular?'

'Wigs,' Annabel says.

'Is it for yourself, dear?' She eyes Annabel's black Uma Thurman number.

'Actually, it's for me,' I say. 'I have the voucher for an NHS one? For chemo?'

'Oh,' says the woman. 'You're very young, dear.'

'Mm-hm.'

She gestures towards the half-empty shelves behind her. 'Is there anything in particular you're looking for?'

I scan the room. There are no more than twenty wigs in varying shades of brown. Most of them are long and curly, or mullet-like things that remind me of Pat Sharp in his *Fun House* days. All of the mannequin heads are white-skinned and dead behind the eyes.

'Do you have anything a bit more . . . colourful?' The way Annabel says 'anyfink' reminds me of Mum, and I can't help thinking of the yellow headscarf that Aunty Cath bought her. We'd laughed so hard when she tried it on, because she looked like a pineapple. In fact, we used to affectionately refer to her as Pineapple Head. The thought makes me smile.

The woman scans the shelves again and shakes her head.

'Something a bit more . . . modern?' I say, looking at her and then at Annabel.

'This is all we have,' she says. 'There's plenty of choice. We have a few more models coming in soon. What would you like to try?'

Annabel shoots me a look of despair and then smiles. 'You've always wondered what you'd look like with a mullet, haven't you Jess?'

'That was the look I was hoping for, yeah,' I say. I point towards the top shelf at the longest, curliest, muddy-brown mullet number.

Huffing and puffing as if we've asked to try on every wig in the shop, the lady reaches it down with a hook-a-duck stick and fiddles with it, handing me a hair net and holding the wig open for me to try. I tuck my long red hair inside the net and slide it on top, followed by the wig, which smells fusty and needs rearranging.

'How do I look?' I say, turning to Annabel and striking a pose.

Annabel can barely keep from corpsing. She purses her lips with raised eyebrows, nods vigorously and then quickly turns away, towards the door, pretending to fumble with a pile of leaflets.

I snigger as I slip the wig off and hand it back to the lady, who tucks it back over the ill-looking mannequin head.

'Think I'll leave it for today, thanks.'

We burst into fits of laughter the moment the door is closed behind us.

'You looked *hideous*,' Annabel says, and I love her for not just telling me what I want to hear, like everybody else.

Pausing at the hospital's front entrance, we stand side by side like school kids, preparing for the cold. I zip up my fur-lined parka as Annabel pulls a furry hat with hanging bobbles over the top of her black bob. Then she reaches into her coat pockets, pulling out fleece gloves with the ends of the fingers missing and slipping them on until her black nails pop out the ends.

'You got plans today?' Annabel says, as we step out of the stuffy foyer into fresh, crisp December air.

'Well . . .' I said I'd be back at the office right after my appointment, but I really want to spend more time with Annabel. I guess I could take a bit longer. 'I have a meeting at three so I could take a couple of hours off.'

'I have an idea,' she says. 'Come on.'

We walk along the river towards Blackfriars, weaving through the hordes at Borough Market, past the Golden Hinde and the Globe theatre. Outside the Tate Modern, the Christmas market is in full swing, with couples clad in hats and gloves sipping their cups of mulled wine and eating bratwurst on wooden sticks.

Everything around here reminds me of uni, the halls in Waterloo where I lived in my first year and the student union just across the river. I've lost count of the nights we tottered across Waterloo Bridge in stupidly high heels and then ambled back barefoot and drunk with our shoes in our hands. If I'd got lucky, I'd sometimes get a piggy-back ride home but I'd usually pass out in my clothes before there was any action.

'Where are we heading?' I ask as we swipe into Blackfriars station.

'Peckham,' Annabel says.

I stop walking and put my hand on her forearm to halt her. 'Peckham?'

'Three stops,' she says. 'It's hardly the end of the earth.'

'I know where Peckham is,' I say, smiling. 'That's where my mum was from.'

117

'Serious?' she says. 'Mine too! My parents still live there. Do you know it well then?'

'Went there a lot as a kid. I stayed there with my Aunty Cath after uni but she moved after she got divorced.'

'All the more reason why my plan makes sense then,' Annabel says, leading me onto an empty train. She has a badge that reads 'Cancer on board', just like the ones that say 'Baby on board', so she can get a seat on the Tube.

'Do you still live in Peckham then?'

'Nah, I live in Camberwell, but it's not far. What about you?'

'Clapham.'

'South of the river girls,' she says, giving me a little fist pump. I feel like an eight-year-old in the playground, thrilled that I have something in common with my new friend. Something besides cancer. 'Where'd you grow up then?'

'Yorkshire,' I say.

'Thought you were northern.'

'Yeah, my mum moved up there when she met my dad, before I was born. I came down here for uni and never left.'

'Your parents still live up there?'

'My dad, yeah,' I say, then I hesitate. 'Mum died.'

'I'm sorry.'

'It's OK.'

We sit in comfortable silence for a few minutes while the train goes through Denmark Hill. I remember the pack of Haribos and offer it to Annabel. She takes a jelly ring and pops it into her mouth.

She keeps fidgeting, one minute ripping off her hat, coat and gloves and fanning herself with a leaflet from the hospital, and the next minute pulling her coat back over her lap and placing her hands under it for warmth.

'Hot flushes,' she says.

'I remember, from my mum,' I say.

'Did she have breast cancer too?'

'Bowel.'

Annabel does a single nod and takes a fried-egg sweet from the bag.

'Do they bother you? The hot flushes?'

'You get used to it.' She shrugs.

We walk down the station steps at Peckham Rye and out through the railway arch. After my work experience as a teenager, I stayed with Aunty Cath again after uni, when I did a whole year of unpaid internships. It's been a few years since I've been back, but everything feels so familiar. It's changed since I was younger, the fishmongers now competing with hipster coffee shops and trendy bars, but there are still the same open stalls with their overflowing piles of yams, the tummy-rumbling smells of smoking meat and jerk chicken and the late-night barber shops and salons that are as much for socializing as they are for weaving hair.

Annabel is out of breath as we turn the corner and she leads me down the street past bus stops, pound shops and a McDonald's that is heaving with lunchtime punters. She gestures ahead of us at a window display that couldn't be more different from the one inside the hospital. Rows and rows of mannequin heads are piled on top of each other: black ones, white ones, their expressions lifeless, wearing every colour and shape of wig. Afro, silver, pink, blue, long, short, diagonal. The colourful heads disappear into the back of the shop.

'Creepy as hell, innit?' she says.

I grab her hand as we step into the shop. '*Now* you're talking.'

It's exactly the sort of place Mum would have taken me to. She always shunned the stuffy department stores and took me to the indoor market in our nearest town. We would buy penny sweets from the stall in the middle, weighing them in silver trays, and then eat them from paper bags while trying on all the clothes in the discount shops. Dad would roll his eyes when we'd come home, laden with shopping bags, but Mum would proudly announce how little it had cost, giving me a sideways wink.

For the next five minutes, Annabel watches me pick out the most conservative hairpieces in the shop, from shoulder-length auburn to full-on wavy ginger, the closest to my natural hair as I can find. I try them on over my full head of hair, tucking it into a net like the ones they wear in the supermarket bakery. Then I stand still as the shop assistant tugs and pulls the wig into place.

'Smells like burnt plastic,' I say, looking at Annabel for approval. 'What do you think?'

'It's going to look different when you've got no hair. You won't have these side burns, for a start,' she says, touching the side of my face.

'What about the shape?'

'You can wear whatever you want to wear,' Annabel says, then she pauses. 'But you're only bald once . . . hopefully. Why not have a little fun with it?'

Annabel slips her fingers under her own black bob and slides it gently off her head, placing it down on the countertop. Her scalp is whiter than the skin on her face, as if it has never seen the sun, and I can make out the faint outline of her skull through the thin, greyish-looking skin.

I catch myself staring. 'Sorry, I don't mean to gawp.'

'Look all you like,' she says. 'It's a shock at first, but you get used to it. Want to touch?'

She reaches forward, takes my hand in hers and guides it towards her head.

I run a single finger down the back of her skull, feeling as if

I'm committing the most intimate act with this girl I've known for only a week. Her scalp is silky soft, completely hairless, with only the tiniest bit of stubble. It feels like a baby's head, only bigger, with all the contours and bumps, fragile and precious.

Annabel shivers.

'Sorry.'

'It's fine. Tickles a bit, but it's quite nice. Probably the most action I'll get all year . . .'

'Tell me about it.'

'Can I try that one?' Annabel says, pointing towards a ball of curls on one of the higher-up shelves.

The shop assistant looks relieved to have something to do besides watch us two awkward chemo misfits touching each other's heads. She takes down the wig with a hook-a-duck stick like the one in the hospital, picking out the hair net and setting it to one side. Annabel won't be needing it.

Annabel pulls it onto her head and adjusts it over her eyes until she can see. Then she pulls a duck-face pose. 'How do I look? OK, now your turn.'

'What colour do you reckon – yellow, green, maybe pink?' I say.

Annabel shakes her head, pointing towards a vibrant, electric-blue bob with a fringe, similar to her own black one. 'Of the many things I hate about breast cancer, the colour pink is right up there.'

'Tell me about it. Breast cancer needs a rebrand.'

She laughs. 'Try the blue. Blue is my favourite colour.'

'Mine too!' I say.

'This one?' says the shop assistant, gesturing towards the wig. I nod.

The woman lifts the mannequin head from the shelf and carefully removes the hair piece, placing it in my hands. I put it on all wrong at first, ending up with hair all over my face like Cousin Itt. Annabel helps me adjust it, her cold hands touching my face.

When I'm fully wigged up, she takes her phone from her coat pocket and presses the button to turn it to selfie mode. 'One, two, three!'

We both strike the same pout and collapse into laughter. Annabel captures the whole burst of frames and we laugh even harder when we see the results. My eyes are half-closed in a demented pose in one of the shots, yet we could almost be sisters. 'That's your new profile pic right there,' she says.

We spend the next twenty minutes trying on everything in the shop – yellow wigs, bum-length red ones, curly grey, shiny purple, jet black straight. Everything I try on feels scratchy, but they're cheap enough that I can afford to keep one in the drawer if I don't wear it.

I settle on the blue bob with the fringe to match Annabel's, and an auburn one that's closer to my natural colour. As I swipe my card, the shop assistant folds each wig flat and slides it into a plastic packet, pressing it closed with a popper, then slipping it over the counter.

'God bless you, ladies,' she says as we walk out the door.

Boxes

'Where did this come from?' Johnny says, picking up my blue wig with his thumb and forefinger and holding it away from him like it's a dirty dishcloth.

'I made a new friend,' I say, smiling at the thought of my shopping trip with Annabel. 'We went wig shopping.'

'A guy at work told me there's this thing called cold-cap therapy that his wife had, where you don't have to lose your hair,' Johnny says. 'Maybe you could try that?'

'I've heard of it,' I say, remembering how Nurse Rose talked me through the options. 'But they say it's like sticking your head in the freezer for three hours, it's really painful. And you know what I'm like with the cold.'

Johnny stays silent, fiddling with the synthetic fibres of the wig.

'What is it?' I say, patting the bed so he'll come back under the covers with me.

He gets in beside me and leans back on the headboard. 'I'm just finding it hard.'

'What do you mean?' I take his hand under the covers.

'The thought of you losing your hair. You know, after your mum . . .'

The image flashes through my head of the first time I saw Mum bald. Johnny was the one who would drive me to visit her, then comfort me when we got home. He found it as tough to see her like that as I did, and now he has to go through it again.

'Hey, it's OK,' I say, snuggling into his arms. 'I'll still be me. I'll still be your Ginge, remember?' Except I won't be Ginge any more, not when I lose my hair.

He strokes my head as we sit in silence for a few minutes.

'Maybe we could do something today – go to the ice rink?' I say, sitting up in the bed. I'm determined to get back to being Fun Jess and devote some proper time to fixing this relationship before I start chemo.

'I thought you knew I had to work?' he says.

'On a Saturday?'

'It's this case we're working on. It's never-ending.'

As soon as he says 'we', my heart sinks. I know that Little Miss Avo is safely out of reach in Manchester, but he's due up there again next week and I know she'll be asking about my cancer, probably doing the head tilt and telling him she'll always be there for him, whatever he needs. He'll probably fall into her perfect, just-stepped-out-of-the-salon hair as soon as I'm bald. I snap the image away.

'It's today I start the hormone jabs,' I say.

'Shit. Can we do it when I get home?'

'What time will that be?'

'I don't know. You know what it's like.'

Sometimes he works until nine p.m., even on weekends. Sometimes he pulls an all-nighter. But sometimes he finishes early and spends the entire afternoon in the pub.

'It's fine,' I say, shaking my head. Johnny hates needles anyway. 'Don't worry, I'll do it myself.'

'Are you sure?'

'It'll be easier this way.' The thought of injecting myself gives me the shivers.

'Could you get Lauren round?'

'Maybe,' I say. The injections have to be done at the exact same time every day for ten days, followed by a final 'trigger' injection.

'I'll be back as soon as I can, promise,' he says, pulling on his socks.

'She's called Annabel, by the way,' I say, as he leaves the room. 'My new friend.'

Kate's house looks like a bomb has hit it. Boxes piled on top of boxes, creating a gangway barely big enough to navigate sideways, let alone with a buggy. Off the entrance hallway is a utility room with every inch of surface area stacked with more boxes that spill over with a mix of tools, cleaning items, pegs and God knows what else. On the floor is a mountain of clothes, possibly washed, possibly unwashed.

'Told you it was a shit tip,' Kate says, leading me through to the kitchen, where baby Ella sits in her highchair.

'Don't worry about me,' I say, grateful to be out of the house instead of sitting at home, thinking about Johnny and Mia.

'I'll make you some brunch,' she says, pushing her thumb into an avocado to check it for ripeness. 'Avo on toast?'

'Let me do it,' I say. I feel awful expecting her to provide for me, but it's the only way I get to see her, now that she has a kid.

Kate sits back down with Ella, passing her blueberries, which she sucks and then presses back out of her toothless mouth in the form of bright purple pulp. I search around for a chopping board, finding one in the sink and giving it a wash before slicing into the overripe avocado.

'So how are you feeling?' I ask. Lauren and I have both noticed changes in Kate since she had the baby, but she clams up every time we ask her about it.

'I'm great,' she says, brushing it off as usual. 'I mean, completely sleep-deprived and I've lost all my social skills, but apart from that, great.'

'What about your NCT friends?'

She makes the sort of stubborn I'm-fine-about-it face you might make if you were picked last for the netball team. 'They're all doing brilliantly. Some of them are even back at work. I have no idea how I'm going to cope with going back.'

'Have you thought about getting therapy?'

'We can't afford it,' she says. It's something that sits oddly every time I look at their vast, four-bedroom Dulwich house, but then I suppose the debt is half the problem.

'It's probably worth the sacrifice,' I say, wishing I could make her better. The old Kate, the events planner extraordinaire who was always there for everyone, always planning the most fun-filled dinner parties and get-togethers, has been absent since the day Ella came along.

'How are things with Johnny? Did you tell him about you-know-what?'

'Not yet,' I say, just as keen to deflect the conversation away from my relationship as she is to avoid her own problems.

I tell her about the egg preservation and wig shopping with Annabel as I attempt to poach four eggs, accidentally breaking the yolk of the first one so that it spreads out in white and orange streamers through the water.

'She sounds nice,' she says. 'It must be good to meet someone who's in the same boat as you.'

'It really is,' I say, putting the plate with the unbroken eggs in front of Kate and taking the massacred one for myself. The yolk makes a crumbly, stringy mess on top of the avocado.

'So, it looks like we've found a date.'

It took approximately thirty-six emails and several online surveys before we settled on a weekend for Lauren's hen do, with only three casualties unable to attend due to other hens, holidays and childcare commitments. Now all we need to do is plan the activities and sort the logistics of payment for those attending for one day or two, drinking or not drinking and so on and so forth.

We run through the options – trip to Barcelona, spa weekend, cookery class, country house retreat with butlers in the buff, weekend in Prague. Presumably all foreign trips are off now that I'll be having chemo. On Kate's hen do, while her husband Colm had a wild time paintballing with his stags in the New Forest, we spent our time making 'sparkle crowns' and fascinators, a whole sixty minutes of my life I will never get back. The last thing I want is another mindless crafts session.

'A spa weekend sounds like heaven,' Kate says, picking up bits of blueberry mush that Ella has thrown on the floor. My plate is clean while Kate's perfect poached eggs sit cold and untouched as she tries to calm the now-crying baby.

'I think Lauren wants to go out-out,' I say, picturing her face as we tell her we're spending the entire weekend in robes and no make-up.

'You're right.' Kate hauls Ella out of her highchair. 'Maybe we could do a bit of both. Spa day and then big night out in London?'

'Love it,' I say. 'Let me take her. You finish that.'

She hands me the baby and I hold her across my forearms and swoosh her around like an aeroplane. Within seconds, she is bawling, and I have no choice but to hand her back to Kate, who abandons her brunch entirely.

'Ssh,' she says, navigating the boxes in the hallway until they're both out of sight.

I want to ask Kate how it's going with Colm, how she feels towards Ella and going back to work; to give her time to really get into how she feels. I want to talk to her about Johnny, about the embryo freezing and how it's the scariest thing I've ever done. But it's clear from the sound of Ella bawling from the top of the stairs that, once again, I have lost her.

I've just about steeled myself to do my first injection. I sit with Oreo in front of the TV, a blanket over my legs and feet. Then I fish out the instruction leaflet from the assisted conception unit and open the individual packs, laying out the vial of liquid, the syringe and the plunger.

I puncture the top of the vial with the needle, pushing it to the bottom and sucking the solution into the syringe. Then I remove the needle, putting the empty vial to the side.

I hold the needle between my thumb and forefinger, wracking my brain to picture how Sinéad did it in the demo. She told me to flick my finger on the side of the syringe, making sure there were no air bubbles. But there's still a tiny bubble that doesn't seem to want to go. I wish I had someone to tell me if I'm doing it right.

I feel like the needle will slip out of my hand with the amount I'm sweating. I pull up my T-shirt and sit with my top resting on both nipples, exposing a section of skin down to my navel. I prod softly at my belly, looking for the fattiest bits, then I squeeze a section of flesh below my belly button and hold it between my thumb and forefinger with my left hand.

With my right, I pick up the needle again and hover it close to the section of flesh I've clamped in my left hand. A sharp intake of breath and I jab the needle at ninety degrees, plunging the syringe all the way down until it stops. I pull it back out and watch as a dark bead of blood appears at the surface.

Relaxing my muscles now, I reach for one of the cotton wool pads I've only ever used to remove make-up and I dab hard at the circle of blood on my belly, pressing down for two minutes while I stare ahead at the picture of Mum on the mantlepiece.

I ease myself out of the chair, carrying the empty syringe and dropping it into the yellow sharps box the hospital gave me, hearing it touch the bottom. Oreo laps at my feet. Good job, Mum. One down, nine to go.

Secondaries

By day seven, I'm so bloated and tearful I want to give up. My belly feels like it could pop like a water balloon. Aisha has borne the brunt of my increasingly fraught relationship with Tabitha, who seems hell-bent on trying to sabotage my work every time I leave the office for a couple of hours for hospital appointments. I've sobbed into my Pret tomato soup on more than one occasion with Aisha, who is trying to persuade me to take some actual time off.

I wonder if it would be so bad if I just left it all to fate. If I can't have kids after cancer, maybe I'm not supposed to. It's not like I'm desperate to have them. It's just that I've always thought I'd be *able* to. You're a woman, you have kids. It's a given.

And then there's being an only child. I'm the only one who can carry on my mum and dad's genes, and Johnny is the only one who can continue his. Mum would have loved a grandchild. Dad would too. In some ways, it feels wrong to continue my legacy if I might have a faulty breast cancer gene, but I can't help feeling an instinct to do it anyway.

I put my hand on my swollen belly. It seems cruel that the side effects of the egg stimulation are similar to pregnancy itself. The cramps, the painful bloating, the way one minute I feel like dancing and the next I just want to cry. All the side effects of pregnancy, but without the baby at the end.

I'm walking down the main corridor after my latest egg check just as Annabel emerges from her appointment, looking as downhearted as I feel.

'You alright?' I say, wondering what news she has just received.

'Don't want to talk about it,' she says. 'Tell me about you. And no holds barred – we'll be hair twins soon, so no secrets, OK?'

My shoulders drop with relief. Johnny has been so preoccupied with work lately that I need someone to give me their undivided attention. We walk down the corridor to the hospital branch of Costa Coffee, where she orders a flat white for me, a latte for her and a large slice of red velvet cake to share.

'In a few days' time, I'm meant to be freezing an embryo with Johnny,' I say.

'You don't sound so sure . . .'

Considering I've only known her for a month, it's amazing how comfortable I feel with Annabel, like I could spill my greatest fears and she wouldn't judge me at all. We've been texting back and forth since the wig shopping. Mostly, she sends me anti-inspirational bullshit memes that say things like 'Let me be the first to punch the next person who tells you that everything happens for a reason'. There's something so truthful and honest about her.

'I found out he cheated right before I was diagnosed,' I say.

'Mate, I'm so sorry. What a dick.'

'Well, it's not quite so simple,' I say, desperate for Johnny not to come across as the bad guy.

'Tell me everything. I'm all ears.'

And so I tell her everything, beginning with Mia and

Marcus, then the modern-day fairy tale in reverse. How Johnny and I met at a wedding, two northerners in London with ambitious plans for life. How he'd been the ultimate boyfriend throughout my mum's illness, even though it knocked him for six. How we moved in together, saying goodbye to our respective flatshares and renting our lovely little place in Clapham. And how he came home one day not long after Mum died with Oreo in a little box, just waiting to be loved, saying he thought the cat could be a stepping stone before we had kids of our own.

'Sounds like you were love's young dream,' Annabel says, slicing off a small piece of cake and spooning it into her mouth.

'We were.'

'So what happened?'

I stare at the crumbs on her plate. In many ways, things were great. When Johnny was on form he was the life and soul of the party, the one who had everyone in stitches at dinner parties. But it only took the tiniest knock back and he'd be straight into a slump, calling himself a failure, like his father. The sex was 'meh', but who still has knee-trembling sex after five years? And the drinking . . . I knew Johnny drank more than your average thirty-something, but I figured he'd grow out of it.

'Has he ever had therapy?' Annabel says.

'God no,' I shake my head. 'Johnny is one of those stubborn northerners who thinks therapy is for wimps.' He associates any kind of asking for help with weakness, but he's been through a lot. I often wonder if he missed out on his childhood, taking on all that responsibility when his dad left.

Mum's death was hard for him too. Although I lived with Lauren at the beginning of her treatment, Johnny was my rock, visiting Mum with me and keeping Dad company. My parents have always been his 'couple goals'. Johnny never got over his father leaving him – it weighs on everything he does. It's certainly part of the reason he wanted to become a solicitor, to prove he's not just a 'useless drunk' like his father.

'Maybe I could have found more time for him when Mum died,' I say.

'That seems very generous of you,' Annabel says.

'I don't know.' I sigh as I force myself to think about something that still feels so painful. 'When Mum died, I sort of cut myself off from everything that reminded me of her. For the first year, I threw myself into work and I was even promoted to editor of my old magazine. But I haven't been able to face baking since she died, and I slowly fell out of love with *Perfect Bake*. Then when the job at *Luxxe* came up, I jumped at the chance, but of course it meant spending all my time grafting for this new position, and I think I pushed Johnny away in the process. I think I've pushed away everything that reminds me of Mum. My dad included.'

Annabel gives me an empathetic look. 'Did he actually say that's why he cheated?'

I shrug. 'Sort of, yeah. He did say I wasn't there for him enough. I always think when someone cheats, it's because there's something wrong in their own relationship. I know I'm not blameless.'

'It's true that no one cheats if their relationship is perfect, but maybe there's more to it,' Annabel says. 'I mean, is it possible you weren't spending time with him because you didn't *want* to? Does he make you happy?'

'Umm . . .' The question catches me off guard. Does Johnny make me happy? It's not like the early days when he'd meet me after work and my stomach would do somersaults when I saw him coming up the escalator. We no longer spend hours people-watching in parks, in fits of belly laughter as he puts on voices for all the different people, imagining what they're saying. But that sort of magic isn't *supposed* to last. What matters is we're comfortable in each other's company, he's a brilliant dad to Oreo and that makes me think he'll be a brilliant dad to my children.

'We've been together a long time,' I say. 'He's not perfect, but he'll make an amazing husband. I love that we come from similar backgrounds, so we get each other, you know?'

'But does he make you *happy*?'

'Of course he makes me happy,' I say. Yes, yes, he definitely makes me happy. Just because he's not entirely happy himself all the time doesn't mean we're not happy overall.

'As long as you're sure,' she says. Then she looks off into the distance, as if remembering something. 'If cancer has taught me anything, it's to recognize the people who really care about you and the things that actually matter.'

'Are you talking about an ex?' I say, not wanting to probe too much into what I assume is a painful subject.

She opens her mouth to start to say something, then closes it again and sighs. 'Something like that, yeah.'

I hate to imagine the sorts of things she's been through, but I can tell she's not ready to open up about it, so I change the subject. 'So what about you? Did you freeze your eggs?'

Annabel's face turns serious, and suddenly I see how exhausted, faded and grey she looks.

'What is it?' I say.

'Um . . .' She pauses. 'I did freeze some eggs, but I'll never be able to have kids.'

'What about when you finish treatment?'

'Jess. I have secondaries.'

I remember Mum's secondary diagnosis like it was yesterday. She'd had two years' grace between that and the big C bomb.

We'd thought, after her chemo had finished, that things were back to normal. There was a brief period where she was even more appreciative of life than before, seizing the opportunities and feeling grateful for the simplest of things – cups of tea, reading the papers, watching *Strictly*.

Then she got sucked back into normal life, worrying about the tea rooms, their finances and her health. Every little thing to her was a sign that the cancer had come back – a headache must mean she had a brain tumour, a backache meant she had cancer in her spine, a cough meant she had it in her lungs.

In the end, it was the only symptom she hadn't thought to equate to cancer – the breathlessness she felt walking up the stairs, which she'd put down to gaining weight and getting old. The breathlessness was the final sign that the cancer had spread, and by the time Mum finally went to get it checked out, it was everywhere. Her two years of grace had ended – they'd ended for us all. With secondaries, there is no cure.

I always thought she was old, because she was my mother. But Mum was fifty-seven when she was first diagnosed, sixty when she died. Only a couple of years have passed but I still can't get my head around how young she was.

And now here is Annabel, twenty-seven years old, the same age I was when Mum was first diagnosed and I thought my entire world had ended. To know that you're going to die of this, that you're never going to have kids . . . I can't imagine how that feels. And yet she's so positive, so full of life and energy. I wonder if that's why she's so easy to talk to, why it feels like she'll never judge. I guess if you weren't afraid any more, if you knew you weren't going to be here forever, you'd open yourself up to all kinds of possibilities.

I can't allow myself to change, like Mum did. I can't allow

myself to be paranoid about every ache and pain or I'll fritter away the only life I've got. From now on, I'm going to be more like Annabel. I'm going to manage my own future, be positive and open to everything that's to come. No more feeling sorry for myself.

One last time

Three days before the egg retrieval, Johnny comes home from work on time. He runs me a bath with candles and orders me to relax while he makes a fish pie, one of my favourite dishes. He's been making a real effort in the last week or so, and even shortened his monthly trip to Manchester so that he wouldn't have to stay overnight. I leave the bathroom door open so I can listen to him pottering about, humming away to himself in the kitchen.

I lie back in the bath and rest my chin on my chest to look down at my breasts. You wouldn't know there was something inside one of them that could kill me. It's only been a month since the diagnosis but the chemo couldn't come sooner.

I move my thumb in firm circles over the right breast, the one that doesn't contain the lump. I want to make sure there's nothing in there, even though I'm certain it would have showed up on the scans if there was anything to worry about.

Soap suds crackle, tiny bubbles burst against my skin, creating a silky film. In a few months, I'll be having surgery and my body will no longer look the same. If I can get through chemo and the op, I promise to myself I'll never complain about my looks again. I'll never take advantage of this body. I'll show it off and be proud of it, the way I did the night we found the lump.

*

We'd gone to Tuscany the first week of September, mostly to avoid the school summer holidays.

I'm a different person on holiday; we both are. All it takes to unwind is a glass of red and the chance to get my summer wardrobe out. Add a bit of sunshine and I can wash away months of uptightness and work worries. And there's nothing Johnny finds sexier than 'Unstressed Jess'.

That night, he kept filling my glass so I wouldn't know how many I'd drunk, kissing me over and over until I couldn't resist him. Snogging like teenagers, you'd think we'd been together four and a half weeks, not four and a half years.

'Let's go home to bed,' he said, nodding at me to down my last drop of wine while he finished off his whisky.

We stumbled out of the cab and in through the gate of our villa, me struggling in my heels on the cobbled driveway until he picked me up and carried me to the front door. I flicked off my shoes and followed him up the spiral staircase to our bedroom, which was still warm from the afternoon sunshine.

I started to take off my dress, so used to stripping on auto-pilot to get the sex finished and prolong my night's sleep for work the next day. But this time he stopped me, placing a hand on top of mine and moving it away. I started to speak but was silenced by his finger across my lips, swiftly removed and replaced with his own.

'Let's do it like we used to,' he says. 'Like in the Lakes, remember?'

I remembered it. Our first weekend away together – the lacy underwear I'd bought specially, the expensive champagne he'd paid for at dinner and the oysters I'd tried for the first time and pretended to like. But it wasn't so much the long nights of fucking that I remembered – it was the hours of talking in between.

That weekend was the first time he opened up about his childhood and the hazy memories he had of his father's drinking before he left. I remembered how heartbroken I felt for that little boy who suddenly became, at the age of six, the man of the house, the one responsible for keeping his mum safe from harm.

But of course, the sex that weekend was pretty good too. I knew by then that the more he let me in emotionally, the more I wanted to give him physically. We barely left the bed and breakfast, staying up until four in the morning and falling asleep in each other's arms.

That was before everything changed. Just a few months later, Mum would be diagnosed with cancer and our passionate beginnings would be cut short. Sex marathons would be replaced with sleepless nights where he'd listen to me talking about Mum, about my fears that the chemo wouldn't be enough, that I'd lose the person I loved the most. We never really returned to the carefree times we had at the start.

Now he slipped a finger underneath the strap of my dress and slid it over my shoulder, bending to kiss me once, twice, three times, from my shoulder to my neck to my earlobe. I moaned as I willed him to take off the rest of my clothes.

I tilted my head to one side to allow him to continue kissing my neck and soon felt a hand inside my dress, pulling down my knickers and letting them drop to the cold stone floor.

Then he was pulling up my dress, raising it over my head so I was standing semi-naked in front of him, only my bra remaining. He spun me around so that my back was facing him, then released the hook of my bra and slid it from my shoulders, watching it fall to the floor with my knickers.

He started undressing himself, not in the functional way he does at home, but with desire and purpose. I twisted my neck to look over my shoulder but he held out an arm to stop me. 'Stay there,' he whispered; the room was so quiet it seemed too much to speak at volume.

His belt and trousers fell to the floor with a clink and he threw his shirt on top of the pile. Then his skin was against my skin, his erection pressing into the small of my back while a finger caressed its way from one nipple to the other, then slowly down between my legs, where it felt its way inside me. I was panting now, out of breath and enveloped in his love for the first time in a long time.

Keeping his hands on my waist, he knelt on the hard floor, resting his knees on the pile of discarded clothing. I felt his nose press up against my butt cheeks as he pushed at my inner thighs, motioning for me to spread my legs wider, then turning me to face him. Then he was against my clit, pushing and probing inside me with his tongue and then with two fingers until I came, loud and hard.

I pulled him towards me now, stretching out on the bed and allowing him to slide inside me, making me gasp. He groaned into my neck, moistening the strands of hair on my skin.

He was whispering into my ear when he came. I felt his whole body against mine as he lost control, coming loud and heavy and melting into me. I pulled his body to me then. I wanted to keep him close for as long as possible.

'Fuck,' was all I could manage as I wrapped my arms and legs around his torso, enjoying the feeling of being crushed slightly by his weight. He was still panting on top of me, still breathing heavily, the boom boom boom of his heartbeat against my chest.

'Fuck,' he said, finally, bursting into laughter. 'Now *that's* the girl I signed up for. I get so fucking turned on when you lose control like that.'

'We'll have to do it more often, then,' I said, closing my eyes. 'Stay here on top of me, don't go anywhere.'

Ten minutes later, I was on my back with the thin bed sheet pulled up to my waist, straddling the wet patch between my legs while I waited for him to smoke his cigarette, a habit he allowed himself only while on holiday.

I turned onto my right side and propped myself up on one elbow, facing the balcony where Johnny was smoking, his back to me as he looked out into the pitch-black countryside.

My breasts looked milky white against the uneven streaks of lobster-red sunburn around where my bikini top had been. I scolded myself for getting burnt. No matter how diligent I am with the factor 50, I always miss those bits around the edges, the patches of skin that have rarely seen sunshine, aside from the one time we found a nudist beach in Thailand.

I ran a finger over the red line underneath my left breast. It smarted from my touch and I could feel the heat emanating from my skin. I placed a full palm on my chest, feeling the cool flesh in contrast to the burnt skin around my rib cage. I pressed down for a moment, the pressure from my hand some-how soothing the pain from the burn, and the feeling of my breast cupped in my hand a sudden comfort.

Then I felt it. A hard sphere, like one of those rubber bouncy balls we played with as kids. Not poking out of my breast, not visible from the outside, but sitting comfortably beneath the flesh, closer to my collar bone.

'Come feel this,' I said, sitting up and pulling the bed sheet around me.

'You are a horny little thing tonight, aren't you?' he said, turning to face me on the balcony, cigarette still in hand, his cock hanging flaccid.

'Serious,' I said. 'I think I've found a lump.'

'What?' He stubbed out the cigarette, shuffling his bare feet across the cold floor and plonking himself down on the bed next to me. 'Let's see.'

His hands were cold and a little damp as he squeezed and poked at my breast.

'There's nothing there, what are you on about? I would have noticed.'

'There is. Look,' I said, feeling around until I found it again and placed his finger on top of it. He touched the bouncy ball softly as I held it in place. His expression went from jovial to sober.

'Does it hurt?' he said, moving his finger away and looking at me with his big almond eyes.

'I don't think so,' I said, prodding it further to check.

'I'm sure it's nothing. We'll go to the doctor's together as soon as we get home.'

Neither of us slept that night, just like in the good old days. Only this time, we weren't having fun.

'You haven't drowned in there, have you?' Johnny shouts from down the hallway.

I emerge from the water, splashing around as I grasp the side of the bath and pull myself up.

'Not quite,' I shout back.

'Five minutes till pie time.'

'Coming.'

I stand up slowly and watch in the mirror as the suds of soap slide down my legs and collect around my ankles. I stare for a few moments at my body, clutching my hands around my swollen belly, as if there's a baby inside. In a couple of days, a doctor will take out my eggs and fertilize them with Johnny's sperm. It's such an invasive, clinical way to go about future parenthood, so far removed from the loving sex I'd imagined leading to a pregnancy one day.

This is it now, there's no going back. And suddenly I feel the overwhelming loss of my mum, the acute pain of something physically absent. I'm making one of the biggest decisions of my life, and all I want is my mum.

'So have you made any progress on the business plan?' I say, fishing around for the chunks of smoked haddock in the middle of the fish pie.

It's been a month since I last broached the topic of Johnny going for partner, and I figure now is a good time, since he seems on better form than he's been for the last few weeks.

'No chance,' he says, taking a sip of his wine. 'Not until we finish this case.'

'Maybe we can sit down and look at it when I start my chemo?' I say. 'I'll be bored if I can't go to work.' I'm concerned he'll leave it to one side then another opportunity will come around and he'll be devastated again.

'Erica is calling me,' Johnny says, looking down at his phone, which is buzzing on the table.

'Leave it,' I say, putting my hand out to stop him.

He looks antsy as he lets the phone ring off, then reluctantly turns it to silent.

'So?' I say, when he picks up his fork again.

'So what?'

'Will you let me help you with the business plan?' It's not like I have a lot to offer, but I figure the act of sitting him down and helping him to focus is a start.

'Will you give it a rest?' he says, taking a larger swig of wine. 'I've got so much on my plate with this case and then worrying about you and . . .'

'Alright,' I say, taking my signal to stop nagging. 'Sorry.'

'No, I'm sorry,' he says. 'I'm just having a hard time.'

Something clicks.

He's having a hard time? *I'm* the one with cancer, *I'm* the one who's been cheated on and *I'm* the one who might lose the greatest job opportunity I've ever had because I'm too busy dealing with cancer, but *he's* having a hard time? I've been kicking myself these last few weeks about how I should have been there for him, how I've been a bad girlfriend and led him to go elsewhere, but he's not taking responsibility for what he did.

Suddenly I'm back to that night, sitting across from him at this bench, hearing all about Mia.

'I cheated on you,' I say.

His head shoots up. 'What?'

'After you told me about Mia, I kissed a guy from work.'

He drops his knife and fork in the middle of his plate and crosses his arms over his chest. 'What are you talking about?'

The confession floods out of me. The dating app, snogging Marcus in that bar, how I wanted to get back at Johnny.

'You went on a *dating site*?' He emphasizes the words as if the act itself was worse than Marcus running his tongue around my mouth.

'I wanted to hurt you,' I say, less emotional than I expected to feel.

He stands up, swinging his legs over the bench, one after the other. He backs towards the stove, pouring himself a huge glass of wine.

'What the fuck?' He picks up a tea towel and starts flicking it towards his thigh, making a slapping sound.

'I'm sorry. You said that thing about making us even and you were in Manchester with her and I just . . .'

'Jesus. I told you I wanted to *marry* you! I've even been

thinking about leaving the firm because of you!' His nostrils flare as he downs his glass of wine and pours another.

'Really?' He hasn't mentioned anything about this. I immediately feel guilty.

He nods. 'Yes, because I love you. Because I know how much it upsets you that I'm still working with her. Because I want to show you how much I love you.'

'I'm sorry,' I say, clutching my hands around my swollen belly.

He lifts his chin in a nod towards it. 'So what are we supposed to do about that?'

'I don't know, Johnny.' I wish we had more time. More time to work things out before the embryo freezing, more time before chemo.

'Fuck, Jess,' he says, storming out of the room.

'Where are you going?'

'Out.'

The front door slams and he is gone.

Trigger happy

I lie on my side on the bed, pyjama bottoms pulled down, bum cheeks exposed. I've managed to get through ten injections in my own belly, but this is the trigger one and I can't do it on my own. It's excruciating for both of us, but it has to be done.

'Sure you know how to do this?' I say, looking over my shoulder.

'The target is big enough.'

'Dad!' I turn and slap his hand. I know he's trying to sound confident, but his voice is quavering. He hates needles.

'Going in,' he says.

I clench my buttocks and fists at the same time, waiting for the pain to hit. But there is nothing. The bed moves.

'Relax, love,' he says. 'I can't bloody do it if you're sat there with your arse like a stick of rock.'

I start to laugh, loosening my muscles everywhere. That's when he does it – I feel the needle plunging in and I squeal a little. It hurts.

'Almost done, hold on,' he says.

It's agony. Fuck, it hurts.

Finally, he draws the needle out. I feel every single millimetre as it slides out of my flesh.

Dad turns to face the door and shuffles away with a loud 'ahem'.

146

'I'll go make us a cup of tea, love.'

Great, and we'll pretend this never happened.

Thirty-six hours to go. That's the last of the drugs, the big one done before the egg retrieval.

I join Dad in the kitchen a few minutes later when I've taken a moment to pull up my pants and compose myself.

He is busy making a brew. 'I reckon we should get a take-away tonight, what do you fancy?'

'Great idea,' I say. 'You choose.'

We sit in front of the TV with the tray of sushi on the coffee table in front of us. Dad used to think he hated sushi, could never understand why you'd want to put 'that disgusting raw fish' in your mouth, but Mum loved it and would seek it out every time she visited me in London, even if was just from Itsu. When she finally persuaded him to try it one year, it turned out Dad had a taste for it too, and it became a little family tradition. We felt too guilty eating it after Mum died, like we were somehow betraying her, but I think tonight is his way of telling me she'd want us to move on, have our little bonding session together.

When Johnny didn't come home last night despite my three thousand missed calls, I realized he might not be back in time for the egg extraction at all. He finally replied to say that he was staying at a mate's for a couple of days to clear his head, but I'd already asked Dad to drive down and help me administer the final injection and be here to hold my hand the day after tomorrow, in case I need it.

Oreo watches avidly as I dip a piece of salmon nigiri into a pot of soy sauce and slip it into my mouth in one, savouring the salty-sweet umami taste. I won't be allowed raw fish or runny eggs while I'm on chemo, so I better make the most of it while I can. Dad coughs as he swallows a bit too much wasabi.

'Flippin' 'eck, that's spicy!'

I give him a little pat on the back and hand him a glass of water as he half laughs, half coughs his way through the spice attack.

We stream a show of a stand-up comedian who's talking about her recent trip to Marbella, and I reheat the miso soups to sip as we stretch our legs out on the sofa. I'm stuffed, but happy.

After the show ends, we stack the sushi boxes and scrape the leftovers into the bin. Dad rinses the plates as I reorganize the fridge.

'He'll be back, love, I know he will.'

Dad knows Johnny and I are fighting, but I haven't actually told him about Johnny's cheating – he'd want to throttle him if he knew the truth. I don't want to give him more to worry about than he has already, so I brushed over the content of our argument when he arrived.

'You think?' I say, remembering Johnny's rage when I told him about Marcus.

'That lad is as stubborn as your old Dad, but I know how much he loves you.'

'Well, he's not here now,' I say, noticing an ancient jar of olives at the back of the fridge.

Dad turns to face me. 'You know you don't have to go through with it?'

'Go through with what?' I say, unsure whether he means embryo freezing or staying with Johnny for the long haul. I make a face as I drop the heavy jar of mouldy olives into the bin.

'This egg thing.' Just like we can't quite say the word 'breast' in each other's company, we're not quite acknowledging the insemination of my eggs either.

'Dad,' I say, picking up a carton of milk and putting it back into the exact same spot. 'It's fine. It's only a sedation, it's not like I'm going under.'

Last time we went through anything like this together, we were stood outside the operating theatre, saying goodbye to Mum and putting on brave faces, telling her we'd still be there when she woke up. I know how it feels to be scared shitless that the person you love most in the world could die on the operating table. All you can do for the next few hours is picture the moment when the doctor comes out to deliver the bad news, and I know full well my Dad must be thinking the same about me now.

'It's a big ordeal, love.'

'It might be my only chance to have kids.'

I know he loves me and he's looking out for me, but he can't understand the prospect of never becoming a mother.

'Your mum and I lost a baby,' he says, out of nowhere.

'What? When?'

'Before you were born.'

I shut the fridge and lean against it, feeling weak.

'I didn't know.'

'She was only a couple of months into the pregnancy. We hadn't planned it, but we wanted it.'

His eyes are filled with tears.

'I'm sorry.'

'We tried for years after that. We weren't desperate the first time round, but we wanted you. And then you came, and you were perfect.'

I look down at the floor.

'Your mum and I would have done anything to give you a little brother or sister.'

'Really? Did you try, after me?'

'We tried for years, love. Nothing. You were our little miracle. We'd have done anything for you.'

'I want to be a mum someday, Dad. I want to give you and Mum something to feel proud of.'

'We're already so proud of you, love,' he says. His voice breaks and he turns towards the sink, wiping his eyes.

I tear off a sheet of kitchen roll and hand it to him.

'Ta,' he says, blowing his nose. 'I just want you to be safe, you know that. It's all well and good wanting a little one, but the most important thing is keeping you here.'

I purse my lips and nod my head, unable to speak. When I was twelve years old, I wrote an essay about how when I grew up, I wanted to marry a man just like my dad. My classmates laughed and Miss Kingly said it was 'adorable', but I meant it. I wanted a husband who would drop football with his friends to pick me up from a night out, so I didn't have to get a taxi on my own. I wanted a man who would lie on my side of the bed to warm it up before I got in. I wanted someone who'd drive two hundred miles just to eat sushi with me and tell me everything will be OK.

I want someone who loves me as unconditionally as Dad loved Mum. That's who I want to have a child with, some day.

I spray the worktop with kitchen cleaner, squeezing my eyes shut to keep from crying.

Nil by mouth

On the day of the embryo freezing, I wake at two in the morning to the sound of pounding at the front door. I peel open an eye that is stuck together with sleep.

Thud, thud, thud. 'Jess! Let me in!'

I leap out of bed, desperate to get to the door before Dad wakes up. But it's too late, Dad is already standing in the living-room doorway, rubbing his eyes.

'Go back to sleep,' I say, gesturing at him to head back to the couch.

'Jess! I know you're in there!'

'Sssssh,' I hiss as I turn my key in the lock and open the door. Johnny must have been leaning on the door frame, because he stumbles across the top step, practically falling into the hallway.

'Jesus, what happened to you?' I say, looking at him with a mix of pity and disgust. 'Where are your keys?'

'It's two in the bloody morning,' Dad says, taking a step towards us. 'She's got her hospital appointment in a few hours!'

'Dad, let me handle this,' I say, shuffling him back into the living room.

'He's bloody paralytic, love, you can't have him treating you like this.'

'I'll handle it,' I say, trying to remain calm before I gently shut the living-room door and head back out to Johnny.

I corral him into the kitchen so we can close the door and talk while I try to sober him up.

'I need a hug,' he says, throwing his arms around me.

I don't fight it. I feel his strong body against mine and close my eyes as I breathe in the familiar smell of whisky, smoke, sweat and Johnny. My arms hang limp by my sides as he holds me.

'I'm sorry,' he says, sobbing, his head bobbing on my shoulder. 'I'm so sorry, I'm sorry, I'm so sorry for everything.'

I wriggle free, wrapping an arm around his shoulder so I can manoeuvre him down the hallway and into the bedroom. He's too drunk to have a proper conversation.

I have to push him with all my might so that he falls onto the soft bed, lying in a heap until I rearrange him into the recovery position so he can breathe. Then I turn off the lights. He's not supposed to drink before the embryo freezing, but Johnny's bloodstream is already ninety per cent whisky, so I doubt it'll make a difference.

I turn away from him and try to shut my eyes, but the tears are already rolling down my cheeks.

'What do you think she's in for, inability to get dressed in normal clothing?' Dad whispers in my ear, gesturing towards a woman on the other side of the waiting room who is wearing an oversized silver puffer coat that I'm sure is on trend but nevertheless resembles one of those Arctic sleeping bags.

'Dad!' I say, jabbing him with my elbow, even though I can't help but smile. It's the sort of fashion that wouldn't pass up north, even though no one bats an eyelid in London.

I'm nil by mouth and the guy opposite is driving me insane, sipping loudly on his latte. Every smell is torture, from the milk in his coffee to the buttered toast from the Costa just down the corridor. I'm anxious to get this over with so I can eat.

Dad and I were both up at six, thanks to insomnia on my part and a lumpy sofa bed on his, so I had plenty of time to chat to him before Johnny got out of bed. After an awkward reunion at the breakfast table, the three of us decided we'd go to the hospital together, even though Lauren had insisted on coming too. Fortunately, Johnny can feign sobriety even after the most mammoth night on the booze.

Lauren gives Johnny a cursory nod, then turns to Dad and throws her arms out for a hug.

'Geoff!' she says, pulling him in. 'How are you? It's been ages.'

Johnny and I leave Dad and Lauren to catch up on the village gossip while we fill in all the required forms. *Name, date of birth, address, next of kin. Is there any chance you could be pregnant? Are you a smoker? Have you ever had cancer?*

'I might go and get a cup of tea,' Johnny says, after we've handed in the forms.

'Actually, I'd like a word with Lauren. Do you mind, Dad?' I gesture towards him and Johnny.

'I was just going to stretch my legs anyway,' Dad says. 'You girls need anything?'

We shake our heads.

As soon as they're out of ear shot, Lauren comes up close to me. 'You OK?'

'I'm not sure I can go through with it.'

She tilts her head. 'Oh Jess. It's a bit late to change your mind.'

I'm welling up for the eighty-fourth time this week. 'It's a lot of pressure to freeze an embryo with a guy who cheated on me a couple of months ago. How do I know he won't do it again?'

Lauren shakes her head and sighs. 'I've been trying to think what I'd do if Charlie did the same to me. But I just think, what if it's your only chance to have kids?'

A nurse emerges from a room in orange crocs, dragging them along the lino floor like slippers.

'What if he leaves me for Mia and I'm locked into this embryo with no chance of having a baby with anyone else?'

Lauren puts her arm around me. 'First of all, I just want you to be happy, so go with your gut. But secondly, that is not going to happen. Johnny loves you.'

'Thanks hun,' I say, giving her hand a squeeze. Right now, the only thing my gut feels is the urge to run to the bathroom and puke.

Another nurse appears in front of our row of seats. 'Miss Jackson? We're ready for you now.'

I look at Lauren, unable to speak. She nods at me to go ahead.

'Whatever you do, it'll be the right thing. I'm here for you, OK?'

I take a deep breath and walk towards the nurse.

I wake from the sedation feeling as if I've been hit by a truck. It takes a moment to register where I am, what I'm doing here. Everything comes back to me in waves . . . the cancer, losing Mum, Johnny cheating . . .

Oh God. What am I doing? I'm freezing an embryo with someone who, just over two months ago, went behind my back and committed the cruellest betrayal, someone who is gaslighting me into thinking I'm a bad girlfriend when all the while *he's* the one who cares about no one but himself. I remember the question Annabel asked me and I realize I've known the answer all along.

Johnny doesn't make me happy.

I feel around for the panic button. Where's the nurse?

A second later, she walks in, the same woman who talked me through the procedure and told me her sister had recently survived breast cancer.

'You're awake,' she says. 'Let me just—'

'Did you already fertilize?' I say. 'Please say you didn't. Please don't. Please.'

'Hold on.' She comes to my bedside.

'It's urgent,' I say. 'You need to make sure you don't do the embryos. I don't want to do it.'

The nurse stands over my bedside and looks at me, smiling.

'Don't worry,' she says. 'First of all, the procedure was successful. We collected twelve eggs.'

'You don't understand,' I say, heart pounding, hands shaking. 'Please, please don't fertilize them.'

She holds out a hand to steady me. She talks in a calm, soothing voice.

'It's OK, Miss Jackson,' she says. 'We haven't done it yet. Would you like me to bring your partner in so you can discuss this?'

'Yes,' I say. 'Please. Johnny. I need to talk to him.'

He walks in minutes later, looking confused. 'Is everything OK?'

I ask the nurse to give us some privacy.

'J,' I say, gesturing for him to sit beside me and take my hand. 'I can't go through with this.'

'What? But haven't they just taken your eggs?'

'Yes, but I don't want to fertilize them.'

'I don't understand. I'm sorry about last night, but it will never happen again. I was hurt. I just needed to get it all out of my system.' He fiddles with his key ring, running his thumb along the smooth metal.

155

I try to sit up in the bed so I can address him better. 'What happened with Mia . . .'

He interrupts me. 'It's over with Mia! It was nothing, I swear. Please don't let her get in the way of our future.'

'Let me finish,' I say, holding my hand like a stop sign. 'What happened with Mia showed me that you and I weren't right. I think I'd had a niggling feeling for a while, but so many things about us were great and . . .'

'So many things about us *are* great,' he says.

'No, let me finish. Johnny, you're not making me happy any more. I'm not making you happy either. You won't let me in. You hate your job, but you don't listen when I try to help you. You just drink your way through it, pretending everything will be fine. But I can't help you if you won't let me.'

'Because everything's so perfect for you,' he says. 'You're so talented and hard-working and everyone loves you. You can go on stage and light it up and apply for any job you want and you'll get it. Whereas I'm just average.'

'My life isn't perfect!' I say, gesturing down at the regulation blue-and-white gown and the fact that I'm lying in a hospital bed. 'For the last few weeks, I've been petrified about starting chemo, but I've spent the whole time consoling you! You're acting like you're the one who has cancer.'

As the words leave my mouth, I realize how much of a burden he has been. I've tried to support him but I'm actually making him worse.

I'm still in a haze from the sedation, but everything is crystal clear. The only way to help him is to let him go.

'The last thing I want in the world is to hurt you,' I say, keeping my voice as soft as I can manage. 'But I think I knew the moment I found out you were cheating that we weren't right for each other. When the cancer came along, I was in a bit of a daze. But I'm stronger now. I can do this alone.'

He stares at me, like a beaten dog.

'But Jess . . .'

I shake my head. For the first time in weeks, I'm sure about this. 'I'm sorry, Johnny. It's over.'

Ten minutes later, Lauren and my dad pop their heads around the door.

'We heard what happened,' Lauren says.

'You OK, Jessie?' Dad says, his heart in his mouth as he sees me curled up in the hospital bed.

'I'm fine,' I say. 'Weirdly relieved.'

I mean it. I didn't know how suffocated I was until it came to the point of no return.

Walking out to Dad's car, I feel sapped of all energy. I stop mid-way across the car park.

'What if I've jeopardized my chances of being a mum?'

There's comfort in those twelve eggs, but from everything I've read, there are many things that can go wrong between freezing, storage, thawing and implantation.

'You haven't jeopardized anything,' Lauren says, lacing her fingers through mine and holding my hand tight. 'You've got a dozen eggs on ice, and at least you're not tied to someone you're not in love with.'

'Thanks, Lauren,' I say, leaning my head on her shoulder and feeling the tickle of her furry hood on my neck as I pull her into a hug.

'That's what I'm here for,' she says.

Travelling in opposite directions

'I'm going to miss you, little guy,' Johnny says, rubbing Oreo's neck as he writhes around on the carpet, angling to get his white tummy stroked.

Leaving Johnny's family WhatsApp chat was one of the hardest things I've ever had to do. I called his mum to tell her how worried I am about him, that I wish I could help but I know we're making each other miserable. She cried down the phone, saying I was the best thing that ever happened to him, begging me to give it one last try.

Johnny wept when we got home from the hospital last night, pleading and pleading for another chance. It took all my strength not to cave in. It would be easier to stay and agree to work on this relationship, but I know I have to take the harder route.

And yet somehow, seeing Johnny break the news to the cat is the thing that finally tips me over the edge.

I had thought, naively, that getting a cat together was as good as saying we'd eventually get married. We'd only gone to the adoption shelter for a look, because I was having withdrawal symptoms from Frostie. But when Oreo pointed his little black head in our direction with a look that said, 'please don't leave me,' we both fell in love, and then Johnny came home a week later, surprising me with him. Now I feel like I'm breaking up my poor little creature's home.

'So what happens to the flat?' Johnny says, not even twenty-four hours after we return from hospital, shell-shocked.

I haven't thought this far ahead. For the last two years, Johnny has been paying two thirds of the rent, since his lawyer salary far outstrips my journalist one. That was part of the agreement when we found the place – I could never afford to live on Abbeville Road on my salary alone.

Before I moved in with Lauren, I'd spent my early twenties moving from flat to flat, being interviewed by Antipodean housesharers who asked whether I wore a bra at home and whether I minded baths because they needed the shower to keep the marijuana plant moist. When I moved in with Johnny, I thought I'd found somewhere I'd be for a long, long time.

'I-I don't know. I start chemo next week,' I say, terrified at the thought of going through treatment while sofa-surfing or sharing a house with Kate, Colm and their screaming baby or, worse, Lauren and Charlie with their constant bickering.

My hands have gone clammy. I don't know if I'll still be able to work in a month, whether I'll even keep my job when I'm having chemo every three weeks. Even with my job intact, I can barely afford to rent somewhere on my own. The prospect of going back to housesharing with a bunch of randoms makes me heave.

Johnny stares at the wall. 'Look, it's my fault. I'm the one who fucked this up. I'll go to Mum's for Christmas and then I'll see if I can rent somewhere closer to work. You can stay here till the contract runs out in May.'

'But the money,' I say. 'I can't afford to pay for this place on my own.'

'It's fine,' he says, back to being the rational, calm lawyer

159

LAURA PRICE

Johnny I've seldom glimpsed lately. 'I'll keep paying my bit until the contract runs out, it's the least I can do. I'll always support you, whatever happens.' His voice breaks on this last bit and I can tell he's stifling his tears.

I start to say something back, but he quickly scoops Oreo into his arms and carries him out of the room.

My inbox taunts me. There are two hundred and fifty-three unread emails, at least half of which relate to Lauren's hen do. I've been ignoring it for weeks, but suddenly it's more appealing than thinking about where I'm going to live come May, or proofing the pile of magazine pages on 'the women who found love against all odds' that sit beside my keyboard. Surely this is rock bottom.

Mass-deleting the clothes-shop spam and countless daily newsletters that I never read, I locate the latest in the chain whose subject line is Re: re: re: re: re: LAUREN'S FABULOUS HEN!. I click into the email and start from the bottom up.

A full-on dispute about payment and attendance has been escalating for weeks. Lucy loves the idea of a spa day but has a christening on the Sunday and wants to pay for one night, not two. Kate has requested she pay the full amount by Friday lest she shoulder the rest of us with the much higher amount of £326 each, and Rowena has chimed in saying she can't get a babysitter and needs to cancel (I'm sure the other mummies will agree it's tough to get a whole weekend off.) Kate's response is that activities and hotels have already been booked and late dropouts won't be tolerated.

No wonder my phone has been blowing up. With a large gulp of my coffee, I open the Lauren's Hot Hens WhatsApp group, which I'm tempted to rename Lauren's Hot Mess. I scroll to the beginning of the unread notifications.

A message reads:

160

Lucy Barnett has left

There is firefighting as Kate tries to calm the increasingly agitated women, while Lauren's mum offers to shoulder the extra cost. One hen has made matters worse by posting a meme that reads: 'Keep calm and suck from a penis straw'.

I finish my coffee while clicking through the spa website and noting the eye-watering cost of each treatment. Then I take a deep breath and log in to my internet banking.

Shit. There are several inbound payments from Lauren's hens, but all that is going out with the balance I need to pay on the hotel and spa. After that, I'm left with just enough to pay my rent to Johnny, but there's never going to be enough to rent on my own.

I open another browser tab and google 'flats in Clapham'. I navigate to Rightmove and search for studios. There's barely anything for less than a grand a month. I broaden my search to within ten miles and enter my maximum budget.

I laugh out loud. There's a studio resembling a prison cell in Golders Green, available at seven hundred and fifty pounds per calendar month, or a room in a flatshare that looks like it hasn't seen a lick of paint since the 1900s. I could live in a mansion in Yorkshire for the price of a shoe box in London.

'Jess, got a minute?'

I minimize the screen just as Tabitha approaches my desk.

'Sure, what's up?'

'Um, just wanted to check how you're getting on with those pages, because we need to send them off in an hour.'

I glance down at the pile of papers, which has been sitting untouched since first thing this morning. 'On it,' I say.

'You sure? Because it looked like you were browsing spa retreats and houses.'

'Excuse me?' I stand up to face her and lower my voice so

161

that the rest of the office doesn't overhear. Aisha has looked up from her desk.

'It's just, you know, normally we'd have this all done by now.'

I sigh. It's fine when she's calling her kid's nursery all day long asking whether they've got the vegan lasagne on the menu, but because I'm single and childless, I'm not allowed five minutes off work. I need her off my case.

'Look, if you must know, I broke up with my boyfriend.'

'Oh my God,' she says, softening her tone and putting a hand on my arm. 'Why didn't you say something? Shit, Jess, I'm so sorry. If there's anything I can do . . .'

I nod my head, fighting back the tears. I put my heart and soul into this job, and I feel like I'm letting the team down.

'Hey,' she says, looping an arm through mine and leading me to one of the glass-walled meeting rooms. 'Come on, let's talk it through.'

A second later, Aisha joins us.

'I told her about Johnny,' I say, wanting to intercept in case Aisha thinks I've told her about the cancer.

'Ahh,' Aisha says. She shakes her head. 'Such an arsehole.'

'If it's any consolation, I went through a load of arseholes before I met my Billy,' Tabitha says. 'The right one will come along when you're least expecting it.'

A tiny smile forms on my face as I catch Aisha rolling her eyes.

'It's fine,' I say. 'At least I'll be able to focus a bit more on work now.'

Tabitha hands me a bunch of tissues.

'You know . . .' Tabitha says, then stops herself. 'No, it's probably too soon.'

'What?' I'm willing to hear anything that might distract me from thoughts of Johnny and impending homelessness.

'Well, just thinking out loud. Aisha, weren't you looking for new columnists for the sex and relationships section? Well, what if Jess were to write about dating after a long-term relationship?'

Aisha catches my eye and we both burst out laughing. Trust Tabitha not to realize how much of a diss this is towards Aisha, who has been single and dating for eons.

'I, er . . .'

'Go for it,' Aisha says. 'If we're going in-house then I can't think of anyone better.'

I laugh, imagining me dating with a wig to cover my soon-to-be-bald head. 'Thanks for thinking of me, Tabitha, but it really is too soon.'

'I don't mean now, obviously. But maybe in the new year, when you've had the chance to move on a bit?'

'It's really not that bad of an idea,' Aisha says.

I dry my eyes and open the meeting-room door for us. If it weren't for the fact that I've just broken up with Johnny, it would almost be funny. At any other point in my career, I'd have killed for a column in this magazine. I just never imagined I'd have to lose my future husband to get it.

Fifty first dates

Annabel meets me at a cafe on Abbeville Road, just moments away from the flat and the Common. Johnny said it was one of the selling points from the estate agent who told him that 'Abbeville Village' was Clapham's star attraction with its rows of gorgeous shops and restaurants. When we first moved in, I pictured us on weekends sipping smoothies in one of these lovely spots, but I can count on one hand the number of times we actually had coffee outside the house, and the rent is three times higher than somewhere five minutes away.

It's the sort of cafe where the yummy mummy brigade sit around in their activewear eating smashed avo on gluten-free toast and drinking flat whites while their toddlers sup baby-ccinos, so I'm grateful for the presence of my fellow misfit, who steals off to the loo as soon as she arrives to inject herself with one of the many different medications she has to take for her cancer.

'So you still haven't told your work?' Annabel says, nursing a hot cup of cocoa between both hands.

I shake my head. 'The publishing director knows, obviously, and my friend Aisha. I told Tabitha about the break-up with Johnny to get her off my back. I don't need more pity.'

'What did she say?' She spoons a tiny marshmallow that has melted to pink goo around the edges.

I laugh when I recall the conversation. 'She suggested I start a dating column.'

'Seriously? Are you thinking about dating then?'

I make a face, remembering the encounter with Marcus and the weird feeling of unfamiliar lips on mine. 'God, no. Not yet, anyway.'

'Good,' she says. 'You should definitely see what it's like to be single for a while.'

I smile, realizing how little I know about Annabel. 'What about you? Do you ever go on dates?'

She snorts. 'And write what in my profile? Dying girl, twenty-seven, seeks guy for dead-end dates?'

I catch myself starting to cock my head and quickly correct it. The last thing she needs is pity.

'Any guy would be lucky to have you, Bel,' I say, realizing it's the first time I've shortened her name in this way, like we've crossed a boundary into proper lifelong friendship. Whatever lifelong means.

'It's really not fun watching a guy's face drop when you tell him you're never going to get better.'

'Has that happened?' I say. I know there's something – someone she hasn't talked about, but I'm reluctant to open up her wounds.

She looks at the table and nods. 'My ex, Mark.'

'I'm sorry,' I say, touching her hand. 'What happened? I mean, only if you want to talk about it.'

'He wanted kids,' she says, almost in a whisper, and I can tell she's fighting tears. 'We were young, you know. We got together when we were twenty-five, a year or so after my first diagnosis, when I'd finished treatment and I thought I could put it all behind me. Mark was one of those guys who's amazing with kids. He had three little nephews who we used to babysit, and they'd run to him like he was their favourite person in the world. He wanted at least four of his own.'

I gulp. 'What about you?'

She nods. 'Yeah, I wanted them too. I managed to freeze some eggs after the first diagnosis, but I was young enough that we should have still been able to have them naturally. And then . . .' She shakes her head. 'Then we found out it had spread, and that was that.'

My heart sinks as I try to imagine how it must have felt to be told the news that your cancer is now incurable and you can no longer have kids. 'There's really no way?'

'They took out my ovaries.'

'Shit.'

'And then we broke up.'

Fuck. How have I managed to bang on about my pathetic problems when this girl has been through so much? I thought my situation was bad, not knowing whether I'll be able to have kids, but at least I have *hope*. The finality of having her ovaries removed must have taken away every bit of hope Annabel had.

I make a face, unable to fathom how anyone could break up with someone as lovely as Annabel, let alone when she had cancer. 'He left you?'

She shakes her head again, clearly still in huge amounts of pain. 'I couldn't let him stay. Not when I knew how much he wanted kids.'

'But what about the frozen eggs? What about adoption?'

'Come on, Jess,' she says. 'They don't let you have IVF, let alone adopt, when you're dying.'

It makes sense, but it's so cruel. 'I'm so sorry you've had to go through all this.'

'It's fine,' she says. 'It's just another thing to deal with when you have secondaries. It's not like we can go back to normal life, like the "survivors".' She makes air quotes with her fingers.

I make a mental note never to refer to myself as a cancer survivor, even if I do get the all-clear. When Mum had her secondary diagnosis, in some ways it was the worst day of my life. But in others it was almost a relief; to end that cycle of wondering, worrying, not knowing.

'Don't let yourself get the fear,' Annabel says, stirring the marshmallow goo into her hot chocolate. 'Live your life, Jess. Seriously. If there's one thing I would do differently, it would be to spend that year or so when I was cancer-free having even more fun instead of worrying about the bloody cancer coming back.'

'I will,' I say. I owe it to her, I owe it to Mum, to live my life instead of spending it worrying.

'And don't spend your life dating total dickwads either,' she says, deadpan.

I burst out laughing, relieved to have broken the curse of the cancer chat.

'I'll put that down as my New Year's resolution,' I say. 'No more dickwads.'

Annabel laughs. 'Listen, do you want to come to ours for Christmas?'

I notice the way she says 'ours' and I wonder who she means. I've been so absorbed in my own problems, I hardly know the first thing about her.

Annabel nods her head a few times, preparing to explain. 'Me and Joe, my brother, we always spend it together. Mum and Dad have worked pretty much every Christmas Day for the last fifteen years, so we kind of developed our own thing.' She smiles and shrugs with a proud look on her face as she says 'thing'.

'They work every Christmas?' I can't imagine spending such

an important day away from my dad, or Mum when she was alive.

Annabel nods more enthusiastically this time, clearly on board with her family's arrangement. 'They work at a care home. Mum is the chef and Dad's a care assistant. They have this whole vibe going on. Every Christmas, they dress up as Santa and Mrs Claus, and Mum does this mad feast that morphs into a karaoke night for the oldies. I think my parents were entertainers in another life because it's the highlight of both their years.'

'That's so sweet,' I say, picturing Bel's parents keeping all the old folk smiling with their fancy dress and gourmet dinners. 'But don't you miss seeing them on Christmas Day?'

She shakes her head. 'No, no, we have a whale of a time. We go round theirs on Christmas morning and do presents before they go to work, then we do Christmas all over again on Boxing Day. But in the meantime, we do our own sibling thing. We used to spend it with our grandparents, but they're not around any more.'

'I'm sorry,' I say, putting my hand on her forearm.

'It's OK,' she says. 'Gramps died a few years ago, heart attack. He was only seventy-five. And then my nan died a few months later, on their golden wedding anniversary. I'm pretty sure she died of a broken heart.'

'Oh, hun.' *Please don't cry, please don't cry, please don't cry.*

'It's the reason I got cancer the first time round, I'm sure of it,' she says, staring off at the doorway, where a woman has just walked in with a yoga mat and a pushchair.

'What do you mean?'

'The stress and the heartbreak from losing them and then helping my parents to deal with all the legal and financial shit. That's what gave me cancer.'

'Really?'

'Stress weakens your immune system. I'm not saying their deaths caused my cancer, but it could have aggravated something that was already there. There's no medical proof, but Dr Deep thinks I'm onto something.'

I wonder if stress could have contributed to my cancer. Mum's illness, worrying about Dad being on his own. Did I know deep down that something was wrong between me and Johnny? I guess so, maybe, but I doubt it could have given me cancer. And my job is stressful but I'm hardly running the country. I remind myself of what the oncologist told me at my last appointment – how it's difficult to know what caused my cancer, but I certainly shouldn't blame myself.

'I'm really sorry, Annabel,' I say. 'If there's anything I can do . . .'

I feel so fortunate that I haven't had it as bad as her, but there's something comforting about knowing we're both sort of in the same boat. She's the only person I know close to my age who's been through this, the only person who understands how it feels to be told you might never have kids. I squeeze her hand across the table, then look away with a sniffle.

'Don't be a dick,' she says, wiping a tear from her cheek and laughing. 'Anyway, there *is* something you can do. Come to ours for Christmas, you won't regret it. Joe's beer can chicken is insane.'

'You have beer can chicken on Christmas Day?'

'Oh yeah,' she says, looking animated. 'And Coca-Cola ham. It's pretty epic. We'll shove a can of fizz on whatever meat we can find and we usually invite my elderly neighbour for the lolz. The more, the merrier.'

I love the idea of a Christmas spent with a full house of misfits and more food than we could ever possibly eat. That's the sort of Christmas we used to have with Mum. She was the queen of the slap-up feast, laying out the table with her legendary goose-fat potatoes, special-recipe sprouts and the most absurdly creamy swede and carrot mash. She'd invite people willy-nilly, from widowed customers she'd met in the tea rooms to the occasional randomer she'd met at Zumba. Our family never felt small when there were twelve people squashed around the dinner table.

When Mum died, Christmas changed completely. It usually began with an argument between Johnny and me over whose house we'd stay at on Christmas Eve – his mum's in Manchester or my dad's on the other side of the Pennines. Either way, it was always quiet.

'I'm in,' I say. 'Although, um, it's probably cheeky but . . .'

Annabel raises a pencilled-in eyebrow.

'Is there any way my dad can come? He's pretty unfussy and he's usually passed out by the Queen's speech.'

'Papa Jackson is one hundred per cent invited,' she says, beaming at the idea of more people to entertain. 'Now what course would you like to make?'

'I do some killer bacon sprouts,' I say, thinking of Mum's special recipe.

'Great,' Bel nods. 'We don't do presents, by the way. Just Secret Santa. Maximum spend, ten quid.'

'Who am I buying for?'

'I'll let you know. It'll probably just be me, you, Joe, your dad and then a couple of old dears . . . I want to set up this sweet old widower from the estate with a lady I know from the chemo ward. We call her Aunty Mags.'

'A bit of festive matchmaking?' I say. 'Sounds fun.'

'It is, only Mags kind of has Alzheimer's in addition to the chemo brain. I've already tried to set her up with a few old boys from the hospital, but she forgets every time. It's like *Fifty First Dates*.'

'Sounds like just what I need.'

When you have kids, you'll understand

Lauren meets me at the hairdresser during the final lunch break before Christmas. It was Nurse Rose who suggested I cut my hair short before chemo, to lessen the shock when it starts falling out. Initially, Lauren wasn't keen on me changing the aesthetic of her dream bridesmaid line-up, but then she realized it will all have fallen out by April anyway.

'Have you spoken to Johnny?' Lauren says, while the hairdresser spritzes water all over the back of her luscious, long locks.

I tell her about the conversation with his mum and the fact that I've exited the family WhatsApp chat and even unfriended him on Facebook.

'Sounds like closure,' she says. 'Maybe this is your chance to have a go at the single life. Who knows, maybe you'll meet an eligible bachelor at my wedding?'

'What, with my bald head?' I say. 'Not sure I'm going to be the most in-demand of the bridal party . . .'

We both laugh, but the truth is I'm dreading watching Lauren walk down the aisle when I'm halfway through chemo and looking like Mr Potato Head.

'That's if the wedding even goes ahead,' she says, trying to put on a jovial tone.

'Why, what's happened now?' It's been a while since

Lauren's said anything about Charlie and his jealousy. I had figured things were going better between them.

'It's actually ridiculous,' she says. 'I was telling him about you and Johnny and I let slip about the thing with Marcus. I didn't think you'd mind since you've broken up and all.'

'No, it's fine,' I say, though Marcus's name makes me flinch.

'Anyway, he properly kicked off.'

'About what?'

'I was defending you, saying you were on a break because Johnny had literally cheated on you, and that of course it was totally within reason for you to snog someone. But he kicked off, being like, "so you're saying if we had an argument, it would be fine for you to go and pull someone else?" And I'm like, "no, that's not what I'm saying *at all*. This is a totally different scenario." But once he's on one, he won't let it go. He's so insecure.'

'That sounds draining,' I say.

'So draining,' she agrees. 'And so tough to keep telling him I love him, that he's the only one for me, that I'm never going to cheat, that I want to marry him. I just can't wait to get the ring on my finger – he might start believing I actually mean it.'

The second hairdresser appears in the mirror, behind my chair. No going back now. I show her the magazine cuttings of cute pixie cuts, where the models look boyish and beautiful, their big eyes emphasized.

'This one will suit you,' says the hairdresser, touching the top of my head and sweeping my fringe across my forehead.

'You'll look great with a pixie,' Lauren says.

We sit in silence for the rest of the time. I'm grateful that Lauren doesn't want to talk weddings today, and even more grateful that the hairdresser isn't interested in my non-existent holiday plans.

Red hair falls to the floor in chunks. I feel the chill as soon as it is gone above the ear. When she is done, she takes out an electric razor and gently buzzes around the back of my neck, tickling me lightly.

Finally, she holds up a mirror for me to see the back of my head. It looks good – different, but good.

As I get up and unfasten the velcro on the cape around my neck, I notice the piles of red hair on the floor. Thirty-one years of growth, never cut above shoulder length.

'Wow,' Lauren says when she sees me. 'You look amazing.'

'You think it's OK?' I say, running my hands around my neck as I get used to the feeling of nakedness.

'I can't believe you didn't do this years ago, it's so you.'

'Thanks,' I say. 'Shame it won't last long.'

'Oh my actual God,' Aisha says, as I approach the long table where the team are sitting, clad in their festive jumpers. 'This look is insane.'

She puts down her wine glass, throws her arms around me, then draws away to get a better look at my pixie cut. 'Seriously, Jess. Why didn't you do this sooner?'

I smile away the compliment, squeezing into the empty seat opposite Miles and Tabitha. I haven't got used to the feeling of my bare neck yet.

'It suits you,' says Tabitha, the only one who hasn't worn a festive jumper for our Christmas drinks. 'Is this in preparation for your new dating life?'

I laugh off the question, as if I would only contemplate a new haircut to impress a man.

'Just fancied a change.' I eye Miles and Aisha, conscious they know my secret.

'Well I can highly recommend it. Being a mummy, I'd never go back to long hair.'

Miles waves a wine glass and gestures at the bottles in front of him. 'White or red?'

'White please. Just a small glass.' Once I start chemo, I won't be able to drink much, but it's Christmas, after all.

A waiter clad in a Santa hat brings over a tray of spicy, sticky chicken wings and maple-glazed sausages to share. He plonks a plateful of crispy-fried vegan chicken bites in front of Tabitha.

'So I thought we could go around the table and say one thing we'd like to do differently next year,' I say, determined to take our team Christmas bash in a positive direction. 'Aisha, want to start?'

As Aisha bites into a chicken wing and starts talking about how she wants to get more involved in our fashion shoots, Tabitha's phone goes off and she excuses herself from the table. I listen to Aisha's full answer before I turn the question to the features writer, then the interns.

When it comes to my turn, Tabitha still isn't back, and I can see her talking on her mobile by the doorway, looking stressed.

'I'll go get her,' I say, wanting to make sure she hears my well-prepared spiel about team collaboration and more structured meetings.

When I approach the doorway, I can hear her talking heatedly.

'I've told you three times, they were in the fridge, top shelf. If you couldn't find them, you should have called me. She's vegan, for heaven's sake. I'm not paying you to feed my daughter ham and chips.'

Tabitha sees me waiting and gives me a nod.

'Right, well I'll make sure my instructions are even more detailed next time. Yep, yep, fine, I've left you the money. Yep, OK, have a good Christmas.'

'Everything OK?' I say.

Tabitha huffs and pushes past me, back towards the table. 'When you have kids, you'll understand.'

Moving on

Dad arrives on Christmas Eve with a car full of bags and boxes.

'Are you staying for a month?'

'Look, love,' he says, stopping in the hallway after dumping an overflowing carrier bag full of what look to be clothes. 'I've held off bringing it up after everything you've gone through lately, but it's really time we talk about this.'

Not now. Not on Christmas Eve. I do not want to talk about getting rid of my mother's belongings the night before Christmas.

'Sweetheart,' he says. 'I've been trying to talk to you for months.'

'Dad, it's *Christmas Eve!*' As I shake my arms out in exasperation, I realize I might as well have stomped my foot like a moody teenager. I sigh. 'At least let me make us a brew first.'

I give him a hand with the luggage, bringing in boxes of books and a small suitcase that jangles as I carry it. I imagine Mum's jewellery scattered around inside it, probably all tangled from the drive down.

Half an hour later, Dad sits on the sofa and I'm on the floor, eking out the dregs of my ginger and lemon tea because I know as soon as I finish it, he's going to want to discuss it.

'We have to talk about it sooner or later,' he says. He puts his mug down and joins me on the floor so that we are both surrounded by bags and boxes.

'Dad . . .' I can't bear to look inside them. Not tonight.

'Love,' he says, patting one of them. 'You haven't visited the house in a year.'

'No, it hasn't been . . .' I think about it. Has it really been a year? He's right, I haven't visited my childhood home since last Christmas. I've been so busy throwing myself into work that I've neglected my own father.

'I get that you're busy. You've got a life to lead. But it's been two years, Jessie.'

Two years without Mum. In some ways, it feels like a lifetime, but in others it's nowhere near long enough to consider getting rid of her stuff.

'Dad . . .'

'Love, I'm not suggesting we throw her things away. I'm not suggesting we forget her. You can keep anything you want, anything that means something to you. But I have to move on, as painful as it is.'

A tear drips down my cheek and I brush it away with a single finger. 'I don't want you to move on, Dad.'

He shuffles along the floor until he is right beside me, and he holds out his arms for me to hug him. 'I know, love, but I have to.'

'But why? Why do you have to? It's not like you have to sell the house, it's not like you have someone else moving in.' I'm sobbing on his shoulder now, my tears soaking into his scratchy woollen jumper.

He tightens his arms around me, suppressing my sobs in his strong grip. 'Sweetheart, I've met someone.'

I pull away violently, wiping my face with my sleeve. 'What?'

'Love, it had to happen someday.'

'*Who?*' It feels like Johnny and Mia all over again. Betrayal.

'A lovely lady from the village. She's a widow herself.'

No. My dad cannot be dating. He cannot be kissing some other woman, parading her around the village where Mum was so loved by everyone.

'Since when?' I can't look him in the eye, so I fix my gaze on one of the boxes.

'We've known each other a long time. She was a customer.'

'Do I know her?'

'You might have seen her out and about. Her name's Elizabeth. Lizzie, we call her.'

Lizzie. The minute he says her name, I know who she is. Lizzie used to come in to the tea rooms with her husband when I was a child. She used to tell me I had pretty freckles and that I'd be batting boys off with a pencil case when I was old enough. It must be ten years since her husband died.

'No.' I shake my head. I do not want to talk about this.

'Jessie, love,' he says.

But I'm already turning to storm out of the room. 'Leave me alone.'

The gift that keeps on giving

I arrive at Annabel's tiny flat in Camberwell to find Mags, the Alzheimer's lady, already sitting in an armchair in the living room, watching a black and white film on TV, her hair tied up in a colourful scarf.

'Merry Christmas!' I say, throwing my arms around Annabel's skinny frame and following her through the narrow corridor to the kitchen, where the smell of roast chicken is already wafting through.

'This is Joe,' she says. 'My other half. Joe, Jess. Jess, Joe.'

Annabel's brother, clad in an apron and with knife in hand, turns around to greet me. He's the spitting image of her, the same huge, beaming smile, bright blue eyes and totally symmetrical face, only taller, stronger. His sandy brown hair is cropped just above a military-style buzz cut, so I can see the shape of his round head. I wonder if he shaved it in support of Annabel.

I go to shake his free hand but he leans in for a kiss on the left side, then the right, and I mess it up like I did when I met Stephanie Asante, almost kissing him on the lips.

'Sorry.'

'My fault,' he says, wiping his hands on the side of his apron. 'Too much time in France.'

'Joe lived there with his ex,' Annabel says. 'He missed his little sis too much so he came home.'

Joe rolls his eyes in faux mockery and starts towards the fridge.

'What can I get you, Jess? Tea, coffee, juice . . . vodka?' He says this last option with a wink.

'Just the tea for now, please,' I say. 'My dad'll be in in a second, he'll probably want a strong black coffee. I can make it.'

'No, don't worry,' says Joe. 'Go sit down and I'll bring it through.'

Annabel walks towards the door as Dad enters, jangling his car keys. We've managed to avoid the topic of his new girlfriend so far this morning.

'Nice little place,' Dad says, glancing around before properly looking at Annabel, then going to shake her hand. 'Geoff, nice to meet you.'

'Lovely to meet you too, Mr—'

'Geoff,' he says, shaking her hand so firmly I think he might break her.

Annabel takes Dad through to the kitchen to meet Joe and I walk back through to the living room where Mags is.

'Hello Mags!' I say, waving my hand in the old lady's face, trying not to obstruct her view of the TV. 'I'm Jess-i-ca.'

'She's not deaf,' Annabel says, entering the room behind me. 'You can say your name at normal speed and volume. You just have to be prepared to repeat it fifty times.'

Mags's baggy, pale skin reminds me of Mum's in her final days, although she's about twenty years older than Mum was. I hope this isn't too difficult for Dad.

I take a seat on the sofa, patting the cushion and gesturing for him to join me. He sits, cautiously, nodding to Mags, who has barely looked up from her film.

A moment later, Joe walks in, carrying a tray of teas and

coffees and a box of mince pies. It's the first time I've ever been away from home at Christmas, aside from the visits to Johnny's family home. Since Mum died, I've been chief cook, and even before that, I would always assist.

'Want to help me in the kitchen for a bit, Jess?' Joe asks, reading my thoughts.

I jump at the opportunity and follow him into the kitchen.

As soon as the door is closed, he speaks to me in a voice barely above a whisper.

'She's been poorly this morning,' he says, looking me straight in the eye. 'She was up all night and she's putting on a brave face. Mind doing me a favour and making sure she doesn't do too much?'

'Of course,' I say. My heart goes out to him. Annabel looking sick is the only way I've ever known her.

'Thank you,' he says, patting me on the arm. 'It's so nice for her to have a mate like you, you know. I've heard so much about you.'

It's funny to hear it, because I've never heard Annabel talk about other friends – in fact, I've barely heard her talk about anyone at all, as if she's shut them all out of her life. I remember how cagey she was about her ex, how she said she pushed him away, and I wonder if she pushed away her friends and family too.

'All good, I hope?'

Joe smiles. 'It's good for her to have someone who gets what she's going through. I imagine my stubborn-ass sister probably listens to you more than she does me. Maybe you can persuade her to have a sleep before lunch? I know you're ill too and you need to rest so just, well, let me know.'

'Oh I'm not—' I don't know how to describe my situation. Does he think I'm terminally ill too? I certainly don't feel sick, especially now the hormone treatment is over. But I still have all the chemo and radiotherapy to come. 'I feel fine. I can help with anything you like.'

'Want to chop a few carrots and then you can go back in and tell her I'm all set and find some way for her to get a nap in?'

For the next half hour, I play sous chef to Joe, watching him chop veg with the niftiest knife skills I've seen outside of *Masterchef*. In the time it takes me to peel a small bag of carrots, he's prepped a whole mountain of potatoes.

'The perks of having a cook for a mum,' he says, when he catches me mesmerized by his knife action. 'Before the care home, she used to cook school dinners, so she had the whole mass-production thing down.'

One glass of wine in, I start describing the preparation of my bacon sprouts as if I'm Nigella Lawson. 'And now,' I say, elongating the word with my mouth in a wide 'o' shape. 'A sssatisfying sssqueeze of lemon . . .' I hiss the 's's as I crush the citrus from a height, then slowly suck the juice from one finger in comedy-seductive fashion. It's something Mum used to do with me when I was little, and it has Joe in stitches.

Forty-five minutes pass and we've talked about pretty much everything, from accents to politics to what Annabel was like as a kid and then about my job, which seems to thoroughly impress him. Joe talks me through his weird career trajectory, from volunteering in Africa to a mind-numbing few years in recruitment, a quarter-life crisis that saw him retrain as an English teacher, a move to Paris to be with his ex and, now, a side hustle to the teaching job, creating an app to help people change careers. It sounds exhausting, but I'm so absorbed in his life story that I have to remind myself it's Christmas Day, I'm in someone else's house, and I'm without Johnny.

Johnny would never have helped me in the kitchen, not that that was an issue. I liked having him out of the way. He might have popped in to steal a burnt bit of bacon from the corner of the turkey tin or pinch a sausage from a cooling tray. I'd have slapped his hand, but I wouldn't have minded.

When I poke my head around the living room door to check on proceedings, I find not only Annabel but also Dad and Mags fast asleep, snoring at varying volumes. Somehow Annabel has ended up leaning her head on Dad's shoulder, and I'm reminded of how Mum must have felt when she'd come in and find me and Dad sleeping off our Christmas lunch with an entire living room full of people. Bel is dribbling a little from the corner of her mouth while Dad's head lolls forward in his seat. Mags has dropped the TV remote on the floor and the film is still going. They all look so content.

I return to the kitchen with a smile on my face. 'Mission complete.'

I pour myself a second glass of wine at the dinner table. Mr Wade, the widower, has been dropped off by the hospital bus and the table is complete, the six of us filling our plates with Coca-Cola ham, beer can chicken, roasties and of course mum's famous bacon sprouts, which I'm confident will be a hit.

Conversation centres largely around the matchmaking of Mags with Mr Wade, who is charming in his flat cap and button-up gilet. I somehow doubt that Annabel will ever achieve her quest to get the two pensioners together, but I love that she's so invested in the challenge.

'You're looking very glamorous today, Aunty Mags,' says Annabel. 'Isn't she looking wonderful, Mr Wade?'

Mr Wade doffs his cap and gestures towards the old lady. 'Ravishing,' he says.

'You're making me blush,' says Annabel. 'Get a room, you two . . .'

'Jess, these bacon sprouts are incredible, what else did you put in them?' Joe asks, scooping up another spoonful of chopped shallots, crispy bacon and moist sprouts.

'Secret recipe,' I say, thrilled that the master chef himself is impressed with my one measly dish.

'She'll never give that away,' Dad says. 'It's her mother's recipe. Our Jess is probably the only kid who ever liked sprouts as a five-year-old. Couldn't get enough of them. Her mother snuck her that recipe on her deathbed, didn't she love?'

'It wasn't *quite* as dramatic as that,' I say, still angry at him for his betrayal. 'But yeah, Mum was a legendary cook.'

'Well, cheers to that,' Joe says, raising a glass to the table. Mr Wade raises a shaky hand to join in the toast, while Mags has to be nudged by Annabel before she understands what's happening.

I knock back my second glass of red. As soon as Christmas is over, it'll be chemo for the next few months and I can't imagine I'll be able to drink much then, so what's a glass or two on Christmas Day?

I don't realize quite how tipsy I am until I get up for the loo. I sit on the toilet for some peace and quiet and flick through my phone. There's a message from Aisha asking whether it's OK to fancy her cousin. A selfie of Lauren and Charlie with the words:

Merry Christmas Jess! I know this year hasn't been the best for you, but I promise the next one is going to be a squillion times better. Here's to good health and amazing girlie adventures. Love youuuuu xx

I skip onto Facebook, where Lauren has posted the same photo of her and Charlie. This time the caption reads:

Celebrating our last Christmas together before we become Mr and Mrs Kenny xx.

I feel selfish for thinking it, but I'm terrified Lauren will

183

start talking about trying for a baby as soon as she gets married, and I'll end up losing her. She's already been different since she got engaged, and I can't help wanting to keep her all to myself. Even Aisha will settle down eventually. I feel so grateful to have Annabel, but then an awful thought occurs to me. This could be her last Christmas.

There's nothing from Johnny. For Christmas, I had bought us tickets to see The Killers and I was looking forward to seeing his face when he opened it. I'd already wrapped it up inside a shoebox and hidden it at the back of the wardrobe so that even if he found it, he wouldn't guess what it was. We'd bonded over music at that first wedding. 'Mr Brightside' was our song.

Right about now, we'd be kicking back on the sofa with wine and Quality Street, fighting over the last Green Triangle while wearing our new pyjama sets and commentating on the Queen's speech. Dad would be snoring on the sofa.

I wash my hands and lean into the bathroom mirror to inspect my skin. My pupils are dilated and my eyes a little bloodshot. My new pixie cut surprises me every time I see it, it's so different from every hair style I've ever had. I squish my hands to the sides of my face to try and see what I'll look like bald, but it's hard to imagine myself with no hair at all.

I open the bathroom cabinet in search of a cotton bud to fix my eyeliner. I can't find any, but the cabinet is overflowing with bottles and bottles of pills with unpronounceable names, each with Annabel's prescription sticker. *Take one per day, take two each morning, swallow tablets with food, do not chew.*

I can't imagine how her body must react to all these foreign things, her veins pumped with different powerful chemicals. I've always tried to avoid taking drugs wherever possible. I'll ride out a headache until I really can't bear it any longer, but now I have to accept everything the doctors throw at me. I hate the thought of the chemo flooding my system.

By the time I return to the living room, Annabel is explaining the concept of Secret Santa to Aunty Mags.

'So we sit around in a circle and open them one by one,' says Annabel. 'You have to guess who your Secret Santa was, and if you get it right . . . well, then you're extra special.'

'Mags, do you want to go first?' Joe says.

I look from Joe to Annabel and back again. I love their dynamic. I would have done anything for a brother or sister.

Mags claws at the glossy red paper and pulls out a bright pink lipstick and eyeshadow set, the sort you would find in the teenage beauty aisle.

'Lovely!' says Annabel. 'Now can you guess who your Secret Santa is?'

Mags looks baffled as she slips her fingers into the fold of the cardboard box to open it.

'I'll give you a clue,' says Annabel. 'The person who gave you that present is sitting in this circle, and it's a girl. Who do you think it was?'

Mags slowly cottons on, pointing her finger at me. 'You!' she says. 'I don't know your name, your boyfriend . . .'

'My boyfriend?' I say, my heart suddenly pounding.

She points at Joe.

'Ah,' I say, giving Joe an embarrassed smile. 'No, no, he's not my boyfriend.'

'Roll with it,' he says quietly, giving me a little wink.

Annabel makes a loud 'ahem' noise. 'Actually Mags, I was your Secret Santa. I'll let you off. I guess me and Jess could be sisters . . . right then, your turn next, Joey.'

Joe rips open the shiny paper. A fake Santa beard, red hat and glasses spill out of the packaging.

'Aha, Santa dress!' Joe says. 'And I'd have to guess my Secret Santa was . . . you, Bel?'

Annabel rolls her eyes. Of course it was her. All the Secret Santa gifts came from Annabel, except for the one I bought, and one from Joe. She's the one thing holding this whole misfit family together.

Dad opens a comedy Rudolph outfit, Annabel gets a child's Disney diary with padlock and key – I'd have bought her a nice leather-bound one but the ten-pound rule seemed pretty strict – and finally it's my turn to open my gift.

What would Bel have bought for me, maybe another wig? I open the soft package and unfold an enormous, neon Pink Panther onesie with full-body zipper.

'Oh wow,' I laugh. 'I've never had a onesie before.'

'It's actually more practical than you think,' Bel says. 'I thought you could wear it for chemo and the winter months when you're shivering your tits off – pun intended. The only thing is we'll have to shove some ice cubes down there for the hot flushes, but we can make you a customized ice-pack bra . . .'

'Hot flushes,' Mags pipes in. 'Used to get them, terrible they were. Ever so sweaty. Lasted five years, they did. Five sweaty years.'

Everyone laughs.

Joe heads off to the kitchen, pulling on his Santa hat. 'I'm going to make coffee,' he says. 'By the time I get back, everyone needs to be wearing their new props.'

By seven o'clock, the whole gang is wiped out in the tiny living room, Annabel curled up with a pile of cushions and her legs rested over Joe's. It's a show of sibling closeness that I've never known first-hand. They seem so at ease with each other and it's obvious how much he dotes on her.

Mags is fast asleep again and Mr Wade sits formally on a

kitchen chair in the middle of the lounge, reading a paper. I watch in awe as he flips through the pages of a broadsheet, somehow managing not to end up with all the papers folded the wrong way in a clumsy mess. Every so often, he folds the paper on his lap to take a noisy slurp of tea from one of Annabel's quirky vintage cups before replacing it in its saucer.

Snug inside my new onesie, I rest my head on Dad's shoulder as he snores his way through the Jude Law and Cameron Diaz scenes in *The Holiday*. Even though watching the movie reminds me of every Christmas I've ever spent with Johnny, I feel content. This gathering of misfits feels like a proper family Christmas, the best I've had since Mum was alive.

Welcome to Chemo Club

Two days after Christmas, I wake up covered in cold sweat. My head is on the wrong side of the bed – the one that used to be Johnny's side – and my body is at an angle, tangled in the corner of the sheet that has come untucked, and the duvet half on, half off the bed. I barely slept.

Today is the day I'm to have my first chemo, the day my hair follicles will start to die. Today is the day when I learn what having chemo is like from the inside, not as the one sitting in the visitor's chair. Today is the day that my father must watch me going through the thing that together we watched Mum go through. The thing that failed to save her.

I sit up in bed, Oreo jumping onto my lap and pushing his head up against my waist. *Feed me, feed me.* I try to breathe, count to ten, but I can't – I can't breathe. My chest feels like it is frozen, my brain isn't processing. *I can't breathe, I can't breathe, I can't breathe.*

'Jessie?'

Dad pokes his head around the door and brings me out of my trance. I see him now, but I still can't speak.

'You OK, love?'

The back of his hand is on my forehead, feeling for a temperature, the way Mum used to do when I was a kid. He has assumed the role of mum now.

'It's alright, darling, it's alright,' he says, imitating the words Mum used to say. 'Just breathe, it's alright.'

It takes a few minutes before I can respond, before I realize I'm crying, the tears interrupting the deep breaths I am trying my hardest to take. Dad strokes my head while Oreo purrs on my lap, both trying their hardest to soothe me.

I breathe a huge sigh, reaching for the box of tissues on the bedside table and blowing my snotty nose.

'It's OK, love,' Dad says. 'I'm here now.'

I take a moment to process what just happened. I felt out of this world, paralyzed with fear. How is it that my father, this man who for almost forty years relied on my mother for everything, suddenly knows what to do when I'm sick? Did I really underestimate him all that time?

'I'll make you some tea and then we better get going,' he says, patting my knee over the duvet and hauling himself up.

'What time is it? Am I late?'

'No, don't worry. We've plenty of time. Have you taken your anti-sickness pills?'

I shake my head. What would I do without him? I can't cope alone. *I can't cope, I can't cope.*

He puts a hand firmly on my wrist as he sees me start to shake again. Then he looks me right in the eyes. 'Now you listen to me. We are going to get through this. The whole thing, OK? I need you to be strong for me.'

I can see the tiny pools forming in the corner of his eyes but he snaps them shut before I can see him cry.

'I'll be strong.' I sniffle the snot back in. 'I promise I'll be strong.'

I have to be strong, for Dad, for Mum. I have to be strong today.

*

'Welcome to Chemo Club!' Annabel says, hugging me and then Dad as we arrive at our familiar table in the hospital Costa.

'Hi, er . . .' I look around the table and see Mags with another of her colourful headscarves. Next to her is a pretty, dark-haired woman who looks around forty. I'm suddenly conscious of my bloodshot eyes and puffy bags, but when I see the bald heads and absent eyebrows, I realize we all probably have a few things in common.

'This is Priya,' Bel says, gesturing towards the dark-haired girl. 'And you know Aunty Mags. Mags, you remember Jess and her dad, Geoff?'

'Hi!' says Priya, standing up to air-kiss and then hug me, her sweet perfume lingering in the air. As she sits back down, I realize her thick dark hair is a wig. Mags stares at the table.

'Thought we'd surprise you,' Bel says. 'First day of chemo and all, thought you'd appreciate the moral support.'

'You guys came here just for me?'

'Well Mags has chemo today and Priya has her Herceptin appointment,' Bel says, looking at Priya. 'I'm the loser who comes into the hospital on her days off.'

In the three working days between Christmas and New Year, I would normally be curled up on the sofa with Johnny, mainlining coffee and orange cremes while working my way through a shiny new hardback. Dad would be pottering about as usual, maybe doing a spot of winter gardening while the tea rooms are closed. Johnny would catch up with his Manchester mates and stay with his mum for a couple of nights before we'd drive back to London together for New Year's.

This year couldn't be more different. At the flat, Dad has been like a fish out of water with no garden to tend to and surrounded by belongings that aren't his own. Then there was the looming dread of my first chemo, both of us knowing, yet not knowing, what lay ahead. He moved Mum's stuff into the utility room and we spent Boxing Day pretending our little confrontation never happened, watching the Christmas specials on the telly. But we couldn't ignore the entire herd of elephants in the room.

'We all know what it's like,' Priya says, giving me a sympathetic look. 'You're gonna totally smash it though, hun. Annabel has told me how strong you are.'

I look up at my dad, who stands awkwardly beside us.

'I'll go for a walk,' he says. 'Meet you back here in half an hour?'

I nod. In the awkward waiting period between the appointment with my oncologist, Dr Malik, and then the blood tests to make sure I'm strong enough for chemo, I'm grateful for the distraction of new friends. I just hope Dad doesn't spend the next half hour panicking.

'Chemo Club?' I say, as I join the women around the table. 'Is that really a thing?'

'It's just our little bunch of misfits,' Bel says, putting a skinny arm around my shoulder. 'We're here to say fuck you to cancer, aren't we girls?'

Mags raises a wrinkled middle finger with a mischievous smile, making everyone laugh.

'We got you this,' Annabel says, gesturing towards a shoebox-sized parcel, covered in Peppa Pig wrapping paper. 'It's all I had.'

'You shouldn't have . . .' I look around the table before slowly tearing the paper from the box. I lift the shoebox lid to reveal a hamper of items: a couple of gossip magazines, a gratitude diary, a huge bar of organic dark chocolate, a pack of cool-down wipes and a couple of chemo lollipops with plastic wrapped around the lolly part, just like the ones we used to get in party bags as kids. There's also a bottle of black nail polish, some chemical-free bubble bath, an eye mask and a tube of peppermints.

'Your chemo survival kit,' Annabel says. 'Just our way of saying we're here for you.'

'This is so sweet,' I say. 'You really shouldn't have. I feel delighted and depressed all at once.'

'It's a club none of us wanted to join but you've got to find the silver linings,' Priya says, her brown eyes gleaming under long fake lashes as she smiles. 'I have eleven-year-old twins and they both like it better now I've got cancer, because mummy gets to spend more time at home with them.'

I know she means well, but the whole concept of silver linings has always made me uncomfortable. When Mum was sick, I read a lot of articles about women who'd gone through cancer and talked about the 'gift' it had given them – the quality time with their families, appreciation of the little things and greater connection with friends. But cancer wasn't a gift for Mum, just like it isn't for so many people and their loved ones. It ripped her from our world in the cruellest way possible.

'So, you're all having chemo then?' I ask.

Annabel makes an eh-ehhh sound, like the buzzer on a game show when the contestant gives the wrong answer. 'Banned word number one. Forfeit!'

'Huh?'

'First rule of Chemo Club,' Priya says, rolling her eyes to humour Annabel. I can't help but like her. 'We don't talk about chemo.'

'I can get on board with that,' I say. 'So what else is banned?'

'Bloods,' says Bel, screwing her face up. 'Cannula, discharge, pus, catheter . . . all the gross medical stuff that makes you want to puke in your mouth.'

I laugh and cringe at once. 'Never been a particular fan of

those words, to be honest. What about you, Mags, any banned words?'

'Bloody cancer,' she says, making a fist with her age-blotched hand and then sticking up her middle finger again.

All three of us laugh.

'Let's add "battle" to the list,' Annabel says. 'She didn't "lose her battle", she fucking died.'

Priya sticks her fingers in her mouth. 'God, yes. And when people say, "she passed away" or "we lost her".'

'Agreed,' Annabel says. 'No more battles or passing away, and no more losing people, unless you're in the supermarket.'

'So the rule of Chemo Club is we don't talk about anything to do with why we're here and how we're doing?' I say.

'You're a fast learner,' says Bel.

'So what *can* we talk about?'

'Scx!' says Mags, and everyone laughs again.

'Boys are always good game,' says Bel. 'Although only the good ones. There's a banned list. Would you like to add a certain ex to the list, Ms Jackson?'

I laugh. I've exhausted every possible thought I could have about Johnny since we broke up. I could quite happily never hear his name again. I nod.

'Done,' says Bel. 'Every time you mention Johnny, I'm afraid we're going to have to make you ask a stranger on a date.'

I laugh. 'Johnny who?'

I leave the girls in the coffee shop and walk down the winding corridors to find Dad. Inside the chemo ward, cards and tinsel cover the reception area and a tree sits in the corner, decorated with baubles and foil-covered chocolates that no one has eaten. While I wait for my appointment, a rotund lady comes into the waiting room with something that looks like a stick of cinnamon and pokes it into the middle of the tree.

'Keeps it smelling festive,' she says, noticing me watching.

Within minutes, Nurse Rose appears. She hugs me, then draws back and looks me up and down, acknowledging my Secret Santa onesie. 'That looks very cosy. Did you have a nice Christmas?'

'Lovely, thanks, it's been nice to have the daily injections done with,' I say, though I can't say I feel quite as relaxed now. The nervous energy in my stomach ahead of chemo makes me want to be sick, despite the super-strength anti-nausea tablets. 'How was yours?'

'Lots of food,' she laughs, patting her stomach. 'I'll walk you through. It's very quiet. Everyone is still enjoying their mince pies.'

Dad appears beside us, then walks a few steps behind as I follow Nurse Rose through a room that is white and clinical but still light and airy.

'Sit yourself down. The chemo nurse will be through in a few minutes. Have you taken your anti-sickness tablets?'

I nod. Every time someone says chemo, I get a pang of anxiety in my belly. They obviously didn't get the banned words memo.

'And you're feeling OK?'

'Nervous.'

'That's totally normal.' She beams. 'You'll be here for three or four hours. Once you're home you can get lots of rest. It's not as scary as you think. Sometimes it helps to get the first one out the way.'

I wish people would stop saying that and let me get on with it. It's like exam anxiety. It builds up and up until you're in that room and then finally it's not quite so bad. I need to pee again.

I settle into the dentist-style white chair, my legs out in front of me on the padded leg rest, my elbows on the armrests.

Beside me stands a long pole attached to a machine with a white face, a large screen and a number pad. I feel like I'm on death row.

'This is nurse Angelica,' Rose says, as a tiny lady appears out of nowhere. She must be about fifty, but she hardly looks old enough to have finished secondary school.

'Hiiii,' she says in the warmest, friendliest tone of anyone I've met so far at the hospital. She reminds me of a lovely Filipina nurse who used to care for Mum.

'You're in safe hands with Ange,' says Rose. 'She's one of our best nurses, been with us for years, even though she still looks like a teenager.'

I laugh with relief and Angelica joins in with a high-pitched, hysterical laugh that catches on to my father and then to the lady who is silently taking her chemo nearby.

'Oh we are going to have FUN,' Ange says, nodding her head so vigorously and enthusiastically that I wonder if she's on something.

'I'll leave you in the capable hands of Nurse Ange,' Rose says, giving my hand a little squeeze before she heads off out of the ward.

'This must be Dad,' Ange says, doing a sort of curtsey in front of my father. 'Very handsome.'

Dad squirms a little in his seat before Ange moves around and sits down beside my dentist's chair. Please, let's just get it over with.

She goes through my notes and runs through a sequence of disclaimers, checks and explanations. 'Could you confirm your date of birth and first line of your address? Perfect. And you've taken dexamethasone with food at least a few hours ago? Great. And your full blood count looks normal. Great.'

She runs through a series of side effects. *Sickness, nausea, headache, constipation, diarrhoea, light aversion, tiredness, joint pains, high temperature, fever.* 'The most important thing is you call us if you have anything out of the ordinary, OK? And check your temperature every few hours. It really is vital you call us if anything feels wrong – don't wait until it's too late.'

Will it ever end?

Throughout the explanations, she makes little jokes and side comments to Dad, who seems to be enjoying the attention.

Finally, we're ready to begin.

I straighten out my arm and place it over the pillow, clenching my fist as I watch her prepare a needle and some tubes from a tray of instruments. When she comes towards me with the needle, I turn my head to the side, averting Dad's gaze and looking towards the exit sign above the door.

'Sharp scratch,' she says, and I feel the dull pain as the needle finds its way into my inner elbow, pressing down and poking around for what feels like much longer than an ordinary blood test. It hurts, but the pain is a relief compared with the anxiety of waiting.

'Release your fist,' she says, and I do so, praying that my blood is now seeping into the right place so I don't have to go through this again.

Then there is clicking and some slight pulling at my arm.

'All done,' she says, patting the area. I look around and see the tap-like device coming out of my arm. There are two lots of tubes connected to the cannula going into my vein.

'This will allow me to feed you the different drugs so I don't have to keep stabbing you,' she says, laughing her hysterical high-pitched laugh. The contagion starts again, causing Dad and the woman opposite to laugh.

Angelica fetches a large, clear plastic bag filled with bright red liquid and hooks it to the top of my drip pole.

'It will make your pee red, like Tizer,' she says, laughing again. 'Don't worry, it's not blood!'

I can't help thinking of Johnny when she mentions the red pee. He'd have taken the piss out of me – pun intended.

'I'm going to give you an injection of saline,' says Ange. 'It will feel a little cold and you might feel like you're going pee-pee.'

I feel the tickle even before she stops talking. I can taste the saline at the back of my throat. It's not unpleasant, but it's a weird sensation.

Nurse Ange connects the Tizer tube to the dial on my cannula and presses some buttons on the machine. She watches me for a few minutes before getting up.

'All done,' she says. 'I'll be back in fifteen minutes. We keep changing your doses. Press this buzzer if you need me. Bye Daaaaad.'

I look over at Dad, who must have found the whole thing excruciating. My body is tense as I wait to feel some sort of sensation.

'She's a live wire, isn't she, love?'

'I'm just relieved to have the injection bit over with,' I whisper.

'Well, you're done now. I'll go fetch some coffee, what do you fancy?'

Coffee is the last thing I want right now, but I'm grateful Dad doesn't want to sit through this entire ordeal.

'Nothing for me, thanks. Why don't you go for a walk, go find Annabel in the cafe? Take your time, I might have a little sleep.'

I don't intend to sleep, of course. I can't imagine anything less relaxing than sitting with a bag of red liquid being funnelled into my veins while I'm attached to a tube.

'Alright, see you soon love. Call if you need me.'

The moment he is gone, I look up to smile at the woman opposite.

'First time, eh?' says the lady, who looks around sixty and wears a yellow scarf around her puffy scalp, reminding me of Mum and her Pineapple Head.

I nod. 'Hardly a spa trip, is it?'

The woman smiles. 'You get used to it. Goes quickly, I suppose.'

'How many do you have left?'

'I'm on low-dose weeklies,' she says. 'A few more to go but I'll be done by the end of January.'

'Bet you'll be pleased to get your life back?'

The woman stalls, then gives me that oh-you-don't-know look and shakes her head. 'Not much to get back to. Secondaries, you know?'

I slowly acknowledge her answer.

For the next two hours, Nurse Ange bounces in and out of the room like a yo-yo, readjusting my drip, exchanging my Tizer bag, checking my blood pressure and that I'm not about to pass out. *I'm fine*, I keep saying. I actually feel way more fine than I thought I would.

After the second refill, the lady opposite finishes her chemo and a different nurse comes to unhook her and help her into a wheelchair. I wave goodbye and say, 'see you soon,' although I doubt I'll ever see her again.

She smiles and says, 'Nice to meet you. Good luck.'

Dad brings me a cheese sandwich and a plastic container of chopped fruit with a little fork and opens it for me. I eat a few chunks of pineapple, enjoying the feeling of the cold juice down my throat. I try to eat the sandwich, but every bite takes me about five minutes to chew. I don't have the appetite. I guess I'm starting to feel the effects.

As the last infusion trickles through, I see Annabel's black wig appear at the door, her trademark Converse plodding down the corridor. Even a glimpse of her has me breathing a sigh of relief.

'Brought you some tea,' she says, plonking down a cup of hot peppermint on the table.

'Thank you so much,' I say, wondering how she knew how little I feel like drinking my usual tea or coffee.

'How's the spa treatment going?'

'It's been pretty painless,' I lie.

'How long till you finish?' Bel says, looking up at the drip pole.

'Maybe twenty minutes or so?' I lower my voice to a whisper. 'By the way, I think the nurse is hitting on my dad.'

Annabel's eyes light up. 'You got Ange? Brilliant. I love her. She flirts with everyone, even me.'

'Well that's reassuring,' I say, happy to give Bel something to smile about.

Suddenly I hear the sound of a bell ringing and loud cheers and claps. I turn to see the nurses gathered around an older lady. I join in with the clapping, then I notice Annabel's face.

'Hey, you OK?' I say.

She shrugs.

'What is it?'

'The bell,' she says. 'They ring it when someone has their last chemo, like "yay, you're cured, let's have a party". It's a kick in the teeth for those of us who'll never see the end of our treatment.'

'Shit, I'm sorry,' I say, holding out my free hand to squeeze hers. I can't imagine what it feels like to know your treatment will never end in celebration. That it will never end at all.

She shrugs and smiles.

I manage a few sips of the peppermint tea before the last few drips of liquid enter my veins. Then Nurse Ange is back, exchanging greetings with Annabel and winks at Dad before giving me a final infusion of saline and then sliding the long needle out of my arm. She presses a cotton wool ball on top of the entry site. That wasn't so bad after all.

'Rest here for a while,' Ange says. 'No rush, get up slowly, take it easy.'

But I need to pee, so I pull myself up, supported by Dad on one side and Bel's fragile frame on the other.

It's a cold day, but the sky is blue and the spacious toilet is flooded with light. I wriggle out of my onesie, watching it drop to my ankles, and sit as the pee flows into the toilet bowl.

When I finally finish, I stand up and look before I flush. The bowl is full of dark liquid, Tizer red. The smell from the waste that has come out of my own body makes me retch. I wash my hands for at least two minutes as if I'm covered in germs.

'All good?' Annabel says when I return to the chair.

I nod, too weak to say any actual words.

'Come on, let's get you girls some fresh air,' Dad says, holding out an arm either side and linking one around mine and the other around Bel.

Arm in arm, the three of us leave the ward.

The mother of all hangovers

When I wake in the morning, I'm not Jess. My head is pounding, my mouth tastes of metal. Nausea overpowers me. I'm an object, discarded in a heap, immovable, irretrievable. I'm not Jess. Not today.

I stare straight ahead at the wood of my bedside drawers. The patterns on the oak, dark brown, light brown, wavy lines, curvy 'V' shapes, swirling, swirling. I can't look left, I can't look right. No peripheral vision, just straight ahead. Immovable Jess. Not Jess.

Dad knocks and pokes his head around the door. 'Tea, love?'

I can't find the words.

'Jessie?' He pushes the door open a little wider and steps inside, cautious. Oreo makes his way in and I feel his weight as he jumps up onto my legs.

'Oh, love,' Dad says, pitying, as he sees the curled-up heap that I am, sweating, stinking, bed sheets strewn and tangled like spaghetti.

Jess is not here.

'My little Jessie,' he says, setting the steaming tea down on the bedside and stroking my head, slowly, softly, like a cat. 'Little Jessie, little Jessie.'

The milky smell hits me, wakes me, and I gag. I try to speak but only a mumble comes out. *Get it away from me,* I say in my head, hoping he'll hear.

'Sorry,' he says, jumping up, retrieving the mug, marching it out of the room. He understands. Thank God he understands.

'Did you take your steroids?' he says, when he re-enters, moments later. 'Good girl,' he says, seeing an empty banana skin and pill packet on my bedside.

'Sleep, darling.' He strokes me like a cat again. 'Get some sleep, get some rest.'

In the evening, I wake to the buzz of a text message. With some amount of effort, I manage to extend my arm to reach for the phone on my bedside and adjust my eyes to the stream of WhatsApp messages on the home screen.

A text from Lauren:

Hi hun, how are you? Thinking about you loads. Call me if you want to talk. Xx

I drag myself into a sitting position, scrolling to see if there are any more texts, but I realize the only person I want to hear from is Mum. *Oh God, I want my mum.*

Tears fill my eyes as it all comes flooding back. Whenever I was sick or sad, she would know exactly what to say and do. When I got my first period pains, she made me cups of tea with actual sugar lumps and baked me one of her brilliant cakes. Lemon drizzle still reminds me of my teens because it was the only thing that could really comfort me, and my first memory of her custard-filled doughnuts is from when I was very young and cut my head open when I fell off my bike. There was nothing she couldn't solve with a bit of sugary magic.

As long as I wasn't keeling over, she'd make sure I got out of bed and into the kitchen to bake with her. Some people say mild exercise helps heal an illness; for Mum it was being around the stove, cooking with love. Long before they bought the tea rooms, she'd have me kneading bread or stirring coffee cake mixture with a bum wiggle to bring me out of my misery. Of course, it worked. I'd forget whatever headache or pains I had by the time the oven timer went off, almost without fail.

And yet I was never quite able to do the same for her. She gave up on baking at some point. She no longer had the energy, and perhaps I didn't try hard enough to get her back into it. She had all this sadness stored up inside her, but perhaps I could have taken some of it away if we'd only spent some time dancing around the kitchen together. It's not that I didn't try. It's just that she seemed so sad every time she realized she'd lost the strength to do the thing she loved the most.

I see the bedroom door beginning to open and I grab a bunch of tissues to hide my tears from Dad. But it's just Oreo, cautiously sniffing his way into the room and then jumping up onto the bed to headbutt me.

'Oh baby,' I say, stroking his little head and feeling comforted by his purr. 'Mummy feels terrible.'

I scroll through the rest of the messages. There are texts from Annabel, Kate, Aisha, Lauren, Aunty Cath and even Priya. They all want to know how I'm doing but the physical and mental effort it takes to reply is too much. Instead, I open Facebook.

First post: Tara Woodward, uni friend, last seen circa 2007. 'I said yes!' reads the post, accompanied by a sparkling ring and a paradise beach scene. Two hundred and sixty-three likes; ninety-one comments.

Next post: Leah Wilder. 'These two' reads the caption, followed by a blue and a yellow love heart, alongside a picture of her gorgeous wife and baby Milo. Eighty-six likes; five comments.

I click into my status box and make sure it is set to publish to my friends only. Then I start to type.

Survived my first chemo. Surprisingly uneventful and
relatively pain free, but this morning is another story.
If you down ten Jägerbombs, two litres of tequila, a
bottle of wine and six pints, you might go some way
to knowing how I feel. It's the mother of all hangovers,
so don't be surprised if you don't hear from me for
the next few days. Jess x

Notifications come instantly. A mixture of likes, sad-face
emojis and comments pop up underneath the post.

Ophelia Cossack-Daly: That's the hard part over with
hun. One down. You are absolutely #KillingIt. You'll be
on the mend soon, you're a #badass Xx

Cath Elderfield: Proud of you darling. The pain will
pass – get lots of rest and sleep it off. Thinking of
you, love Aunty Cath xx

Simon Brighthouse: jessica my wife had breast
cancer she has loads of tips for chemo including
tumeric and bitter apricot kernels she has loads of
her headscarfs left over if you like she said they were
really comfy though her head used to itch a lot from
the wigs x

Aisha Parker: Smashed it! So proud of you. Next
year is going to be your year, I can feel it. Love
you xx

A text comes through. Annabel.
Saw your Facebook post. Who is this Ophelia Cossack horse
nutter with all her inspirational BS? xoxo
I laugh out loud for the first time since yesterday.

204

Some girl I went to uni with. Could defriend but seems more fun to see what she comes out with next xx

Bel replies. Definitely! How you feeling?

Pretty shit, but guess it's normal. You?

Cancer sucks, darls. Today is the worst day, you'll feel better tomorrow. Joe sends his love too. Big hugs xoxo

I lock the phone and place it back on the bedside table. I've slept for almost twenty-four hours.

I need to pee. I drag myself up, steadying myself with a hand on the wall as I adjust to standing. Everything goes fuzzy for a moment, my vision returning in a slow blur. One foot in front of the other, I pace to the bathroom, a few steps down the hallway, then collapse onto the loo, as if I've been walking for days. The pee flows in desperate gushes, now diluted Tizer red but still pongy, the smell of outgoing chemicals making me retch again.

I sit for a moment before I flush, then step towards the sink, taking a long look at myself in the mirror as I wash my hands with cool, soapy water. Staring back at me is a version of Jess, puffy faced from the steroids with a sweaty grey sheen on her skin.

I turn on the bath taps and begin mixing hot and cold as I pour in a few glugs of chemical-free bath suds from the box of Chemo Club goodies.

The water is too hot and I scald my feet and yelp as it burns. Fuck. It hurts, but at least I can *feel*.

Once the water cools, I submerge myself, lying back until my head is fully under, the water touching my lips and leaving my nose and eyes dry. I no longer feel the sensation of long hair being dragged into the water – just the short mop on my head, immovable, compact. I wonder how long it will be until I have none at all.

I pick up my book and open the first page to start to read,

but I find myself re-reading the first paragraph over and over, unable to take in the information. My attention span lasts about three seconds before my thoughts start spinning off to Lauren and her hen do. My brain isn't functioning as it should.

I close my eyes, dropping the book on the floor next to the bathtub, letting the bubbles surround me, the warm water soothing my body, soothing my tender stomach. If Johnny could see me now, red-faced and swollen, would he still find me attractive? Will any man ever find me attractive again?

I emerge from the bathroom some forty-five minutes later, wrapped in a thick, soft towel that Dad left to warm on the radiator.

I am Jess again, just about.

Let yourself float

Going into the new year like . . . reads the caption below the picture, which shows Tabitha Richardson posing in a red cut-out swimsuit on the edge of an infinity pool, looking impossibly glamorous given that there is presumably a one-year-old baby just off-camera. She has added the hashtags *#paradise*, *#calmbeforethestorm* and *#gifted*. The rest of her feed is littered with sickening posts of her and her perfect family posing in pristine hotel rooms with piles of Christmas gifts.

I shouldn't look at Instagram, but I can't help myself. Having spent the last few days holed up in bed, I'm fully au fait with my friends' and colleagues' Christmas breaks, from Kate and Colm's family gathering in Ireland to Aisha's South London feast with her extended family and Tabitha's perfect trip to Sri Lanka. After all the #ChristmasDinner food pics and magazine-worthy tree shots, the feed has now transitioned to New Year's Eve selfies and inspirational quotes and #goals for the year ahead.

Despite Lauren's pleas for me to join her at Charlie's family's country pile because she's 'bored out of her brain and so out of place with all these poshos', I have neither the energy nor the desire to leave Clapham. It's the first time I've spent Christmas in London and it's lovely to see the city so quiet. Not that I've ventured outside my front door much, but at least there's been a distinct lack of sirens and street noise. Round about now, Johnny and I would have returned to London and we'd be gearing up to attend Kate and Colm's annual New Year's Eve dinner party, a couples' affair through and through. But this year I have a feeling all the invites are perfunctory. Surely no one would want the boring chemo girl at their festive bash?

On the morning of the thirty-first of December, when I'm feeling just about human again, Aunty Cath visits with her two teenage boys. I've been dreading their visit as my cousins are such lightning bolts of energy, but it's refreshing to get dressed and put on make-up. Cousin Kit brings his games console and I play a few rounds of the latest car game before boredom sets in. We plan to take a walk on the rainy Common but I only manage as far as the corner before we have to turn back towards the flat, where I collapse onto the kitchen bench and wait for Cath to ply us with hot tea. By the end of the afternoon, I'm shattered.

Just as the boys are loading their presents into the car, Aunty Cath grabs my hand and pulls me to one side. 'Your mum would be proud of you, you know,' she says.

I'm taken aback.

'The way you've handled things, moving on from that awful Johnny.'

She holds out her arms and hugs me, lightly, as if she knows how much my body hurts.

'You know what your mum told me when I was going through my divorce?'

I nod at her to tell me. I wish I could bottle Mum's wisdom.

' "When you're stranded in the middle of sea, sometimes you feel like you'll never reach the shore. You're kicking and kicking and trying to stay afloat. But you know what? Sometimes

208

you have to stop kicking and let yourself float. It might take a while, but you'll make it to the other side eventually." '

I hold my arms out to hug her again, because I know I won't be able to speak without crying.

'As brilliant as he is, I know it's not the same as having your mum around,' she whispers, nodding towards my father, who stands near the door, ready to wave them off. 'But your dad is suffering too, you know. It's hard for him, but I think he's trying to move on.'

I nod. I know what she means. I just can't quite bear to hear it.

'I know I'll never replace your mum, but I'm only a phone call away.'

She leaves me with tears in my eyes. It's been so long since I've had a mother figure in my life that I didn't realize quite how much I needed one.

In the afternoon, Dad walks in to find me on the living-room floor, surrounded by Mum's stuff. I've been sobbing onto the cardboard boxes for fifteen minutes but I haven't quite summoned the courage to open them yet.

'Jessie,' he says, getting onto his knees when he sees me with all the stuff. 'You don't have to do this, not until you're ready. I'm sorry I tried to force you.'

'No,' I say, wiping the snot from my nose. 'You were right, I need to face up to it.'

'Are you sure? Let me make us a brew.'

He returns a few minutes later with buttered crumpets and piping hot tea. I sniffle a few times and then give in to the chewy, buttery goodness. They taste so good, and I realize how much I've missed home, the smell of freshly baked cakes and the endless food pleasures.

'I've missed you, Dad,' I say, dripping a tear into one of the doughy holes.

'Not as much as I've missed you, eh.'

We lick the butter from our fingers and set to work on the boxes. I might not be ready to discuss Dad's new girlfriend but I think I can just about look through Mum's stuff.

I start with the carrier bags full of clothes. A slim-fitting, stripy jumper dress, a cream fitted jacket with shoulder pads, an old pair of leather trousers, the ones she used to wear for nights out with her pals, before she put on weight from the treatment. Then my hand rests on something silky. I pull it out. It's the slinky, plunging red dress she'd bought for her fifty-fifth birthday because 'who says fifty means frumpy? I'm going to be sexy at sixty, I'll show you!' I smile as I recall it.

That was the thing about Mum. She didn't save her best clothes for special occasions; she wore them around the house. She was your woman in a magazine shoot who *actually* baked a lemon pie in a glamorous polka dot dress. Mum was the definition of 'you only live once' before YOLO was even a thing.

I draw the dress to my lips, taking in the smell. It's mostly must from sitting in the cupboard but if I sniff hard enough, I can summon a faint *eau de Mum*.

I put the dress to one side as I sort through another bag.

'I thought you could maybe keep a few favourites, then we give the rest to charity,' Dad says. 'What do you think?'

I'm absorbed in the second bag, gasping as I pull out the beautiful sequinned dress that she wore for the *Strictly Come Dancing* live audience. I hassled every single person I knew to enter the draw for Blackpool week so we could try and get Mum tickets for her sixtieth birthday. It was Lauren who scored the two tickets in the end, and I'll never forget the joy on Mum's face when she opened the envelope and realized we were heading to the Blackpool Tower Ballroom.

'She was so happy that night,' I say, remembering how we'd called Dad right after the show, dying to know if he'd seen us on the telly. I'd given the tickets to both of them but Dad had insisted I go with Mum – she'd enjoy it more with me there, he'd said.

'She was,' Dad says, getting to his feet and taking my hand to waltz with me around the room for one step, two steps, three.

'She never stopped banging on about her split second of fame on primetime TV,' I laugh, recalling how she'd made me get hold of the clip and blow up the blurry glimpse of the side of her head behind Bruno Tonioli so she could put it on the wall in the tea rooms and proudly tell all the customers about it.

Dad swirls me around, the two of us silently remembering Mum as we weave in and out of the piles of clothes, bags and boxes.

Then my foot bashes against a box and I stub my toe, falling to my knees.

'Love, are you OK?' Dad crouches down again and reaches for me.

I fall into his arms, sobbing this time as if my heart has been sucked from my chest. It's not the pain in my foot that hurts.

'I miss her so much,' I say. My whole body bobs up and down as I sob and sob and sob.

'Me too, love. Every single day.'

We stay like that for a long time, until eventually we can speak again, and sort through the rest of the boxes. I salvage the sequinned dress and the red one, her favourite blue earrings and a box of books. When I agree to donate the rest to a charity shop, Dad suggests he can drop them in North London on the drive back home so I never have to bump into anyone wearing my mother's clothes.

'Better still, I can drop 'em off somewhere around the Watford Gap,' he says. 'Not like you'll be going north of there any time soon.'

'Very funny,' I say, lightly punching his arm. I don't have the heart to tell him all charity shop collections are centralized anyway. 'I'll visit more often next year, I promise.'

But as soon as the words leave my mouth, I remember the reason I've been so reluctant to visit. 'Are you sure you want to sell the house and the tea rooms?'

He nods, and I see for the first time that he is resolute. He was just waiting until I was ready to accept it. 'It's too big for me on my own, and it's your mother's project, but I'm not doing it justice. I've found a little bungalow that's perfect for me.'

'You're not leaving the village?'

'No, love. It's on Laywood Lane, down the little ginnel where you used to play as a kid.'

'I love that lane,' I say. 'Those little cottages with the apple trees?'

'That's the one,' he says, his face lighting up.

An apple tree for Dad to tend to, and a little cottage where he won't have to worry about the stairs when his knees pack in.

'It sounds perfect,' I say.

We spend the evening on the sofa watching films and eating Dad's festive bubble and squeak. By ten o'clock, he is asleep and I'm scrolling through Instagram, watching Aisha's Stories as she dances up to the camera, panning around a nightclub with vodka in hand.

I shuffle my toes in my socks and lay my head on Dad's shoulder.

I wake him up at the end of Jools Holland, just as the

fireworks are about to start over the Thames. Dad opens a sleepy eye and acknowledges the television.

'What does this bloke even do for the other three hundred and sixty-four days of the year?' Dad says.

'God knows,' I laugh, clinking my mug against his empty whisky tumbler. 'Happy New Year, Dad.'

He puts his arm around me. 'Good riddance to the last one,' he says, and promptly falls back asleep.

Swipe right

On New Year's morning, I wake, hangover free, feeling better than I've felt since chemo almost a week ago. Dad set off early to go back up north and, now that I've finally got the flat to myself again, I feel like I can snap out of being the sullen teenager I become in his presence.

New year, new me.

There's something about the first of January that feels as satisfying as opening a brand new issue of a glossy magazine. The pages aren't yet smudged with fingerprints, the images are crisp and intact and there are fresh possibilities with each page. This year is a new start. No wasting time thinking about what could have been with Johnny, no feeling sorry for myself. I'm going to get back out there and start dating, and be the best editor of *Luxxe* I can be.

I lay out a load of old copies on the bed and make notes in a pad that says 'Twenty-first century laptop' on its cover. I'm done with the formulaic profile of the Woman Who Went Through Some Shit and Finally Feels Comfortable in Her Own Skin. It always starts with them turning up at the Chateau Marmont in Los Angeles, wearing scruffy jeans, slouchy jumper and no make-up, and ends with them transforming into a flawless butterfly with zero problems.

But life isn't that straightforward. I want *Luxxe* to be

accessible to every woman. I want us to cover strong, power-ful leaders who aren't necessarily at the top of their game yet, and who certainly aren't done with their problems. I want us to write about women who are still dealing with shit; women like Stephanie Asante, who survived an abusive childhood on a council estate and somehow went on to run a women's em-powerment network, where she now helps people from similar backgrounds. I want us to profile women of colour, people with disabilities, trans women, people who didn't even make it to sixth form, let alone Oxbridge. I want to cover those who don't have the same opportunities.

As I look through the old issues, I come across the sex and relationships pages. There are articles about destination wed-dings, keeping the passion alive after the 'eleven-year itch' and 'bringing up baby'. Six months ago, these were the sorts of pieces I loved as I looked ahead to a future with Johnny. It's not hard to see why the magazine was skewed towards rela-tionships, marriage and motherhood with Leah at the helm. But now that I'm single, the gaping hole is obvious.

Suddenly, Tabitha's suggestion that I write an online dating column for *Luxxe* doesn't seem like such a distant possibility. I don't have to be celibate for the rest of my life just because my hair is about to fall out.

I make myself a slice of toast and download Happn again. Poised to recreate my profile, I'm surprised to see it is already there. Huh. I guess when I deleted the app, I didn't actually delete my profile.

There are three new messages.

Ben, 25 *Hey*

Kyle, 42 *Hi*

Rick, 30 *Are you Jewish? Because Israeli nice to meet you*

According to the details under Ben's profile, we crossed

paths at the hospital. I could meet all kinds of doctors and patients on here.

Then it strikes me. I'm a woman in the midst of my problems. Tabitha was right – perhaps I can write about my dating experiences, not in the sense of naming and shaming the misfits I meet online, but in genuinely trying to find love. That's what I want, isn't it? I'm not going on these apps for a one-night stand. I actually want to find love again. And if I can show how hard it is when you're in the thick of it, maybe I can make other women feel less alone.

I do some research into traditional dating sites and download four new apps in addition to the ones Aisha mentioned, to make seven in total. That's it – I'll go on seven dates in seven days from seven different dating sites and write about my experiences. There's no way I won't meet *someone* decent.

The rest of the afternoon is lost in the excitement of trying to find my best angle for selfies, finding a selection of photos that make me look friendly, active and popular, and providing proper information about myself as well as criteria for the men I'm looking for. I fill in my vital statistics and complete an extensive, Mensa-like survey. Then I'm left with an empty box that reads: *Tell us something about you.*

There's a minimum character count, and it turns out 'will write something here later' doesn't meet the threshold. I sift through as many profiles as I can find and realize there's a formula to follow, which involves brevity and lists. I write some variation of the same profile across all seven sites. I am nothing if not efficient.

Hi, I'm Jess, I'm thirty-one and single, but you probably gathered that. I'm looking for someone who's funny, smart and preferably still has his own teeth – I'm not asking for much, right? I'm a magazine editor and I love a good list. So, on that note . . .

Likes: Custard doughnuts, Sunday roasts, nineties and noughties pop throwbacks (see: Destiny's Child, Girls Aloud, Mis-Teeq), tequila-based cocktails and men who 'get' feminism.

Dislikes: Over-ripe bananas, people who list the number of countries they've visited on their profile, aggressive umbrella-wielders and the Northern line.

By the time I've completed my profile on the seventh site, I have an inbox full of messages on one of the non-swipe apps.

3:15 p.m.
to: SayYesToJess
from: CariocaDreamer
Hello, I am Brazilian! My name is Ricardo! This is my first time using a dating site! I hope you like my pictures! I'm into surfing but I'm not keen on the cold water in England. I'm looking for a girl who would like to visit Brazil with me some day. Don't be shy, send me a message let's see if we get on! Ric!

3:21 p.m.
to: SayYesToJess
from: Loves4Foolz
Hey. So that's not my pic in the profile – I've used a model 2 protect my identity cuz I'm married. Up 4 some fun?

3:38 p.m.
to: SayYesToJess
from: AdamandSaira
Hey Jess, we loved your profile! We're a couple in a loving relationship for over ten years and we're looking for another

217

woman to join us for occasional, harmless fun, nothing too kinky. Saira is a lawyer and I'm a broker, so we rarely get much time at home together but on the weekends we sometimes spice it up with a third person. We can FaceTime to get to know each other first if you like. Adam and Saira x

3:48 p.m.
to: SayYesToJess
from: Adonis123
U r so sexy. Wanna cum 2 mine?

I've always wondered what it would be like to go on these sites. Online dating was around before I met Johnny, but I was far too busy being twenty-something and meeting guys in bars with Lauren. At some point during our relationship, the internet became the *only* way to meet people. Since then, I've heard everything from the success stories, like Lauren and Charlie's engagement, to the horror stories, mostly via Aisha – the latest being a bond trader who allowed her just three minutes of foreplay before rudely declaring that his 'pants won't take themselves off'. Needless to say, she pulled a typical Aisha and kindly removed his underwear before throwing all of his clothes out of her bedroom window and giving him no choice but to leave her place in the nude.

Despite the more negative tales, I always thought it would be fun to date online. But I never expected it to be *quite* so addictive – there are literally thousands of choices, albeit most of them unsuitable.

There are badly lit bathroom mirror shots, photos of bulging boxers, the occasional full-frontal dick pic and more guys posing with sedated tigers than there are tigers in India. Then there's Adam and Saira. Their first picture is taken from the side so you can't make out their faces, then there's a selfie of

218

them on a beach somewhere, and clear head shots of Saira in smart work clothes and Adam in a suit. Even if I was in the market for a threesome, I wouldn't risk it with a lawyer who could move in the same circles as Johnny and Mia.

The profiles differ wildly across platforms, offering a window into the sorts of demographic on each. The men on the apps tend to have better spelling but use fewer words, while those on the websites write whole paragraphs but have a lax approach to grammar. One has specified he has 'no tolerance for time waisters', while another states 'no boars'. It's hard to know whether to plump for those who lack any grasp of spelling and grammar yet have made a real effort, or the ones who have a PhD yet whose profiles seem to actively repel women.

Of all the messages I've received, only a couple have referred to things I wrote in my profile. Aisha was right – people really do only look at the pictures. But there's one, FiremanMike83, who has actually read my profile and put some care and thought into his response.

FiremanMike83: *Hey Jess . . . massive Sunday roast fan over here! I can even cook it for u, how's about that? Big fan of nineties choons too. Does TLC Waterfalls make your hit list? Mike x*

I'm so relieved that someone has actually read my profile, I reply straight away.

SayYesToJess: *Hi Mike! Of course Waterfalls is up there – absolute banger! So when are we doing the roast?*

FiremanMike83: *As soon as I've worked out whether ur a nutcase or not lol x*

Note to self: add 'lol' to my list of dislikes.

SayYesToJess: *Er, you get a lot of nutcases on here then?* I try not to sound too offended.

FiremanMike83: *God yeah. I mean, u sound quite normal*

219

but there's loads of girls on here that ask for stuff and say they'll date u under one condition.

SayYesToJess: *What do you mean?*

I really am sheltered when it comes to dating.

FiremanMike83: *They ask you to buy them clothes. Dresses and stuff. They send you the link. Some of them make a living from it. Poles mostly. x*

SayYesToJess: *Erm . . . sorry?*

I'm lost.

FiremanMike83: *The thing is, even if you buy the dress, half the time they won't even have sex with you x*

Oh. Wow. OK. Perhaps I need to re-examine my judgement. This feels like the right moment for my first ghosting.

I move to one of the friendlier apps, the so-called feminist one. There's a new match, a good-looking guy called Frank whose profile indicates he shares my love of food.

I click into the box to compose a message.

Hey Frank, nice to see you on here. Fancy a drink sometime?

His reply comes within seconds. *I could do tonight? x*

Foodie Frank

Frank, 33. Project manager and massive foodie, looking for a nice girl to dine with me. I'm tall so ideally you're not a midget but other than that I don't have a 'type'. IG: @Frank_About_Food
    PS We can lie and say we met in Tescos x

In the time it takes between arriving outside the restaurant and Frank showing up, I spot at least six people who could be him. A bearded guy in a trilby hat who is not dissimilar to Tom Hardy, a pony-tailed man whose height matches Frank's but who looks at least ten years older and a spotty, nervous-looking chap in specs who stops outside the entrance, glances down at his phone and back at me, before discounting me. Then I spot the lanky guy in a leather jacket crossing the street. I check the avatar in the app. It's him.

Shit. It's far too soon for this. Even before I left the house, I felt exhausted. The effort of showering, putting on make-up and squeezing into my skinny jeans and boots was more exertion than I've had in the week and a half since chemo. If Dad was still at home, I'm sure he would have told me it's too soon. I avoided the Tube and got a taxi because of the risk of germs, like Dr Malik advised, but I'm so weak that my knees could crumble. I wish I was at home in my pyjamas.

I look for a way out – if I put my head down and go left, he won't notice me. He hasn't seen me yet. How do people do this, casually meeting perfect strangers for dinner like it's the easiest thing in the world?

'Jess?'

I look up to see the almost seven-foot totem pole that is Frank, his hair cut far too short for his face, hovering above me. Up close, I see that one of his eyes looks slightly to the left while the other faces forward.

'Hey,' I say, leaning in for an air kiss. There was none of this awkward introduction stuff back when I met Johnny. Just a series of Jäger shots during wedding speech bingo, then a night of grinding on the dance floor. Simpler times.

'How you doing?' he says, without waiting for me to answer. 'I'm excited to try this place.'

'Must be good, judging by the queue.' I'm desperate to sit down, my legs already weak, not to mention the energy required to keep warm in the freezing cold. The biting wind makes my ears ache.

I gesture towards the line of people in front of us, making a show of rubbing my hands together to keep warm. 'Sure it's worth the wait?'

'Let me see what I can do,' he says with a wink. 'Connections.'

Frank slips through the queue and pushes his way to the front, saying something to the lady on the door with her high ponytail and clipboard. A shake of the head. He speaks again, but she has already moved on to the next couple, escorting them inside.

'No luck?' I say, when he returns, sheepish.

'They'd usually let me in, but with tonight being opening night, they've got a load of other VIPs in the queue so . . .'

'You're a VIP?'

222

'Influencer,' he says, waving his phone by way of explanation.

'What's your handle?' I say, pulling off a glove to open Instagram.

He looks hesitant, then peers over my shoulder and watches me type, as he says, 'At Frank underscore About underscore Food.'

'Frank About Food?' I say, clicking on his profile from the dropdown. 'Cool name.'

I glance at his grid and make a mental note to do a proper stalk later. He has five hundred and sixty followers.

'I only just made the account public,' he says, waving a hand over his short hair. 'That's why I don't have many followers yet.'

'Sure,' I say. 'So, what about your day job?'

We talk about work, moving half a step forward every few minutes. Frank goes straight in asking whether we do guest takeovers on *Luxxe*'s Instagram.

'How did you know I work at *Luxxe*?' I say, racking my brain to remember if I put the name of the publication in my profile. I'm sure I didn't.

Frank looks rumbled. 'Google image search.'

'What do you mean?'

'I reverse image searched your profile pic?' He says it like it's a question. 'Most people use a photo they've also used somewhere else. It took me about three seconds to find your LinkedIn.'

'Oh,' I say, making a mental note to make myself a bit more incognito. Not that I mind him knowing where I work, but I'd rather we discover these things about each other through actual conversation.

I tell Frank I've only been at *Luxxe* for a month or so and that I'm not responsible for social media, though of course

I know I could get him exposure if I wanted to. He keeps pushing to find out which of my colleagues handles our socials.

When we reach the pony-tailed lady at the front of the queue, Frank says, 'Thanks Anikka.' She looks baffled, but escorts us to two stools at the counter around the steamy pasta kitchen.

'She gave us the best seats,' he says, adjusting his stool and placing his phone face up on the counter. 'Perks.'

I'm pretty sure she gave us the only available seats, but I don't want to burst his bubble.

Moments after I step inside the restaurant, I feel my cheeks starting to burn and a damp, hot sweat on the back of my neck. I fling off my coat, beads of sweat forming a blanket of heat over my entire body.

My first hot flush, on a first date. I shouldn't have left the house. It's too soon for this. My skin is burning.

Frank is saying something, but I can't hear it. My whole body is focused on cooling itself down, and I'm peeling off my jumper, wishing I could strip down to my bra and knickers.

'Jess?' he says, looking impatiently from me to the waitress, who is standing behind us. 'White or red?'

'Um, red,' I say.

Then I'm shivering, my arms suddenly covered in tiny goose bumps, my hair standing on end. I reach down for the jumper I threw on top of my coat under the stool.

By the time I've resumed normal body temperature and a modicum of composure, I'm relieved to see that Frank is still engaged in a thorough interrogation of the server. After five minutes of tasting different wines and rejecting them, he settles on a bottle of Pinot Noir. Just as she's about to leave, he says, 'Actually, we're ready to order food?'

I open my mouth to speak but he is already reeling off

small plates. Burrata, olives, sourdough, salumi (what even is salumi?), ravioli, lobster linguini . . .

'Anything else?' he says, after dictating an entire order for the both of us.

I make a vague noise of protestation before deciding resistance is futile. Johnny always let me order.

The food arrives all at once. Small plates of burrata and Italian sausage, fresh ribbons of pasta with chunks of lobster and plump pillows of ravioli. I pick up my fork to stab into a slice of sausage, but a hand quickly swats it away.

'Woah, woah, woah,' Frank says, giving me a stern look. 'Pics first, yeah?'

I put down my fork and watch as he gets off his stool and stands over the counter, removing all cutlery and arranging the plates into a collage. He takes a test photo, then shakes his head – 'too dark' – and gets out another piece of equipment from his pocket. A portable flash.

Frank continues with his photo shoot, eventually asking me to vacate my stool because I'm causing shadows. I give an apologetic nod to the lady beside me as I elbow her on my way down.

The lobster linguini looks longingly at me, the rising steam gradually slowing to regular air.

'It's probably going a bit cold?' I pose it as a question so as not to be too demanding.

'Almost done,' he says without looking at me, turning his phone to portrait and panning across the whole flat lay of plates, then switching to selfie mode and introducing the restaurant.

Finally, he puts the flash back in his pocket and climbs onto his stool. I pick up my fork to resume eating. Again, I'm interrupted.

'Hold on,' he says. 'Just got to do a story.'

I glance down at his phone as he tags the restaurant, adding hashtags and clicking through the fonts on Instagram Stories. Finally, he presses send, leaving the app face up on the counter as he picks up his fork and reaches across me to cut into the burrata.

'Sorry,' he says, his mouth full of food. 'You have to do these things at the start of the meal to build up engagement.'

'Mm-hm,' I nod, finally biting into lukewarm linguini.

'Plus if the restaurant knows you're here, there's more chance of being comped.'

I look up at the pasta chef and am pleased to see he's not listening.

We pick from the plates with our fingers, knives and forks, initially careful not to take too much of each other's share and then slowly stepping up the competition until we're vying for the last slither of salumi.

'I like a girl with a good appetite,' he says. 'Shall we order more?'

I fork the last bite of lobster into my mouth, licking the sauce from my lips and ignoring the patronizing comment.

'I'm stuffed,' I say, patting my food baby. 'Thanks though, it was delicious.'

'Would you like dessert?' the waitress says, reaching for the last of the plates and piling the cutlery on top with a clatter.

'We'll have the chocolate brownie,' Frank says, handing the menus back to the waitress without even looking at me. I start to open my mouth again but she is already gone.

'I'm just nipping to the loo,' I say, looking forward to reading the messages from Aisha and Annabel that are stacked up on my home screen.

I slump onto the toilet, all energy gone straight to my stomach. I open Frank_About_Food's Instagram and click on his Stories. He must have filmed a selfie video before meeting me.

'*Hi guys! This is Frank and I've just been invited to the opening night at the most exciting launch of the month, Lucia's. Stay tuned to see what I'm eating!*'

I play it again, realizing he must have stood at the front of the queue to make it look like he was going straight in, before going to the back of the line to meet me. I can't help but laugh as I forward the video to Aisha.

When I return to the counter, there's a minuscule scrap of brownie remaining on a plate that is strategically placed between me and Frank, with a fork on either side.

'Saved you some,' he says.

I lift my fork to take the one small biteful that isn't crumbs.

'You can have that whole bit,' he says.

I chew the tiny piece of brownie as Frank returns to Instagram, clicking into his stats and replaying his own Stories.

When the bill arrives, Frank opens it and looks around as if searching for someone to amend it.

'What's the damage?' I say, reaching down for my purse.

'I can't believe they didn't comp us,' he says. 'I usually get at least a free glass of bubbles.'

Five minutes later, after splitting the bill, we're outside saying goodbye before he heads off for the Tube and I hail a taxi.

'It was soooo nice to meet you,' he says, kissing me quickly on the cheek, then looking down at his phone again. 'Don't forget to intro me to your colleague about the Insta takeover, I just love *Luxxe* as a brand.'

'Sure,' I say, making a mental note to tell Aisha and the social team to avoid him at all costs.

On the ride home, I check the rest of Frank's Stories. He has recorded another selfie outside the restaurant, thanking Lucia's for its 'amazing service and amazing staff'.

I keep checking my phone, waiting for an acknowledgement

of an enjoyable meeting, a fun date. After five years, I became accustomed to Johnny's habit of monitoring my journeys to make sure I got home safely. It's the least I would expect.

By the time I arrive home, Frank has posted the flat lay of dishes on his feed with a long description and twenty hashtags in a separate comment. I click through to the restaurant's handle and see that he has left a comment there too:

Amazing opening night, thanks for having me! Follow @Frank_About_Food for my Stories! #FollowforFollow

He seems to have had plenty of time to curate his Insta, though not quite enough to check I got home safely.

Seven dates, seven apps, seven days

Back on the singles market after a five-year relationship, Jessica Jackson tries her hand at online dating

Not so long ago, tinder was something you threw on the fire and the 'gram was a unit of measurement in baking. Fast forward a decade and getting a date is as easy as ordering a gluten-free, vegan cheese toastie for same-day delivery. But how easy is it to find actual love? I gave myself seven days to find out.

*Names have been changed to ~~protect the innocent~~ stop me from being trolled.

Monday – the Follow Me Back Guy

Vitals: Fred, project manager, 33
We met on: Bumble
I love food – I love eating it, making it and talking about it. So when I matched with a foodie on the app where women make the first move, I was only too happy to ask him out.
Pros: He scored brownie points by picking a cool new restaurant.
Cons: He ruined it by gobbling the brownie at the end.

He was pretty much as billed – friendly, smart, good-looking. But it turns out he was more interested in face-less followers than following me up to bed.

What I've learned: Get to know someone online before you invest an entire evening in their company.

Tuesday – the Empty Profile Guy

Vitals: Jai, founder of 'own company', 39
We met on: Inner Circle
I'll admit it – I was sold on his three photos:
  - Jai on stage, TED-Talk style in suit and tie
  - Jai on surf board with torso on show
  - Jai attending wedding with arms around mother and sister

Was I concerned that his profile was blank but for a series of emojis? Nah – I figured it would make getting to know him more fun.

Big mistake. It turns out a guy who has nothing to say in his dating profile will have nothing to say on the date, nor will he make any effort. You can be the hottest man in the world but if you're too self-involved to make conversation, I'm not interested.

What I've learned: Empty profile = empty future. (Note to self: review own profile)

Wednesday – the Smartarse

Vitals: Jared, research fellow and Everest climber, 36
We met on: Tinder
Sapiosexual, noun: a person who finds intelligence sexually attractive or arousing. Admittedly, I had to google it. But I figured yeah, that's me. I fell for my ex not only for

his moves to 'Party Rock Anthem' but also for his drive and ambition, so while I found Jared's profile a little off-putting, I figured in real life he was what I wanted. Not so. From his opening question about my parents' education, I felt like I was in a university admissions interview. If I want to be tested, I'll sign up for Mensa.

What I've learned: Never date a man capable of writing: 'Swipe left if you draw your eyebrows on with a felt-tip pen' #Next.

Thursday – the Married Guy

Vitals: Elliot, whisky importer, 32
We met on: Hinge
Me: 'So who do you live with?'
Him: 'Oh I . . . live with my family, actually.'
Me: *adopts poker face* 'You still live with your mum and dad?'
Him: 'No, I, er . . . I live with my kids and my, er, wife.'
Me: —
Him: 'I know what you're thinking, but she's totally cool with this.'
What I've learned: Find out a guy's intentions before the date – a simple 'are you single?' should suffice.

Friday – the Friend Zoner

Vitals: Niall, English teacher, 29
We met on: Match
The first thing he did when he saw me was compli-ment my leather jacket – and reveal that his ex had the same one. Within minutes, he was tearfully recounting how said ex left him for his best mate, and we were

swapping stories about our shared heartbreak. Half a bottle of wine in, we were belly-laughing over everything from Uber ratings to the fact that he still co-parents a lizard with his ex. It was clear we'd friend-zoned from the start.

What I've learned: Maybe my ex wasn't so great after all. It's been years since I've laughed like I did on this date – I guess we're different people now than when we met.

Saturday – the Peacock

Vitals: Alejandro, polo player and banker, 30
We met on: Happn
He showed initiative by inviting me to his birthday party on a Soho nightclub rooftop. Unfortunately, I wasn't the only one who'd been invited as his date. Enter: a whole harem of women who thought the same. I only spoke to him once, but no bother – I spent an hour chatting to a glamorous Ukrainian before she revealed she was eighteen years old and met 'Ale' in a strip club. I then spent a fortune on a round of sixteen-pound cocktails for a large group of 'chicas' who by the end of the night were referring to themselves as 'Ale's angels'. (See Insta Stories for evidence)
What I've learned: There are guys out there who treat the apps like it's Kickstarter. Next time you want to get bums on seats at your party, maybe try crowdsourcing, hun?

Sunday – the No Questions Asked Guy

Vitals: Bryan, photographer, 31
We met on: POF

Me (after exhausting all other lines of conversation): 'Do you have brothers and sisters?'
Him: long, unexciting story about his sister.
Me: waits for him to say 'And you? Any siblings?'
Him: *sips pint*.

It's a good job I'm a journalist because if I hadn't asked all the questions, there'd have been no more than three words uttered the entire night – yet he was capable of wanging on about himself ad infinitum. Is it me, or has social media shattered our ability to care about anyone other than ourselves?

What I've learned: I want to be with someone who is not only interestING but interestED – someone who'll remember a few key facts and give sufficient shits to follow up next time.

As I write this in my PJs with my blistered feet in tatters, I apologize to every man or woman I've ever envied for being single in the time of apps.

Dating. Is. Exhausting.

Sure, it's exciting and fun, and yes, there are some lovely, normal people on these sites, but it takes tremendous effort to introduce yourself time and time again to someone you might only spend a few hours with – not to mention the toll it takes on the wallet. (Thank God I was mostly drinking Coke.)

But it was worth it, because I've learned as much about myself as I have about these apps and the people on them. I've learned that my 'type' isn't just tall, dark and kind. My type is someone I can talk to, someone who truly makes me laugh and who genuinely cares about me.

Most of all, I've learned that I probably won't find lasting love on an app that uses geo-technology to find strangers to fuck. No, I'm going on thirty-two and I'm done with time-wasters. I'm looking for the one, and I'll do whatever it takes to find him. Anyone know of a young, eligible bachelor?

Drop-outs who ghosted me: 3
Hours of my life I'll never get back: 35
Total funds spent: £323.87

Unfollowed

'So when's the next instalment?'

I walk into the office on the first Friday after Christmas to find Tabitha peering over Aisha's shoulder, examining the analytics on the website.

'Did it do OK?' I say, approaching the line of desks without looking at Aisha's screen. I sent the column on Monday and have spent the entire week fretting about the response.

'Meh,' Tabitha says, moving her hand in a 'so-so' gesture. 'I really loved the piece but I think it'll take a while to build up engagement. Plus it's January.'

I whip off my coat, feeling the now-familiar wave of a hot flush chasing through my body. I slump into my chair, spreading my legs to mitigate the heat.

'Can we turn the air-con up? It's boiling in here.'

'Are you in the menopause or something?' Tabitha says, laughing.

If only she knew. Dr Malik explained that chemo will cause my periods to stop and I'll have hot flushes and perimenopausal symptoms for some time. Super-fertile Tabitha joking as if the menopause is something to be ashamed of makes me feel like I've failed as a woman. But I laugh it off.

'I might need to take some time off dating,' I say, even though I'd be glad not to swipe through another app for the rest of my life. My little project might have made for a good story, but it took every bit of energy I could summon post-chemo and it knocked me for six. I didn't even make it to brunch on the weekend with Kate and Lauren because I couldn't find the strength to drag myself out of bed.

'Well, you've started something now,' Tabitha says, frowning. 'Readers are going to want to know what happens next. Plus, you did say you wanted to find someone.'

'I'll think of something,' I say. I have my second chemo next week and it's only a matter of time before my hair falls out. How will I go on dates then?

Every morning, I check my pillow for signs my hair is falling out. I've seen the films. I know the scene where the character touches the back of her head in the shower then looks down to find a pile of hair in the plug hole. Just because I'm expecting it doesn't make it any easier. Every day, I put a hand to the back of my head, pinch my fingers together and pull gently at a section of hair. When it doesn't budge, I breathe a sigh of relief. I'm spared for at least one more day.

I click into my inbox. There's a message from a PR.

Jess, we loved your dating piece so much. Is this going to be a regular thing? We'd love to send you on an all-expenses-paid trip for two to Rathmore House. We have a couples package that we think you'd love, and it'll be perfect for Luxxe x

I flick to my Instagram inbox. There's a message from Frank_About_Food.

Jess. I saw your piece. Nice that you thought I was trying to use you, but don't flatter yourself. For what it's worth, I wouldn't date you again either. Have a nice life. #Unfollowed.

I make a face. *Of course* Frank saw the piece. He spends his entire life online. Well, I guess I deserved the unfollow.

I navigate to *Luxxe*'s Instagram, where Aisha has posted a picture of me taken at a shoot for the baking magazine, looking down as if pondering which cake to choose. Beneath it is the caption, *Our acting editor went on seven dates in seven days to see if she could find love. Link in bio to find out what happened.*

Below the post are twenty comments, around half of which are love heart emojis or spam. Then there are a few genuine comments.

@Aisha_Parker_ Yass girl! So proud of you for doing this. Your dating efforts put mine to shame! xx

@Life_after_luvv Adore this piece. Good on you for getting out there. I've given up on men . . .

@JillyheartsLondon Where did you get your top from? x

@Jj781th2 She's not that pretty

The last comment stings. I put my heart and soul into writing that piece and it seems all people care about is what I'm wearing and whether I'm attractive enough to write a column about dating. If they knew how much effort it took to put myself out there after a round of chemo, perhaps they'd say something different. But I don't want pity.

January always passes slowly. Gloomy weather, dark evenings and low bank balances make for skint friends and miserable colleagues. By the time my birthday rolls round, no one is up for doing anything. But this year has been different. The first week of the year was a whirlwind, with dates every evening and being comatose overnight while trying to keep up with the crazy new-year workload. It barely seems like a week has passed, but now my birthday is here, and my second round of chemo shortly after.

People say having a December birthday is a curse, but January is worse. I rarely do anything other than a nice meal with Johnny to celebrate because all my friends are too busy giving up booze and detoxing while they wait for that elusive pay cheque. This year, Lauren is too absorbed in wedding planning, Aisha is on a spending ban and I don't want to bother Kate when she's so stressed and tired with the baby and going back to work. I've made a vague arrangement to go for dinner with Kate and Lauren but the likelihood of it happening before next Christmas is slim to nil, since it hinges on finding a date that all three of us can do. Even though I have zero plans, I still want my hair to hang in there for the milestone.

For all my wishing, hoping and deliberately not washing, three days before my birthday, my hair is falling out in clumps. It starts with a few extra strands here and there – on the pillow, in my hairbrush, barely noticeable. But when I do the tug test, I pull away a whole section. It doesn't hurt to pull out the hairs but my scalp feels sore, as if it's sunburnt.

It's time.

I wish I could make it to my birthday without losing my hair. I could not wash it for the next couple of days but my head is itchy and my hair feels greasy. It's like a tooth that is hanging on a string and I know it'll feel so much better when it's out.

I scratch at my scalp. Another clump falls out, floating down onto the pillow. I scratch again. It feels good, satisfying, to scratch the itch.

I want to wash it so badly. I want to pull it violently out of my head. The hair is already dead. Like with the tumour, I just want it out.

Slow-braised lamb

The morning of my thirty-second birthday, the weekend before chemo number two, I wake up to find the biggest pile of pillow hair I've seen so far, a mound of red locks that must have left a hole the size of a fifty pence coin on the back of my scalp.

I sit up in bed and feel around the back of my head and down to the nape of my neck. The sunburnt feeling has mostly gone and although I can feel a thin patch, there's still hair covering all parts of my head.

I switch on the bedside lamp and walk to the full-length mirror, sitting down on the floor facing it, hairbrush in hand. As gently as I can manage, I brush through a tiny section, attempting to make some semblance of a hairdo.

But it's no use. Hair comes away on the brush with every stroke and there is more sitting loose on my scalp. If I shower, the weight of the water will wash it away.

My heart pounds. I need to do this.

I plod into the bathroom, Oreo hot on my heels. I open the door gently, careful not to wake Dad on the sofa, since he got here so late last night. I squeeze a little bubble bath into the tub. As it fills with water, I strip off my pyjamas and take a long look at myself in the mirror. The hair cut makes me look like a boy. It felt feminine at first, with the fringe styled sexily across my face by the hairdresser, but the greasier and more lifeless it gets and the longer I have to deal with it, the less it looks like it did then.

I will never look like this again.

I run my right hand through my hair with my fingers spread out like a comb, knowing what it will do. I close my eyes and softly yank. The pain is minimal. It is satisfying to pull out a chunk, like peeling dead skin after sunburn or picking a scab.

I scan the bathroom for somewhere to put the handful of hairs that have come away. I see a cardboard coffee cup that Dad must have discarded on the windowsill after his long drive back. The perfect disposal unit.

I set the cup down on the floor beside the tub and poke one foot into the water. The temperature is just right, so I lower myself in, easing back until my hair touches the water – the last time I'll feel this sensation for a while.

Allowing the water to envelop me, I relish the feeling of soaking the greasy crop that has weighed my head down for days now. I've been trying so hard to last until today but I can't put this off any longer.

When I'm ready, I run a hand across the top of my head once, then again, this time taking a section of hair between my fingers. It comes away effortlessly, like slow-braised lamb falling off the bone. I pick the wet, lifeless clump out of the bathtub, wring the water out and push it inside the coffee cup.

By the time I've finished pulling every last strand from my head, the cup is full to bursting. I push down the mush of strands as if I'm compressing the contents of a bin bag. The cup feels heavier than if it was filled with coffee, the hair is so dense and wet.

Closer to my scalp there are stubborn sections and I feel as if I'm pulling endlessly. Eventually I can feel my whole skull with my fingers, just a few soft tufts remaining on my head.

I squeeze a blob of shampoo and rub it between my palms,

then gently over my scalp. It feels like a baby's head, soft and rounded.

Then I plunge once more, lying back in the tub until the water surrounds my face, staring up at the cracks in the ceiling. *Don't fall asleep in there, Jess.* I hear Mum's words in my head.

I know that as soon as I stand again, I will see my reflection in the mirror, and there will be no turning back. No way to reverse this, no way to put the hair back on my head.

I sit up, blacking out for a second and grabbing onto the side of the bath. When my vision adjusts, I see myself.

My head is a canvas of white skin with uneven tufts of soft, light hair springing up in random places. I look like a newborn chick, not quite ready to face the world.

By the time I've plucked up the courage to leave the bathroom, it is eight a.m. I try to wrap a towel around my head in the usual way but it doesn't stay in place without a mop of hair to hold it. Eventually I secure it with a hand and walk cautiously down the corridor, crawling back into bed and picking up my phone to text Annabel.

I'm bald

Annabel's reply comes immediately.

Shit. You OK? xoxo

Surprisingly relieved.

Being bald is liberating, right?! xo

I have a bit of a situation. Hang on . . .

I hold the phone up to my face and take a selfie to capture the random sprouts of hair.

Annabel is typing . . . reads the screen. Then it stops. Starts again. Stops. Great – now even my fellow cancer patient doesn't know what to say to me.

Finally, her reply comes.

241

Welcome to the club, Tweetie Pie! Just shave that shit off. You're going to look beautiful xoxo

I take a deep breath and walk to the living room, where Dad is still asleep. I tap gently on his shoulder until he stirs.

'Jess,' he says, peeling one eye open.

I stand in front of him with the towel wrapped around my head while he adjusts his vision.

'Happy birthday, love,' he says, sitting up on the sofa bed. 'You OK?'

I pat my hands on the towel, indicating my head.

'Please don't be shocked . . . I'm bald.'

I wait for the reply. One second, two seconds, three seconds . . .

'Oh, love.'

'Promise you won't laugh?'

He looks at me with an expression that says, 'as if I would', and waits for me to take the towel away.

I turn my back to him as I peel the towel from my head. Then slowly I turn to face him on the sofa.

He has tears in his eyes.

'Bloody hell, Jessie,' he says. 'Only you could look this good.'

Hampstead Heath

I don't want to burden Dad by asking him to come with me to the hairdresser, so I call Lauren. She wishes me happy birthday and says she's up for seeing me tonight and will text me later with a plan, but right now she's busy with wedmin and can't decide between the arancini balls and the miniature Yorkshire pudding canapés. I tell her to go with the Yorkshires – *always* go with Yorkshires – and then hang up, feeling a little dejected.

I text Aisha, knowing she's always up for joining me. She's probably only watching *Saturday Kitchen* in her pyjamas anyway.

Oh mate, I'm so sorry, she replies. Date last night with the DJ was amazing, but I have the worst hangover. I literally feel like I'm going to die x

So much for those films where the friends offer to shave their heads for the one who's going through cancer treatment. Apparently mine are all too busy to care.

Annabel is the last person I message. It's not that she's my last choice – far from it – but I don't want to burden her when she's going through so much herself.

She jumps at the chance.

I thought you might be busy with your friends but I was hoping we could meet up . . . I have a surprise for you. xoxo

*

243

I open the post while I wait for Annabel to arrive. There are cards from Aunty Cath, various other distant relatives and a few of Mum's friends. Cath and the boys have sent a gorgeous hamper filled with thoughtful, healthy food gifts – almond butter, sesame seed bars and the all-healing kale chips. She's also enclosed a new cake recipe book that I saw featured in *Perfect Bake*. I suspect she's joining the band wagon of trying to get me back into baking.

Dad gives me a cat-themed card, in which he has written: '*Thirty-two years of taxi rides, interest-free loans and tearing my hair out with worry, but I wouldn't change it for the world. The best of years to my best girl. Mum would be proud. Love Dad XX* '.

He has enclosed a cheque to contribute to 'the next big adventure'.

Then, with a cautious look on his face, he hands me something wrapped in green crepe paper. I gasp as I open Mum's old recipe file, the one where she scribbled all her recipes by hand, the pages blotched and sticky with flour stains.

'Oh Dad,' I say, gulping as I trace the pad of my index finger over the cover. Just holding it in my hands takes me back to baking with her in the tea rooms.

'For when you're ready, love,' he says, with a wink.

Annabel arrives at ten a.m. with a package in her hand. I can see Joe waiting in the car behind her, his buzz cut hidden under a cream-coloured beanie.

'Happy birthday, old woman!' Bel says, throwing her arms out when she greets me on the doorstep.

'Aw, thank you,' I say, putting my hand on my head to check my woolly hat is still there. 'Does Joe want to come in?'

'He's our chauffeur for the day,' she says. 'Let me talk you through the plan and then we're off.'

'Shall I put the kettle on?' I motion for her to come in and give Joe a wave.

'No time,' she says, handing me the small package. 'Here, open this.'

We go through to the kitchen, where she greets Dad with a hug. I rip open the paper and pull out a handmade card on top of another package. The card is printed with stamped letters, and reads, 'Ten things to do when you're thirty-two'.

'What is it?' I say.

'Have a look!'

I open the card and realize it's a booklet, with each left-hand page listing an activity and each right-hand page with four little photo corners waiting for a picture. The first page reads 'Hair twins' and the second says 'Breakfast of champions'. I start to turn another page but she puts out her hand to stop me.

'Each page is a surprise,' she says. 'You can only see the next thing on the list when you've done the one before it. Now open your proper present.'

I set the booklet down on the kitchen table and start to open the gift. Dad observes the proceedings, looking amused.

I pull out a box and see that it's a Polaroid camera with a set of film. It's too much.

'Annabel, you really shouldn't have . . .'

'What's the point of me getting my disability benefits if I can't spend it?' Bel says. 'We're going to take a picture of everything that happens on your birthday and stick them in this book. Something you can keep forever.'

'This is amazing,' I say. I'm lost for words. It's the most special gift I've ever received.

'Ready for the first item on the list?' she says.

I nod. 'Hair twins' makes me think she's taking me wig shopping again.

'Alright,' she says. 'Ready to go properly bald?'

She takes an electric razor out of her bag.

'Where did you get that from?' I'm getting goose pimples on my arms.

'It's Joe's,' she says. 'Don't worry, I'm a pro. I always do his hair for him. And since I'm on palliative chemo tablets now, my hair gets super thin but doesn't fall out completely, so I shave it.'

She gestures for me to sit at the kitchen bench in front of her. Dad brings over two cups of tea – we're going to need them after all.

I sit still as the razor stirs to life. A moment later, the feel of a light tickle against the nape of my neck as it skims its way over my head. Dad has left the room.

It takes all of two minutes as she gently removes the tufts of hair from my scalp, then switches off the razor to perfect silence.

'All done,' she says, coming around to the front of the chair. 'How does that feel?'

I run a palm over the top of my head and down to my neck. There are a few tiny bits of stubble but apart from that it's smooth – the hair has fallen clean out at the roots.

'It feels like . . .' I can't find the words. Truly all I feel is relief, but I need to see it for myself.

We walk through to the hallway mirror and she puts a hand on my shoulder for support as I approach to get a good look. My eyelashes, still intact for now, look longer than ever.

'I actually kind of love it.'

'It suits you,' she says.

I turn towards her and give her a hug.

'Ready for the first pic?'

She retrieves the Polaroid from the kitchen and leaves her

own black bob on the table. Then we put our heads together and take a selfie.

She wafts the photograph as it dries and we watch as the first image emerges. With our bald, white heads, we really do almost look like sisters.

'Hair twins, see?' She hands me the booklet and I slot the Polaroid picture into the first page.

'We better get going,' she says.

'What should I wear?'

She looks me up and down. I'm wearing jeans and a T-shirt, while she has on a cute top with tiny shorts, thick black tights and her Converse.

'It's your birthday, why not throw something nice on? I'll wait in the car.'

I ransack my room looking for something comfy enough to wear around all day but nice enough in case we're going somewhere special. Ten minutes later, I've decided on a floaty, thigh-length electric-blue dress that Mum bought me with my cosy leather jacket, black tights to match Annabel's and some sturdy black boots that have seen me through many a winter.

I stare at myself in the mirror as I consider whether to go out like this, with my bald head on show. It looks almost cool with the leather jacket, but I'm not sure I'm ready to brave the world with it just yet, not to mention I'll be freezing. Then I remember the blue wig and fit it onto my head for the first time since our shopping day in Peckham.

Without my hair to pad it out, the wig looks perfect and the colour matches my dress almost exactly. It's as if Mum knew what was to come. I feel confident as I stride out to the car with my blue dress and wig and a heap of mascara to emphasize my lashes while I still have them.

'Gorgeous,' Annabel says, when I reach the car.

Joe gets out to greet me, throwing his arms out for a proper hug and wishing me happy birthday before driving off towards our first destination.

Stop number one is Maltby Street Market, where Annabel buys us custard doughnuts and horseradish-laced Bloody Marys for breakfast. We sit in the sun at the end of the narrow lane of stalls selling every kind of bread, pastry and coffee, and we snap a selfie of the three of us holding up our doughnuts and cocktails.

As soon as I bite into the custard-filled pillow of dough, I am taken straight back to baking with Mum in a way that I haven't revisited since she was alive. It's the way the sugar catches in my throat and coats my lips, and the combination of the soft, chewy dough with the smooth, cool custard inside.

'You alright there, Jess?' Joe says, catching me in my moment of pleasure.

'Mmm,' I manage, closing my eyes and raising my shoulders in exaggerated ecstasy.

'They're good, aren't they?' Annabel says. 'You have to get here early to get the doughnuts before they sell out.'

'Annabel has been dragging me here since it opened a few years ago,' Joe says, finishing off the last of his doughnut and slurping his cocktail. 'You won't find a better doughnut in London.'

'Well,' I say, raising an eyebrow.

When the two of them look at me with the same 'go on then' expression, I realize how alike they are. It's something about the cute little button nose and swimming-pool blue eyes. Peas in a pod.

I shake my head. 'No, it's nothing. I just, I used to make doughnuts with my mum. Very similar to these ones, in fact. The best.'

'Is that right?' Annabel says. 'Well, I think we'll be the judge of that, won't we Joe?'

Joe looks at his sister and laughs. 'You have two willing testers right here, whenever you need us.'

I smile. Being here with the two of them is bringing back my urge to bake.

'Come on,' Annabel says, springing up and holding out two hands to help Joe and me up.

A few minutes later, we're inside a quirky antique store, where every inch of space is crammed with curious relics. Enamel lampshades hang from the ceiling and there are rugs and prints on the walls.

Joe looks down at his phone and hovers his finger over a button. 'Whoever finds the most hideous object wins a prize. You have two minutes, starting NOW.'

Annabel runs off around the corner and Joe crouches down to scrabble through a wooden chest. I'm clearly at a disadvantage as they must have been playing this game for years.

I round a different corner and start poking through shelves of ornaments that look like the sort of junk we found in my grandad's place when he died. I settle on a suitably hideous gravy boat shaped like a squirrel.

When the two minutes are up, Joe and Annabel reappear, each looking sheepish, with their hands behind their backs. I copy them, hiding the boat behind my back too.

'Alright, you go first,' Joe says.

I present my squirrel and hold it up for inspection.

'Not bad,' Joe says. 'Go on then, Bel.'

With a look of pure glee, Annabel reveals her item: a taxidermied weasel, its mouth open to reveal sharp little teeth, as if frozen mid-hiss.

I take a step back. 'That's so gross.'

Joe laughs. 'Taxidermied animals. Every. Freaking. Time. You're obsessed!'

'What?' she says, grinning. 'She's cute. I think I'll call her Winnie.'

Joe mock-sighs. 'Alright, you guys ready? Close your eyes.'

We both nod and shut our eyes, until he instructs us to open them on the count of three.

What I see in front of me is truly hideous. Joe cradles a porcelain doll with curled white hair like a barrister's wig and teeth that jut out in every direction. The most haunted part is its eyes, which stare straight ahead, blank and blind.

'That. Is. Evil,' Annabel says, backing away.

'Well I think it's clear I win,' Joe says, with a Disney villain laugh. 'Alright, let's do a pic and head off.'

As we cram together to pose for the Polaroid, a shop assistant appears from around the corner with a loud 'ahem' and points to a sign that says 'Do Not Touch'.

We quickly take the picture and apologize profusely, before running out of the shop and collapsing into giggles on the street.

Three hours later, we park on a side street near Hampstead Heath. I know what's coming, and I'm not looking forward to it. In fact, I'm dreading it almost as much as my next chemo.

'It'll be fun!' Annabel says, as we walk through the park towards the Mixed Bathing Pond. 'Once you get over the initial shock.'

On the one hand, it's a terrible idea. I'm not supposed to swim in pools during chemo because of the infection risk. Annabel insists an outdoor pond is less germy, though I suspect duck shit is worse than human bacteria. But she says there are men and women as old as ninety who swim in the pond, and if they don't have a heart attack from the cold then

I'm sure I'll be fine. Besides, given that she's up for it with incurable cancer, I can hardly protest.

We arrive at the pond to find people giggling and squealing as they strip down to their swimming costumes and woolly hats. There's an atmosphere of camaraderie that makes me glad we came.

'I forgot to mention that my prize for winning the Hideous Antiques Olympics is exemption from going in,' Joe says with a smug look on his face, as we find a spot on the jetty where we can take off some layers and dump our clothes.

'Joe never goes in,' Annabel says, looking at me and shaking her head.

'Because only a certified nut job would want to swim in seven-degree water that's full of pond scum and God knows what else,' he says.

'Ignore him,' Bel says. 'I started wild swimming when they told me I was going to die. It's good for mental health, apparently. I'll take that.' She shrugs.

We stand shivering for a minute before it's time to approach the platform and jump into the murky water, where men and women bob up and down in their colourful hats, shrieking and screaming while posing for photos. I find myself wishing the pond had iced over so we'd have an excuse not to go in.

Annabel turns to me, putting her hands on my forearms. 'Ready?'

'Not. At. All.' My teeth are chattering just thinking about plunging into the cold, dark water. I'm afraid I'll have a heart attack and be too far from an ambulance to get help. But then I look at Joe in his woolly beanie, holding two cosy-looking towels. He gives me an encouraging nod, as if giving me permission to indulge Annabel in the thing that brings her so much joy.

Annabel puts her arms around me and jigs up and down,

trying to transfer some body heat. 'The more we wait around, the colder we'll be. Just do it.'

She separates from me then takes a step away. Within a moment, she's in the water, squealing with the cold before laughing and shouting 'Come in! It's like a jacuzzi!'

New year, new start.

I grit my teeth and hold my nose as I step forward and plunge, going against all my instincts.

The shock is instant. I try to move my legs but everything is numb from the waist down. I flail my arms around, feeling like I'm going to drown.

Annabel swims up and grabs hold of me. 'Breathe,' she says. 'Stop trying to kick for a second and breathe. In, out.'

I remember Mum's advice to Aunty Cath – stop kicking, just float. I breathe with her for a moment, doing my best not to panic. Within seconds, I start to feel the life back in my limbs. Everything is tingling, my hands, my toes, my fingers.

'You OK?' she says.

I manage a nod, barely able to speak.

I start to kick to keep myself warm and Annabel does the same. Then I become aware of the laughter, giggles and screams again as the people around us enjoy the sensation of pride and achievement.

Soon Annabel and I are laughing and shrieking too, and for a moment I feel like everything in life is as it should be.

'WE'RE ALIVE!' she shouts, throwing her arms out and back into the water.

'We're alive!' I shout.

Within moments, the people around us are joining in, and a buzz runs through me at the echoes and echoes of 'We're alive!'

'Hey, girls, over here,' Joe says, waving from the jetty with the camera in his hands. I tread water beside Bel and do my best to grin through the cold as Joe snaps the photo.

Annabel starts to swim towards the ledge and I follow her, copying as she uses her arms to pull herself out. Joe holds out the towels and envelops us in their warmth, reminding me of getting out of the bath into my mother's arms as a kid.

My teeth are chattering and Annabel's lips are blue but I've never felt euphoria like it. My skin is tingling. I feel radiant, inside and out.

'I meant what I said, you know,' she says. 'I know everyone thinks I'm dying, but I'm not dying, I'm alive.'

I'm too numb to speak but I know exactly what she means.

We dry ourselves off and pull on our clothes before following the crowd to buy hot chocolate and warm up our hands. Inside the toasty cafc, we get talking to a group of older women who also braved a dip.

When one of the ladies comments on how young and sprightly we are, my instinct is to keep schtum. We don't need to tell them we have cancer to know we've done something to feel proud of. But when Annabel casually tells them we're cancer patients, they're anything but pitiful. Two of them have had cancer too, and the conversation quickly descends into a kind of chemo bants. We talk for ages about how amazing and freeing it felt to be in the water, even if we were only in there for a few minutes.

For the rest of the afternoon, my head feels clearer, my mind calmer, and I'm positive about the year to come. I can see why Annabel loves it. I feel like I've massaged my soul.

By seven o'clock, the book is full of Polaroids. Breakfast on the Maltby Street Ropewalk with matching blue and black wigs and Joe in the middle, a stunning shot of the whole of

London from the peak of Hampstead Heath, the photo of us with blue lips in the pond, and then champagne and finger sandwiches over afternoon tea at Claridge's. We've covered more of London in one day than I've done in the last ten years.

Joe has accompanied us everywhere, carrying our bags like a patient sherpa and pepping us up with refreshments and good humour. Only the tenth page of my book remains unopened.

'Can I look yet?'

I'm not sure what to expect, though I'd be perfectly happy to slouch on the sofa and watch a movie with our feet up. If this is how exhausted I am, I can't imagine how Bel must feel.

'Not yet,' she says, snatching the book from my hands. 'We need to nip home to get changed.'

In the car, I check my phone and realize that Lauren still hasn't texted me. She couldn't even make more than a half-hearted suggestion to meet me on my birthday. Thank God for Joe and Annabel.

We pull up outside my flat and all three of us get out, Joe following us down the path to my front door. I put the key in the lock but I'm met with resistance. Then it opens from the inside.

'Dad?' I say. I can smell something odd, incense maybe.

Before I can take two steps into the flat, there are lights flung on and sudden music and . . . 'SURPRISE!' Lauren jumps out first, hugging me with the most ridiculous grin on her face.

'Oh my God, I . . .'

Charlie stands behind Lauren, then there's Kate and Colm, Aisha, Clara from next-door, Aunty Cath and my cousins. Even Priya and Mags are here. There's a huge disco ball hanging over the floor and everyone is wearing neon accessories, including Mags, who wears a big pair of yellow rave specs. In the corner, there's even a DJ, my cousin Kit, wearing a fluor-escent headpiece.

'Turn the page,' Bel says, thrusting the booklet into my hands.

I turn it. It reads 'Family'. She brought them all together to give me the birthday party I never expected to have. I can't possibly think how I'm going to thank her.

Everyone congratulates and hugs me, handing me gifts and prosecco, while Charlie dispenses homemade whisky sours from a makeshift bar in the corner.

'I felt sooooo awful lying to you this morning,' Lauren says, giving me a guilty face. 'This was all her idea.'

She points to Annabel, then steps forward and gives her a hug to properly introduce herself. Aisha does the same.

'But how did you . . .?' I turn to Annabel, trying to work out how she managed to contact all my friends and family and still keep this a secret.

'I have my ways,' she says, patting her nose with her index finger.

'This is the best present ever, thank you,' I say, hugging them in turn.

'You deserve it,' Annabel says, hugging me back. 'We need to take your Polaroid.'

She shouts to the group to get in formation, then Joe directs us into the picture. Dad steps in to grab the camera to let Joe get in the shot, but Joe turns it around to take a selfie.

'Three, two, one, cheeeese,' Joe says, pushing the button.

The picture plops out and Annabel waves it around in her hand until it dries. We stick it in the book together, the perfect memento from the perfect day.

The evening descends into a blur of cocktails and dancing, with Lauren and I heckling DJ Kit to play old-school disco tunes like 'Oops Upside Your Head', then coaxing the entire party into the accompanying row-the-boat clapping routine on the floor. When Eminem's 'Without Me' comes on, Joe and Annabel launch into a flawless rendition of the entire rap, and I can picture them as kids, practising together in front of the mirror. Just as I'm about to collapse on the sofa with Annabel, Joe gestures for me to grab his hips and instigates a mini conga around my tiny living room, which has everyone in stitches. Mum would have loved the entire night.

I fall asleep almost as soon as my head hits the pillow, Oreo equally exhausted from all the activity. The only thing stopping this from being the best birthday ever is wondering how many Annabel might have left of her own.

When life gives you lemons

For the first time in years – since before we knew Mum was really sick – I open the pantry door and reach for a heavy bag of flour. I have to use both arms because I'm so weak from the second chemo, but I manage to get it down, a cloud of flour puffing out of the bag as I set it on the worktop with a thump.

It takes me some moments to remember what comes next. I had the routine down to a tee; I'm proud of the fact that I never needed to consult Mum's hand-written recipe book – this was one she'd taught me and I'd learned off by heart, but now I'm struggling to recall it.

I step back into the pantry and reach for sugar, sea salt, yeast. Surely if I lay it all out, it'll come back to me.

I'm struggling to remember how many grams of flour to use. Then I recall Mum's voice in my head singing, 'I would walk five hundred miles and I would walk five hundred more'. Of course. Five hundred grams, how could I forget?

I open my phone and stick on an album of seventies tunes that I haven't listened to since she died, and I'm instantly transported back to our little baking ritual.

I measure out the required amounts and stir together the flour and water with my fingers. Sticky dough latches on to my skin and I enjoy the feeling as I scrape it off with a spatula, nicking at my fingers as I go.

It isn't long before the dough takes a familiar form, the yeast smell fills the air and I'm back in my comfort zone. I section the dough into balls and then loosely, gently, roll and knead, roll and knead. It's hard not to see the comparison between these perfectly rounded lumps of pale dough and the breast reconstruction photos that Nurse Rose showed me in a catalogue of mastectomy options. Mum would have laughed at the comparison, perhaps held the dough balls up to her chest and sang 'Like a Virgin'.

We always liked to sing while we baked. It was something I grew up with, the time just for Mum and me, singing along to songs and doing silly voices. On the best days, Mum would let me help in the tea rooms and Dad would go out and leave us to it. On the best days, Mum would dance around the kitchen with a wooden spoon. She taught me always to dance while cooking because it helps put love into the food.

I stick the balls on the side and wait for them to prove, lapping up the nostalgic scent of yeast permeating through the kitchen.

After lunch, I make myself a peppermint tea and log in to my work emails. It's been six days since the second chemo and I'm starting to recover from the migraine-level headaches, light aversion, constipation and sickness. For several days after each round, I lose my appetite for tea and coffee, which makes the headaches even worse because I'm effectively going cold turkey from caffeine. I should see it as an opportunity to give up caffeine for good, but it's a part of my routine that makes me feel normal. I can't remember the last time anyone invited me to meet them for herbal tea.

As I sift through my emails, I can tell the team are buckling under the added workload and I know I owe them an explanation. Whereas last month I told them I was taking the week off for a 'medical procedure' and this time I told them I had to deal with 'a few health issues', I know there's only so long I can keep it a secret, especially now I've lost my hair. Plus, after seeing the way those ladies responded to Annabel's openness at the Hampstead ponds on my birthday, I'm no longer sure that keeping it a secret is the best option.

For the rest of the afternoon, I while away the time doing admin for Lauren's hen do. Kate has mostly resolved the issue of the non-payers – there's nothing like a cancer bombshell to guilt people into action. I check my bank account with gritted teeth and breathe a sigh of relief. True to his word, Johnny has continued to pay his part of the rent. At least I still have a few months before the contract ends and I have to find a new flatmate.

Now I'm tasked with creating a photo book for Lauren, which is not a bad job, given I'm going to be holed up in bed for another day or two. While a routine Facebook stalk usually leaves me feeling miserable, this time looking through pictures of me and Lauren over the years puts a smile on my face. We've had so many laughs, from falling on our faces in surfing lessons to getting blackout drunk in Temple Bar in Dublin. It's good to remember the fun Lauren, not just the wedding-obsessed version of late.

I move from Facebook to a box of old albums, going back to our sixth-form days and our first holiday together post school. The outfits we wore back then make me snigger – if Dad had known I essentially went out in nothing more than my bra and knickers, he'd have grounded me for life. We went out dancing every night in tiny boob tubes and hot pants, tottering around on far-too-high heels and drinking jelly shots from strange men's bellies. There are pictures of Lauren with her arm draped around various conquests, from the Scottish holiday rep we met at our villa to a Swedish guy with blonde

curtains who she shagged on the beach. Kate and I lived vicari-
ously through her, queueing up at the payphone to call the
guys we were dating back home every day.

I enjoyed watching Lauren when she was young and wild
and free, but the truth is I've always preferred the buzz
and security that comes from being part of a two. I realize
now that I miss it. I miss the regularity of having someone's
arms to wrap around me, someone who cares about me
and looks out for me. I miss being able to kiss, being able
to feel. It's only been a month since I broke up with Johnny
but I feel like we fell out of love a long time ago. Of course I
loved him, but in hindsight, I don't think I'd been *in* love for
a while.

I always thought that Mum being diagnosed with cancer
at the very start of our relationship brought Johnny and I
together, but now I realize it also tore us apart. Our honeymoon period was cut short and, after those first few months
of carefree fun, we were weighed down with hospital appointments and chemo sessions. By the time Mum was in remission,
we were too serious and settled to return to the twenty-four-
hour sex marathons; we were like an old married couple. Then
no sooner had we started to make time for ourselves, Mum
was diagnosed again and deteriorating fast.

Looking back, I think Johnny's suggestion that we move
in together just before Mum died was a sticking plaster to
keep us together. A flat of our own, a cat of our own, but
none of it was enough in the end. I'd been going through the
motions, picturing our future together – marriage, kids, the
works – partly because that was what everyone did. I realize
now that I was grieving Johnny while we were still together,
and I'm finally starting to feel OK. I'm finally starting to feel
ready to move on.

*

The next morning, I make my way down to the kitchen to find the proved balls of dough, glistening as the sun streams in. I dust down the fryer and boil the kettle while I wait for it to heat up. Then I take out lemons, butter, sugar and eggs and start to make the filling, licking my fingers as I go.

I plop the doughnuts into the sizzling vat of oil and watch as they float on top like buoys bobbing out at sea, browning on one side for two minutes before I flip them over to brown on the other.

When they're done, I take them out and rest them on baking paper for the fat to drain off until they're cool enough for me to handle. Then I dip them in a bowl of sugar, tossing and turning until they're covered in white powder.

I lick my fingers and then my lips. Refined sugar mixed with the taste of freshly baked dough. Nothing reminds me more of Mum.

I savour the taste for a few more moments then make a hole in the first doughnut and push in the nozzle of the piping bag, funnelling in lemon curd until it pops out the top like a nipple. I fill six with the curd and another six with raspberry jam, finding one of the professional-style cardboard boxes I used to buy to take my doughnuts in for the *Perfect Bake* team.

'Doughnuts for breakfast?' Dad says, appearing in the doorway.

'How long have you been standing there?'

'Long enough to see you're back to your old tricks,' he says.

'Well, surprise!' I say. 'Just kidding, I'm going into work today so I thought I'd make a batch for the team. You know, see if I've still got it.'

'That's nice of you, love,' he says. 'Saved one for your old Dad though, I hope?'

'Of course,' I say, ushering him into the living room as I promise he can have tea and doughnuts as soon as they're done.

Ten minutes later, we sit side by side at the kitchen bench, eating the doughnuts and silently sipping our tea.

'Your mum would be so pleased,' Dad says. 'I wasn't sure if you'd ever bake again.'

'I promised her I would,' I say. 'Some things just take a little time, you know?'

Dad nods slowly, as if pondering his own promises to Mum.

'You know, she'd be happy you've moved on too,' I say.

He turns to face me, a little alarmed. 'Do you mean . . .?'

'I'm sorry for how I reacted before. It's been two years; you're entitled to fall in love again. It's just . . .' I don't want to cry, I really don't, but I can't stop the tears from falling. 'It's just hard.'

'I know,' he says, putting down his doughnut. 'Just because I've found someone, doesn't mean I've forgotten your mum.'

'I know.'

We sit in silence for a minute. Dad pats a wet finger on his plate to dab the remaining bits of sugar and lick them off.

I copy his move, sucking the sweet granules from my fingers.

'So what's she like?'

He looks at me, surprised.

'Lizzie,' I say. 'Tell me about her.'

'Oh, love,' he says. 'She's a good companion.'

I know he's playing it down, making out like she's just a friend, that she'll never match up to Mum. 'But what's she *like*? Does she make you laugh?'

He smiles. 'She's kind and she's thoughtful. And she cooks a ruddy good chicken and mushroom pie.'

'Well why didn't you say so sooner?' I laugh.

Dad puts his tea down and turns to look at me.

'It's good to have the old Jessie back.'

Inspirational

'Oh my days, Jessica Jackson, is that what I think it is?' Aisha moves towards the box of doughnuts with her arms outstretched, then opens it, pokes her head inside and inhales for about twenty seconds.

She straightens up and throws her arms around me. 'I cannot even tell you how welcome this is right now. I've missed you so much this week. Tabitha has been insufferable.'

I laugh. 'I can imagine. Has she said anything about me being off?'

I glance over at our row of desks across the floor, where I can see Tabitha typing away at her computer.

'She was trying to get it out of me, why you were off. I think she still thinks you're preggo.'

'Ha.'

'Cute hat, by the way.'

I pat my blue woolly hat, my pulse racing as I remember what I'm about to do. Underneath it, I'm completely stark bald.

'Hey, you'll be OK,' Aisha says, touching my arm and giving me a reassuring nod.

We walk over together to the team, where I'm greeted like a returnee soldier after a war, even though none of them knows the reason for my mystery sick leave.

'Not only do we have the pleasure of Jess today, but she also brought us her famous doughnuts, and let me tell you, once you've tried a Jessica Jackson doughnut you will *never* go back,' Aisha says.

Tabitha looks up from her screen. 'Nice to have you back in our *presence*.'

It's not what she says, but the tone in which she says it, the emphasis on the word 'presence', as if I've been skiving in the Seychelles instead of stuck in bed in agony after chemo. I can feel my blood beginning to boil. But I realize I can hardly blame her since I haven't exactly been honest.

I dump the box on the spare desk and people start to gravitate towards it, reaching in to select the fattest ones. I'll need to master the vegan version so that Tabitha can try them too.

As I watch them bite into their doughnuts, holding out their palms to catch the dripping fillings, I try to work up the courage to do what I'm about to do. I glance at Aisha, my heart pounding.

She nods and gives me an encouraging smile. I summon the image of Annabel, flailing her arms about in the middle of the Hampstead pond on my birthday, shouting at the top of her lungs.

I'm alive. I have nothing to hide.

'I have a little announcement to make,' I say.

A row of eyes look up at me from half-eaten doughnuts. Even Tabitha swivels in her chair to face me.

I put my hand on my bobble hat, trying to find the courage to take it off. It's as if my hand is glued to my head.

'About this,' I say. 'I know certain people on this team might feel I've been shirking my responsibilities lately.'

Tabitha looks down at the floor.

'I want you to know this magazine is my number one priority and I'm working around the clock to do the best job I can.

There are reasons why I didn't tell you this before, but, well, now I realize I was wrong.'

Tabitha looks up at me now, confused, expectant.

I take a deep breath and use the bobble to lift the hat off my head, like a butler lifting the silver dome from a platter of food. I feel so exposed, my head cold and breezy. I can't help running my hand over it.

'So yeah, I have cancer.'

I wait for the penny to drop, the faces to fall. I glance up and see that the intern is crying and the features writer's mouth has fallen open. But it is Tabitha's expression that gets me.

In this moment, every bit of rivalry falls away. Tabitha's face runs through guilt, then sadness, then compassion. She stands up from her desk and takes a step towards me.

'Why didn't you say something sooner?' She looks at my bald head, then back to my eyes, shaking her head. 'I would have helped you, I would have . . .'

'It's OK,' I say. This is exactly what I didn't want, pity. But seeing the way Annabel has embraced her life has made me want to make the most of mine too. Cancer is not something to be ashamed of.

'I don't want you to feel sorry for me,' I say, addressing the team. 'If I'm here right now in the office, it's because I feel good enough to be here. I have chemo every three weeks so I'll need to take at least a week off every three, maybe more. And the good news is there's only four rounds to go. But I love this job, it keeps me alive, and I'm doing fine, so you don't need to worry. Any questions?'

There's the usual silence that comes when anyone opens up questions in a presentation, before one person opens the flood gates and the questions pour out. *What is chemo like? Did it hurt to lose your hair? Will it grow back?*

Aisha and the intern make tea and we sit in a circle of office

,, t

chairs while I answer their questions in a sort of Audience with Jess.

I didn't know I wanted to share it, but it all comes flooding out. The hot flushes, the steroids and the jabs I now have to take to keep my white blood cell count up. Aisha flinches as I describe the self-injections, but I'm used to it, what with the fertility treatment and now this.

'And about the air-con,' I say, eyeing the dial on the wall that has long been the subject of Office Air-Con Wars. 'I get hot flushes as a side effect of the chemo. So if you see me stripping off or turning it to Arctic, that's why.'

There are wows and 'I just can't believe its' as the news sinks in across the team, until finally I tell them we need to get back to work, but that they can come to me if they have any questions, rather than gossiping behind my back.

'Of course,' Tabitha says. 'I'm so glad you've told us. We're here to help you through your journey.'

I cringe at the word 'journey'. It reminds me of the kids on *The X Factor* who burst into tears and say, 'My nan died and if I don't become a singer by the time I'm fifteen I'll *literally* die because I've wanted this my *whole life*.' I make a mental note to add it to the banned words list at Chemo Club.

'Actually,' I say, figuring I should start as I mean to go on. They won't know if I don't tell them. 'I've learned there are certain things you shouldn't say when someone is going through cancer. I've been guilty of this myself but from now on, at this magazine, we don't use the word "battle". Saying that someone "lost their battle" or their "fight" against cancer suggests that they failed in some way, that they didn't have enough willpower or strength. It's not something you can train yourself up to beat.'

'So what should we say instead?' Tabitha says, genuinely open to my advice.

'Write that the person died,' I say, realizing I've learned a lot from Annabel in these past couple of months. A lot about acceptance. 'We don't often talk about death, but it's the only thing that's certain in life. We need to learn to talk about it.'

Tabitha nods, both eyebrows slightly raised, for once really listening to what I'm saying.

'And can we not say "journey" either?' I add, with a grin this time. 'Sorry Tabitha, that one's just a personal pet peeve.'

Aisha holds up a notepad where she's been writing down the list of banned words. 'I'll circulate this in a bit so you can reprimand us if we don't adhere.'

'Thanks Aish,' I say, laughing at her organization.

'Thank you for being so open with us, Jess,' Tabitha says. 'And let me know if you want a hand in the fashion cupboard. It's like a junkyard in there but I promise it's an organized mess. I think we have some cool hats somewhere.'

'Thanks Tabitha,' I say. For the first time ever, I can see that she genuinely wants to help.

'You did great in there,' Aisha says, tearing off a chunk of her baguette.

I blow on my soup and nod in thanks. 'How did Tabitha get on this week?'

Aisha makes a face.

'That bad?' I laugh.

'Nah, she's great. She's just struggling without you.'

'Without me? But I've barely done anything.'

'Are you kidding me, Jess? You're the poster girl around here, everyone talks about you all the time. If I wasn't your bestie, I'd be jealous.'

I frown. 'But I haven't *done* anything. I just sit on my arse all day feeling sorry for myself.'

'You don't get it, Jess,' she says, waving her finger at me. 'You're inspirational.'

I frown again. 'What do you mean, *inspirational*?'

That might be another word for the banned list. It irks me when people bandy it around when referring to cancer patients, just because they've kept a smile on their face during something that happened *to* them. It's not like I've found the cure for cancer. Now *that* would be inspirational.

'Well, first of all, you've managed to get two bloody jam-packed issues to press when anyone else would have been sobbing into their pillow after everything you've been through. Second of all, you've got us all thinking differently. We were pushing out so many interviews with second-rate celebrities that no one gave a shit about and you've really made us think about the stuff that matters. You've been a mentor to me.'

'But how can I mentor you? I've hardly been here.'

She looks at me as if I'm dumb for not getting it. 'Jess, look at you. You've got your shit together more than anyone else I know. You don't need to be in the office to be a mentor. You do it by being who you are and reacting to the situation how you have done. Anyone else would have taken full sick leave if they got diagnosed with cancer, and I still think you should, by the way. But you've *volunteered* to keep working. Going on a dating site the day after you find out your boyfriend cheated? You just power through, Jess. You're so fucking strong, you always have been.'

'But . . .' It feels weird to hear Aisha saying these things. Aisha, my ballsy friend who stands up to arseholes on dating sites and says exactly what's on her mind. I never thought of myself as being like that at all.

'I know you can't see it,' she says. 'But I've looked up to you my whole career. You do realize we started as interns together?

And now look at you, powering ahead as *editor*, managing a team when I know full well you're sat in your bed feeling sick as a dog from chemo, and then coming in here and taking that hat off like "don't fuck with me"? That's *brave*, man. I fucking love you.'

'Aw,' I say, welling up for the millionth time. 'When you put it like that . . . Thank you.'

She finishes her baguette and gives me a troubled look.

'It's made me take a long, hard look at my own situation, to be honest.'

'Really?'

'Jess, I think I'm going to hand in my notice.'

'What?' No. If Aisha leaves, the whole magazine is screwed, not to mention I'd miss my work wife more than anything.

She keeps her voice down. 'This whole "you only live once" thing. You know I love being digital editor but it wasn't exactly what I set out to do.'

'So what? You're going to become a fashion designer?'

'I've applied to go back to uni,' she says, giving me a tentative look. 'Central St Martins.'

'Aish! This is amazing.' I put my spoon down and wrap my arms around her. She's been talking about wanting to go to fashion school ever since we first met, but I never thought she'd take the plunge.

She looks vulnerable and scared as she draws back from the hug. 'I don't know if I'll get in, it's a bit of a gamble.'

'Aish, of *course* you'll get in. Have you *met* yourself?'

She laughs. 'Even if I do get in, it won't be till September, so Leah will be back by then and hopefully you'll get a permanent job as well. Promise I won't screw anyone over.'

'Screw the rest of us,' I say. 'This is about you. I'm so, so pleased for you.'

'Well, if it all goes wrong, you're the one I'm blaming,' she says. 'There's no one else who could inspire me to quit my job and become an impoverished student again at this age.'

'I'll take that as a compliment,' I say, giving her a nudge and passing her a tissue. 'How will you manage with money and stuff?'

'Well, I was going to talk to you about that,' she says. 'I need to find somewhere cheaper to live, for starters. Maybe a bit further out. I don't suppose you fancy a houseshare?'

I'm so relieved I almost burst into tears. I knew I needed to sort my housing situation, but I don't think I realized quite how desperate I was until she said it.

'God, yes,' I say. 'If I'm not going to be working with you any more, I *definitely* need to be living with you. Otherwise my Aisha withdrawal symptoms are going to be extreme.'

'Thank fuck,' she says. 'I don't think I could handle any more rejection right now.'

'As if I would ever reject you,' I say, already picturing the girlie nights in at our cosy new flat somewhere. I need to get away from Clapham and the memories of Johnny and chemo.

'Deal,' she says. 'Do you think you could, er, make me doughnuts for breakfast on the reg?'

I pretend to ponder it.

'Sure, if you give me first dibs on all your new fashion finds.'

'Consider it done, roomie.'

Single Bald Female

Hi there,

I'm Jess. Thanks for clicking on my profile. I'm guessing either you're into bald chicks or you're just curious. Whatever works for you.

So . . . I could write the usual glossy spiel about how I'm some 'beautiful, funny, well-travelled, intelligent woman seeking down-to-earth, hilarious guy for in-depth conversations, a nice glass of wine and absolutely no pressure for a relationship', but there'd be a hefty disclaimer: I was diagnosed with breast cancer two months ago and I'm soon to be a wonky-boobed wonder. I'm also bald as a baby and just out of a long-term relationship . . . oh, and I don't know if I'll be able to have kids.

Still with me? OK . . . well, I'm just plain old Jess, hoping my hair will grow back luscious and thick à la Meghan Markle, except ginger. (Did I mention I'm ginger?) I love food but I hate the word 'foodie' and I'm not quite ready to embrace veganism yet. My pet hate is the word 'lol', so if you use it, chances are I won't reply. Lol.

I don't really know what I'm looking for right now, except that I'd like to go on a few dates with someone

*funny and kind, who doesn't mind me being bald for
a while. I've put a selection of photos on here – some
were taken today; the others from when I was younger
and hotter . . . and had eyebrows.*

Hope to hear from you,

Jess x

I read the profile to Annabel. It feels good to write something real, something totally honest. It's an exercise in 'what
would you do if you weren't afraid?'

'Do I sound like I love myself?' I say, spinning the MacBook
around and sliding it across the kitchen table towards her.

'Nah,' she says. 'You're saying you have cancer and you
don't give a fuck. Guys will love that.'

'You don't think I should sound a bit more . . . humble?'

'Trust me. Guys want a girl they can take care of. But
they also want someone sexy and confident who has her shit
together. You're ticking all the boxes.'

'You really think it'll work?'

'Of course it'll bloody work,' Annabel laughs, passing the
laptop back to me. 'Any guy would be lucky to have you. And
if they're put off by the bald thing then they're not right for
you anyway.'

I take a deep breath and hit 'Submit'.

*Congratulations! Your profile will be reviewed by our team
within 24 hours. Happy dating!*

8:20 p.m.
to: SingleBaldFemale
from: SweetLikeChocolate84
*Hi Jessica, just reading your profile and felt compelled to say hi!
Like you I am a cancer survivor. I was diagnosed after finding a*

lump on my testicle. Luckily it was detected early. They removed my testicle as a precaution and gave me an implant. How has the crazy world of online dating been treating you? Ryan x

8:35 p.m.
to: SingleBaldFemale
from: IrishHeart69
Hay I am not really looking at the moment (have been dating someone for a bit . . . six dates . . . shock horror) but just wanted to say fair play to ya! You are a lovely looking girl, seem to have a personality to match and love your honesty. If I wasn't seeing somebody already then I'd love to meet u.
Sorry but I have a bit of a dark sense of humour. With your possibility of infirtility think of the money we could save on condoms! LOL (just kiddin' LOL haha)
Take care, Finn

9:51 p.m.
to: SingleBaldFemale
from: SpanishEyes23
Hola Jess! Wow, so inspired by your story. You are very brave. And beautiful eyes! If you haven't guessed by my username, I'm Spanish, new to this country and new to this site. Would love to talk to you. José x

I sift through profile after profile. Annabel was right. They're hardly a catalogue of stunners but there's a surprising amount of interest in my profile and most of the guys seem pretty, well, *normal*.

There are still plenty of bathroom mirror selfies and sedated wildlife, but on the whole, the guys who have messaged me this time are much more polite and genuine, and there's a distinct absence of indecent proposals.

Take Spanish Eyes, for example. According to his profile pic, he's tanned with a nice figure and big brown eyes, he's five foot ten and 'looking for a relationship'. And Spanish – what's not to love? I hover my finger over the Reply button on José's message and ponder what to write. Is he really interested in bald Jess or have his mates put him up to it?

I decide to keep it short and simple.

Hi José, do you fancy meeting for a coffee?

'Jess?' says a tentative-sounding voice, pronouncing my name like 'Yes'.

I turn to find a smiling, brown-eyed boy, eyebrows thick like hairy caterpillars, dark hair framing his tanned skin.

'Hi,' I say, a little too gleeful, sticking my arm out to shake his hand while I go in for the left-sided air kiss, then the right. 'I'm Jess nice to meet you how are you I'm fine thanks,' I say, all in one breath, before I realize I'm still holding his hand. Christ, I'm nervous.

'Is a pleasure,' he says, emphasizing the 's's like 'sh's.

He retrieves his hand from my clammy one, and we stand for a moment, just smiling, taking each other in. I was worried I wasn't up to this, I'm still so weak from the chemo, but the minute he smiles at me, it feels worth it.

'Yes?' he says, and it takes me a second to realize he's saying my name. 'What would you like? Coffee? Tea? Some cake?'

I feel the familiar sensation of a hot flush coming on, a Mexican wave of heat that spreads from my thighs up to my neck.

'Just water please,' I say, wriggling out of my coat, one arm half-stuck inside a fur-lined sleeve.

I stumble out the front door into the cold, fresh air, collapsing onto a bench. I start to strip off the rest of my coat and jumper, then tug to rearrange my wig. By the time José joins me two minutes later, the hot flush has passed and I'm freezing again.

'You are OK?' he says. 'You are sick? Would you feel better to reschedule?'

I take a proper look at him for the first time. He is handsome – so much dark, dark hair, with eyes that are big and round and kind.

'I'm fine,' I say, feeling a little livelier as I start to pull my jumper back over my head. But as I do so, the tight neck of the jumper pulls my wig back a few centimetres, revealing a slither of milky white scalp as it comes away from my forehead. No matter how much I want to feel confident, it hits me straight away – I'm vulnerable and naked, like the little girl in the playground who cried when the boys tried to pull her skirt down.

'Let me help you,' he says, coming towards me, but I turn away from him, adjusting the wig to its rightful place with both hands.

'Does my hair look OK?' I joke, swishing my blue bob as I turn back towards him.

'It's biutiful,' he says, pronouncing it like the name of the Javier Bardem film. 'Your eyes, they are biutiful. You can wear no wig and I still think you are biutiful.'

Johnny would take the piss if my wig fell off mid-date. He'd make a joke of it, something about multiple personalities, gingers having more fun, kinky wigs . . . he'd say something to make me laugh, to make me feel better. But as far as first dates go, I'm fine with being *biutiful*.

'So you are a foodie?' he says, pronouncing the 'd' softly, so that it sounds like 'smoothie'.

'I guess,' I say, taking a split-second to remember what I wrote in my dating profile. 'I love food. Bit of a sweet tooth. What about you?'

'I am more of a salty foods kind of guy,' he says.

'Savoury,' I say.

'Yes, savoury,' he says. 'I need somebody like you to correct my English.'

'Always happy to do that,' I say.

'Do you cook?'

I get a pang of joy as I remember baking those doughnuts. I can't believe I left it so long.

'I bake,' I say. 'Doughnuts, mostly.'

'I would like to taste your doughnuts,' he says, narrowing his eyes. 'I'm sure they are berry good.'

'They're decent,' I say. I should bake another batch soon, and I need to work on the vegan ones. 'What about you, do you cook?'

'I like to make a lot of Spanish dishes and I am making very famous *croquetas*. Since coming here I start to make some English food and I learn to make the curry. I'm not quite making the fish and chips yet.'

I laugh. 'Fish and chips are not something we really cook at home. *Croquetas* though? Now you're talking. You guys have some of the best food in the world.'

'I know,' he says, beaming at the compliment. 'I miss the cooking of my mother. But I try to learn English ways now. English food and English girls.'

'You know a lot about English girls?'

'I am hoping I find out,' he says, raising an eyebrow. 'You are the first one I date.'

'No pressure then,' I laugh. He has a way of making me feel at ease. 'How am I doing so far?'

'So far, so great,' he says, and I can't help feeling a little buzzy.

He leans in slightly, and for a moment I think he's going to kiss me. Then his look changes to concern. 'You are tired,' he says, and I remember the chemo for the first time in at least ten minutes.

'I'm OK,' I say. 'I'll have a coffee and I'll be right as rain.'

This is not strictly true. I'll go to sleep as soon as I get home and I won't wake up until morning.

'Right as rain,' he repeats. 'A good English phrase. You are teaching me a lot today, Yess. I will get you some coffee!'

He jumps up, delighted to be able to help.

When he returns five minutes later, he is carrying my flat white plus a slice of ginger cake, good for nausea, as if somehow he knew.

'I *love* ginger,' I say, my mouth watering at the moist-looking slice in front of me. 'How did you know?'

He holds a hand out to touch my blue wig, and I feel a tickle against my neck. 'I take a guess, from your pictures,' he says, with another of his flirty smiles.

His hand lingers longer than is comfortable and his face turns serious.

'Tell me, Yessica, you are single for your cancer journey?'

That word again. *Journey.* Cancer is not a journey, like some road trip on Route 66. Cancer is a fucking nightmare.

'I'm single, yeah,' I say, biting my tongue, because he's trying to be nice and English is not his first language. 'I broke up with my ex a month or so ago.'

He takes my hand, picking it up like it's some sort of precious jewel. Then he holds it in both of his, looking down at my hands and back up to my face.

'Yess,' he says, his eyes drilling into mine. 'You are not alone. I am here now. I will look after you.'

Fuck cancer

'He actually said that?' says Annabel, giggling by the side of my chemo chair.

'He was dead serious,' I say, enjoying how happy she seems, listening to my dating tales.

'Andalusia sounds like a great place for a wedding,' she says, and we both laugh.

I tense my hand as Nurse Ange tightens the dial on my cannula, then I smile back at Annabel as I try my hardest to concentrate on the story.

'I mean, he is really sweet . . .' I pause as I feel the tingle in my crotch and the metallic taste of saline in the back of my throat, already making me feel sick. 'But I must admit it was *slightly* cringe when he started getting all soppy.'

'You're definitely going on a second date though, right?' says Priya from the other side of my chair.

'I think so. I mean he seems like a nice guy and he's interested in me when I look like this, and I'm not sure if I've mentioned he's absolutely gorgeous? It just depends how I feel after this next round of chemo.'

'Jess, you're a total catch,' Annabel says. 'Chemo or no chemo. Seriously. No one else could rock that wig.'

'You are beautiful, just like your father,' Nurse Ange

interrupts, looking down from my drip as she hooks up a goldfish bag of the Tizer-red stuff.

Priya and Annabel snigger.

'Do you reckon José would be good in bed?' Annabel says.

I do a mock eye-roll. 'It's all you bloody think about, isn't it?'

'A good shag from a sexy Spaniard might do you good,' Bel says. 'You know what they say about Latin men.'

'Have you *seen* me?' I say, gesturing once again towards my head, my cannulated arm and my body, which feels weaker by the day. 'There is no chance I'll be doing anything remotely sexy any time soon.'

Nurse Ange gives me a wink as she sets the red drugs to feed into my veins and heads out of the room.

'What about you, Priya?' I say. 'How's it going with hubby?'

'Yeah,' Bel chimes in. 'Have you persuaded him to shag you yet?'

Priya's face drops and, as she tries to speak, she starts to cry.

'Hey, you OK?' I say. 'I didn't mean to . . .'

The question triggers something in Priya and soon there are tears flowing down her cheeks, ruining her perfect flicks of eye liner.

'I don't even know what to do,' she says, half laughing, half crying. 'Sorry, I'm pathetic. It's just, if I even try to kiss him, he pulls away. I've not felt this unsexy since the twins were born.'

Bel walks round to Priya's side of the chair and wraps an arm around her, pulling her to her bird-like frame.

'Of course he bloody fancies you,' Bel says. 'It'll probably just take him a while to get used to your new body.'

'But what if he never does?' Priya says, sniffling like a toddler.

'He will, of course he will,' I say. 'He loves you.' But I don't know that, do I? I've never even met the guy. He might be cheating on her, like Johnny.

'I just can't wait to finish this frickin' treatment and get my hair back so he can fancy me again,' Priya says. 'He's treating me like some fragile doll he daren't touch.'

'He probably doesn't want to hurt you,' I say. 'Have you talked to a counsellor?'

Priya explains about her husband Guj's stubborn streak. As a pharmacist from a family of medical doctors, he can't see the benefit of talking therapy and – much like Johnny – he thinks counselling is for wimps.

'But *you* could still have therapy,' Bel says. 'I can lend you Dr Deep if it'll help?'

'You guys are sweet,' Priya says, managing a smile through her sniffles. 'I'd like that a lot.'

'Consider it done,' Bel says, handing over a wad of tissues for Priya to blow her nose.

It strikes me that cancer has messed up all our lives. It's not just the physical effects on our bodies, but the emotional collateral damage too. For Priya, it's the strained relationship with her husband and making them both feel differently about her body. For Annabel, it's being told she would never have kids, losing her boyfriend and living with the knowledge that she's going to die from this disease. And for me, it's the fact that all the things I took for granted have been thrown into doubt – that I would settle down, get married and have kids. Now I don't know if I'll ever be a mother. I don't know if I'll ever fall in love again, if anyone will find me attractive. I just want to find someone who loves me for who I am.

'Fuck cancer,' says Bel, as if she's read my mind. 'Fuck cancer and everything that comes with it.'

Biutiful

My periods have stopped. A lot of women my age would be overjoyed at a missed period – the first sign of a pregnancy. But for me, it means chemo has shut down my ovaries and I'm further from motherhood than ever.

The effects of the third round of chemo have been no better than the previous ones, but at least I now know what to expect. Not that it makes it any easier to wake up with a head that feels like it's been slammed between two iron bars. I have felt so sick I've wanted to puke my guts up, but the anti-sickness pills stop me from getting that relief. Then there are the hours of staring at the wall because I'm too brain-tired to read a book and too light-averse to watch TV. Instead, I scroll endlessly through my social media feeds, hate-liking mushy Valentine's Day missives and pictures of my friends' flawless offspring.

On my last check-up, the chemo mid-way point, Dr Malik confirmed the news I'd been dreading. Even though the scans show the tumour is shrinking successfully, I'll still have to have a mastectomy to give me the best possible chance of surviving until I'm old and grey. As he went through the options, I zoned out, picturing the scars and imagining having to explain them to a partner one day. I tuned back in to hear him explaining the nipple-sparing process, something I'm eligible for because my breast is small enough to allow blood to travel to the nipple post-operation, meaning it won't become a scab and fall off. I'll be spared from having to wait a year without a nipple, before having my skin twisted and tattooed at a later date. I suppose that's something.

The fact that my periods have stopped is the nail in the coffin, just in case I wasn't already feeling maximum horrendous. What if they never come back? I scuppered my chances of freezing an embryo and now here I am, alone, no hair and no periods, not an ounce of womanhood left. I feel so ugly and unfeminine. The idea of being in a new relationship feels more unlikely than ever.

And yet, a week and a half after my third chemo, José has sent me twenty-eight text messages and called me three thousand times, constantly checking up on my temperature and state of health, as if I might keel over at any moment.

He's consulted Dr Google and seems to know more about breast cancer than I do. On the one hand, this is mildly irritating and deeply unsexy, but on the other it's nice to know he cares. It's hard to imagine dating anyone else who would be so tolerant of my flaws.

'Can I ask you something?' he says, calling me the night before our second date, when I'm just about over the worst of the chemo.

'Go on . . .'

'Is it OK, if you feel comfortable, to come without your wig? I would like to see your bald.'

I feel as if he's asked me to fulfil some deep sexual fantasy, but in truth I'm relieved at the idea of not having to wear an itchy wig for another night of sweaty hot flushes. I've pretty much ditched it at home, in lieu of cotton hats that strip away every ounce of femininity.

I may have vowed to be new, positive, self-loving Jess, but

without my wig and make-up, I look like an alien. I still have a few eyelashes left, but my eyebrows have almost completely disappeared, leaving my face like a blank canvas. Chemo is meant to get rid of the cancer and make me better, but when I wipe off my make-up and look in the mirror, I see a cancer patient staring back at me, looking balder and sicker than ever.

Going out bald feels terrifying, but in the spirit of 'take me or leave me' I've agreed to José's request. I put on big earrings, bright red lipstick and as much super-length mascara as I can decant onto my few remaining lashes. By the time I'm ready to go out, I look passable.

Pottering around the house is one thing, but entering a pub bald is another. I feel as if I've stripped naked and everyone is staring as I walk through the door, desperately searching for José so I won't look like a loser loner cancer patient.

I spot him at a corner table, waving his hand at me, and my heart thumps in my chest as I approach. What if he hates it?

'Yess!' he says, jumping up and throwing his arms around me as I reach the table. 'Wow! My God! You are so biutiful.'

He pulls back and puts his hands on my forearms, examining me like a precious painting. 'Wow.'

Any thoughts of this being a joke evaporate. The dude can't take his eyes off me.

'You are OK?' he says as I put my bag down and ease into the comfy sofa seat.

'I'm fine, honestly,' I say.

He goes to the bar and I use the time to text our new Chemo Club WhatsApp group, which has been the recipient of many a paranoid message over the last twenty-four hours.

Told you he'd be hot for it! Annabel writes, when I report the positive reaction to my bald look. He must be gagging for you. Enjoy! xoxo

José returns with a glass of wine for me and a lager for him, then sits very close to me on the sofa. We sip our drinks as we talk about everything from work to food to favourite films, finding a few things in common and a lot not at all.

As we start on our second glass each, he puts his hand on top of mine and gives me one of his intense looks.

'Can I kiss you?'

I barely have time to reply before he lunges forward, planting a wet, full-mouthed kiss on my lips and sending a tingle down my body. I taste my own breath, metallic, winey. I remember the chemo, the taste of saline rising up my throat. Then I catch the salt on José's lips, the hoppy taste of lager and the warm attack of saliva from his tongue.

José pulls away slightly, moving his mouth to my neck, nibbling softly.

'Your bald is so sexy,' he murmurs, barely hiding the arousal in his voice. 'I can touch?'

I make a vague murmur as he reaches over and runs his hand along my scalp. I flinch. I know what this feels like. It's addictive to touch, comforting, like stroking a cat. But having him caress me feels both unnerving and a tiny bit arousing.

I pull away and he removes his hand, placing it back on top of mine and leaning in, as if to kiss me again. But just as I turn to kiss him, he goes right past my lips, turns his mouth towards my head and takes a deep, loud inhalation.

He is sniffing me. In public. On a second date.

As freaked out as I am by the public head sniffing and mildly obsessive approach to my 'bald', I can't help wanting more of Spanish Eyes. Two weeks after chemo number three, I'm distinctly horny, despite all the online cancer forums' attestations of how chemo will kill your sex life through a whole host of terrifying side effects, like vaginal dryness. I figure if

I'm going to get my post-cancer body out, it should be with someone who is respectful and fully appreciative of it. José is definitely that.

He arrives on my doorstep five minutes early, bottle of Tempranillo and bunch of tulips in hand. The smell of the tulips makes me gip. I put them down on the kitchen worktop. I really must buy a vase.

As I go to the cupboard to find glasses, he reaches me from behind and kisses me on the neck. His kiss feels tender but it takes me by surprise.

'You are looking biutiful!' José says.

I do feel a million times more biutiful than I did several hours ago, having invested in a warm bath and an hour's worth of YouTube make-up tutorials. It's not like I need to spend time getting my hair ready, and the one advantage of chemo is the natural and pain-free Brazilian bikini and leg wax, so I don't even need to shave. Small perks.

Dinner is the simplest curry I can manage, though it feels weird cooking for someone who isn't Johnny or Dad. Afterwards, we retire to the living room and I suggest watching a film, handing him the remote to scroll through my Netflix account.

Oreo jumps up onto José's lap and he pushes him off aggressively.

'I hate cats,' he says.

I make a point of coaxing Oreo back, stroking him until he purrs. José's reaction is alarming, but then Johnny didn't like cats much when we met either and he grew to love Oreo like a human baby.

'Let's watch this one,' José says, picking *The Girl with the Dragon Tattoo*. Before I have a chance to protest the choice of a sexually violent thriller as our first film together, he has already pressed play, and the preamble to the opening credits egins. I try to adopt the position I always had with Johnny

for film nights – me with my head on the perfectly moulded
spot in his shoulder, my knees curled up against his legs – but
José's shoulder is too bony, and he seems to want to put his
arm around my neck so that I have to sit forward, in pain.

He gasps and commentates throughout the film. I try to
communicate through silence that I'm not up for conversation, but he keeps on talking. Even when I take a ten-minute
loo break to scroll through my phone, he doesn't get the hint.

When the film ends, he leans over to kiss me. I've got to give
this a chance, I think, so I kiss him back, trying to slow the
pace as I feel him warming up, his arousal apparent. Before I
can register what's happening, he has pushed his tongue into
my mouth and is making an 'o' shape, circling his tongue
around mine like a washing machine. There's so much saliva
I could do with one of those tiny mouth hoovers they use at
the dentist.

Fingers run across my naked scalp, making the back of my
neck tingle, and I'm relieved when his mouth moves to my
neck, making its way slowly down to my collar bone, my . . .

'Stop,' I say, pulling back, as his kisses stray too close to
my breasts.

'I'm sorry,' he says. 'You are OK? It is too much?'

'It's not you,' I say, although it is you, and I want you to
leave now. 'I don't feel comfortable. I'm sorry. I think it might
be better if you go.'

'I understand,' he says, apologetic and wounded. 'You need
time. Take as much time as you want. I will go now.'

But I realize it's not time I need. It feels sacred, being intimate with someone for the first time after Johnny, the first time
with no hair, like losing my virginity all over again. I need it
to happen with someone who's not going to be a passing fling.
I need it to happen with someone who completely gets me,

AURA PRICE

286

someone who I want to be with for a long, long time. And as kind and considerate as he is, José is not that person.

'José, I'm sorry. I'm not ready for this, for us.' *Half truth, half lie.*

'It's OK, Yess,' he says, taking my hand again. 'You are going through a hard time. Take some time and call me if you want to see me again. Yes?'

'OK,' I say, though I know I won't be calling him.

We hug goodbye at my door, and as he draws away he takes one last look at me and says: 'You are biutiful.'

And just like that, he's gone from my life, the sweetest, kindest guy I might never see again. A guy who fancied me even without hair, who desired me even though I feel broken.

Coming out

After a shock diagnosis at thirty-one years old, our acting editor and columnist Jessica Jackson reveals why she's no longer hiding her illness

Let's just say 'Have Cancer' was not on my list of things to do before I'm thirty-five. Settle down with nice guy, yes. Travel the world, sure. Be diagnosed with breast cancer and have to freeze my eggs? Big Fat No.

Turning thirty was a milestone. Thirteen-year-old me thought I'd be bossing it *Devil Wears Prada*-style and living in a castle with unicorns by then, but I had barely figured out how to put a duvet cover on without suffocating myself inside it, let alone climb the elusive property ladder. But however much or little I'd achieved from my imaginary list, I wasn't expecting this.

Three months ago, I was told I had breast cancer and that chemo could send me into early menopause. Like the gynaecological equivalent of PPI, I was given the option of freezing an embryo with my then-boyfriend's sperm in case the treatment leaves me infertile. So far, so good. Only then I realized just how daunting it was to lock him in for life when I wasn't even sure our relationship would make it through the next year.

288

Reader, I didn't go through with it. We broke up and I froze my eggs on my own, with no guarantee they'll ever turn into a baby.

At first, I hid my illness from work and the wider world. I was sick of the pitying head tilts and that phrase 'But you're so young'. I didn't want my colleagues to think I couldn't handle my job, but I was taking one out of every three weeks off work with little explanation. I was lying to our readers and my team.

Worst of all, I was lying to myself.

Not long ago, I met a beautiful soul called Annabel. (She told me that being featured in a glossy magazine is on her ~~bucket~~ Fuck-It List, so here you go, Bel.) Annabel has stage four breast cancer – that's the incurable kind. But you know what? Bel is the most alive person I know. She may be approaching the end of her life, but she's not dying. She's living. And if you met her, you would probably wonder why you ever complain about anything, because her zest for life is so infectious. She takes every day as it comes and she doesn't treat cancer like it's something to be ashamed of.

Spending time with Bel has taught me that I don't have anything to hide either. I might need to wear more make-up to cover for my lack of eyebrows, and I certainly need more sleep than I once did. But I am no less capable of running a magazine.

It was terrifying to walk into the workplace of my dreams and reveal my bald head, but the truth is it's been liberating. It's not just about taking my wig off when I want to or telling my team I feel physically weak. It's about being my whole self, not the fakey-fakey image I've painted of myself online. People only pity you if you let them.

So if cancer has given me anything, it's this. The freedom to tell the truth, to be the real me.

This one's for you, Bel.

Boxes of Kleenex used: 12
Times I've been told I'm 'too young for cancer': 9
Superheroes in the NHS: 1.3 million

Annabel Sadler: You've made a ~~dying~~ living woman very happy! Love you xoxo

Aisha Parker: Jessica Jackson, you are everything and more. So proud to call you my friend and future roomie x

Cath Elderfield: It's so true you have to make the most of the life you've got, there were so many things your mum put off for retirement that she never got to do. Sweetheart, go out and live your life and do everything that you want xx

Ophelia Cossack-Daly: Wow Jessica, you are so #brave! x

I turn to the comments on *Luxxe*'s Instagram, below a selfie of me with my bald head and big earrings.

@Becka_Becka Your article has inspired me to tell my manager about my bipolar disorder. Wish me luck! X

@Minnieshouse22 Awesome story! It's so important to bring your true self to work. Congratulations to this wonderful woman x

@RandyPanda123 Dare I ask – do the, er, carpets match the curtains? LOL

Killing it

'Jess, have you seen? Your column is killing it.'

I walk into the office on Wednesday morning to find Tabitha and the social media assistant gathered around Aisha's desk, peering at her screen. I've barely had the chance to remove my coat before they start hammering me with stats.

'It's gone viral, look,' Aisha says, pointing at the screen.

'Ten times more hits than Vegan Suzie,' Tabitha says, tapping on a box with a load of numbers.

'And you should see the comments we've had on social. The inbox is going mad.'

I need to sit down. I was so nervous about this post going live, but it seems to have been received much better than I ever imagined.

'Have you got a sec, Jess?' Tabitha says.

As I follow her to the meeting room, I can't help feeling dread in my stomach. Maybe Miles has complained about me using the site to wang on about myself. Or maybe I've made some massive mistake in the issue that's just gone to print. My brain has been all over the shop – 'chemo brain' really is a thing.

As she goes to take the seat opposite me, she shakes her head and pushes in her chair, walking over to the other side of the table to sit next to me instead. Then she pulls out the chair so she is facing me in a way that is totally contrary to her body language of the last few months.

'I owe you an apology,' she says, sighing into her hands. 'A huge apology.'

I'm taken aback. This is not what I expected.

'Jess, it's no secret that we've butted heads over the last few months. In fact, I wouldn't be surprised if you've been tempted to throw coffee in my face on more than one occasion.'

I laugh and shake my head. 'You've probably had the same thought about me.'

She puts her palms on her lap, as if laying it all on the table, opening up her body language to me.

'Look, when Leah first told me she was pregnant, I fully expected to step in as acting editor. I was still on mat leave with Matilda at that point, but I knew I'd be back in time to cover her. So when she said they were hiring you, I was gutted.'

'You went for the job?' I say. I'd always figured because she's the fashion editor, she wouldn't be interested in management, but why wouldn't she? This is Tabitha. She's smart, she's ambitious, she likes to be in control of everything . . . I guess we're more similar than I thought we were.

'I'm a sore loser,' she says, shrugging apologetically. 'To be honest, I've realized now you're the best person for the job. I'm not cut out for managing people. But I couldn't see that at the time.'

I look down at her hands. How could I not have considered how she must be feeling? I always assumed she was jealous, but I didn't think about how I would feel if someone walked in and took the job that I thought was all lined up for me.

'There's another thing,' she says. 'I know I can be harsh sometimes. Defensive, maybe?' She looks at me and I pinch my thumb and index finger together to show that yes, maybe a tiny bit, but I'm smiling so she knows I'm not judging.

'Before I had Matilda, I always knew I'd come back to work. I was at the top of my game. I can do this job with my eyes closed. But taking a year out and spending that time with a kid who can't even speak . . . it changes you, Jess. Don't get me wrong, I love Tilly more than anything in this world. But being a new mum knocks your confidence in ways you never expect.'

I think about walking into the office and removing my hat after chemo, exposing my bald head for the first time. If her back-to-work experience was anything like it was for me, then it must have been terrifying.

'The truth is, returning to work after maternity leave, especially when you know that someone more experienced has stepped into the shoes you thought were waiting for you . . . it's really tough. I put my guard up. I took things out on you, and for that I'm truly sorry.'

'I'm sorry too,' I say when I'm finally able to get a word in edgeways. 'I never stopped to think what it must be like to return to work after having a baby.' But then, thinking about Kate and how she's struggling with Ella and trying to keep her events company afloat, it all makes sense.

I can feel what's left of the hairs on my arms standing on end and I'm not sure if it's hot-flush related or the conversation itself that is giving me goosebumps.

She nods. 'I really admire you, Jess. I know we can work together. I don't want to work against you. I'm happy to look at your idea of covering more underrepresented women, because you're right, we are biased. I don't think we can go entirely against what this magazine has always stood for – it needs to be a smooth transition, but I can help you with that.'

'Thank you, Tabitha,' I say, and I mean it, 'for your honesty.'

She throws her arms up in the air. 'It was entirely driven

by *your* honesty. Coming into the office and removing your hat like that? Are you kidding me? You're the bravest person I know.'

We have a little moment, hugging across our chairs. I have to admit, it feels good to crush the tension that has been building between us for three months.

As we're about to return to the rest of the team, an idea comes to me. I stop still in the doorway. 'Hey, can I run something by you?'

'Of course,' Tabitha says, perching on the edge of the desk.

'This is going to sound crazy, but why don't we profile *ourselves* in the anniversary issue?'

'What, like me talking about coming back to work after mat leave?'

'And me talking about how petrifying it has been to come out as a cancer patient when I work for a glossy magazine that celebrates strong women who have their shit together.'

Tabitha looks unconvinced.

'Think about it,' I say, drawing an imaginary cover line in the air with my hand. 'It could be like, "These women are at the top of their game, but they're scared shitless". We'll get some others involved too. I could ask my friend Kate. She runs her own events company and I think she's suffering from post-natal depression, and then there's my friend Annabel, who is living with stage four cancer. And maybe someone like Stephanie Asante, talking about how she escaped her domestic situation and how she now empowers others who are going through similar stuff?'

'I don't know, Jess. What if it ruins our careers?'

'Then we're both in it together?' I laugh. 'Seriously, I think this could be a really positive way to make our readers feel seen. We see their flaws, we see their imperfections, and we've got their backs.'

Tabitha blows out a puff of air. 'I guess . . .'

'We could put Matilda in the mag too, if you like? Whatever you like. We'll make it beautiful.'

Tabitha thinks for a moment, but then I see she's coming round to the idea. 'So like, underneath the cover of the women pretending they have their shit together?'

'Exactly,' I say, feeling proud that we've reached an agreement on something for once. 'We could theme the whole issue around breaking with the fake, showing the sides of ourselves that we don't share on Instagram. No air-brushing. We could call it The Truth Issue.'

'You know what?' she says. 'I love it.'

Show and tell

'Wait, he *sniffed* you?' Priya says.

'Yep! He was like –' I lean in close to Annabel on the sofa and bury my nose in her wig, inhaling deeply.

'I'm assuming your words were "get the fuck off me"?' Bel says.

I shrug. 'I think I was dumbstruck.'

'Complicit!' Bel says. 'This is absolutely brilliant.'

'That's the best dating story ever,' Priya says.

It's so good to see them both laughing. Priya, with her husband who won't sleep with her, and Bel, whose treatment is literally endless. In a world where everyone else wants to ask if I'm OK, it's refreshing that these two just want to talk about sex and boys and boys and sex.

Bel and Joe's flat looks different from the last time I saw it, when the huge dining table was crammed into the tiny living room with Mags and Mr Wade around it. A Camberwell bolt-hole that they rented when he moved back from Paris and she got her secondary diagnosis, it sits in the basement down steps that are protected by iron railings. In front is a green park where marijuana fumes share space with young professional mums and the occasional jogger. It's not quite as yummy mummy as Clapham, nor as rough and ready as Peckham.

There's barely a male touch here. It's clear Joe allowed his sister to dictate the decor. The shelves are filled with plant pots and piles of books, though there are tribal trinkets from Joe's travels and pictures of him in kayaks and on top of mountains. A plateful of Priya's raw brownies sits on a tiny coffee table next to the sofa.

Bel's bedroom is at the back of the flat, looking out onto an overgrown garden, while Joe occupies the living room, transforming the sofa into a bed by night. There's a rail in one corner that constitutes his wardrobe, a mix of colourful T-shirts and white shirts.

'Mind if I smoke?' Annabel says, as she opens a wooden box and starts rolling a spliff.

'I'm surprised your oncologist hasn't told you to stop,' Priya says, giving her a look.

'It's medicinal,' Bel says, taking a drag and passing me the spliff. 'Besides, my onco says I should do whatever it takes to feel better.'

I take the joint. I haven't smoked since my teenage years in the bike sheds behind school. I'm not sure I even still know how.

'Does it help with your pain?' Priya says, as we pass the joint between us.

'Totally,' Bel says. 'Not sure what I'd do without it, to be honest. It helps my mind as well.'

Her body has relaxed into the sofa after just five minutes of the stuff, and I instantly feel lighter than before.

Priya shrugs. 'I mean, it kinda goes against my healthy eating but I suppose it's rare I get a night off the twins, and you only live once, right?'

She reaches for the spliff and takes a cautious drag, then performs an over-the-top sigh as if it's instantly gone to her head.

'So what's in these raw brownies of yours?' I ask, sinking

my teeth into a gooey bite that tastes nothing like a real brownie.

'Dates, almonds, coconut oil, raw cacao . . .' Priya says. 'You like it?'

'They're good,' I lie, between hard-to-digest mouthfuls of cardboard.

'Probably not a patch on your doughnuts, I'm sure,' Priya says.

'These famous doughnuts you keep mentioning,' Bel says. 'You're all talk.'

'Oh yeah, want to try them?'

I reach for the box that contains my latest batch of doughnuts and place it on Annabel's lap. Then I reveal a separate, smaller box with my experimental vegan version, and present it to Priya.

'Come to mama,' Bel says, opening the box and taking a sniff. 'Bloody hell, these look good.'

'Jess, this is so sweet of you,' Priya says, picking up one of the misshapen vegan doughnuts. It took several attempts and a whole lot of mess, but eventually I managed a decent version using almond milk from a recipe I found on the *Perfect Bake* website.

While Priya samples the one in her hand, Annabel digs into the regular doughnut box and bites into the pillowy dough. Her eyes light up with pleasure.

'Fuck me, these are everything,' Bel says.

Priya makes orgasmic noises. 'You'll have to give me the recipe!'

I'm so pleased they love what I made. It was Mum's thing, the satisfaction of providing enjoyment for loved ones. It brought her real joy.

'Your mum and my mum would have got on well,' Bel says, and I feel a surge of love for her and grief for Mum, all at the same time. Annabel reminds me of Mum in too many ways to count – her passion for life and the way she would never deny herself something that might bring pleasure. Her utter selflessness and the joy she gets from making others happy. She and Mum would have been thick as thieves.

I take a deeper drag on the spliff and put my feet up on the pouffe next to the sofa. The fairy lights around the top of the living room are starting to look like real fairies. There are three picture frames with a black-and-white photo of what must be Annabel and Joe's grandparents, a photo of the two siblings, then the whole family together.

'I'm not being funny,' Priya says. 'But can I show you my boobs? I'm convinced I'm still wonky.'

'Is this about Guj again?' Bel says.

'Partly. I mean, I'm sure he thinks I'm a freak. But also, I think my surgeon is taking the piss, saying my boobs are even when they're not.'

'Go on then,' Bel says. 'We're all friends here.'

Priya grabs the joint from Bel and takes a drag. She peels up her blouse and holds it in place just below her neck, revealing two very different breasts. On the left is her original one, full and rounded, the nipple erect from the sudden exposure. On the right, the reconstruction, a smooth mound with a red scar across the centre and another, fresher one, below it. The breast is visibly higher on the right-hand side than the left.

'Be honest,' she says. 'Is this side higher than the other?'

'Yeah, maybe,' says Bel. 'It doesn't look bad though.'

'You look gorgeous,' I say. 'There is no way he's not sleeping with you because he finds you unattractive.'

'I just want them to do it right,' Priya says, starting to cry again. 'I'm thinking about asking for another operation.'

'I had three surgeries before they got mine right,' says Bel. 'I actually asked for a different surgeon because the first guy kept telling me it was perfect and it wasn't. The second one was good, Mrs Redfern. Maybe get a referral to her?'

'Can I see yours?' Priya says. 'I mean, if you feel comfortable.'

'I've whapped these bad boys out in front of enough strangers to last me a lifetime,' says Bel, pulling up her top and raising it over her arms, dumping it in her lap.

I'm not prepared for what I see.

Annabel's body is a patchwork quilt. While one breast is reconstructed after her first cancer operation, the other is completely gone. But instead of the flat, scarred chest I had imagined, she is covered in lumpy bits of skin, bulging out around the scars on each side like a hunk of raw meat tied up with string. There are scars along her stomach, under her arm, all over both breasts. The truth is, she still looks so beautiful.

'It's –' I struggle for words, simply in awe of Annabel and her ability to cope with so much.

'This is Freddy and this is Flo,' Annabel says, cupping her hand under each breast to introduce them.

Then the three of us are in fits of giggles, the awkwardness gone.

'Mind if I touch?' Priya says.

'Anything for you,' Bel says. 'I know you haven't had any for a while.'

I watch as Bel guides Priya's hands from Freddy to Flo and back to Freddy, comparing the two. 'Press harder if you like, I don't have any feeling,' she says. 'Jess, want a go? Can't have you left out of the threesome.'

'You've twisted my arm,' I say, running my fingers along the scars.

When the two of them put their tops back on, I confess that I feel like a fraud. My breasts are fully intact, but I have all this still to come, and I have no idea how mine will look after surgery.

'You'll be fine,' Priya says. 'I wish I had your figure. Child-birth and breast cancer will wreck a woman.'

'She's right,' says Bel, slurring her words a little. '*Biutiful!* No wonder the sexy Spaniard couldn't get enough of you.'

I laugh.

'Seriously, Jess,' Bel says. 'You don't realize how stunning you are, big C or otherwise.'

'You two are like my personal cheerleading squad,' I say. 'I've honestly no idea what I'd do if I hadn't met you.'

'Mate, tell me about it,' Annabel says, giving my hand a little squeeze. 'I wish my friends got it like you do.'

It's the first time I've heard her mention other friends. I know how close she is to Joe, but I've been wondering for a while if there's anyone else. Someone this wonderful should have a whole crew around her.

'Did something happen?' I don't want to upset her, but equally I want to give her space if she wants to talk. 'With your friends, I mean?'

Annabel lets out an exasperated sigh. 'How long have you got?'

I squeeze her hand back. 'Hun, we've got all the time in the world.'

Bel finally opens up. When she was first diagnosed, at twenty-four, she had to take six months off her job as a social worker. By the time she went back, she'd missed out on opportunities, and her friends were moving on in their careers, leaving her behind. She had a small group of girlfriends she'd known since school who were supportive throughout her chemo and radiotherapy. But when the treatment finished, they couldn't understand how she wasn't OK. They wanted to go out drinking and partying but she was a shell of her former self, anxious, depressed and struggling at work.

'They tried for a really long time to snap me out of it,

especially Tarn,' Annabel says. 'But there's only so long people stick around when you're pushing them away.'

By the time she met Mark, some of her confidence had returned, but it wasn't long before she received her secondary diagnosis. She had to quit her job for good this time, losing the thing that had been keeping her going – helping others. Then she was told she could never have kids, and she pushed Mark away as well.

'For ages, he kept saying "I'm not going to leave you" and I kept telling him to go,' she says, wiping away a single tear as it drips down her cheek. 'I couldn't let him do that, so I kept insisting, but deep down I wanted him to stay. And then one day . . .'

She breaks off, and I wrap an arm around her, wishing I could do something to take away her pain. I'm devastated for everything she's had to go through.

When Priya goes home to her kids, Bel and I retire to her bedroom. I snuggle my head into her lap and we talk until we can't keep our eyes open. She tells me she adores Priya, but that it's hard for someone with kids to understand the pain of being told you can never have them. Even though I don't have that same finality as she does, I do have some inkling of what it feels like to have that taken away.

'That's why I'm so grateful to have you,' she says.

I barely sleep for worrying about Bel. Beside me on the bed, she can't stop coughing – the kind of painful, incessant chesty cough that can only be associated with lung cancer. She gets up several times to go to the loo and there are blood-stained tissues on her bedside table.

When I wake up, sunlight is streaming through the window and Bel is fast asleep by my side; the smell of bacon wafts through from the kitchen. I plod through in just my T-shirt to find Joe at the stove.

'Morning, sleepy head,' Joe says. 'Hope I didn't wake you.'

I feel a sudden self-consciousness as my hand goes to shield my bald head. I really didn't want him to see me like this.

'Not at all,' I say, tugging at the bottom of my T-shirt to pull it down over my knickers.

'Bacon?'

'God that sounds good.'

'Knowing Bel, she won't be up for hours. She was coughing blood again last night, wasn't she?'

So he knows. I feel the weight of responsibility lifted, and immediately feel guilty for it. As long as her brother knows, I don't feel like I need to report her to the cancer police.

'I was worried about her,' I say. 'I guess it means it's in her lungs?' I think of Mum in her worst days, when the cancer had spread to her lungs as well.

'It's pretty much everywhere at this stage,' Joe says. 'She plays it down.'

He pushes mushrooms around the frying pan as if we're discussing the football scores, not the fact that his sister is dying.

'So you guys had a fun night?' He makes a smoking gesture as he says this.

'We did,' I say. 'What time did you get home?'

'I snuck in at midnight and you were already asleep. Well, you were, anyway. Bel was coughing her guts up so we sat in the kitchen for a bit.'

'Is it the smoking that makes her cough? She said it helps with the pain.'

'I don't know if it makes a difference. She's been coughing like that for months.'

'Hmm,' I say.

'So how's the dating going?'

I take a chair and curl my legs up to my chest, pulling the T-shirt over my knees.

'Oh, you know, so-so.'

'Annabel told me what you did with your dating profile, posting a photo with your bald head and all. I think that's so cool.'

'God, how embarrassing,' I say, feeling suddenly shy. It was one thing posting my dating profile to a load of strangers I haven't met, but it feels intimate discussing it with Joe.

'It's not embarrassing at all,' he says. 'I would be straight in your DMs if I saw that. Makes a change from all the fakes on the apps.'

I look away. I think I might be blushing.

'Anyway, Annabel told me about this Spanish guy who's into you? Are you going to see him again?'

I'm grateful for the change of subject. 'He's a nice guy, but nah, I'm done.'

'Sounds like you could do with a nice guy.'

Joe spoons mushrooms onto two plates and adds bacon, buttered toast, baked beans and a perfect poached egg.

'Fancy yourself as a bit of a cook, don't you?' I say as he puts the plate in front of me and twists black pepper over the top.

'I've been known to cook a few meals for the ladies.' He gives me a flirtatious look.

'So what's your speciality, besides these delicious-looking breakfasts?'

'I don't get to cook these delicious-looking breakfasts for anyone other than my sister these days,' he says, just as I'm wondering which girl may have been lucky enough to sleep over last. 'But I do a mean roast.'

'And your Christmas dinner . . .'

'Maybe I'll cook something for you some day, if it doesn't work out with the online dating.'

I can't look at him after this last comment. Surely he'd never be interested in his little sister's cancer-patient mate.

'So what was Mark like?' I feel as if I'm going behind her back, but Annabel is so cagey about anything other than the plain facts when it comes to her ex.

Joe acknowledges the question like he's heard it many times before. 'That prick? I don't know what kind of human being thinks it's acceptable to leave a woman when she's just been told she has incurable cancer.'

'Was it that soon after?'

'Nah, he let it hang for a while, after they told her she'd never have kids. But we all know that was his reason.'

We both go silent.

'She's had a lot of shit in her life, my little sis,' Joe says. 'And I wasn't here for any of it.'

'What do you mean? You've always been there for her, haven't you?'

Joe lifts a forkful of bean-soaked toast into his mouth and indicates he's about to speak. Eventually, he finishes chewing.

'I ran away to Paris after our grandparents died. My ex, Aurelie, she never intended to stay in England for long. I figured Bel would be fine – she had Mark and Mum and Dad. But I was kidding myself. She doesn't like to bother our parents with stuff – they work so hard and she wants to protect them, so she never lets them go to her appointments. I'm the only one who sees her vulnerable side. When all that shit happened, I wasn't there for her.'

'You stayed in Paris because of Aurelie?'

He shakes his head. 'Nah, we were over a long time ago. I was just scared to come back.'

305

I feel for him, having to make the decision to move back to London when he knew he'd have to watch his sister die.

'It must have been hard for you,' I say.

He shrugs. 'I'm trying to be a good brother after all the time I spent running away from our shit,' he says. 'Thing is, I don't think we've got long left.'

The C bomb

I sit in my robe at the side of the pool and watch as Lauren, Kate and eight other women hold hands and jump into the shallow water with shrieks and shouts. I shield myself from the splash as they giggle and disperse around the pool, some of them getting straight out the other side and into the jacuzzi. I touch my hand to my head. The swimming cap feels slimy against my naked scalp.

Lauren swims up to the side and puts her elbows on the tiles to talk to me. 'Sure you can't come in for a bit?'

I shake my head. A spa day for the hen do seemed like a great idea. Hair, nails, massage, swim, sauna . . . But that was before I found out I can't have massages during chemo, mustn't swim or use the sauna or steam room. My body is so susceptible to germs that pretty much everything is banned. So instead I'm sitting at the edge of the pool with a turmeric latte, watching the others have the time of their lives.

I untuck my legs and rest my back on the sun lounger. Lauren's friend Erin, five months pregnant, floats on her back with the curve of her pregnant belly just visible under her halter neck swimsuit.

I close my eyes and try to drift off. I'm constantly tired, my rickety body making me feel ninety years old. I never imagined chemo would be so prohibitive – no sushi, no runny eggs, no soft cheese, no spa days. All the restrictions of a pregnancy but without the happy ending.

Back at the hotel in the evening, the girls descend on the room I am sharing with Lauren and Kate for the 'pre-lash' before we head into Soho. Two women curl their hair with straighteners, while others gather around the bathroom mirror doing their make-up and speculating what their husbands and boyfriends might be up to this weekend. Kate is anxious about her first full night away from Ella and is calling Colm every five minutes to check up on her. Ten bottles of prosecco line up on the dressing table and I can barely breathe for perfume.

'Can I do your make up?' Kate says, noticing me feeling sorry for myself. I feel downbeat, seeing them all hyped and excited for a night out, but I'm too self-conscious with my hairless face and eyes and the knowledge that I might break out into hot flushes any minute. I'd rather stay in the hotel and watch a film while they go out tottering in their heels.

But I reluctantly agree, as I know Kate is trying to make me feel better. She plonks a filthy, overfull make-up bag on the bed and starts swiping at my face with a powder brush that must be home to millions of chemo-threatening germs. I feel myself tense as her fingers touch my face, nearing my eyes and then my lips.

'Relax,' she says. 'I'll make you look gorgeous.'

I try to relax my face muscles. If I'm going to catch something, I've probably already caught it.

'Falsies?' she says, waving a pair of fake eyelashes and a little tube of glue in my face.

'If you can manage it,' I say. I'm not sure I have enough eyelashes left to support the weight of the falsies. But Kate is already applying glue and ordering me to look down as she presses the lash against my eyelid.

After three attempts on the left side, it isn't working. My eyes are streaming and the tears stop the glue from sticking. Before I realize it, I'm crying.

'You guys go without me,' I say. 'I can't even get false eyelashes on; I'm not going to be any fun.'

Lauren comes rushing over and puts her arm around me, patting me on my back like she's trying to burp a baby. 'We're not going anywhere without you, you're my maid of honour!'

Her kindness only makes me want to sob harder. I feel useless, I can't even get myself together for one night.

'Ssh,' she says, rubbing my back. A few other girls stand over me, giving me sympathetic looks. Then they're holding up earrings and belts and tubes of glitter in a bid to make me feel better.

'Let me have a go,' Lauren says, taking the eyelashes from Kate and holding out a bunch of tissues for me to dry my eyes.

There is glue all over the edges of the lashes. Lauren wipes it carefully on the cardboard box and presses my eyelids down with cotton wool pads. She reapplies glue, waving and flexing the lashes in her hand to dry them.

'Look down,' she says.

I obey, staring at my hands, which are dry and cracked from the chemo.

Lauren presses the first line of lashes onto my right lid, sliding it closer into the corner and holding it down until I feel the wet glue once again. She keeps it there for thirty seconds before cautiously drawing her hand away.

'Now open your eye really slowly,' she says.

I peel it open. The lash feels heavy on top of my lid and the glue makes the skin around my eyes feel tight. But for now, it sticks, so Lauren repeats the process on the other side, allowing me a quick break to blow my runny nose.

'There you go. Beautiful,' Lauren says, holding up a mirror so I can admire her work.

It's true, I do look better. Now I just have to try and go the whole night without crying . . .

'Thanks, hun,' I say, reaching for a sip of my prosecco.

'Alright girls, five minutes till games time!' Kate calls. 'Give me a hand, Jess?'

I join her as she shuffles around with a laptop and various wrapped gifts. Within five minutes, the girls are assembled on the bed, sipping from plastic penis straws, as Kate plays a video of Charlie answering questions about whether he or Lauren is more adventurous in bed and after how many dates they first had sex. When she correctly guesses his response, Lauren wins a point, but more frequently she gets it wrong and has to down a shot of tequila.

Twenty minutes into the games, Lauren is progressively drunker and louder, and is encouraging everyone but her pregnant friend to drink, drink, drink. I've mostly been pretending to sip the same glass of prosecco all evening.

Lauren takes a video call with Charlie in front of the group, where she pans the phone around the room and gets each of us to blow him a kiss. When Lauren assures him there definitely *won't* be any strippers tonight, she performs an exaggerated wink towards the girls, but I catch Charlie's face as he sees it. He doesn't look best pleased.

At the end of the games, I present Kate with the gift I've organized from all of us to thank her for stepping in to organize the hen do. She seems genuinely touched as I hand over the hamper of pampering goods we thought would help her take a break. I can see she has tears in her eyes, but when I try to comfort her, she brushes me away.

'We have a little something for you too,' Lauren says, taking me by surprise.

'For me? But I've barely lifted a finger.'

Kate reaches into her bag and hands me a package, which I tear open. I can feel the eyes on me as I pull out a beautiful, baby-blue leather diary with gilt-edged pages and a matching leather passport case.

'Oh my God, you really shouldn't have,' I say, tearing up again.

'Do *not* cry!' Lauren says, and I flap my heavy eyelashes to bat away the tears. She wraps her arms around me and squeezes me far too tight. 'We love you, Jeeeeess.'

'You've been trying so hard to make us all smile with your amazing columns, but maybe you need somewhere private to write down how you're really feeling?' Kate says. I suspect Lauren was meant to say all this, but she's too drunk to know what's going on.

Kate is right. As much as I'm trying to be honest, my articles are never going to be the warts-and-all version I tell my friends.

'And this is for our adventures,' Lauren says, aggressively punching her finger on top of the passport cover while leaning her head on me for support. 'No men, just us girliiiies.'

'I don't know what to say.' I try to smile so that I won't cry. 'Thank you so much.'

One of the girls starts to clap and they all come over one by one to hug me, telling me how much they admire my bravery.

I'm so touched by the sentiment that I almost forget how ugly I feel underneath the layers of make-up and fake eyelashes.

By nine p.m., Lauren is so drunk she's slurring her words. I try to get her to eat some of the chips we ordered from room service but she's determined to keep herself light and in the mood for dancing. In the bathroom, one of the girls has a 'tactical

311

vom' before we head to the club. I wait until the last moment before we go out to put on my wig – the ginger one this time. I'm not in the mood to stand out.

It takes twenty minutes to get the whole group from hotel room to street level. People keep forgetting their bags and tiaras, running back up to the room while the rest of us wait in the lobby. It's pouring outside and I seem to have developed a full-blown cold.

Lauren jumps in the first lot of Ubers and goes ahead with some of the girls, while I rest on a sofa in the warmth of the lobby with pregnant Erin and a couple of the others. I seize my moment to talk to Kate, who spills her feelings about the fight she had with Colm before she left the house, and how much she's struggling with Ella. For once, I feel like the strong one.

By the time we get out of the cab, there's a queue around the block for the club and it really is pouring. We walk towards Erin and the others near the back of the line.

'Jeeesss,' Lauren slurs, when she sees me. 'Just in tiiiime!' She grabs my hand and leads me to the front of the queue, nearly tripping over someone's feet and receiving a chorus of tuts from the others in the line.

'What are we doing?' I ask, my heels already killing me.

She stops in front of the bouncer and gestures towards me.

'My friend Jess has cancer, she's dying,' she says, sticking out her bottom lip in an exaggerated sad face. She stumbles slightly and has to put a hand on my shoulder to stop from falling. 'This could be her last night out, but she can't stand up for long. I don't know if she can wait in this queue.'

I stand on the spot, stunned. 'Lauren,' I say, nudging her, a warning tone in my voice.

The bouncer looks me up and down. 'She doesn't look like she's dying.'

'Show him, Jess,' Lauren says, pulling at my wig like a toddler trying to get her mother's attention.

'Lauren!' I plead, glancing at the long line of people behind us.

'Show him under your wig,' she says, leaning on me for support.

The bouncer's eyes bore through me, giving me a 'come on then' look.

I take a deep breath and peel back the wig, raising it just enough to show him that I'm bald underneath. Lauren reaches out and puts her palm on top of my head, giving it a stroke.

'See? She's bald.'

As she does so, she loses her footing, her ankle doubling over on her heel so that she falls, taking my wig along with her.

It all happens in a split-second. I'm scrambling to help Lauren to her feet before I realize I'm standing completely bald in front of a line of people. Everyone is staring.

I drag my wig out of the puddle, but it's soaked. All I feel is shame as I pull it back over my head, the cold, wet hair sticking to my face.

'You can go in,' the bouncer says, giving me a look of pure pity.

Lauren starts towards the door, but the bouncer holds an arm out in front of her.

'Not you,' he says. 'Too drunk.'

By this point, Kate and Erin have come to the front of the queue to see what all the commotion is. Kate tells the bouncer she is Lauren's older, more responsible sister, and that she will take her straight to the bar for a pint of water. The bouncer remains unconvinced, but she explains that it's her little sister's hen party, and she's a giggly drunk, not an aggressive one. It would mean the world to her if he would let us in . . .

'Fine,' he says, reluctantly lifting his arm to let us through.

Once inside, Lauren attempts to high five me, but misses. 'We should drop the C bomb more often,' she says, leaning her weight on me again.

I push her off, stunned. Kate is torn between staying with me to check I'm OK and going with Lauren in search of a pint of water. She gives me an apologetic look as Lauren pulls at her hand.

Erin stops to check if I'm alright. I tell her I'm fine; I'll catch up with them later. I need to find the loos to sort out my wig. Lauren and Kate disappear into the dark, misty room.

I work my way through the mass of bodies grinding against each other, flailing their hands in the air to the latest Calvin Harris floor-filler. I squeeze through, arms out in front of me like a shield.

A hot flush. I want to rip off my coat, but there's no space, I'm stuck in the middle of the dance floor, hemmed in between sweaty bodies, bumping and grinding. A guy squeezes my arse. I turn to shout at him, but his plastic pint glass is flying through the air, covering my already soaked wig in beer.

I shake my arms in shock, trying to get the beer off, but my elbow somehow hits someone behind me.

'Watch where you're going!' A blonde girl, high heels, short dress, fish lips, gives me a death stare.

And that's when I crack. Standing still in the middle of the dance floor, I pull a chunk of strands at the bottom of my wig and let it topple from my head, instantly freeing me. As a small circle of strangers forms around me, I shut my eyes and fling my hands in the air.

Then I scream.

I scream for my best friend, who should be right here by my side, holding my hand.

I scream for Mum, who I miss so much it sometimes feels

as if my stomach has been hollowed out and emptied, leaving nothing but blank space.

I scream for Annabel, who deserves to live.

'Jess,' says Erin, rubbing my back to try and snap me to my senses.

I brush her off, picking my wig off the floor for the second time.

Then I turn back the way I came, tears flowing down my cheeks. *I have to get out of here. I have to go back to the hotel.*

On the street, shivering from the cold, I plug in the hotel address for an Uber. But when I picture the ransacked room with empty bottles and perfume stench and a dozen tried-on and discarded outfits, I know I can't go back there. I want my own bed, but I don't want to be alone. I want Annabel.

Hey Bel, you there? xx

I wait for the reply, but none comes.

Shit night, need a hug. If you wake up and see this, let me know xx

Just as I'm redirecting the Uber for home, there is a ping on my phone.

She's asleep but I'm here. Could do with a hug too. Come over. Joe x

I don't need more to take him up on his offer. I redirect the cab to Annabel's.

There are several missed calls from Kate. I text her to tell her I've bailed, then I switch my phone off. I'll deal with the consequences tomorrow.

Joe is wearing his pyjamas when I arrive. He sweeps me into his arms at the door. His voice is croaky and he looks as if he's been crying. 'She's out for the count,' he says, gesturing towards Annabel's room as he leads me through to the living room, where his sofa bed is out.

'I'm sorry to come round like this, I've had the worst night.'

'You look, er . . .' He takes in the wonky, sodden wig that is half-stuck to my face, the false eyelashes that are already peeling away and my way-too-tight dress.

'It's been a day,' I say, and it's all I can do to laugh at how ridiculous I must look. Joe starts to laugh too. 'Don't suppose I could borrow something more comfortable?'

'Hang on, I'll find you a T-shirt.'

Joe rummages in his clothes rail while I discard the ginger wig and tug at a fake eyelash. It feels so satisfying to peel it off, like picking PVA glue from the table in art class as a kid.

He hands me a baggy T-shirt and a mustard-coloured hoodie. 'Put these on, get comfy. I'll make us a cuppa.'

I turn away from him as I pull down the top half of my dress. Then I sit on the edge of his bed and undo the buckles on my heels, feeling instant relief as I kick them off. I slip Joe's T-shirt on, wriggling out of the dress underneath it. It smells like lavender.

I poke my head around the kitchen door. 'Don't suppose Annabel has any make-up remover?'

Joe nods and leads me to the bathroom, handing me a pack of wipes from the cupboard. I follow him to the kitchen, where he takes two mugs and waits for the kettle to finish boiling. As he makes the brew, I wipe off my make-up, trying to remove the glue from my eyelids as I inhale the clean, cucumber smell.

Joe leans against the door frame and laughs as he watches me wiping away my face.

'You know you don't need all that stuff,' he says.

Maybe he's right. I look like a cancer patient without it, but at least I'm not pretending to be someone I'm not. But then I can't imagine Lauren's face if I'd suggested going on her hen night with no make-up and no wig.

As I talk him through the horrendous evening, Joe ushers me back towards the living room and puts the two mugs of tea on his bedside table. He pulls back the duvet and gestures for me to sit in his bed. 'There's a new series I was about to watch. Fancy it? Promise I won't try any funny business.'

I climb inside, tucking my bare legs and feet under the warm duvet as he climbs in beside me. Having stripped off my wig, fake eyelashes, make-up, heels and dress, I feel like myself again. I hate all that false shit. This is home.

I nestle the mug in my hands and lay my naked head back on the pillow, telling him all about Lauren and her friends and the spa day, the drinking games and the club. It's exhausting just replaying the story.

'I'd have walked out a lot sooner,' he says, staring at me in the dim light of his bedside lamp.

'Sucker for punishment,' I say. 'I can't wait till the wedding's over so I can get my friend back.'

'When is it?'

'It's a month and a bit away,' I say. 'Beginning of April.'

He sighs and puts an arm around me. 'Want to watch a few episodes?'

'Sure.'

I notice the box of tissues on the side table. He's definitely been crying.

'Are *you* OK?' I say.

He sees me eyeing the tissues.

'Ugh, just protective big brother stuff.'

'Is she . . . I mean, is she any worse?'

Joe removes his arm from around me and rubs his eyes. He shakes his head, then nods. Then he shakes his head again.

317

'The chemo tablets aren't working, Jess. She's been told to stop taking them.'

I feel like I've been punched in the chest. Annabel hasn't said anything about this to me. She must be distraught.

'But if the chemo isn't working, surely there's something else she can try?'

'She's still having some other treatments, but she's not going to get better. I just wish we had more time.'

Putting my mug down on the side table, I find the back of his hand under the cover and brush mine against it. We sit like this for a moment, just touching our hands together, not moving, leaning in to each other. Then his finger twitches, touching the valley between my middle and index fingers, then slowly pushing its way between the two.

As the pad of his fingertip runs down the inside of my middle finger, tingles of electricity course through me. He traces a U shape, slowly moving the soft pad of his fingertip up the inside of my index finger, finding nerve endings I didn't know existed.

Then his hand rolls outward towards mine, while mine moves towards his until eventually all ten of our fingertips touch, and I'm fourteen years old on the coach back from Hadrian's Wall with the lights turned off, my hands finding the warmth of Tommy Riley's as we both discover desire for the first time.

I gulp as our fingertips give way, the palms of our hands gravitating towards each other until they meet, my stomach doing somersaults I didn't think were possible. Then his fingers are intertwining with mine, my nerve endings pulsing as his inner fingers brush mine, slotting into the valleys. Then his fingertips come to rest on the back of my hand and mine on his, our hands fully interlocked.

I lean in towards his body to cushion my head on his neck.

He looks down at me in the dim light and I can almost taste his scent. 'You OK?' he whispers, just centimetres from my mouth.

I can't speak, I can't breathe, but I move a fraction forward and find his lips with mine. And then we are kissing, turning our bodies together, running hands beneath the covers, feeling skin on skin.

'Are you sure?' he says.

'Yes.'

Piña coladas and pixie hair

The morning after the hen do, I'm up and out at the crack of dawn so that Annabel won't realize I slept in Joe's bed. There are seven missed calls and eleven voice notes on my phone. I listen to the string of drunken voice notes from Lauren, starting from midnight. It took her over an hour before she realized I'd gone, before Kate told her I was safe. She is singing along to 'Mambo No. 5', shouting down the phone as she gets to our favourite bit: 'a little bit of JESSICA here I am . . .' Then she is saying 'we missed you, where did you go?' and then it's three a.m., they're back at the hotel, they've realized I'm not there and they're panicking. By five a.m., the voice notes have stopped.

Then there's a voicemail from my dad. 'Jessie love, I'm sure everything's fine, but I've had a call from Lauren saying you're not with them. Call me when you get this.'

Thank God he only saw Lauren's missed calls this morning – he'd have been panicking all night. I'm so stupid to have worried him.

I call him back right away.

'Jessie.' He sounds concerned.

'I went to stay with Annabel because the hen do was awful, I'm sorry.'

'It's OK,' he says.

'Sorry I panicked you.'

'Reckon Lauren might have a sore head this morning.'

'Yeah.'

'Anyway, I'll be down tonight. Ready for tomorrow?'

The thought of chemo fills me with dread, but I feign being relaxed. The next three rounds are a different type of drug and it's the unknown that worries me the most.

'See you tonight, Dad.'

Even though I feel she's the one who needs to apologize, I decide I should call Lauren, at least to let her know I'm OK.

'Oh Jess, I feel like death,' she says. Her voice is hoarse, hungover. 'Where did you get to?'

'I went to Annabel's. I'm sorry, I should have texted you.'

'We were so worried,' she says. 'Why did you run off like that? Kate got your text, and we thought you'd gone back to the hotel. But when we got back and you weren't there . . . we were up half the night worrying.'

'I'm sorry, it all got a bit too much.'

'Well you could at least have said bye.'

'I'm not sure you'd have noticed.'

'Of course I'd have noticed. You're my best friend.'

The image comes into my head of me, holding my sopping wet wig outside the nightclub. 'Best friends don't use their friend's cancer to get into clubs.'

Lauren falls silent.

'You told the bouncer I was *dying*,' I say.

'Oh my God, I'm so sorry. I really didn't mean to . . .' she says. 'I was off my face.'

'Sure.'

'I just wanted to get us in so you didn't have to wait in the rain. I *really* didn't mean to upset you.'

'It's fine,' I say, remembering the beautiful diary and the way she held my hand as I cut off my long hair.

321

Lauren begins to cry. 'I'm sorry, Jess. I've been awful, haven't I?'

'Um . . .' How do you tell your best friend she's changed since she decided to get married?

'Look, Jess, to be honest, the whole cancer thing has floored me. I was so scared it would be like with your mum . . .' She doesn't have to fill in the gaps for me to know what she means. 'I know it probably seems like all I care about is the wedding but I've been worried sick about you. Just ask Charlie.'

'I know,' I say. I believe her, but I don't have the energy to talk about it.

'Jess, I'm so, so sorry. I've been wrapped up in the wedding and . . . if I'm honest, I don't know how to be around you any more. I don't know what to say to you sometimes.'

It hurts to think of my best friend tiptoeing around me. If this is how she feels now, I can only imagine how it will be after she marries Charlie and starts talking about 'trying' and then some day has a kid. I can't help feeling we're growing apart.

'I'm still the same me,' I say. 'Just be the same as you always are.'

Lauren keeps talking, telling me how afraid she's been, how much she loves me and wants me to be around forever. I wish I could go back to the way we were.

Before Lauren got engaged.

Before Mum died.

Before cancer.

Annabel paints my finger and toenails black in preparation for the second half of chemo, to stop them from falling off. I've seen pictures on blogs of women's nails that have gone yellow and black from the chemicals. She says the dark polish stops sunlight from getting to them, helping them to stay intact.

322

Today's Chemo Club has a record turnout, with Annabel, Priya and Aisha in and out of the ward bringing cups of tea and bars of chocolate, anything to make me feel comfortable. Joe sent a sweet text to let me know he's thinking of me.

'Why are you smiling so much?' Aisha says when Dad goes to fetch tea. 'Is it a boy?'

I keep my mouth shut, shaking my head.

'You kissed a boy on the hen do, didn't you? Oh my God, you did!'

Nurse Ange comes to the rescue as she bounds into the ward, holding what look to be giant foam gloves, like the ones at baseball games. As she starts speaking, Aisha nudges me. 'Don't think you're getting out of it that easily, young lady.'

'We're going to put these ice gloves on your hands and feet to protect your nails, OK?' Ange says. 'It's going to be very cold but it will help with the side effects.'

The thought of the cold makes me nauseous. I can't bear cold showers or ice against my skin.

'Pop your hands out for me,' says Ange, slipping the enormous blue gloves over my hands, then my feet. It doesn't feel too cold at first. 'I'll leave that for twenty minutes for your hands and feet to adjust. Then we'll get the chemo started.'

I can already feel the cold building up inside the gloves, like the cumulative effect of holding my hands in the ice baths that Johnny used to take when he still went cycling. There was a threshold where it became unbearable and I'd have to take my hands out, but in this case I can't.

My feet feel even worse, my toes tingling with numbness and the pain rising to my head, like an ice-cream headache, amplified.

'Think warm thoughts,' Priya says. 'You're on a desert island, surrounded by warm sand, palm trees, the sound of the waves. The sun is blaring down on you in your red bikini and you can feel the rays on your belly and thighs. There's a sexy guy in hot pants coming along with piña coladas and Bloody Marys . . . which one will you go for?'

'Can I have a hot chocolate?' I say, squeezing my eyes shut, trying to picture the scene.

'Jess, it's boiling. You're on a desert island and it's forty degrees. You definitely don't want a hot chocolate. Anyway, the hunky man is wondering if he can have your number. He particularly likes your pixie hair and your red bikini. What do you think?'

'Am I alone on this island?' I ask, desperately trying to play along when all I can think about is the splitting pain of the ice surrounding my hands and feet.

'You're with your girlfriends but we're a little way down the beach in our own private paradise and you've come out today to check out the local talent,' Aisha says. 'This guy is just your type . . . he's tall, dark, ripped and very strong, very muscular. And he wants to take you in his hot tub.' Annabel giggles.

'Now you're talking,' I say, laughing as I open my eyes.

The gloves are starting to warm up and the pain is easing off slightly, just as Ange comes to replace them with fresh ones. My muscles tense and I bite my teeth as she slides the new ones onto my hands and feet.

'So you were going to tell us about the boy who's making you smile?' Aisha says.

'There's no boy,' I lie. 'I was just thinking how lucky I am to have such wonderful friends.'

Box sex

During my 'good' week after chemo number four, I send Dad back home and invite Joe round for dinner and a walk on the Common. He insists on cooking while I put my feet up. Annabel has gone to stay at their mum and dad's and she thinks he's out with a mate. I feel bad lying to her, but until I know what our status is, I don't know what I would tell her.

I walk into the kitchen to find a pack of frozen peas in a glass dish next to my place setting. 'What's this?'

'Your personal ice pack, for the hot flushes,' Joe says, turning from the stove to grin at me.

'You really have thought of everything, haven't you?' I say, stepping over to him and kissing him, while I run my hand over the soft layer of hair on his head. He kisses me back and then pulls away.

'Don't make me ruin the fish cakes.'

'Never,' I laugh, picking up my glass of wine and settling at the kitchen bench to watch him cook.

'Forgot to ask, you're not allergic to anything, are you?'

'I'll eat anything. Shellfish, offal, insects, you name it . . .'

'I'll note that down for next time,' he says, turning over the fish cakes with a spatula.

Next time. A good sign, surely, that he's thinking about a future with me. I love that he makes me feel so secure.

'I could get used to this,' I say, my chin in my hand as I rest my elbow on the table.

'I'll cook for you any day, you know it's my one true love,' he says.

'How come you never became a chef, like your mum?'

'Well, the careers counsellor at school told me I should be an undertaker, which set me off on a slightly different path. Then I ended up with an English degree and then, well, somehow I ended up in recruitment. It paid the bills for a while, but I wanted to teach. Plus, have you seen how much chefs earn? You don't do it for the money.'

'I don't think you teach for the money either, do you?' I say.

'Not at all, and teenagers can be absolute bellends, but I wouldn't change it for the world. What about you, is there a plan B?'

It's a question I've rarely been asked in the last ten years. Even though I've written less since I've been an editor, I've always made sure I keep up some kind of writing, which is why it's so great having a column. After all the unpaid internships and hard graft, I don't think I'd ever change, as long as I can write. 'I love it, especially at the moment, writing my column.'

Joe steps away from the stove, puts a hand on my neck and pulls me into a kiss, as if he couldn't stop himself. 'It's the passion I love about you.'

Love. Love about you. I try to hide the grin on my face. I mustn't get ahead of myself.

He returns to his cooking. 'So if you won the lottery, would you stay at the mag?'

I think about the piles of old *Perfect Bake* issues stacked up in my living room and how proud I still am every time I see my name on an editor's letter. Even though I get tired of the office politics, the deadlines and the endless meetings-that-could-be-emails, I don't think I'll ever get over the buzz of opening a fresh magazine that I put together or seeing my byline on the page.

'You know what, I'm not sure I would,' I say.

'You'd never want to sell your doughnuts?'

'I wouldn't mind having one of those little weekend market stalls one day. That'd be cool. What about you?'

Joe presents two plates of perfectly cooked fish cakes with peas and sweet chilli sauce and takes the seat opposite me. 'I'd set up a foundation for kids in Southeast Asia, teaching them how to cook and stuff. You know, the shit they don't really teach you at school. Social skills, food, nutrition, life.'

Ugh, is there any box this man doesn't tick?

'The Sadler Foundation has a nice ring to it,' I say, biting into a fish cake and moaning my approval.

Joe nods. 'I've done a bit of research but I need to travel more first, get to know the region.'

'You don't stay in one place for long, do you?' I say. He seems to change careers and countries every couple of years. I wonder how easily he changes girlfriends.

'Well, Mum and Dad always encouraged us to travel. They didn't have much growing up but they've worked hard to be able to afford the occasional trip. Mum was always daydreaming about exotic places like Borneo and Costa Rica, so as soon as I turned eighteen, I've always travelled.'

'Southeast Asia next then?'

'Definitely,' he says. 'I really want to spend more time in Thailand and see if I can find a place to set up a project. Maybe next year.'

'What about Annabel?' *What about me?*

'Jess,' he says softly. 'She's not going to be here next year.'

327

'You don't know that. I've heard of people living for ten years with some types of cancer.'

He puts his fork down and looks at me.

'I'm being realistic. I'm not going anywhere while my sister is still alive, put it that way.'

He leans over to kiss me and takes my face between his palms.

'You can come with me if you like.'

'To Thailand?'

'Sure, go travelling. The whole shebang. It'll be fun.'

I manage a half-smile. Part of me longs to go.

But backpacking with Joe would mean that Annabel was dead.

The rest of dinner is filled with laughter and I barely notice it's gone eleven. Soon I'm leading him by the hand to the bedroom I shared for so long with Johnny.

I sit up in bed, half-clothed, Joe lying by my side. We chat for hours, interrupting our laughter with kisses, never going too far. He touches me cautiously, brushing my breasts but never pressing too hard.

'Does it hurt?' he says, running his finger over the lump.

'No,' I say. I've asked myself the same question count-less times, pressing on the lump to see if it is getting smaller from the chemo, or if it hurts more than it did before. It's hard to tell how much it has changed, but Dr Malik is confident the treatment is working.

I'm grateful Joe has seen me before the mastectomy. After seeing Annabel and Priya, I can't help worrying about the lumpiness, the scarring, the weird-looking nipples.

'Will you still fancy me, you know, after my operation?' I say, hugging the bed sheet up to my neck.

'Are you kidding me? You're gorgeous now and you'll be

just as gorgeous after.' He kisses me on the neck and moves his hand down the top of my cleavage.

'Seriously though,' I say, pulling his hand away. 'I'm worried it'll freak you out . . . that you'll look at me and see cancer.'

'Look,' he says, peeling up the front of his T-shirt to reveal a long, white scar that runs the entire way up his chest, from his belly button to his nipple line.

'What happened?'

'Massive operation when I was sixteen. I'll tell you about it another time, but I was out of school for half a year. I was totally paranoid about anyone seeing the scar, so I avoided even flirting with anyone until I was eighteen. And by that point, I was kind of behind.'

'Oh.'

'When I started having sex, obviously no one gave a shit about my scar, and I wished I hadn't left it so long. So let's not waste any time,' he says, kissing me again.

In the morning, I wake in a cosy tangle with Joe, his hairy legs tickling against my hairless ones. He is snoring, a glaze of sweat on his forehead. When I try to extricate a leg, he stirs, peeling one eye open.

Without saying a word, he shifts sideways towards me, wrapping one heavy arm around my waist as I slot into a safe, warm, Sunday-morning spoon.

Dear friends with kids

In her latest column about newfound singledom and dealing with breast cancer in her early thirties, Jessica Jackson writes an open letter to the sisterhood

Dear friends with kids,

It's not that I'm not happy for you. I am. It's just that I'm also unhappy for me.

I'm happy for you because you're experiencing, with your partner, the most profound and ultimate joy that anyone can ever experience, with a child of your own. I'm unhappy for me because I don't know if I'll ever have that, and because as you gain a little human who you love more than anyone in the world, I lose another friendship.

I know I won't *lose*-lose you. It's just that you have other priorities now, and you'll never be able to pay me the same attention you did before. We'll never again sit on my parents' kitchen floor eating the leftover contents of the fridge after a wild night out. You won't be there to hold my hair back the next time I'm puking into a pan, because you'll be cleaning up your baby's puke instead, and because there won't *be* any more wild nights out.

There'll be no more sleepovers and we'll never have those hour-long phone calls with the telephone wire wrapped around our fingers and the door shut so our parents can't hear us talking about our crushes.

It's not that I don't, or won't, love your child. How could I not, when she's a tiny extension of you? When your kid puts her hand on my leg for support when she's learning to walk, I feel a love that I can't explain. When I feel the bump kicking in your belly, it makes me well up with happiness for you – I share your excitement, like a sister. And when your baby laughs with me for the first time, I am filled with so much love for her, just like I love you, my friend.

What I want you to understand is that I'm not just miserable and jealous, I'm left out. You've joined a club I might never be part of. More and more of my friends are joining by the day, and I'm not sure if I'm eligible for membership. If it wasn't enough that you're all paired off and having couples-only dinner parties, now you're part of this new thing, an exclusive club with 'NCT friends', 'expressing' and burping. I know that poonamis and sleepless nights aren't glamorous things, but they're things I want to be a part of.

So please, friend, fit me into your new life. Don't forget me. Don't assume I don't want to hear about 'latching on' and the damage to your perineum, but in the same way do remember to ask me, just ever so occasionally, how I'm doing.

Love, Jess x

Times I've been the bridesmaid, not the bride: 3
Bouquets I've caught: 0

Aunties who've approached me at weddings to ask whether I'll be next: 362

I feel a burning in my chest when the piece goes live because I know this one will be controversial. But I hear Tabitha's voice in the back of my mind: be honest. Other people are feeling this too.

I've forewarned Kate about the piece, but she calls me in floods of tears when she reads it anyway.

'Oh Jess, it kills me that I can upset you so much from having a baby, but I'm so glad you wrote this.'

'Kate, it's not about you, like I said before. It's this whole cumulative effect of Lauren getting married and then Tabitha and Leah and Priya and every other person I know with their perfect lives. It's the endless Facebook posts and all the stuff I'm left out of.'

'I get it,' she says. 'Before we had Ella, I felt exactly the same. And you might not think it now, but the grass is always greener.'

I understand that she can empathize with me, but I still don't see how she can really 'get it'. She has a child so she doesn't have to worry about it any more.

'Jess, I know I have less time for you and Lauren since I had Ella, but what you might not realize is I actually need you *more* than I did before. This has been the hardest year of my life.'

'I know,' I say. I'm crying already. This is exactly the effect I didn't want to have, to upset Kate.

'The time with Ella, it's so *lonely*, Jess. When I'm at home with her, the days seem to go on forever and Colm is never home. And when I'm back at work, I just feel constantly guilty for not being there for her.'

'I'm sorry, I know it's been hard.' I wish I could do something to help her.

'And I know you've got it tough with the chemo and Lauren

SINGLE BALD FEMALE

is out of action with the wedding of the century but Jesus, Jess, I need my girlfriends more than ever.'

'I'm so sorry I haven't been there for you.' I'm such a shit friend.

'You *have* been there for me,' she says. 'What I'm saying is I want to spend *more* time with you. I want to have girlie nights in and forget about the fact that I'm a mum for a few minutes. Sometimes I feel like it's sucked my whole identity away.'

It's a perspective I haven't seen before, and it suddenly clicks into place. Of course she's still the same Kate she was before. I've got it into my head that she's changed since she got married and became a mum, but she misses the person she used to be just as much as I do.

'Listen,' I say, seizing my chance. 'I don't suppose you'd be willing to be interviewed for the magazine? It's kind of short notice because the shoot is next week, but we're doing this piece about truth and honesty and sharing our problems so that other people won't feel so alone and . . .'

'Get my face in *Luxxe*? Are you kidding? Jess, I'd bloody pay you to put me in there.'

'Are you serious?' I never thought she'd go for it. I've been putting off asking her.

'Will they give me a makeover? It's been so long since I've felt even vaguely attractive.'

'Of course,' I say, relieved that I haven't offended her. 'We can mention your events agency as well, maybe give it a little bit of a boost?'

We make a plan for the interview and I promise I'll make sure she gets full hair and make-up and access to the wardrobe. With kids a similar age, I can picture her getting on well with Tabitha too.

I feel so good after speaking to her that I call Lauren as soon as I hang up.

'I just read your piece,' she says, before I even get to 'hello'. 'Shit, Jess, I get it. It's half the reason Charlie and I are getting married – otherwise I'd still be shagging my way around Magaluf.'

I laugh at her comment because it's true, she was always the most likely to end up single because she was so addicted to the good life.

'You do know I was miserable for the first few months after I moved in with Charlie because I missed living with mates so badly?'

I had no idea – but I felt the same. I hated feeling like I couldn't slob out with cream on my moustache because Johnny might stop fancying me.

'Shit got boring, didn't it?' I say.

'Tell me about it. When was the last time we had a big night out? I mean, let's forget about the hen-do disaster.'

I seriously can't remember the last time the three of us did anything together that wasn't a midweek meal or a weekend brunch.

'When did we relegate our friendships to weekdays?'

'I don't know,' she says. 'I mean, no offence to Charlie, but you and Kate are *way* more fun on a Saturday night. I feel a bit repressed.'

'Well let's do something then,' I say. 'When I'm better.'

'Like what? Clubbing in Marbs?'

'Marbs schmarbs,' I say. 'Let's go to California, do a road trip.'

Lauren sounds animated. 'Jess, I cannot tell you how much I want to go on holiday with you. Married life just seems like . . .'

'You're not having second thoughts, are you?'

She makes a relaxed sound. 'No, no. Charlie is amazing. I just don't want marriage to mean I have to be divorced from my friends.'

334

'This is easily rectified,' I say, feeling warm with the love I thought I'd said goodbye to when she got engaged.

'Well, I'm glad we've sorted this one out. Next time you write an article for half the world, come to me first.'

I laugh. 'Anyway, speaking of your wedding . . .'

'You're not going to say you hate the dress, are you? Because I don't think I can handle . . .'

'Actually, I was wondering if there'd be a space for a plus one.'

'Oh my God, are you serious? *Of course* Joe can come. So it's official then?'

I feel weirdly shy saying it out loud. 'Well, we haven't had the whole exclusive chat yet, but it's going well. He's such a lovely guy, you know?'

'I can't wait to get to know him better, Jess. He seemed so lovely at your birthday. And he's cute! I'm so happy you've found someone.'

I hang up the phone with my chest bursting, for the first time in ages, with love. I can't believe all it took was a couple of phone calls to my friends.

Just before bed, I read the comments and messages from the article I shared on Facebook.

Aisha Parker: I am sooooo with you, girl. Crazy cat ladies together forever xx

Annabel Sadler: You know you can always count on this girlfriend for eternal, childless singledom xoxo

Tabitha Richardson: This piece made me cry. I wouldn't trade Matilda for the world, but us mums are just as jealous of the single life sometimes. Big hugs x

Gamma knife

Joe and I sit in silence on plastic seats as we wait for Annabel's treatment to end. I hate being on the other side, being friends and family instead of the patient. It's all just waiting, helpless, wishing it was me instead of her.

I pick up my book but I can't read more than three lines before my mind wanders to Annabel, lying beneath a big machine, her head in a frame, trying to remain as still as possible while having her brain zapped.

'How long will it take?' I say. I really want to organize something nice for Annabel, to take her mind off all this, at least for a while.

'Last time it was hours,' he says. 'That's the worst part, not knowing where she's at. Endless waiting.'

'How was she afterwards?'

'In shock,' he says, without really looking at me. 'She played it down, of course, but she wasn't expecting it to be so painful.'

'Is it really that bad?' I imagine jolts of power going through her brain like an electric shock.

'Well, the name gamma knife sounds worse than it is,' he says. 'It's just radiation to specific spots in the brain to target the tumours. There's no cutting involved, and it's not painful. But she said it hurt when they fixed the frame to her head.'

'That's something,' I say. 'How you feeling about everything?'

He leans his head on my shoulder so I can smell his banana shampoo.

'I'm OK,' he says. 'Just helpless, you know? But glad to have you here. We both are.'

Annabel emerges an hour later, her temples marked from the pins that have been holding her head frame in place.

'How was it?' I say, both Joe and I standing up from our seats to greet her.

'Don't want to talk about it,' she says, almost a whisper.

Joe puts his arms around her while I stand beside them.

'Shall we get out of here?' I say.

We walk to the car park in silence and I open the boot to reveal my surprise, another batch of doughnuts. Raspberry jam flavour, Bel's favourite. She manages a half-smile as Joe helps her into the passenger seat.

Back at theirs, the three of us squeeze onto the couch, Bel on one end, Joe on the other and me in the middle, covering ourselves with a blanket.

I lift one of the jam-filled pastries and hold it up to Bel's mouth. She takes it, licks it, licks her lips and savours the sugary sweetness. I see the beginnings of a smile in the corners of her mouth. Then she goes back for a bite, and jam squirts out onto the blanket.

All three of us laugh.

'Hey, I want one too,' Joe says, brushing his arm against mine as he reaches into the box on my lap.

He bites into the doughnut, making heavenly eyes at me as he does so.

Annabel puts her doughnut down, exhausted, before she can finish it. I pick up one of the trashy magazines on her coffee table.

'Want me to read to you?' I say.

She nods her head, almost imperceptibly.

I flick through the pages and pick an article about the latest celebrity break-up, where the author speculates that the actress may turn to a sperm donor for a baby.

'They've made this up,' I say, shaking my head.

I turn to the next page, holding it closer to our faces to look at the pictures. 'Ugh, can you believe they managed to get that shot up her skirt? I wouldn't want to be a celebrity; I'd be constantly making a dick out of myself and ending up in magazines.'

I turn a few more pages but Bel is barely responding.

'You OK?' I say, shutting the magazine and dropping it into my lap, on top of the doughnut box.

Bel stares off into space. I try to see what she's focusing on, but she's staring at nothing.

'What if I forget Nan and Gramps?' she says.

I reach under the blanket for Joe's hand without turning to look at him, then I find Bel's with the other. I'm squeezing so hard I feel I might crush her, so I squeeze tighter on Joe's instead.

'Don't they say you get confused about the present but you remember the significant bits from the past?' I say.

She stares at me, hopeless, helpless. 'If I lose my mind, will you tell me, every day, about Nan and Gramps? I don't want to forget them.'

'Of course we will,' Joe says.

'Why don't you tell us some stories so we can help you remember?' I squeeze harder on Joe's hand to stop the tears from flowing.

'Remember when we tried to teach Nan how to do email?' Joe says, his voice catching as he starts to speak.

Annabel perks up, a grin appearing across her face. 'The netbox! The bleedin' netbox!' she says, doing an impression of her grandmother in a Cockney accent. 'She was always asking how many stamps you needed to send an email. She was flabbergasted when we said it was free.'

'Did you guys go on holiday as kids?' I say, trying to provoke some memories now that Bel is opening up a bit.

'We used to take the caravan down to Brighton,' Bel says, staring off towards the window.

Joe nods, with a childlike look on his face. Suddenly Annabel's shoulders are shaking and I realize she's laughing.

'What is it?' Joe says, the laughter catching.

'The seagull!' Annabel says, putting her hand on her chest, in pain from the laughter. She turns to me. 'Oh Jess, it was so funny. Gramps had bought us all ice creams and we were sat on those stripy deck chairs on the beach. Joe stands up and he's holding his ice cream to the side while Mum rubs sun cream on his back . . .'

I catch Joe's face as he recalls the story and puts his face in his hands, laughing too.

'And suddenly Dad's like "look out!" But it's too late . . .'

'What?' I say, waiting for the punchline but they're both laughing too much to tell it.

'I'm not kidding you, it's like a film. This seagull literally swoops down and nicks Joe's ice cream. And Joe kind of does a double take as he realizes the entire cone has straight-up vanished from his hand. And then he starts WAILING, like literally inconsolable. And I can't stop laughing when I see this seagull hacking away at the cone with all his mates just a few yards away.'

I can't help laughing along now, both of them in happy tears at the memory.

'And Joe does *Not. Stop. Crying.* Well, until Nan finally agrees to take him off and buy him a replacement ice cream,' Annabel says. 'Joe's been shit-scared of seagulls ever since.'

'That's not true,' Joe says. 'I laugh in the face of seagulls!'

'It is so! In fact, it's not just seagulls, it's pigeons too. Any bird. I've seen you flinch when a sparrow even so much as approaches you. Coo, coo!' Annabel leans across me and makes a swooping motion towards Joe, who bats her hand away.

'Don't believe a word she says, Jess.' He shakes his head at me. 'Bonafide alpha male. Zero avian phobia over here.'

'Sounds like you had a fun childhood,' I say, as Annabel tries to calm herself down from the exertion of laughing so hard. She coughs into a tissue and I notice it comes away with blood again.

'Why don't you show me some pictures?'

Joe goes over to the bookshelf and brings back an old photo album. The three of us leaf through the pages, laughing at photos of a young Joe and Annabel posing behind retro photo boards on Brighton pier, their heads popping out of the cut-out holes on the bodies of a mermaid and a diver rescuing her from the deep.

Then we've moved on to pictures of them from an earlier summer, naked in their paddling pool and then wearing corduroy sweaters and leggings. Joe is in hysterics as he recalls the time Bel pooed in the bath.

'He'll never let me live that one down,' Bel says, turning towards me with an eye roll.

Joe laughs.

'What about you two,' Bel says, suddenly serious. She looks from me to Joe, and back to me. 'Will you look after each other?'

I turn to Joe. Is this the right time to tell her? I'm scared she'll think we're taking advantage, or she'll be jealous. Her friend and her brother.

Joe is the one who breaks the silence.

'I'll definitely take care of this one,' he says, making a show of putting his arm round me in front of Annabel. 'Speaking of which . . .'

Annabel cocks her head and raises an eyebrow.

'It's early days but . . .' Joe says.

She pulls a face, waiting for him to spit it out.

'Well, we're kind of, um, together,' Joe says, biting his lip in anticipation of her reaction.

Bel bursts out laughing. 'Jesus, guys, you think I didn't notice? Why do you think I've been going to stay at Mum's? You two have been sneaking around for weeks!'

'It's only just begun,' I say. 'It's not like we're . . .'

'Jess!' she says, her eyes lighting up, the most energy she has shown all day. 'Come on. My brother's been mad about you since the day he laid eyes on you.'

I can barely speak for a second, blushing. 'You're not angry?'

'Angry? How could I ever be angry when my best friend in the world and my big brother are getting together? It's the best news ever.'

I don't know what makes me happiest: the fact that she's pleased for us, or that she called me her best friend.

Brighton Beach

It is another week after my fifth chemo before I'm strong enough to get to the beach, but the timing works well as it falls during Joe's school holidays in late March. I thought if we brought Annabel back to the place where she had all those happy times as a kid, she would refresh the memories of her grandparents and we could even make a bunch of new ones. It will do Joe good too, the chance to do something fun for once, instead of carting his sister around to hospital appointments to receive endless bad news.

Joe drives us to Brighton with Annabel in the passenger seat, covered in blankets, me in the back. On the way, he instigates a game of I Spy while Bel points out the things I barely notice, the colourful houses, the green parks, the trees still barren of leaves.

We park in a space near the sea front and lift Bel into her wheelchair. She can still walk, but she'd rather save her strength for when it matters. We wheel her around the Lanes, stopping to look in shop windows and laughing at silly signs.

'Can I get an ice cream?' she says, when we walk past a shop with metal tubs of colourful flavours on display.

'It's freezing,' Joe says.

'I know, but I want an ice cream. I might not be here come summer.'

342

'Of course you will,' he snaps. 'Please don't say things like that.' But we all know she's right.

We wheel her into the shop and help Bel out so she can look at the flavours. She picks a cone with a mix of salted caramel and mint choc chip, while Joe goes for cappuccino covered in toffee sauce and I get strawberry and orange sorbet. Then we head to a little open courtyard to eat them.

'Look out!' Annabel shouts, making a face of horror to the left of Joe's shoulder. Joe quickly ducks, before he realizes she's taking the piss.

'You're a dick, little sister,' he says, shaking his head in mock disgust. 'I'll get you back for that.'

'Right, first photo op,' I say, getting out the Polaroid camera Bel gave me for my birthday. I thought I could recreate some of the snaps of her and Joe and their grandparents when they were kids and put them into a photo book for her to compare against the old ones. 'Quick, before it melts!'

Joe and I crouch down either side of Bel's wheelchair and pose with our ice creams as I take the first picture. I smile as the image starts to appear. Annabel looks like a child, making come-hither eyes at her ice cream, while Joe focuses solely on his sister, ever the doting big brother. I place the picture carefully into my bag before turning my attention to my ice cream.

The sorbet slides down my throat, soothing the inflammation, powerful enough to relieve the metallic taste in my mouth that worsens with every chemo. Pure joy shows on Bel's face as she chases her tongue around the cone, deep in concentration, catching drips of sticky salted caramel.

We make our way towards Brighton Palace Pier, my shoulders sinking with relief as soon as I spot the iconic pistachio-coloured railings and smell the salty sea air. As we amble down the pier, Joe wraps Bel's blanket tightly around her to shelter her from the wind, removing it only briefly to snap new

343

Polaroids with our heads popping through the cut-out holes on the photo board. I produce the sneaky shot I took on my phone of their nineties' version of this picture, so they can copy the exact poses they made as kids. Afterwards, we hold the new Polaroid up against the old image on my screen and laugh until we're breathless.

Then we head to the amusement arcades. We start on the slot machines, jamming two-pence coins down the chutes and watching as the blocks push the piles of coins just far enough to touch the edge of the ledge but never quite far enough to tumble over it.

Bel is determined to see it rain two-pence coins and perseveres until she's spent three pounds on the one machine. Joe and I roll our eyes at each other, stealing kisses while she's not looking. Eventually it pays off and the pennies pour into the chute.

'Quick, help!' she shrieks as the coins start to overflow, spilling out onto the floor.

I find a spare tote bag and hold it out as Bel scoops up handfuls of coppers, dropping them in with glee.

'I'm rich!' says Bel. 'Shout you guys fish and chips?'

Joe orders three lots of battered haddock and chips at the kiosk on the pier and pours out the heaving bag of coins onto the counter. 'My sister won these on the slot machine, hope you don't mind,' he says, taking a couple of notes from his wallet to supplement the pennies.

I see the server's eyes scanning my blue wig then my pale face, devoid of eyebrows and eyelashes. I see the look of pity and I can tell he thinks Joe is talking about me. I want to correct him, to point to Bel, hidden from view in her wheelchair underneath the counter, but I hate myself for thinking it, as if Annabel is somehow inferior to me just because she's sicker.

Three lots of fish and chips arrive in cardboard boxes. Joe

joins me to open each one and sloshes on heaps of diluted vinegar, cheap ketchup and salt from sachets.

We wheel Bel over to three stripy deck chairs facing the carousel. Joe helps her into one of the chairs and she stabs a chunky chip with her tiny wooden fork and pops it into her mouth. The three of us sit, ploughing the greasy chips into our mouths and licking salt and ketchup from our lips. I steal a candid shot of Bel with her tongue halfway out of her mouth that I think Joe will love.

When I put the camera away, Joe feeds me a chip. I lean to kiss him, just a peck.

Bel makes a loud 'ahem'. 'It's good to see you two bonding,' she says. 'You'll make an honest woman of her once I'm gone, won't you Joe?'

'Annabel!' he warns. 'Stop talking like that.'

'Alright, forget the "when I'm gone" shit,' she says. 'But you'll marry her someday, won't you?'

My knee is twitching. Would she put me on the spot like this with anyone else I'd been seeing for a matter of weeks, or is it just because he's her big brother?

'I reckon it wouldn't be a trip to Brighton if we don't go on the carousel, what do you think?' Joe says. I'm grateful for the change of subject, even though secretly I want to know his answer.

'Yes!' I nod, turning to Bel in her deck chair. 'Reckon you're up for it?'

'I'm not a fucking invalid.' She nods, then makes an awkward face. 'Alright, I am an invalid, but I haven't quite lost the capacity to sit on a horse and hold onto a pole for five minutes.'

We wait our turn before helping her onto the horse. I take the one beside Bel's, and Joe goes behind us. Around us are kids with their parents, a teenager or two. Cold wind attacks my face but I don't mind, breathing in the sea air as we ride the carousel, bobbing gently up and down. I hold out the camera and get a shot of us holding onto the golden poles with our matching wigs blowing in the wind.

When the ride ends, we wheel Bel to the end of the pier and look out to sea, listening to the gulls and the sound of the waves, crashing, far off. Down below, there are people walking on the stony beach, occasional swimmers tentatively dipping toes and shrieking at the cold.

'I want to die by the sea,' Bel says.

Joe nods, just enough to acknowledge her, but not wanting to question further.

'I want to go in,' she says.

'It's freezing in there. You'll die,' Joe says.

'I'm going to die anyway.'

I pray for her to change her mind as we wheel her down the ramp to the beach, but she doesn't. We leave the chair at the bottom of the ramp and she starts to peel off her clothes, dumping them with her Converse.

'You'll come in with me, won't you, Jess, even if Mr Boring doesn't want to?'

I shudder at the idea of getting into the ocean, taking my clothes off in this cold. It's starting to drizzle and somehow it feels even colder than when we went in the Hampstead ponds in January.

But Annabel is already down to her T-shirt, exposing her white legs. I remember the euphoria we felt at Hampstead Heath.

'Wait for me,' I say, unzipping my parka and throwing it onto the back of the wheelchair. I give Joe a look that says, 'What can I do?'

'Bra and knickers,' says Bel, willing me on, jigging her legs up and down to keep warm. It's really starting to rain now, the freezing cold drops landing on my exposed arms.

'We're really doing this, aren't we?' I say, laughing mostly out of hysteria.

'You two are fucking crazy,' Joe says, shaking his head, genuinely concerned. 'I'll look after the stuff. Be as quick as you can.'

'Don't be such a wet,' Bel says with a wink. It's the most animated I've seen her all day.

I wriggle out of my jeans and raise my T-shirt and jumper over my head to reveal a spotty pink bra and unmatching blue knickers. What a day for Joe to see me like this.

Bel is down to her bra and knickers too, and I can see the jagged white scars under each cup, the tied turkey effect on her chest.

'Stop staring, perv!' she says, slapping me hard across the bum before running away from me, doing a little shimmy as she makes her way to the water's edge. It is pouring with rain, the drops hammering the waves and blending into the darkness as they hit the sea.

I turn to see Joe staring at Annabel from behind. He's seen the scars, the gauntness, the fragility. Does he imagine me like this one day?

I walk up, kiss him gently on the lips as if to say, 'I'm still alive. I'm still here.' Then I follow Annabel into the sea, the cold taking my breath away as the water slaps at my thighs.

Ahead of me, Bel is already floating on her back, looking up at the sky.

How to meet a guy IRL

In her latest column, Jessica Jackson explains why she's given up on online dating

I asked my first boyfriend out via telephone. I called his landline (it's like an iPhone but with a long cable that's fixed to your parents' house) and spoke first to his father, then his mother, then finally the fourteen-year-old object of my affection. I lay tangled in phone wires behind a door I'd shut to keep my parents from eavesdropping, and we talked for a whole fifty-nine minutes about whether Mrs Davis from French class was secretly a lesbian. At the end of it, I said, 'Will you go out with me?' He said yes.

I miss those times – the pre-Tinder, pre-internet, even pre-texting days when the only way to reach your crush was via their landline. For twenty years we've had the ability to send flirty texts; for fifteen we've had the ability to 'poke' and for ten we've been able to swipe left and right in a virtual supermarket with shelves full of the opposite sex. Which is great in some ways, but in others it's awful.

It's awful because anything you buy online you can send back to the shop with free postage. Online dates are as disposable as the dress you ordered and changed your mind about when you saw a shorter, more sparkly one. You don't even have to call and make your case for the return – you just pop it in a jiffy bag, bung on a pre-populated label and the money is back in your account in no time. Online dating is the same.

That's not to say it's a bad thing. I don't know how else I would have met anyone in my thirties, when most of my friends are in relationships and my idea of a big night out is a bottle of wine before the last Tube home. In hindsight, it was far too soon, but I signed up online after I broke up with my long-term boyfriend, and put myself through seven dates in seven days on seven apps *(click here to read)*.

It didn't occur to me to tell potential matches that I had cancer and was about to lose my hair – why would I? I wanted to sell myself as the sort of woman I thought men wanted to be with – fertile, young, whole. But guess what? The guys I met weren't the kind I needed to be around as I entered the scariest chapter of my life. It's not that I need a man to take care of me, but I do want someone who'll understand if I'm too sick to leave the house or I don't fancy bodice-ripping sex in the middle of chemo.

Then I realized these men weren't the only ones lying online – I was too. How could I expect to meet an honest guy if I wasn't being truthful about myself? I was vulnerable and weak, broken-hearted and bald. I wasn't going to meet the sort of guy who'd respect me if I masquer-aded as a hedonistic twenty-something in search of a hook-up. So I made a new, honest profile with a picture of me and my hairless head.

The guys who got in touch this time were honest about themselves. Some of them had cancer too. Others said they admired my bravery, so I knew they valued a personality, not just a pretty face. Then there were the ones who just found baldness plain sexy – who knew that was a thing?

I went on a handful of dates off the back of my new profile. The guys I met were lovely, though ultimately not for me. But they taught me that I don't have to settle for second best just because I think I'm damaged goods. It doesn't matter that I'm not perfect – no one is.

As soon as I accepted that, I found someone offline, in actual real life. It's early days but he is good to me, and he makes me feel good about myself. He might even be a keeper. And whatever happens in the future, I'll know I chose a guy who didn't mind being seen with a girl with no hair, and who is with me because of who I am. The confidence I've gained from that is far greater than the confidence I might get from growing my hair back.

Guys whose opening messages simply said 'Hey': 15
Dildos inserted into my vagina for medical purposes: 1
Cups of tea drunk: 233

Ophelia Cossack-Daly: Whoop, whoop! So glad you've met your #PrinceCharming Jessica. Can't wait to hear more! #IHearWeddingBells

Annabel Sadler: Can't tell you how happy this makes me. You are going to be the best sister-in-law ever xoxo

Cath Elderfield: Well I'm glad you've managed to meet someone 'IRL' as you say (I always thought that meant Ireland, maybe that's where I'm going wrong teehee), but I can't say I've had the same success. I'm thinking about signing up for this Tinder malarky

myself, is there an OAP version? There's life in the
old dog yet! Love Aunty C xx

Reply – Kit Elderfield: Over my dead body, Mum!

After the column goes live, I post a picture on Instagram of me
with my bald head and earrings, alongside a line about finding someone who likes me for who I am. I add the link to my
column and include the hashtag #SingleBaldFemale.

Within an hour, I have ninety new followers and the post
has five hundred likes, even more than my red-carpet pic at the
Luxxe Women Awards. There are dozens of comments below
it, mostly from total strangers.

*@NiamhOShea99 Your columns are so inspiring! I've just
been diagnosed with breast cancer at thirty-three and am also
single, so I might follow your example – bit scared to sign up
on dating sites though! Niamh x*

@TiaAdedeji26 Been following your columns in Luxxe *and
am loving your take on modern dating. I've been on apps for
years and it can be painful – it's good to know I'm not on my
own. Wishing you loads of luck in love x*

I keep checking Instagram in between uploading pics to
Annabel's photo book. The likes and comments keep on
coming, but it's a totally different crowd from Ophelia et al.
Most of the people commenting seem to have gone through
something similar – whether breast cancer or disastrous
dating. Even Stephanie Asante has left a lovely, sweet message
about how beauty is only skin deep and empowerment comes
from within.

Even though the comments are mostly from complete strangers, I feel a weird affinity with them. It's far more comforting
to hear kind words from someone halfway across the world
who also has breast cancer than an estranged Facebook 'friend'
who knows nothing about it. I feel like I'm finding my tribe.

#SheSaidYes

The morning of the wedding, Lauren is more stressed than ever. I thought she'd be relieved to be back in the Yorkshire countryside with almost nothing left to organize for the big day. Instead she's been fidgeting all morning, worrying her make-up is going to look too dramatic and anxiously checking the weather app to see if the dark clouds will turn to rain.

Kate serves eggs Benedict with Buck's Fizz and we lounge around in matching pink pyjamas to a romantic playlist while we take it in turns for make-up and hair – or freshly washed wig, in my case.

It takes the make-up artist forty-five minutes to put my face on, but she manages to fill the bald area above my eyes with real-looking eyebrows, and applies fake lashes with minimum fuss. She tones down my puffy, blotchy skin with some sort of green corrective concealer and creates a healthy glow with blusher and eye shadow. If it weren't for the fact I'm completely bald, no one would know about the chemo.

When she sees me, Lauren looks half happy, half sad. 'Jess, you look stunning.'

Her voice breaks and tears fill her eyes.

'No,' she says. 'This bride is *not* going to cry on her wedding day.'

'I'll get us some tunes,' Kate says.

Moments later, Justin Timberlake is pumping from her phone and our prosecco glasses are topped up.

Kate and I stand over Lauren, swigging from our glasses, as she relaxes into the chair and lets the hairdresser curl her hair.

'I know I said I'm not going to cry, but can I say something, before I get my face on?' Lauren says, craning her neck to look up at us both.

'You're not going to get all soppy on us, are you?' I say.

'Last night was the first proper girlie sleepover we've had since Kate got married. I've really missed it.'

Kate and I nod. 'It really was fun,' I say. We spent the evening eating pizzas, dancing around Lauren's hotel room and gossiping about everything from old boyfriends to chin hairs. Lauren seemed on edge at first, but she relaxed after a couple of glasses of wine.

'We should take a vow not to break up our girlie nights just because two of us are married,' Kate says.

'Hard yes,' I say, putting my prosecco flute into the ring to cheers them both. 'It shouldn't take a wedding for us to get together like this, should it?'

'Well,' Kate says, raising a cheeky eyebrow. 'Unless you've got something you want to tell us, Jess . . .'

'What, me and Joe? Don't be ridiculous.' I laugh at the idea of us getting engaged. But the truth is, I'm thrilled at the thought. I know it's far too soon to say it, but the word 'love' has been on the tip of my tongue a couple of times. Feeling how right things are with Joe has made me see how wrong they were with Johnny.

'I'll make sure I aim the bouquet in your direction,' Lauren says with a wink.

'Very funny,' I say. But once she's put the idea into my head, it's hard to get it out.

*

I briefly interrupt my bridesmaid duties to meet Joe in our room. I've neatly arranged my bathroom products on one side of the sink and hidden my dirty underwear. It's our first time staying in a hotel together and I'm irrationally nervous.

He knocks on the door and I pause before I open it, losing all my nerves the moment I see his smiling face. He steps into the room with his wheelie suitcase in one hand and his suit bag in the other.

'Look at you,' he says, and for a moment I'd forgotten about my over-the-top wedding make-up.

'Is it too much?' I say, kissing him then going up close to the gilt-edged mirror for a better look.

'Let me see,' he says, putting down his luggage. He puts his hands on my hips and draws me in to his body, kissing me softly so as not to ruin my red lips. 'You look radiant.'

I moan as he draws away from the kiss. 'I wish I could stay a bit longer so we could enjoy all this.'

He walks further into the room and we admire the claw-foot bath with the beautiful view of the gardens outside. 'We can have some fun in here tonight, can't we?'

'Maybe you can help me scrub my make-up off later,' I say, perching on the edge of the bath and pulling him towards me.

I try to kiss him again, but he is wary of my make-up, so he puts his arms around me and hugs me instead.

'I better get back to the bride,' I say, seeing the time. 'Will you be alright on your own?'

'I'm quite sociable when I want to be,' he says, taking off his coat and unzipping his suitcase. 'I better get my glad rags on in preparation for charming all the mums and nans. I'll have you know, mums *love* me.'

I force a smile. My mum would have loved Joe, but she'll never get the chance to know him.

*

354

'Can you see him?' Lauren says, standing beside her father as Kate and I peer into the church at the rows of assembled guests.

I spot Joe before I see Charlie. He is standing on the third row from the front, on the bridal party's side. I never imagined he would scrub up quite so well in a tux. He looks so handsome with his buzz cut and suit, I can barely take my eyes off him, but I remember I'm supposed to be looking for Charlie.

'Groom. Check. Best man. Check,' I say, turning to Lauren in her stunning marshmallow-white dress. For all my moaning about the bridesmaid dresses, I have to admit she was right all along – we are perfectly coordinated. I brought both my wigs to Yorkshire, having promised Lauren I'd wear the rescued auburn one so as not to stand out in the photos. But as soon as I tried on the electric blue with the marshmallow-pink dress, it was a no brainer – Lauren said she'd be thrilled for me to wear it.

'Ready, girls?' Kate says, holding the hands of Lauren's two little nieces in their adorable miniature matching dresses. She gives them each a gentle push, as if launching two ducklings into the water, and they're off, taking a few cautious steps down the aisle. There's a chorus of 'aww's from the congregation.

Seconds later, Kate gives us one final smile and wishes Lauren good luck before she marches down the aisle behind the flower girls.

'This is me,' I say, turning around to give Lauren a hug before I leave her to walk down the aisle with her father. It is starting to spit with rain.

But Lauren is staring towards the entrance to the church, as if in a trance. On the floor beside her, she has dropped her bouquet.

'Lauren?' I say, stepping in front of her and taking one

355

of the hands that hang limp by her side. 'Sweetie, it's time to go in.'

In slow motion, she raises her head to meet mine, but she looks dead behind the eyes. I give her dad a little nod and gesture for him to step away for a moment.

'Lauren, Charlie is in there waiting for you. I'm about to walk down the aisle. Are you OK?' I'm anxious she's going to get wet out here in the rain.

She starts to shake her head, slowly at first, then speeding up, her nostrils flaring. I take her hand and guide her gently towards the entrance to the church. I'm supposed to be halfway down the aisle by now, but I need to make sure Lauren is OK.

As I step towards the threshold, I feel her tug on my hand. I turn around.

'I can't do it,' she says, letting go of my hand and backing towards the stone wall.

I peer in at the congregation, where everyone is staring expectantly at the entrance. Then I look back at Lauren, who is now slumped on the soggy grass, her wedding dress bunched up at her feet. I *knew* something wasn't right.

'Could you go in and stall them for a bit, say we're having a dress malfunction?' I say to Lauren's father. 'Last-minute jitters.'

He looks at Lauren and gives me a nod, heading into the church.

I crouch down beside her and talk in the same voice I used to use with cousin Kit when he would come home crying with cuts and scrapes. 'Sweetie, the love of your life is in there waiting to marry you. What is it, what's wrong?'

She is hyperventilating now, the tears pouring down her cheeks, leaving streaks of black mascara down her face like rain tracks on a car window.

'Hey,' I say, pulling out a bunch of tissues from my clutch bag and pressing them underneath her eyes. 'We don't want to ruin this make-up. Come on, take a deep breath.'

I try to get her to count with me, focusing on the numbers as we take deep breaths in, then out, in, then out. But by the time we get to five, she blurts it out.

'I can't marry him,' she says, with complete clarity. 'I thought I could do this but I can't.'

I sit properly on the floor beside her now, stretching my legs out in front of me, conscious I'll ruin my dress but also knowing it's over. As I try to console her, I hear the organist shift to filler music to pass the time. Lauren's dad emerges, having pacified the guests.

'Tell them it's off,' Lauren says, sniffling as she looks up at her dad.

He crouches down beside her and takes her hand. 'Surely you don't mean that?'

'Please,' she says. 'I'm sorry, I'm so sorry. I can't do it.'

I try to keep her calm while her father disappears into the church, but I can't get any sense out of her.

A few seconds later, Charlie comes running out of the church. I step back and lead Lauren's dad down the path to the road to give them some space.

It feels like we're watching a romcom-gone-wrong as we eye them from across the church gardens, trying to make out what they're saying. I keep expecting Charlie to pick her up and wipe the tears from her eyes, kiss her and tell her everything will be OK. No matter about the bad luck from seeing her before the wedding, or the fact that her dress will be covered in mud. At least he'll have talked her down from the ledge.

But that doesn't happen. After five minutes of Lauren crying and Charlie trying to calm her, she drags herself to her feet

357

and shakes her head at him. I watch him put both hands on her arms to try and stop her, but within seconds she is running away from him, towards me and her dad, back towards the same car that dropped us off fifteen minutes earlier for the best day of her life.

Settled

In my hotel room, Kate boils the kettle while Lauren picks at the kirby grips in her hair, removing them one by one and dropping them onto the bedspread. Her wedding dress lies in a crumpled heap between the bed and the window, while Lauren sits in her bra and knickers underneath the duvet. We had to send her mum out of the room until she could stop crying hysterically.

Kate brings over a cup of tea and sets it by Lauren's bedside, stirring in two sachets of sugar and a capsule of milk.

'Here, let me help you,' I say, motioning for Lauren to move in front of me so that I can help her extract the grips embedded in her up do.

Like the monkeys we once saw in India picking out fleas from each other's fur, Kate and I work on removing every trace of wedding day from Lauren. Kate wipes at her face with cotton wool pads while I work my way through her hair, which is crispy and hard from so much product.

'You don't have to tell us now, if you're not ready,' Kate says, blowing on Lauren's tea and encouraging her to take a sip. 'But we're here for you whenever you are.'

Lauren manages a tiny sip of the sugary tea, and eventually sighs.

'I think I knew all along that it wasn't right,' she says,

turning her head sideways to acknowledge me sitting behind her. 'But it really clicked when you found out Johnny had cheated.'

I let go of the kirby grip in my hand and drop it into the pile, then I crawl across the bed so that I'm facing her, beside Kate.

'When I met Charlie, you guys were both so loved up. Kate, you were getting married and Jess, you'd moved out of our place and in with Johnny. I felt like I'd lost you both, like I was the only single person on the planet.'

'I know that feeling,' I say, squeezing her hand. I never thought I'd be the person who finds a relationship and neglects her friends, but there was a period after Mum died and Johnny and I had moved in together that I barely saw Lauren. I thought she was busy having the time of her life, going out and getting drunk with her single pals. It breaks my heart to think of her being so lonely.

'I felt like you were both leaving me,' she says, wiping at the tears that are falling down her cheeks. 'When I started seeing Charlie, I was let into the group again. I got invited to your couples' dinner parties and had a plus one for weddings. I even got a couples' discount on my frigging gym membership, for god's sake.'

The three of us laugh. I'm already hatching a plan for a feature on how discriminatory the world can be against single people.

She reaches for a wad of tissues and blows her nose. 'Charlie is amazing. He's so sweet and kind and reliable. But I don't think I've ever really been in love with him, you know? I just sort of *settled*. And his whole jealousy thing, all the insecurity and the fighting, it's because deep down I think he knows I don't feel the same way about him as he feels about me.'

I must admit, I was surprised when Lauren accepted Charlie's proposal after just a year of dating him. She was the wild one at school, skipping classes after all-night benders and always dating the bad guys, the unavailable ones. Charlie wasn't the sort of guy I pictured her settling down with, neither exciting nor exotic enough for her tastes. I thought maybe she'd realized she needed someone who was more like marriage material.

'And when you told us about Johnny's cheating and how you realized people only cheat when their own relationship isn't right, something clicked. I still look at other guys, I still fancy people. It's like I still think of myself as single.'

Kate reaches for her cup of tea and cradles it in her hands, taking gentle sips. 'Do you love him?'

Lauren sighs. 'I do, yeah, but I'm not *in* love with him. I don't know if I ever was. And when I look at you guys, well, you and Colm, and now you and Joe, I feel like I'll never have that. And I'm scared I'm nearly thirty-two and I'm going to be single forever and I'll never have kids and . . .' She is sobbing again.

'Of *course* you'll have that,' I say, taking the hand that isn't held by Kate. I wish Lauren could understand how much I relate to what she's feeling. For the last few months, I've felt like I'm destined to end up a lonely old cat woman spinster, and bald to boot. It's only since I met Joe that I've started to think that marriage and kids could be a possibility again.

When she's ready, Kate and I leave Lauren alone so that Charlie can go into the room and talk to her. He looks crestfallen in his wedding suit as we meet in the corridor, shaking our heads to confirm that no, she hasn't changed her mind. I feel so sorry for him, having to hear that the woman he loves has never really felt the same.

I arrange to meet Joe in the hotel bar, since Lauren and Charlie are in our room. When I get there, he pulls me into a hug and orders me a lemonade as he talks me through his version of events. He says that watching Lauren's father address the congregation to tell them that his daughter would no longer be getting married was one of the saddest things he's ever seen.

I can't shake the guilty feeling. If I'd been there for Lauren over the last couple of months, perhaps I could have helped her. She said it was mine and Johnny's break-up that led her to doubt her marriage to Charlie, and the cancer that stopped her from talking to me about it. What if I'd been a better friend, had pressed her on why she'd been behaving so out of character? Lauren was by my side when Mum was sick, the best friend a girl could have. It should have occurred to me that it's not like her to go bridezilla, to try and persuade me to freeze an embryo with Johnny when we both knew it was the wrong decision. I've been so preoccupied with work and men and cancer, I haven't been a good friend.

For the rest of the afternoon, I flit between gathering all the parts of the wedding that belonged to Lauren – the photos she'd attached to every table to represent the different parts of her life, like 'Yorkshire massive', 'Uni crew' and 'Gap yah' – and listening as she frets over all the things she needs to sort out. Reverse wedmin, she calls it, cancelling the honeymoon, giving back the gifts, paying Charlie's parents back the debt she now owes them, not to mention finding a place to live. It feels far too soon, but I'm happy to offer up the possibility of her moving in with me and Aisha. Silver linings and all that.

By the time Lauren's parents persuade her that it's better if they drive her back home with them, she is like a child at the end of her own birthday party, too exhausted from adrenaline to do anything but comply.

Joe and I decide to stay at the hotel and drive back to London tomorrow as planned. We order BLT sandwiches and crisps from room service and eat them in bed. I'm utterly spent.

'I know it's going to sound weird, because this has literally been the worst day ever,' I say, twisting my neck to look up at Joe from my position snuggled into his chest. 'But it's been really nice having you here.' I mean it. Somehow, experiencing this together has only made us feel closer.

Joe strokes my head, and I realize I feel more secure in two months with him than I did in five years with Johnny.

I sit up and face him. The feeling is stronger than anything I've felt in a long time. 'I mean it. I think . . . I'm falling in love with you.'

Joe stops stroking my head and freezes, his body turning to stone.

'Shit, I'm sorry,' I say. What was I thinking? It's far too soon for the 'L' word.

'Ssh,' he says, putting his finger to my lips and turning his body to face mine. 'I'm crazy about you, Jess. I'm falling for you too.'

Falling for you. Definitely not *falling in love*.

'It's fine,' I say. 'Forget I said it.' I shuffle into a sitting position and crawl under the covers, pulling the thick white duvet up to my chest.

'Jess, look, I know tonight is not the right time, but there's something I need to say.' Joe scrambles for his T-shirt from the floor. Why is he getting dressed? My chest feels so tight I can barely breathe.

He sits on top of the duvet instead of getting under it with me. 'I really am falling for you. These last few months of

363

getting to know you have been incredible. I love the way you make my sister feel. You've brought her back to life. You've brought *me* back to life.'

'But . . .' I say. There's always a but.

'My sister is dying, Jess,' he says. 'She's my number one priority, and I can't help thinking the more time I spend with you, the less I spend with her.'

'But we can spend time with her *together*, me and you and Annabel.' There's nothing more that I want. I love her as much as I love him.

'Jess, I promise you, there is no one else I'd rather be with than you. But I'm not ready. I don't think I can be in a proper relationship right now, not with everything . . .'

His face crumbles, his brow creasing up and his nostrils flaring as the tears start to pour. It is clear what he means. He can't go into a relationship when his sister is dying.

'Oh Joe,' I say, putting my arms out and drawing him in. He takes the invitation, resting on my one good breast, his head bobbing up and down as he sobs and sobs.

When I wake up, the sun is streaming in through the window. I can barely open my eyes, my head feels as if it's been hit by a truck. I groan as I roll over, my entire body sore from a day on my feet. Then I realize I'm alone. Joe has gone.

I adjust my eyes and slide sideways across the bed to reach for the note he has left on his bedside table.

Jess, I'm so sorry for everything I've done to hurt you, but I can't do this. You deserve to be loved in a way that I just can't give right now. I am so sorry. Joe x

I collapse back onto the bed and weep.

The final straight

'Good news,' says Dr Malik. 'Your blood count is perfect. Ready for the last one?'

'As I'll ever be,' I say, turning to Dad.

Four months ago, I never thought this day would come – the sixth and final chemo. I'd been planning on making doughnuts for everyone and handing them around the ward to celebrate what will hopefully be the last time I ever have to do this. I planned to wear a blue dress with my blue wig – something to make myself feel pretty, a nod to getting better and growing my hair back. But in the two days since the wedding, all I've felt like doing is curling up under a rock.

Joe has been calling and texting, asking if we can speak, but I've ignored all his attempts. He said what he needed to say, and I know deep down he's right. He's in an impossible situation, going through the worst thing imaginable. He needs to give himself time and space.

But that doesn't ease the feeling of heartache. *Right person, wrong time.* Or maybe he's not the right person at all – if he really cared about me as much as he said he does, surely we'd make it work somehow.

How many more times can my heart be broken? I know we weren't together long, but it was real. I'd already made us an 'us' in my head. I wanted him in my life, I wanted all of him,

I wanted to introduce him to everyone I know and proudly show him off. Joe didn't see me as damaged goods. He liked me for who I am.

I don't blame him for not being able to handle it. I wouldn't wish what he is going through on anyone. But I'm sorry for me, for having to start from square one, when I feel like I have nothing. No hair, no life, nothing going on with work because chemo has put *everything* on hold. The cumulative heartbreak of the last six months – Johnny, Joe, Lauren and Annabel – is too much for me to take.

'Come on then, love,' Dad says, prompting me to leave Dr Malik's room and walk to the ward.

My steps are slower now, my life interrupted by chemo and the ageing effect it has had on my body. It's hard to remember being able to spring out of bed now that I can barely clean my teeth without needing to sit down on the edge of the bath.

'Final one,' says Nurse Rose, giving me a hug and glancing at my bald head. 'You must be excited to get this over with.'

I try to smile, but it only brings tears to my eyes. It's hard to feel excited about anything now. The other side of chemo feels like an endless empty space.

I slip into the chemo chair and wait for Nurse Ange to arrive with my ice gloves, while Dad goes on a tea run.

'Delivery for you,' says Rose, holding a huge bunch of flowers.

My mind shoots to Joe. Could he really have changed his mind?

I read the note. *Smash it, Jessie J. Always here for you, love Aish xxx*

My heart sinks when I realize it's not from Joe. Of course he hasn't changed his mind. He's not like Johnny, wanting me one minute and someone else the next. Joe is a good man. That's what makes this even harder to take.

Nurse Ange comes in, her usual chirpy self, butchering the lyrics to a Rihanna song in her loveable way. I try to smile, but I can barely respond as she goes about her business. With the ice gloves on my hands and feet, I feel the burn straight away, and all I want is to be at home in a nice warm bath. When I feel the dull pain of the cannula being forced into my tender skin for the last time, I start to cry.

'Are you OK?' she says, still fiddling with my inner arm and fixing the tubes with tape. 'The last chemo can be emotional.'

I shake my head. I don't want to talk about Joe. I feel like an idiot for telling so many people about him, getting excited about a relationship that barely began. What was I thinking, taking him to my best friend's wedding when we barely knew each other? I don't know why he agreed to come along if he knew it wouldn't last.

'You are so nearly there,' Angelica sings, fixing the bag of chemicals to my drip pole and pressing a series of buttons. 'Just one to go, nearly done now.'

She hands me some tissues and I dab my eyes with my free hand. I don't want to be here. I want to fall asleep and never wake up.

'Knock, knock,' comes a voice from the doorway. I turn to see Priya pushing Annabel in her wheelchair, with Dad following closely behind.

I sniffle and dry my eyes as they approach my chair. I don't want Annabel to see me like this. My tears are pathetic compared with what she's going through.

Dad greets them and excuses himself, saying he'll take a walk outside.

'How you doing, hun?' Priya says, pulling up a seat and sitting next to Annabel, beside my chair.

'Fine. Emotional,' I say, too teary to manage any more words.

Annabel starts to haul herself out of her chair and Priya gets up to help her.

'Don't get up on my account,' I say, seeing the effort it takes for her to get onto her feet. Annabel looks weak. She's lost even more weight and her voice is croaky and rasping.

'I just wanted to give you a hug,' she says, leaning into me and putting her bony arm around my neck. 'Sorry about my dickhead brother.'

Priya excuses herself to do the tea run.

'He told you?' I say, as she sinks back into her chair.

She nods. 'He didn't tell me what happened, but I guessed. For what it's worth, I think he really likes you. Too much, possibly. And I know he doesn't want me to know this, but I think he just can't handle getting into a relationship when I'm like this.'

She gestures towards her body in the same way you might if you were showing off a new outfit. I feel bad for being able to worry about a two-month relationship ending when she's nearing the end of her life.

'Forget it,' I say. 'We don't have to talk about this.'

'I'm sorry,' she says. 'If I could change things for you . . . Maybe when I . . .'

Maybe when I die, you could be together.

I shake my head. 'Sssh,' I say. 'Let's not talk about this. It's too . . .'

It's too close to home. Just looking at Annabel's eyes, I see Joe. And suddenly I realize I've lost both of them. With Joe in my life, I thought I would keep a piece of Annabel once she dies. Without him, I lose them both.

'I'm sorry, Jess. You know I . . .'

'Stop,' I say, looking away from her, suddenly mad at her for existing, for coming into my life that day, when everything could have been simpler.

'Jess . . .'

I shut my eyes. 'I'm sorry, Annabel, I can't talk about this right now.'

I can feel her hurt as I squeeze my eyes shut. I know I'm being cruel and stubborn. I should reach out and hug her, but I don't.

I can hear her starting to open her mouth and close it again, and feel the movement as she reaches out towards my chair then pulls her hand back. Then I hear the wheels in motion as she spins away from the chair.

I open my eyes just in time to see Bel leave the ward.

'Where's she off to?' Priya says, walking towards me and setting her cup down on the table between us.

I shrug, like a stroppy teenager, unable to speak.

'Is she coming back?'

'We both got a bit upset.' She won't be back.

Priya furrows her brow, like she understands.

'Well, we were meant to give this to you together, but since she's gone . . .' Priya pulls out a wrapped gift. 'It's no biggie, just a few things we thought you might like.'

'It's from Annabel too?'

Priya nods. I gulp down the lump in my throat. I'm a terrible, terrible person.

I open the wrapping and pull out a blank journal with the words 'The next chapter' on the front. I finger through it, finding pages with titles of lists: 'Goals for the year', 'Places I want to visit', 'Things that make me happy'.

In the 'Things that make me happy' list, someone has already written 'hanging with my Chemo Club girls'. A tear drips down my cheek as I recognize the handwriting as Bel's.

'We figured you love a list,' Priya says.

'It's amazing, thank you,' I say.

I feel like a total bitch.

369

Human pin cushion

On the fifth day after chemo, just as the prickling pain in my bones is easing, I find myself pulling up the covers, shivering with cold. I do my hourly temperature check, having pretty much maintained a stable temperature for the last three months. It says 38.6 – and I'm sitting under a thirteen-tog duvet. *Shit*.

I would normally call Dad for his opinion, but it's late and he's just gone back up north, thinking I was done with the worst of it. He'll be asleep in bed with Lizzie now, and I've kept them apart long enough. Lauren stayed last night, the two of us sharing in each other's misery, watching feel-good films on the sofa, but I don't want to bother her when she has work in the morning. I can't wait to move in with Lauren and Aisha next month so I don't have to be on my own any more.

My next port of call is Annabel, but we haven't been in touch since the day of my chemo. I know I need to apologize, but every time I pick up the phone to text her, I picture her face and then I picture Joe. I can't face either of them.

'Shit,' I say, to no one other than Oreo, who jumps up from my lap, disturbed.

I check my temperature a few more times and eventually haul myself out of bed to get dressed and order a taxi. Every muscle and bone in my body aches.

The journey to the hospital is quick. At eleven thirty, there are only late-night revellers, people running for Tubes, some of them probably only just going out. There's a queue outside a nightclub on Clapham High Street, drunk girls smoking in the street, young men with boy-band haircuts. It reminds me of the awful night of Lauren's hen do, my wig in a puddle on the floor, my head exposed.

By the time I arrive at the hospital, I'm shivering with cold. How can I possibly have a temperature? I put my palm to my forehead to see if I'm burning up, but all I feel is cold.

'Let's get you in for some tests,' says a nurse I've never seen before, leading me to an unfamiliar part of the hospital. She gestures to a chair and I sit down, peeling off my coat and sweater.

'My veins are pretty uncooperative,' I say, accustomed now to feeling like a human pin cushion.

'We'll find a way to get some blood. Sharp scratch.'

She is rougher than Ange, squeezing my arm too tight and poking the needle in once, then twice, with no warning the second time.

I daren't look down but I know there is no blood, because she's still prodding my inner arm.

'Do you usually have trouble?'

'My veins are uncooperative,' I repeat. 'I've been on chemo for four months.'

'You should have said. I'll have to call a senior nurse.' She says it like it's my fault.

Another nurse arrives ten minutes later, a guy this time, but he doesn't introduce himself. 'Tough veins?' he says.

'Hi,' I say. 'Yes, there are only a couple of veins that will work now. I'm a bit sensitive.'

'Don't worry, we'll get there,' he says, reapplying the tourniquet and aiming again at my inner elbow.

371

When the needle fails for the third time, I start to cry. 'Please, please can you make sure you bring someone who can do this?'

'I'll have to get a doctor,' he says.

'Great,' I say, tears in my eyes, willing them to treat me like a person, not a voodoo doll.

I check my phone while I wait. No calls, no texts. I write a message to tell Dad I'm in hospital but in good hands.

'Miss Jackson,' says a voice, distracting me from my thoughts. 'I'm Dr Stevens. I hear you have a temperature?'

My voice breaks as I try to explain the problem with my veins. This time, he gets it right, piercing my skin so gently I barely realize it's done.

'All set,' he says. 'I'll set up some saline through this drip and we'll get some tests done, look at your blood cultures, determine where the infection is.'

He looks around me, registering the absence of partner, parent or friend. 'Do you have anyone you can call?'

I wish I had Joe or Annabel. Both of them would know what to do, they'd know exactly how to make me feel better. But both relationships are damaged, and I can't expect Annabel to be at my beck and call. Not when I've treated her so badly.

'I'm sure my Dad will come tomorrow,' I say.

I wake up soaked in cold sweat, my legs rustling against the plastic under-sheet of the bed. *Where am I?*

Shit. I'm still in the unfamiliar ward. A man snores like a ribbiting frog a few metres away.

I try to move my hand, but find it attached to the drip pole. I need to pee. I don't know how to pee with this thing attached. Where's Nurse Ange when I need her?

A woman shuffles past the dark corridor and for a moment I think it's Rose.

'Hello?'

She comes over, stands beside my bed. She is not Rose.

'How do I get to the bathroom with this attached?' I say, feeling like a helpless child.

'You take it with you,' she says, sullen-faced.

'Can you help me, please?'

'Of course,' she says, but she sounds resentful. Was she on the way to another patient, or perhaps going for her break?

'Just take the pole with you,' she says, softening as she holds out an arm to help me. I swing my legs carefully down onto the floor. 'Hold on to me. There you go.'

I use my free arm to steady myself on the bed and stand. I must've been asleep half the night. It's five a.m.

Once I'm on my feet, I nod at the nurse to release me, and secure the pole with one hand while dragging it to the loo with the other. I'm shackled to a machine.

I stare at myself in the bright white light of the bathroom mirror. My eyelids are puffy, my face still blotchy, my eyes bloodshot. Bald head, barely a hair on my face now, a ghost of a woman.

I lie back in the bed, struggling to get comfy as I rustle around on the sheet, which is soaked with my sweat. All around me, machines buzz and whirr, my roommate ribbits and every time I approach falling to sleep, I'm disturbed by someone new entering the room.

Nurses arrive to take my blood pressure with plastic readers they place over my thumbs. People take my temperature. Cleaners swab the floor, poking their heads around the door. Each time a different face, each time checking my notes at the end of my bed.

I try to sleep but all I can think of is Joe and Annabel, and how much I miss them both. I hadn't realized quite how much I'd come to love having them in my life.

Knowing I shouldn't, knowing I'll never sleep if I do, I press the home button on my phone and watch as the screen lights up the entire ward. I click onto Annabel's Instagram profile and browse through the feed. It's like an homage to our friendship, every post a picture of our three smiling faces – me, Joe and Annabel, the three musketeers. Underneath the pictures of us at Hampstead Heath, Joe has commented with two emoji hearts.

How could I have been so selfish? Annabel has months, maybe weeks, to live, and yet she has dedicated them to making me happy. She dropped everything to give me the best birthday I've ever had, and she's gone out of her way to include me in her plans with Joe. In return, I tried to take her brother away.

I realize how unfair I've been. If this is how I feel when I'm stuck in hospital for one night, how must Annabel feel, knowing she'll never have a clean break? If my future seems bleak, I can't imagine how it must feel to have no future at all. I've been so wrapped up in my own problems that I've neglected a friend who only has a short time left.

I pick up my phone to text her an apology, to tell her I'm in hospital and that I miss her and I love her, but when I look at the words on the screen, they seem so pathetic. I owe her more than a text message. I need to see her in person, to wrap my arms around her and tell I'm there for her. As soon as I get out of here, I'll go straight to her.

Quarantine

'Jessie,' says the voice, the moment I open my eyes.

'Dad. Where am I?'

I look around the ward, remembering the infection, the drip, the late-night trip in the taxi.

'How did you get here so fast?'

'I got your message at three a.m., love. I didn't want to call you back in case you were sleeping, so I drove through the night. You should've called the house phone.'

'I didn't want to wake you.' My eyes are filled with tears.

'Jessie,' he says, putting his hand over mine. 'You can always wake me. I'm your dad. I've nothing else to do but care for you, remember?'

I nod, trying to hold back the tears.

'Good morning, Jessica,' comes a familiar voice, a welcome interruption.

'Dr Malik.' My God am I pleased to see him.

'I hear you have an infection,' he says, hovering over my bed. Then, turning to Dad, he says, 'Hello again, Mr Jackson.'

Dad shakes his hand.

'We have your blood results,' Dr Malik says. 'It's inconclusive, we can't see where the infection was. But the bad news is you're neutropenic – you don't have enough white blood cells to fight infection.'

Oh, shit.

'We'll need to keep you in for a couple of days while you recover. You have to be extremely careful with visitors.'

'A couple of *days*?' I need to get out of here so I can see Annabel.

'I'm afraid so. It's just to keep you under observation. You'll need to stay on the drip but don't worry, your temperature is already dropping back down.'

'Thank you, doctor,' I say.

They move me to my own private quarantine with a TV, bathroom and even a window. Another nurse I've never seen appears with a cardboard bedpan shaped like a kidney.

'Take this to the bathroom with you every time you go,' she says. 'We need to measure how much you pass.'

'You mean when I—?' I can't quite bring myself to say it.

'Your bowel movements and urine,' she says.

I sit for ten minutes with the cardboard kidney tray slotted into the toilet bowl, but I can't go. I feel like a toddler potty training, an invalid who can't go to the loo without being monitored. Eventually I fix my eyes on the steady drip, drip, drip of the shower and the pee starts to flow, drumming onto the cardboard like rain on my Velux windows.

'There's a good girl,' says the nurse when I return with the kidney tray of urine and set it down on the floor outside the bathroom. She puts on her gloves and exits the room with the sample.

I wash my hands like a crazed Lady Macbeth, as if somehow touching a tray containing my own piss has made me dirtier. I rub the water and soap gently around the tube coming out of my right hand, then dab it dry, twisting my hand underneath the cable to hold the pole in place.

'I'll go home and get you some stuff, love, what would you like me to bring?' Dad says.

'There's a book on my bedside table. A couple of magazines and my pyjamas, next to my bed, some tops and knickers . . .'

I hate the thought of Dad rifling through my underwear drawer. I tried to do those things for him as much as possible with Mum, so they might retain just a tiny bit of the passion in their relationship. I helped with cleaning, getting Mum in the bath, holding her hair back when she was sick. But I couldn't be there all the time and I think of the moments he had to help her go to the loo, the ultimate humiliation for both of them.

'I suppose you might want some chocolate too, then?'

'I hear it's good at curing neutropenia,' I say, with a smile.

I spend the morning flicking through TV channels – Saturday telly, kids' cartoons, old movies, all the world continuing around me while I remain in quarantine. Outside the window, it's beginning to look like summer, the trees covered with leaves, the sky pure blue.

Dad comes back at lunchtime with my clothes and books and a parcel. I recognize the packaging and rip it open immediately.

'Annajel Does Brighton' reads the title on the cover, breaking up a collage of snaps from our trip. I had toyed with calling us 'Bessica', but felt like Annajel was more inclusive of Joe. But the truth is, both feel trivial now.

I open the first page, relishing the satisfying sound as the hardback cover peels away from the freshly printed pages. I re-read my short dedication: *To Bel, for teaching me to live. Love always, Jess x*

On each of the left-hand pages, I have scanned the black-and-white images of the Brighton trips they took with their grandparents as a child from the album Joe secretly lent me. Then on each right-hand page there is a comparison image from our trip last month. Aisha helped me edit the photos so that it looks like one of those magazine shoots where celebrities recreate iconic images from old vinyl album covers.

I've included captions like '#SeagullGate' and 'Show me the money!' beside a candid shot of Annabel staring maniacally at the slot machines, eyes entirely on the prize.

The final image makes my heart stick in my throat as I see it in print. Joe captured one of me and Bel running into the sea, the ominous, dark clouds and uninviting grey water contrasting against our pasty white arms and legs. On the adjacent page is a shot of Joe and Bel as kids, the two of them playing with sandpits on the same beach, facing out towards the sea in identical blue towelling pants.

I close the book and place it down on my bedside table. I need to see Annabel. I need her to know how much I love her.

When Dad leaves after lunch, I send work an email to let them know I'm in hospital, then I pick up my phone to text Lauren and Kate. I hold my good hand away from me and snap a selfie with my drip and pole in shot, then I send it to them without a filter.

Hey girls, don't panic but I'm in hospital with some sort of infection. Telly recs and bad jokes appreciated. Jess xx

Both Lauren and Kate reply immediately.

Oh my God, are you OK? Can we come and visit?

I tell them about the neutropenia and the quarantine, and how it's probably best if they stay away, but I promise to let them know as soon as I'm on my way home. Lauren lists out seven different TV programmes I ought to be watching, while Kate tells me about a podcast she listened to all the time when Ella was born.

I open Instagram and scroll. Leah has posted a flat lay with baby Milo on a fluffy rug and building blocks spelling out the letters 'I am five months old'. Tabitha has dropped an adorable image of her and Matilda alongside a triumphant account of how difficult she found it going back to work after mat leave, but how she is now at peace with the guilt she feels as both mother and employee. I like both the photos, but they only emphasize that feeling deep down that I might never have kids of my own.

Then I remember Johnny, and realize I've barely thought of him in weeks. I wonder how he's getting on, if he's managed to get himself out of his slump and back on track at work. Knowing I shouldn't, I hit 'unblock' on his account and navigate to his grid. There's nothing, so I take a deep breath and navigate to Little Miss Avo's feed, knowing I will only punish myself by looking at her tanned, taut body when I'm stuck in hospital feeling like death.

And there it is. The image of Johnny and Mia, his arm draped loosely around her shoulders as she poses in a figure-hugging, off-the-shoulder black dress and crimson heels. Next to it is a photo of them, both sweaty and red-faced in their activewear, looking like they've been for a jog together. *A jog!*

Beneath it, the caption says:

We scrub up alright x

So I couldn't persuade Johnny to get himself better, to start cycling again and motivate himself for work. I couldn't help him, but Mia obviously could.

I scroll down her grid to see if there are any more clues, and then I see it.

Can't wait to move down to London to be with this one x

I feel sick. I thought I would feel fine seeing Johnny with another woman – I want him to move on, to be happy. But not with *her*. And I know it's because I've lost Joe and Annabel, but I suddenly feel so hopelessly, desperately alone.

I shouldn't have looked at Instagram. I shouldn't have

tortured myself like this. I delete the app and stick my phone on the bedside table. But I can see it out of the corner of my eye, taunting me with all the fun that everyone else is having while I lay here, miserable.

I'm suddenly filled with a desperate urge to scream and shout and kick and fight, but the only thing in sight is my phone. In an impulse, I pick it up and hurl it across the room with all my strength.

Then I watch as it lands underneath the window with a crunch.

'Someone to see you,' the nurse says, appearing from behind my door.

I crane my neck to see who it is. I wasn't expecting Dad again today.

She appears around the doorway, looking completely different from the last time I saw her five months ago with her baby bump.

'Leah!' I say, taking in her beautiful peach-coloured sweater, paired with jeans and stylish boots, ever the *Luxxe* editor. 'What are you doing here?'

'Breaking with tradition,' she says. 'They said it was fine for me to come in as long as I don't come too close. I don't have a cold, don't worry.'

I fumble for my wig, but it's too far away. With no make-up and my hideous-looking chemo face, I must look like I've been brought back from the dead. Certainly not a good look for meeting the boss for the first time since she went on maternity leave.

'Can I sit?' she says, leaning into the chair against the wall. She looks glowing and radiant, certainly not like a woman with a five-month-old baby.

'Look, the nurses told me how knackered you are, so I

won't keep you long. And I'm sorry for just turning up like this. I did call, but it went straight to voicemail . . .'

I glance at my phone on the bedside table, feeling like a complete fool for my moment of hot-headedness. One of the catering staff retrieved it from the floor but it's shattered into a gazillion pieces and won't turn on.

'My phone ran out of battery,' I say, too embarrassed to admit the truth.

'No bother,' Leah says. 'Much better to see your face!'

I wince at the statement, wishing I was wearing some make-up, a little bit of armour.

'I wanted to show you this,' Leah says, reaching into her bag and handing me a copy of the magazine. 'You absolutely smashed it.'

I gasp when I see it. The Truth Issue for *Luxxe*'s tenth anniversary. I had completely forgotten it was out this week.

The front cover is a grid of alternating black-and-white images of celebrities and ordinary women. On the top left is Tabitha, looking like a porcelain doll with Matilda in her arms. Beside her is Stephanie Asante, wearing her hair out and holding up a sign that reads STRONG. Below that is Kate, looking straight into the camera, vulnerable yet powerful. Then, sandwiched between two A-list celebrities, is Annabel, blue eyes popping in contrast with her shiny black bob.

And right in the centre, bald, is me.

'Wow,' I say, tracing my finger over the cover as my stomach flutters.

I open the magazine to find the feature, each page showing a bold image of a woman and a first-person take on her vulnerabilities and strengths. The pull quote on my page says: *'My hair tells a story, and I wouldn't change that for the world.'*

Then I turn to find Kate's page. We did the shoot right

before my fifth chemo and had a whale of a time in make-up, but it was only through interviewing her that I finally understood a bit of what she's going through. She told me about the loneliness and her constant guilt, how she worried she couldn't love Ella like she was supposed to, and how she has finally plucked up the courage to go to her doctor. Her quote reads: '*I love her more than anything, but when my baby was born, I didn't feel that rush of love I was told to feel.*'

Finally, I find Annabel's page, where she poses in her trademark Converse with her arms crossed over her chest and the wise look of someone much older than her years. In the article, she talks movingly about how we need to learn to talk about death and the lessons she would tell her younger self about confidence. As I cast my eyes over the piece, my whole body aches to be with her.

'It's incredible,' I say, shutting the magazine before I end up in tears again.

'We've exceeded the sales targets, Jess,' she says. 'Everyone is loving this new content.'

'Wow,' I say. 'So Tabitha was right.'

'*You* were right,' Leah says, shaking her copy of the magazine at me. 'Tabitha told me about the way things were for you both when you started. I shouldn't have bulldozed you in without explaining everything to you both first.'

'All that seems like a distant past,' I say. 'Water under the bridge.' I must remember to send Tabitha and Aisha a congratulatory message.

'I know you were worried about editing a women's mag, but you've clearly got a knack for it,' Leah says.

'Thank you,' I say, but I feel guilty taking credit when I've taken so much time off.

'Listen,' she says, composing herself in her chair. 'Miles

wanted to do this in the office together, but he's given me permission to talk to you today.'

'Um, go on,' I say, feeling suddenly nervous. If she's been meeting with Miles, it must be to discuss her return from maternity leave and what happens to me in turn. I could be out on my ear in a month's time and I haven't lined up a new position.

'Jess, I know you've not been able to give it a hundred per cent these last few months, but the amount you've managed to do when you've been having chemo is just phenomenal. You've done a brilliant job and you're a natural born leader. Everyone agrees.'

'Even Tabitha?' I joke.

'*Especially* Tabitha! You'd think I'd done a shit job as editor, the amount she goes on about you.' Leah laughs. 'Anyway, there's been a lot of discussion internally and we've decided to create a new editor role that we'd really like you to go for. We've basically created a position for you.'

I raise my eyebrows. 'But what about you?'

'You're looking at the new editor-in-chief!' she says, beaming. 'Alright, it's mostly a fancy new title, but I'm going to be more hands off on the day-to-day stuff and focus on the bigger picture, including events. I'll have lots of input but you'll effectively be in charge of the magazine. We'll have to give you an interview on your vision for the future, but you'll walk it.'

'What about Tabitha?'

'Well, I shouldn't say this, but between you and me, there's a chance of a promotion to fashion director. That's where she really excels.'

I sit up straight, trying to figure out why I don't feel quite as elated as I thought I would. 'I don't know what to say.'

I wish I could detach my hand from the cannula and get up

and hug her, but I'm aware I'm still a magnet for germs with rock-bottom defences.

'Say you'll think about it. You don't have to decide right now.'

I let out a big breath, as if I've been holding it in for the last six months. This is the opportunity of teenage Jess's dreams, but something is holding me back. I fell out of love with *Perfect Bake* because I couldn't see a cake without dredging up the pain of losing Mum. I jumped straight into *Luxxe*, but I was only running away from my problems, transferring the pain to somewhere new. I'll never deal with my grief if I keep running. Annabel and Joe have taught me that.

'Leah,' I say, putting the mag down on the blanket on top of my legs. 'I'm honoured you've thought of me for this job. And don't take this the wrong way . . .'

She opens her mouth, as if she's about to say something, then she closes it again.

'I don't know if I can.'

'Jess, you've been working like a soldier throughout your chemo. I know you still have radiotherapy and surgery to come. You can take as long as you like. The job will be waiting for you.' She plays with the animal print pop-socket attached to her phone.

'No, I mean I don't know if I'll even apply for this job. I think I want to take a sabbatical. There's some things I need to do.' It's not even something I've thought about, but the words come out on their own.

Joe was right – you can't rush into a relationship or throw yourself into work instead of processing your grief, but that's exactly what I did. It's taken two years to see it, but I need to face up to Mum's death. I need to go home and help Dad part with Mum's stuff, to finally move on and sell the tea rooms. Maybe I'll even go travelling, take some time to figure out what I want and stop living at a hundred miles per hour.

'Oh,' she says. 'A sabbatical? Oh.'

'It's not forever,' I say. But I don't really know if I'll want to go back, or what I'll do with my future. All I know is that I need to slow down.

'Wow,' she says. 'I don't think I've heard of a better idea in ages.'

Learning to dance in the rain

'I'm going home today,' I say, as the head of the catering staff plonks my breakfast tray on my lap. The smell of steaming, sugary porridge wafts up my nose.

'Are you, dear?' She eyes my bald head and grey skin, looking surprised. Then her face changes. 'Well, that's wonderful news. We'll miss you around here.'

'No offence,' I say, 'but I hope I never see you again.'

'I hope so too, love.'

An hour later, as I walk down the corridor and through the double doors for the first time in three days, I feel like a prison escapee. I peer into the kitchen on the way out, calling goodbye to the team, who look at me as if I'm escaping too. Does no one ever leave this place alive?

I walk slowly at first, my hand sore and still bunched into a fist from three nights with the cannula. The skin is grey and wrinkled, as if I've been in the bath for a week.

I walk past Radiology, Endoscopy, Pharmacy, the Prayer Room. Past the Costa, no reason to go there now, no Mags or Annabel or Priya to keep me company. Then I'm through the sliding doors and finally onto the outside.

As the cool air hits me, I open my mouth and inhale, desperately drinking it in as if I've been starved of oxygen for days. Wind on my skin, the delicious smell of London drizzle, even the whiff of smoke from the patients gathered around the entrance, inhaling their cigarettes while still hooked up to their drips. I am free of mine, free to walk on my own.

I savour the time to myself before Dad arrives to pick me up. I finally understand what Mum meant about appreciating the simple things. Birds tweeting, flowers sprouting, the drip of drizzle and the cool British air.

I make my way round to the car park, taking it easy, one foot in front of the other. There he is, ever-faithful, the only man I really need.

But as soon as I see his face, I know something is wrong.

'Dad, what is it?' I stare at him through the open passenger door.

'It's Annabel,' he says.

It takes forever to get away from the hospital. Endless signs in different colours, one-way routes, rows of bins, different car parks, the mortuary. Then one-way streets, scaffolding and road blocks.

'Why didn't they call me?'

Dad shakes his head. 'Joe said he tried but your phone was switched off. He came to the flat late last night, said she went into the hospice in the afternoon. He had no idea you were here.'

Shit. I look down at the shattered phone in my hand. Part of me was relieved it wouldn't turn on, so I didn't have to immerse myself back into the world where everyone is living their perfect lives.

But Annabel needed me, and now it might be too late.

I borrow Dad's phone and click on Joe's name but it rings and rings and he never picks up.

*

It takes an hour and twenty to drive to the hospice in Hove. Every lorry driver in the land seems to have picked today to travel south at a snail's pace.

After three wrong turns, we finally arrive at the winding road that leads to the hospice, the sort of place I never imagined visiting someone who is only twenty-seven.

'I'll wait in the car,' Dad says, and I understand. I understand he can't do this again, not so soon after Mum.

'Are you OK?' the receptionist says, when I appear in the doorway.

'I'm looking for my friend,' I say.

She eyes me suspiciously. 'Which room are you meant to be in, dear?'

'Sorry? No, I'm here to see Annabel Sadler.'

My hand goes to my head. I must look like a patient, escaped from the hospital, the sticky tape from the cannula still showing on my hand, my naked head and bloated face betraying me.

'Annabel Sadler, which room is she in?' I repeat.

The receptionist takes so long to answer that I'm tempted to make a run for it. Finally, she wakes from her stupor and takes me down to a little area with a row of seats. She taps on a door and returns a moment later with Joe.

'Joe,' I gasp. His skin is pale, his eyes red and bloodshot. I can tell he hasn't slept.

He pulls me into his arms, his nose slotting into my neck. I almost collapse as I feel his arms around me.

'What happened? Is she OK?' I say when we finally draw apart.

'She's OK,' he says. 'She had what they call a warning bleed.'

'What? What does it mean?'

'On her brain. They said it usually leads to a bigger bleed.'

388

'Fuck.' My hands are trembling. 'I'm so sorry, Joe.'

I hug him again. None of it matters any more.

'Our parents are here,' Joe says. 'It's been a mad twenty-four hours, I'm so sorry we didn't get to speak.'

Right on cue, a man and woman walk out of the room, holding each other's hands. It's stupid, but whenever I'd imagined Annabel's parents, I'd pictured a rotund Santa and Mrs Claus. But Annabel's mother is the spitting image of Bel, with the same petite frame and smiling eyes. She drops her husband's hand when she sees me and I think she's about to shake mine, but she comes right up and hugs me.

'Jess,' she says. 'We've heard so much about you. I'm Alice, this is Roy.'

I shake Roy's hand. He has a kind face too, framed by grey hair and specs. A vision of a future Joe.

We chat for a minute but I'm on edge, dancing from one foot to another. I need to see Annabel. I need to know she's safe.

Joe senses my unease and suggests his parents take a break and get some tea. Alice takes her husband's hand and leads him off down a corridor, the two of them moving in step with each other.

'Is she, you know, can she speak?' I ask when I have Joe on his own.

'She's not making a lot of sense, but she seems to know who I am.'

'Can I see her?' What if she doesn't recognize me?

'Of course,' he says. Then he puts a firm hand on my forearm. 'I'll wait outside. I'm here if you need me.'

I steel myself as I walk in, preparing for wires and drips and cables. But Bel looks different, almost younger than she did when I saw her just over a week ago. With no wig, I see that her hair has grown back in a short elfin shape. It suits her so well. She looks peaceful.

She recognizes me straight away. I can see it in her eyes, the faintest hint of a smile, even though her body doesn't move.

'Bel,' I smile, touching her with my hand that is still crumpled from the cannula.

She lets out a little squeak. I don't know what she's trying to say.

'Bel, listen, I fucked up, massively. I'm sorry I wasted the time we had.'

'Ssh,' she says, her finger twitching a fraction by her side as if she wants to hold it to her lips. ' 's OK,' she whispers.

'I want you to know I'm sorry and I love you. You're one of the best friends I've ever had. I've spent so much time worrying about stupid stuff when I should have been focusing on you.'

I reach into my bag and pull out the photo book, then carefully place it on top of her chest, holding it for her to read.

I watch her eyes as she reads the words 'Annajel Does Brighton'. She smiles from her eyes.

I turn the pages just slowly enough for her to see the pictures but fast enough that I won't exhaust her. As we reach #SeagullGate, she releases a small laugh, just loud enough for me to know she understands. We finish on the photo of us entering the sea, our backs to the camera before we float belly-up under the grey sky.

She mumbles something hard to make out. I shut the book and move closer, indicating that I haven't understood. She repeats herself. It's a distant whisper, almost indecipherable.

'Storm . . . dance . . . rain,' she says.

I recognize what she's trying to say. It's a quote we saw on a poster together, that day in Brighton. I picture the two of us, flailing our arms about and dancing in the waves as the rain lashed down on top of us.

'Life's not about waiting for the storm to pass . . .' I nod, and her eyes tell me I did good. 'It's about learning to dance in the rain.'

'Dance in-a rain,' she says with tears in her eyes as she smiles up at me.

'Yes,' I say, squeezing on her hand. 'Yes, I will. I'll be dancing for you, every time it rains. I'll be dancing.'

I watch as her eyes slowly close and her chest rises and falls, rises and falls, in time with the buzz and whirr of the machine by her side. I know these are the last words I'll ever hear her say.

Annabel

Annabel Sadler dies on the Friday of her twenty-eighth birthday. She isn't aware of our presence, but we eat doughnuts by her bedside and sing happy birthday with little cardboard party hats strapped to our heads with elastic bands. The only time her hands twitch is when Alice sings a song that Bel recognizes from when she was a toddler.

Just like her nan died on her golden wedding anniversary, I know that Annabel waited for her birthday before letting go. She wouldn't have wanted to miss out on one final moment in the spotlight, with everyone she loved gathered around her.

We are all by her side as she slips away, taking one last, peaceful outward breath before her body lets go. She looks so serene and beautiful, her elfin hair soft around her face like a baby.

Long after she is taken away, Joe and I return to the room to gather her things. We barely say a word as we pick the coloured streamers from the party poppers off the floor, the remnants of what could have been an ordinary birthday celebration. We fill just one small wheelie suitcase with her belongings and take it out to the car.

Afterwards, Joe and I return to the empty room, neither of us saying a word. Instead, we hold each other for a long time.

*

The sun is shining as Joe leads the procession along Brighton Beach, two Fridays after Annabel's death. Alice and Roy follow, trudging along the stones, hand in hand. More people show up than I even realized she knew, from old school pals she hadn't seen for years to friends of her parents and distant aunts, even Mark.

A sea of blue moves together along the coastline, everyone wearing different shades, as requested by Bel. Tabitha opened up the fashion cupboard and we raided it for all the blue items we could find – Aisha wears a cobalt jumpsuit, Lauren a turquoise maxi dress and Kate a sky-blue dress with boots. I wear my wig with my blue birthday dress, the one Bel loved.

Priya and her husband Guj have their arms wrapped around each other, every so often stealing soft, loving glances at each other, the therapy clearly doing its job. Priya wears a tie-dyed blue sari, while Nurse Ange follows in a floaty dress, humming and singing her way through the procession. Aunty Cath sparkles in blue earrings inherited from Mum. Dad walks hand in hand with Lizzie, and for once I'm so pleased he's found someone to look after him. I couldn't bear to think of him going to another funeral alone.

In the afternoon, while everyone else is in the pub, Priya and I sit on the stone wall, looking out to sea.

'How you feeling about everything?' she asks me.

'It hurts worse than anything I could ever imagine,' I say. Worse than Mum dying, if that is even possible. 'But it's also a relief, you know? I'm glad she's at peace.'

'Yeah,' she says, squeezing my hand. 'But I meant, how are you feeling about Joe?'

I picture him scattering Bel's ashes into the sea. There was a moment when he turned back and caught my eye. We shared a look, an eye roll. Annabel got one over on him in the end. One last time in the freezing cold water, much to his disapproval.

But there was something else in that look. A letting go, an acknowledgement that we both need time. That things are going to be OK.

'Actually,' I say, picking up a pebble and throwing it as far as I can towards the ocean, 'I'm going to take the advice of a very wise girl I once knew named Bel. I think I'm going to be single for a while.'

One year later

At six a.m., a horn beeps outside the flat. I bound out the door and run to the car to hug Kate. Colm is behind the wheel, with Ella in her child's seat, wearing the little blue dress I bought for her in San Francisco.

'Oh wow, let me see your hair,' Kate says, gesturing towards my beanie hat, strategically placed to show my hair poking out beneath.

I remove the hat and shake out my almost chin-length crop.

'It looks amazing!' Kate says. 'So where's all the stuff?'

'It's in the hallway. Come inside. Lauren and Aisha are just finishing their breakfast. I'll make you some tea.'

Colm brings Ella into the house and we sit around the kitchen table drinking tea and eating Aisha's homemade banana bread. Now that we're no longer working together, it's lovely to live with her. She and Lauren have been a godsend as housemates, always on hand with tea, cake and bad advice and looking after me throughout my surgery and radiotherapy. Aisha has even started seeing someone, and I've dragged the two of them kicking and screaming to Brockwell Lido for an outdoor swim every Saturday morning.

When Aisha found the three-bedroom flat on Brixton Hill, we all knew it was perfect. Lauren agreed to pay for the big room on her lawyer salary, while Aish and I got rooms just big enough to fit a double bed. We might as well not have bothered with a three-bed, given that we spend half the time with all three of us tucked up under Lauren's duvet watching re-runs of *New Girl*, just like in the uni days.

Everyone helps carry the boxes from the hallway to the people carrier. By six thirty, the car is fully loaded, with Aisha and I squashed into the back row, entirely covered by boxes.

'Excited for today?' Colm says, as he kicks the engine into gear.

'Excited, nervous, all the feels,' I say. The truth is this day couldn't come sooner.

'I can't believe it's been a year, can you?' Lauren says, leaning around from the front seat and giving me a supportive smile.

'Me neither,' I say, barely able to believe how everything worked out. With the rent I was saving from sharing with Aisha and Lauren, I could afford to take some proper time off once my contract ended at *Luxxe*. After my mastectomy operation, I went up north to stay with Dad for a couple of months, helping him sort out the tea rooms for sale. Lizzie was a wonderful carer, making pots of tea, bathing me and helping me dress in a button-down flannel shirt when I was too sore to pull clothes over my head.

While I was still bed-bound, I got stuck into my project to digitize Mum's famous recipe book. The website had a hundred thousand hits in its first month, thanks in part to a piece I wrote for *Perfect Bake* on the power of cooking to heal a broken heart. I also continued my column for *Luxxe*, this time as a freelancer, writing about the pain of survivors' guilt and learning to love my scars. Even though Joe and Annabel both helped me recover from everything I've been through, I think I always needed that time alone.

Six months after the mastectomy and with radiotherapy out

of the way too, Lauren and I made good on our promise to take the ultimate Californian road trip. We whiled away hours in roadside diners, writing actual postcards and letters home as part of our big commitment to an entirely social-media-free trip. When we got back, we printed actual photos into actual albums and sat around regaling our families with tales of our great adventure. After years of being unhappy with Charlie, Lauren is finally back to her old self.

And now I'm preparing to go back to work. With *Luxxe*'s live event programme going from strength to strength, the magazine still has the budget to hire an editor, and Leah and Miles both agreed they need me more than ever. I've loved this last year of freedom – being able to lie in till noon when my body just wants to sleep, going for mid-week swims in the lido and not being bound to the commute. But I'm so looking forward to going back to the office, seeing the team and running that magazine again. I'm even looking forward to seeing Tabitha.

But first, there's something I have to do.

We reach Maltby Street Market to find tens of traders setting up their wares and a mix of smells of fried onions, fresh coffee and just-baked bread.

Aisha fetches coffee from the nearby stall as we survey the area, watching others set up as if they've done this a million times. I'm a bag of nerves, imagining the yummy mums and foodies visiting the stall, *my* stall, in just an hour's time.

Kate and Aisha hold either side of the trestle table as I kick the metal leg to pop it into place. Colm unloads boxes containing paper bags, napkins and cardboard cups, while Lauren entertains Ella.

'Here she is,' I say, picking up the huge wooden board that reads ANNABEL'S.

'It's incredible,' Kate says.

Once the board is set up with everything else around it, we stand back and admire our work. It looks like a real-life stall. All that remains is to set out the boxes of doughnuts in neat lines, separated by filling: raspberry jam, custard and lemon curd, Mum's favourite. We lay out the board with the prices and flavours. One for three pounds, four for a tenner. The result of an entire week's prep and the aid of some trusty helpers.

Ever the stylist, Aisha composes the first photo and posts it onto the @BelsDoughnuts Instagram account with the caption *Open for business.*

I reveal the bottle of prosecco I've been hiding in my kit and pop it open with a bang, spilling the bubbles and decanting it into five cardboard cups.

'Cheers,' I say. 'Here's to Annabel's.'

'And here's to you,' Lauren says, putting an arm around me and drawing me to her.

'Don't look now, but there's someone you might be happy to see,' Aisha says. I can't help but swing round to where she's looking.

My hand jerks to my mouth as I see him, tanned and freckled, his blue eyes sparkling. Goosebumps run all the way down my arms and legs.

'What are you doing here?' I say as Joe walks up to the stand. 'You were somewhere in Southeast Asia two days ago.' I have no shame in admitting I've been Insta-stalking every move of his grown-up gap year.

'I came to see *this*,' he says, throwing his arms out and gesturing at the enormous sign bearing his sister's name. Then he wraps those same strong arms around me, pulling me into a tight embrace. 'You didn't think I'd miss out on being Annabel's first customer, did you?'

Acknowledgements

On 22 June 2012, at twenty-nine years old, I heard those words: 'You have breast cancer'. You could say I was unlucky, but I like to think I'm incredibly fortunate – not only to have survived the last decade when so many didn't, but to have spent it surrounded by the most wonderful, generous and supportive friends, family, colleagues and medical staff.

It seems fitting that this book should be published on the tenth anniversary of my breast cancer diagnosis because it closes what was probably the most defining chapter of my life. There are many people I'd like to thank, not just for supporting me in writing my first novel, but for helping me survive the last decade. Jess wouldn't thank me for saying this but it's been a journey.

To my agent, Sophie Lambert, for your faith in this novel from the very beginning. I am so grateful for the patience and grace with which you tackled the approximately 7,000 drafts I sent your way, even while home-schooling three kids during a global pandemic. You are a bona fide wonder woman and my ultimate champion – thank you.

To my editor, Jayne Osborne, for your passion and love for Jess and Annabel from the start, and for believing so wholeheartedly in this novel. I knew you were the one the moment I realized we shared a love of *Selling Sunset*. Never forget that what you do is so important. Thank you for making my dreams come true.

To all at C&W, and particularly Kate Burton, for securing my first book deal. To Meredith Ford, for loving my manuscript and for giving me a proper Yorkshire welcome on my first publishing house visit. And to Mareike Mueller at Harper-Collins Germany for your incredible enthusiasm for this story. I cannot tell you how much this powered me through.

To all at Pan Macmillan, including Josie Turner, Elle Gibbons, Natalie Young and Sasha Baker. Special thanks to Charlotte Wright for your patience and perseverance with my questions and edits, and to the art team for creating my incredible cover. I'm so fortunate to be in such capable hands.

To the Faber Academy class of 2018. Quite simply, I could not have finished this book without you. I am beyond grateful for your endless support and 'shit sandwiches', and for pointing out the sheer quantity of tea-making performed by my characters in early drafts. Special thanks to Sophie Morris, Sophie Binns, Laura Burgoine, Bryan Glick, Lissa Price, Angelita Bradney and Ben Ross for the early reads and advice. To Tamzin Cuming for all your medical know-how, and to Hannah Tovey for giving me my first cover quote. Finally, to Richard Skinner, for bringing us together.

To my very first reader, Karen Eeuwens, not only for your wildly enthusiastic and generous feedback but also for offering to read it again, and again, and again – your support means so much to me. To Vanessa Fox-O'Loughlin, for your encouragement when this novel was just the seed of an idea, and for allowing me to believe it would be published someday. And to Alice-May Purkiss, for taking the time to do a sensitivity read when you knew it would be painful.

To the entire team at 50 Best, for tolerating the Air-Con Wars and for bringing the lolz even when I was on the verge of tears. You guys are truly the best team I've ever had. Special thanks to Will, my champion since the beginning, for believing in me from the very first draft and encouraging me to spread my wings.

Thanks also to Christine, Gordon and the folk at Facebook in Dublin for doing it right and being so supportive as an employer – and for keeping me well-fed and watered.

To my friends. I may not have a great track record of sustaining romantic relationships, but I've sure as hell made up for it with friendships, so this section might be rather long.

To Danie and Niki, for dropping everything and flying to Dublin to drink margaritas with me the minute you heard the news. To Sophie Austin, my faithful travel buddy, for taking me wig shopping and always asking the right questions – I adore you, and I don't think you know just how wonderful and talented you are. To the Brazil girls – Sophie, Alice, Alexa, Alex, Elsie and Jo – for joining me on an adventure that sparked a lifetime of other adventures, and for still being such fabulous friends twenty-two years later. To Daniela, my Mexican sister – *te quiero mucho, amiga*.

To Maz, for sixteen years of friendship, eighteen months of lockdown walks and thousands of hours of discussion over the merits of Tinder, Bumble and Hinge – you deserve the world. To Camila, for the daily dating debriefs over hours of train commutes – I'm so happy you found love in the end. To Stuart, for finding me on SpareRoom and rescuing me when I'd just about given up, and for indulging me with my turmeric obsession. To Beth, for being so supportive throughout my cancer treatment. And to Lucia, Saz, Eleanor and Alex – even though I seldom see you, I know we'll always go straight back to how we were.

Finally, to the Kavos Chicks – Helen, Michelle, Lindsey

and Vicky – aka the best bunch of friends a girl could have. Over two years of college, twenty-five years of friendship, nine babies and a global pandemic, you've seen me through approximately 96,000 break-ups and you've helped me put my heart back together every time. Special thanks to H, for drilling it into me long, long ago that no man is worth my tears, and the one who is won't make me cry.

Now, to paraphrase Little Mix: shout-out to my ex(es), you're really quite the ~~man~~ men. You made my heart break and that made me who I am. Alright, there were some real rotters, but there were plenty of good eggs too. To the one who showed me early on what proper love is (and possibly condemned me to twenty years of singledom, but hey ...), the one who encouraged me to get the lump checked out and the one who healed me back to life – you know who you are. Thank you.

To the Boobettes of CoppaFeel!, the incredible army of women educating young people about the importance of checking their breasts and knowing the signs and symptoms of cancer. Not only have you been incredibly generous in answering all of my medical questions, you've also been a tremendous support over the years. I am humbled by all that you have been through, and all that you do to help others. What an astonishing bunch.

To the entire team at CoppaFeel! for saving so many lives through your incredible work, and for creating such an invaluable community for those of us affected by breast cancer. To the original turd glitterers, Kris Hallenga and Maren Sheldon, for founding such a brilliant charity and for showing me what it is to truly live. And to Laura Weatherall-Plane and Jon Plane for showing me what it is to love.

To the ones we lost along the way, including far too many beloved Boobettes. To Janet, Lynda, Mary, Marjorie and

Aunty Heather. To my maternal grandmother, Hetty, who died from breast cancer far too young – I reckon we'd have got along famously. To Vanessa and Jodie, aka Vanjo, two of the funniest, most kind-hearted, beautiful-inside-and-out women I have ever had the privilege of knowing. Yours was the greatest friendship love story I've ever witnessed.

To Mr Sharif and Dr Chittalia at the Christie in Manchester, for saving my life, quite literally. To the entire team at St Vincent's in Dublin, the Wythenshawe in Manchester and the Royal Marsden in Sutton – because, oh yes, I get around a bit. A special shout out to Nikki Snuggs and her dream team of nurses, especially Paula, who called me on Christmas Eve 2020 so that I wouldn't have to spend the lonely lockdown Christmas worrying that my cancer had come back. You ladies work your tits off, pun intended.

To all those who read my blogs on *The Big Scary 'C' Word* and the *Huffington Post* and encouraged me to write a book – your feedback and support over the last ten years has been invaluable. Believe me when I say it has powered me through countless days when I've felt like giving up.

To Philip, the best big brother in the world. Thank you for being there when I need you, for not laughing (or crying) when you saw my bald head for the first time, and for giving me the three most wonderful nieces.

To Mum and Dad, still going strong after fifty years. You are my inspiration, my backbone, my shining example of what love should be. Mum, thank you not only for flying straight to Dublin when you heard about my diagnosis, but also for so willingly participating in a rooftop HIIT class set to German techno on arrival. Thank you both for setting the most incredible example of love, for taking care of me when I was sick and for being there for me throughout. I love you both tremendously, and I owe you everything.

Finally, to Mark, for swooping in just in time for my acknowledgements and making a formerly bald, formerly single girl incredibly happy. You take my breath away.

London, January 2022

What happens at twenty-three? Well, if you're lucky, seeing a bit of the world, partying with your pals and having a whole load of carefree fun. And if you're less lucky? Breast cancer. That's exactly what happened to CoppaFeel! founder Kris Hallenga. After finding a lump in her boob aged twenty-two, moving to China for eight months and eventually visiting her doctor three times, Kris was told the news that she had incurable breast cancer. Kris was unaware that breast cancer could affect people in their twenties and it struck her that there was very little information about breast cancer out there for young people. The idea for CoppaFeel! was born.

Although Kris will always live with cancer, she wanted young people to know that catching cancer early means you have a higher chance of surviving and recovering. She wanted people to learn from her story and the stories of others just like her, so she put out a call for young people who'd experienced breast cancer and wanted to talk about it. One of those people was Laura Price:

'Like Kris, I was dismissed by several doctors who said the lump in my breast was probably hormonal and that I was too young for cancer. I became a Boobette to help educate others about the signs and symptoms of breast cancer and to try to ensure as few people as possible are diagnosed at the late stage. Fortunately, my cancer was caught in time for successful treatment and a healthy, happy life. Now, I tell my story to provide hope and inspiration to others' – Laura Price

Breast cancer can affect anybody, but checking regularly and knowing what's normal for your chest could save your life. Here's how to check:

1) **Check regularly:** this will help you get to know what's normal for you. You can use any method you're comfortable with, such as lying down in bed, standing in front of a mirror or when you're showering.

2) **Look and feel:** remember to check all parts of your chest, including your armpits, up to your collarbones and your nipples.

3) **If in doubt, get it checked out:** early detection saves lives, so if you notice anything unusual for you, get it checked out by your doctor.

Visit self-checkout.coppafeel.org to find out more.

 @coppafeelpeople

 @CoppaFeelPeople

 @coppafeel.org